Praise for Tom Perrotta and *L*... W9-BFH-550

a *New York Times*, *Los Angeles Times*, *USA Today*,
San Francisco Chronicle, *Boston Globe*, and *Booksense* bestseller

"What a wicked joy it is to welcome *Little Children*, Tom Perrotta's extraordinary
novel . . . a sterling comic contribution . . . [that] raises the question of how a
writer can be so entertainingly vicious and yet so full of fellow feeling. Bracingly
tender moments stud Perrotta's satire . . . at once suspenseful, ruefully funny,
and ultimately generous. . . . What is Tom Perrotta but an American Chekhov
whose characters even at their most ridiculous seem blessed and ennobled by a
luminous human aura?"
—*The New York Times Book Review*

"*Little Children* offers a generous serving of laugh-out-loud moments. . . . Perrotta
is an astute student of twenty-first century suburban life."
—*USA Today*

"An accomplished comic novelist extends his range brilliantly. Perrotta's best."
—*Kirkus Reviews* (starred)

"With *Little Children*, Perrotta has moved into the suburbs with a wrecking ball.
He has cooked up recipes of depravity that would curl Betty Crocker's hair. If
good satire can generate a corrective jolt, this may be a deadly shock."
—*Christian Science Monitor*

"What distinguishes it from run-of-the-mill suburban satire is its knowing blend
of slyness and compassion."
—*The New York Times*

"[An] intelligent, absorbing tale of suburban angst . . . once again, [Perrotta]
proves himself an expert at exploring the roiling psychological depths beneath
the placid surface of suburbia."
—*Publishers Weekly*

"Perrotta deftly combines the darkness of A. M. Homes with the archness of
Updike in this incisive novel, by turns wickedly funny and deeply poignant."
—*Baltimore Sun*

"Perrotta has crafted a sly tale of children trapped in adult bodies. . . . Perrotta's
scenes sneak up on you. . . . Most satire is fueled by anger. Not Perrotta's. His is
gentler stuff."
—*Los Angeles Times Book Review*

"A dark, satirical tale about sex, lies, and stagnation in the wilds of suburbia. . . ."
—*New York Post*

"A bitingly hysterical exploration of bored young suburban parents. . . ."
—*Entertainment Weekly*'s Must List

"Perrotta wisely refuses to condescend to the world he satirizes, and his masterful
perspective provides the reader with a breezy ominiscience over the characters'
failures in life. The book is disarmingly funny but rueful . . . a brave novel."
—*Esquire*

"Perrotta's most delightful transgression is his unsentimental treatment of what passes for the third rail of suburban reality—the sanctity of child rearing. . . . A–."
—*Boston Globe*

"For a novel with such a deceptively simple plot, Perrotta's *Little Children* is as heavy with multiplicity as the bulging diaper bag of an overzealous new mother. . . . There are enough subtleties and surprises here to keep the author's message from becoming pat."
—*San Diego Union-Tribune*

"An outstanding contribution to the literature of Bad Mommy and Bad Daddy. . . ."
—*New York Times Book Review*

"*Little Children* is satire, Perrotta's take on the gnawing dissatisfactions of family life, the tyrannical control small kids exert over their parents . . . and the inescapable sense that there is something better out there. But, as you'd expect from a writer who's shown the generosity Perrotta has, it's compassionate satire. *Little Children* is a withering take on suburbia but—and this is what differentiates it from all the other withering takes on suburbia—its view is from the inside. . . . The voice is key to what's so good about the book. . . . *Little Children* is certainly Perrotta's most ambitious book."
—Salon.com

"*Little Children* is a skilled and mature study . . . filled with credible characters wrestling with that time in their lives when they sacrifice their ambitions for their children. . . . What is most admirable is Perrotta's feel for his subject, conveyed without condescension."
—*Philadelphia Inquirer*

"Tom Perrotta has been called the American Nick Hornby, and in a lot of ways the comparison's a good one . . . *Little Children* is deft, satisfying social satire. It nudges Perrotta out of the category of talented-but-lightweight writers, into a league of quietly remarkable writers more comparable to Flaubert than Hornby."
—*Montreal Mirror*

"His writing style is warm and lean—an absolute pleasure. *Little Children* is a terrific book."
—*Trenton Times*

"Perrotta is a novelist-as-cultural-anthropologist—Steinbeck without the Dust Bowl, Tom Wolfe without the rhetorical flourishes—and he looks at his fictional world with a dispassionate eye."
—*The Oregonian*

"Darker and more ambitious than his previous four works of fiction . . . *Little Children* is a searing, compulsively readable look at how familial and marital discontent can metastasize into adultery and violence. Combining rueful wit with a wonderfully creepy sense of foreboding, *Little Children* feels like what you might get if Nick Hornby collaborated with David Lynch. . . . Here is comedy that is rooted in sadness. The steady hum that emanates from Perrotta's suburb is not the lawn mowers but the sound of human failure."
—*Newsday*

"In this darkly comic novel, Tom Perrotta reverses Tolstoy's famous dictum and suggests that all unhappy families are unhappy in the same way . . . lively reading."
—*San Francisco Chronicle*

"This wicked and hilarious novel provides a bitterly accurate portrait of contemporary family life."
—*The Atlanta Journal Constitution*

"The sterile horrors of the burbs are overdocumented, to say the least, but Perrotta, an expert with precocious youngsters is never shrill and only slightly vicious in satirizing his infantilized grown-ups."
—*Village Voice*

"He manages to satirize and sympathize at the same time, redeeming all his characters by digging deep for their shared humanity."
—*The Seattle Times*

"This book tackles serious topics . . . with a surprisingly light tone."
—*US Weekly* (Hot Book Pick)

"A fast-reading, wholly engaging novel."
—*Booklist*

"Perrotta's writing style isn't flashy. But his knack for capturing a variety of voices (from a four-year-old boy to an elderly woman) and the way he weaves in telling references to the minutiae of quotidian suburban existence (juice boxes and *Blue's Clues*, book clubs and cybersmut) make for characters who are idiosyncratic but familiar, difficult to condemn, difficult not to empathize with."
—*Boston Phoenix*

"A masterpiece of a comic novel . . . What Perrotta has produced, in the end, is a new literary hybrid—a satire with heart."
—*Tacoma News-Tribune*

"Readers will await the inevitable crash with horrified glee. . . ."
—*Newsweek*

"A story that is timeless and placeless yet rock-solid in its appeal . . . Perrotta has added another layer to what is becoming an impressive and durable body of work."
—*Boston Herald*

"With this novel, Perrotta has entered the land of Updike and Cheever, the messy world of adults who cheat on spouses and fail their children, but unlike those excellent authors who staked out the territory, Perrotta's excursion does not leave an aftertaste of bitterness. . . ."
—*Pittsburgh Post-Gazette*

"With *Little Children*, Perrotta displays a refreshing compassion without sacrificing his trademark understanding of what makes this country tick—and what ticks it off."
—*Nashville Bookpage*

"A funny, smart, and spooky send-up of the void at the center of suburbia. . . ."
—*Creative Loafing,* Charlotte, NC

ALSO BY TOM PERROTTA

Joe College

Election

The Wishbones

Bad Haircut:
  Stories of the Seventies

LITTLE
CHILDREN

TOM
PERROTTA

ST. MARTIN'S GRIFFIN ✤ NEW YORK

LITTLE CHILDREN. Copyright © 2004 by Tom Perrotta. All rights reserved. Printed in the United States of America. No part of this book may be used or reproduced in any manner whatsoever without written permission except in the case of brief quotations embodied in critical articles or reviews. For information, address St. Martin's Press, 175 Fifth Avenue, New York, N.Y. 10010.

www.stmartins.com

Library of Congress Cataloging-in-Publication Data

Perrotta, Tom. 1961–
     Little children / Tom Perrotta.
          p. cm.
     ISBN-13: 978-0-312-36282-9
     ISBN-10: 0-312-36282-X
     1. Parent and child—Fiction. 2. Child molesters—fiction. 3. Married people—fiction. 4. Suburban life—Fiction. 5. Adultery—Fiction. I. Title.

PS3566.E6948L57 2003
813'.54—dc22

                                                              2003015947

First St. Martin's Griffin Edition: October 2006

10 9 8 7 6 5 4 3 2 1

In memory of my father, Joe Perrotta

ACKNOWLEDGMENTS

I'd like to thank my editor, Elizabeth Beier, for excellent advice just when I needed it, and my agent, Maria Massie, for her insight and good humor. Dori Weintraub and Sylvie Rabineau also provided valuable assistance. My wife, Mary Granfield, was, as always, the best first reader I could ask for. Mainly, though, I'd like to thank Nina and Luke for letting me tag along at the playground.

"I have a lover! I have a lover!" she kept repeating to herself, reveling in the thought as though she were beginning a second puberty.

—FLAUBERT, *MADAME BOVARY*

PART ONE

DECENT PEOPLE BEWARE

BAD MOMMY

THE YOUNG MOTHERS WERE TELLING EACH OTHER HOW TIRED they were. This was one of their favorite topics, along with the eating, sleeping, and defecating habits of their offspring, the merits of certain local nursery schools, and the difficulty of sticking to an exercise routine. Smiling politely to mask a familiar feeling of desperation, Sarah reminded herself to think like an anthropologist. *I'm a researcher studying the behavior of boring suburban women. I am not a boring suburban woman myself.*

"Jerry and I started watching that Jim Carrey movie the other night?"

This was Cheryl, mother of Christian, a husky three-and-a-half-year-old who swaggered around the playground like a Mafia chieftain, shooting the younger children with any object that could plausibly stand in as a gun—a straw, a half-eaten banana, even a Barbie doll that had been abandoned in the sandbox. Sarah despised the boy and found it hard to look his mother in the eye.

"The Pet Guy?" inquired Mary Ann, mother of Troy and Isabelle. "I don't get it. Since when did passing gas become so hilarious?"

Only since there was human life on earth, Sarah thought, wishing she had the guts to say it out loud. Mary Ann was one of those depressing supermoms, a tiny, elaborately made-up woman who dressed in spandex workout clothes, drove an SUV the size of a UPS van, and listened to conservative talk radio all day. No matter how many hints Sarah dropped to the contrary, Mary Ann refused to believe that any of the other mothers thought any less of Rush Limbaugh or any more of Hillary Clinton than she did. Every day Sarah came to the playground determined to set her straight, and every day she chickened out.

"Not the Pet Guy," Cheryl said. "The state trooper with the split personality."

Me, Myself, and Irene, Sarah thought impatiently. By the Farrelly Brothers. Why was it that the other mothers could never remember the titles of anything, not even movies they'd actually seen, while she herself retained lots of useless information about movies she wouldn't even dream of watching while imprisoned on an airplane, not that she ever got to fly anywhere?

"Oh, I saw that," said Theresa, mother of Courtney. A big, raspy-voiced woman who often alluded to having drunk too much wine the night before, Theresa was Sarah's favorite of the group. Sometimes, if no one else was around, the two of them would sneak a cigarette, trading puffs like teenagers and making subversive comments about their husbands and children. When the others arrived, though, Theresa immediately turned into one of them. "I thought it was cute."

Of course you did, Sarah thought. There was no higher praise at the playground than *cute*. It meant harmless. Easily absorbed. Posing no threat to smug suburbanites. At her old playground, someone had actually used the c-word to describe *American Beauty* (not that she'd actually named the film; it was *that thing with Kevin what's-his-name, you know, with the rose petals*). That had been the last straw for Sarah. After exploring her options for a few days, she had switched to the Rayburn School playground, only to find that it was the same wherever you went. All the young mothers were tired. They all watched cute movies whose titles they couldn't remember.

"I was enjoying it," Cheryl said. "But fifteen minutes later, Jimmy and I were both fast asleep."

"You think that's bad?" Theresa laughed. "Mike and I were having sex the other night, and I drifted off right in the middle of it."

"Oh, well." Cheryl chuckled sympathetically. "It happens."

"I guess," said Theresa. "But when I woke up and apologized, Mike said he hadn't even noticed."

"You know what you should do?" Mary Ann suggested. "Set aside a specific block of time for making love. That's what Lewis and I do. Every Tuesday night at nine."

Whether you want to or not, Sarah thought, her eyes straying over to the play structure. Her daughter was standing near the top of the slide, sucking on the back of her hand as Christian pummeled Troy and Courtney showed Isabelle her Little Mermaid underpants. Even at the playground, Lucy didn't interact much with the other kids. She preferred to hang back, observing the action, as if trying to locate a seam that would permit her to enter the social world. *A lot like her mother,* Sarah thought, feeling both sorry for her daughter and perversely proud of their connection.

"What about you?" It took Sarah a moment to realize that Cheryl was talking to her.

"Me?" A surprisingly bitter laugh escaped from her mouth. "Richard and I haven't touched each other for months."

The other mothers traded uncomfortable looks, and Sarah realized that she must have misunderstood. Theresa reached across the picnic table and patted her hand.

"She didn't mean that, honey. She was just asking if you were as tired as the rest of us."

"Oh," said Sarah, wondering why she always had so much trouble following the thread of a conversation. "I doubt it. I've never needed very much sleep."

Morning snack time was ten-thirty on the dot, a regimen established and maintained by Mary Ann, who believed that rigid adherence to a timetable was the key to effective parenting. She had placed glow-in-the-dark digital clocks in her children's rooms, and had instructed them not to leave their beds in the morning until the first number had changed to seven. She also bragged of strictly enforcing a 7 P.M. bedtime with no resistance from the kids, a claim that filled Sarah with both envy and suspicion. She had never identified with authority figures, and couldn't help sensing a sort of whip-cracking fascist glee behind Mary Ann's ability to make the trains run on time.

Still, as skeptical as she was of fanatical punctuality in general, Sarah had to admit that the kids seemed to find it reassuring. None of them complained about waiting or being hungry, and they never asked what time it was. They just went about the business of their morning play, confident that they'd be notified when the proper moment arrived. Lucy seemed especially grateful for this small gift of predictability in her life. Sarah could see the pleasure in her eyes when she came running over to the picnic table with the others, part of the pack for the first time all day.

"Mommy, Mommy!" she cried. "Snack time!"

Of course, no system is foolproof, Sarah thought, rummaging through the diaper bag for the rice cakes she could have sworn she'd packed before they left the house. But maybe that was yesterday? It wasn't that easy to tell one weekday from the next anymore; they all just melted together like a bag of crayons left out in the sun.

"Mommy?" An anxious note seeped into Lucy's voice. All the other kids had opened Ziploc bags and single-serving Tupperware containers, and were busy shoveling handfuls of Cheerios and Gold-fish crackers into their mouths. "Where my snack?"

"I'm sure it's in here somewhere," Sarah told her.

Long after she had come to the conclusion that the rice cakes weren't there, Sarah kept digging through the diaper bag, pretending to search for them. It was a lot easier to keep staring into that dark jumble of objects than to look up and tell Lucy the truth. In the background she heard someone slurping the dregs of a juice box.

"Where it went?" the hard little voice demanded. "Where my snack?"

It took an act of will for Sarah to look up and meet her daughter's eyes.

"I'm sorry, honey." She let out a long, defeated sigh. "Mommy can't find it."

Lucy didn't argue. She just scrunched up her pale face, clenched her fists, and began to hyperventilate, gathering strength for the next phase of the operation. Sarah turned apologetically to the other mothers, who were watching the proceedings with interest.

"I forgot the rice cakes," Sarah explained. "I must have left them on the counter."

"Poor thing," said Cheryl.

"That's the second time this week," Mary Ann pointed out.

You hateful bitch, Sarah thought.

"It's hard to keep track of everything," observed Theresa, who had supplied Courtney with a tube of Go-gurt and a box of raisins.

Sarah turned to Lucy, who was emitting a series of whimpers that were slowly increasing in volume.

"Just calm down," Sarah pleaded.

"No!" Lucy shouted. "No calm down!"

"That'll be enough of that, young lady."

"Bad mommy! I want snack!"

"It's not here," Sarah said, handing her daughter the diaper bag. "See for yourself."

Fixing her mother with an evil glare, Lucy promptly turned the bag upside down, releasing a cascade of Pampers, baby wipes, loose change, balled-up Kleenex, books, and toys onto the wood-chip-covered ground.

"Sweetie." Sarah spoke calmly, pointing at the mess. "Clean that up, please."

"I . . . want . . . my . . . snack!" Lucy gasped.

With that, the dam broke, and she burst into piteous tears, a desolate animal wailing that even made the other kids turn and look, as if realizing they were in the presence of a virtuoso and might be able to pick up a few pointers.

"Poor thing," Cheryl said again.

Other mothers know what to do at moments like this, Sarah thought. They'd all read the same book or something. Were you supposed to ignore a tantrum and let the kid "cry herself out"? Or were you supposed to pick her up and remind her that she was safe and well loved? It seemed to Sarah that she'd heard both recommendations at one time or another. In any case, she knew that a good parent would take some sort of clearheaded action. A good parent wouldn't just stand there feeling clueless and guilty while her child howled at the sky.

"Wait." It was Mary Ann who spoke, her voice radiating such undeniable adult authority that Lucy immediately broke off crying, willing to hear her out. "Troy, honey? Give Lucy your Goldfish."

Troy was understandably offended by this suggestion.

"No," he said, turning so that his body formed a barrier between Lucy and his snack.

"Troy Jonathan." Mary Ann held out her hand. "Give me those Goldfish."

"But Mama," he whimpered. "It's mine."

"No backtalk. You can share with your sister."

Reluctantly, but without another word of protest, Troy surrendered the bag. Mary Ann immediately bestowed it upon Lucy, whose face broke into a slightly hysterical smile.

"Thank you," Sarah told Mary Ann. "You're a lifesaver."

"It's nothing," Mary Ann replied. "I just hate to see her suffer like that."

Not that they would, but if any of the other mothers had asked how it was that Sarah, of all people, had ended up married, living in the suburbs, and caring full-time for a small child, she would have blamed it all on a moment of weakness. At least that was how she described it to herself, though the explanation always seemed a bit threadbare. After all, what was adult life but one moment of weakness piled on top of another? Most people just fell in line like obedient little children, doing exactly what society expected of them at any given moment, all the while pretending that they'd actually made some sort of choice.

But the thing was, Sarah considered herself an exception. She had discovered feminism her sophomore year in college—this was back in the early nineties, when a lot of undergraduate women were moving in the opposite direction—and the encounter had left her profoundly transformed. After just a few weeks of Intro to Women's Studies, Sarah felt like she'd been given the key to understanding so many things that were wrong with her life—her mother's persistent depression, her own difficulty making and keeping female friends, the alienation she sometimes felt from her own body. Sarah embraced Critical Gender Studies with the fervor of a convert, taking from it the kind of comfort other women in her dorm seemed to derive from shopping or step aerobics.

She enlisted at the Women's Center and spent the second half of her college career in the thick of a purposeful, socially aware, politically active community of women. She volunteered at the Rape Crisis Hotline, marched in Take Back the Night rallies, learned to distinguish between French and Anglo-American feminism(s). By senior year, she had cut her hair short, stopped shaving her legs, and begun attending Gay, Lesbian, and Bisexual dances and social events. Two months before graduation, she dove headlong into a passionate affair with a Korean-American woman named Amelia, who was headed for med school in New York City in the fall. It was a thrilling time for Sarah, the perfect culmination to her undergraduate voyage of self-discovery.

And then—suddenly and with astonishing finality—college was over. Amelia moved back to Westchester to spend the summer with her family. Sarah stayed in Boston, taking a job at Starbucks to pay the rent while she figured out what to do next. They visited each other twice that summer, but for some reason couldn't recapture what had so recently been an effortless rhythm of togetherness. On the day before Sarah was supposed to visit her in her new dorm,

Amelia called and said maybe it would be best if they didn't see each other anymore. Medical school was overwhelming; she didn't have the space in her life for a relationship.

Sarah had nothing in her life but space, but she didn't get involved with anyone else for almost a year, and when she did it was with a man, a charismatic barista who did stand-up comedy and said he liked everything about her but her hairy legs. So Sarah started shaving again, got fitted for a diaphragm, and spent a lot of time in comedy clubs, listening to tired jokes about the difference between men (they won't ask for directions!) and women (they want to talk after sex!). When she tried to explain her objections to humor based on sexist stereotypes, Ryan suggested that she extract the metal rod from her ass and lighten up a little.

Along with dumping Ryan, applying to graduate school seemed like the perfect solution for escaping the rut she was in—a way to recapture the excitement of college while also making a transition into a recognizable version of adulthood. She cultivated an image of herself as a young professor, a feminist film critic, perhaps. She would be a mentor and an inspiration to girls like herself, the quiet ones who'd sleepwalked their way through high school, knowing nothing except that they couldn't possibly be happy with any of the choices the world seemed to be offering them.

Within a couple of weeks of starting the Ph.D. program, though, she discovered that she'd booked passage on a sinking ship. There aren't any jobs, the other students informed her; the profession's glutted with tenured old men who won't step aside for the next generation. While the university's busy exploiting you for cheap labor, you somehow have to produce a boring thesis that no one will read, and find someone willing to publish it as a book. And then, if you're unusually talented and extraordinarily lucky, you just might be able to secure a one-year, nonrenewable appointment teaching remedial composition to football players in Oklahoma. Meanwhile, the Internet's booming, and kids we gave C pluses to are waltzing out of college and getting rich on stock options while we bust our asses for a pathetic stipend that doesn't even cover the rent.

Sarah could see that it was all true, but she didn't really mind once she adjusted her expectations. Graduate school didn't have to lead anywhere, did it? Wouldn't it be worthwhile just to spend a couple of years reading and thinking, reawakening her mind from a long stupor induced by too many espresso drinks and lame one-liners? She could just get her master's, maybe teach in a prep school after that, or join the Peace Corps, or even figure out a way to climb onto the Internet gravy train like everybody else.

What did her in was the teaching. Some people loved it, of course, loved the sound of their own voices, the chance to display their cleverness to a captive audience. And then there were the instructors like herself, who simply couldn't communicate in a classroom setting. They made one point over and over with mind-numbing insistence, or else they circled around a dozen half-articulated ideas without landing on a single one. They read woodenly from prepared notes, or got lost in their muddled syntax while attempting to speak off the cuff. God help them if they attempted a joke. The faces looking back at them might be bored or confused or hostile, but mostly they were just full of pity. That's what she got from her two semesters of teaching: enough pity to last her a lifetime.

Broke and demoralized, Sarah quit school and landed back at Starbucks, this time with a seriously diminished sense of herself and her future. She was a failure, a twenty-six-year-old woman of still-ambiguous sexuality who had just discovered that she wasn't nearly as smart as she'd thought she was. *I am a painfully ordinary person,* she reminded herself on a daily basis, *destined to live a painfully ordinary life.*

As if to illustrate this humbling lesson, her old lover Amelia walked into Starbucks one chilly afternoon that fall. She looked absolutely radiant, with a strong-jawed Korean husband standing proudly beside her, and a plump, wide-eyed baby strapped to her chest in a forward-facing contraption. The two women recognized each other right away. Amelia froze in the doorway, exchanging a searching look with Sarah across the length of the floor.

Sarah smiled sadly, trying to acknowledge the strangeness and emotional richness of the moment, but Amelia didn't smile back. Her face—it was fuller, less girlish, with a touch of fatigue around the eyes—didn't betray the slightest sign of desire or regret or even simple surprise. All Sarah could find on it was a familiar look of pity, as if Amelia were just another bored freshman who didn't know what the hell the teacher was going on about. She whispered something to her husband, who cast a quick, startled glance at Sarah before mouthing the word, *Really?* Amelia shrugged, as if she didn't understand how it was possible that she even knew this pathetic woman in the green apron, let alone that they'd once danced to Aretha Franklin in their underwear and collapsed onto a narrow bed in a fit of giggles that seemed like it would never stop. At least that's what Sarah hoped Amelia was remembering as the perfect little family retreated out the door, leaving her to fake a smile at the next person in line and explain for the umpteenth time that there was no such thing as "small" at Starbucks.

That, she would have explained to the other mothers, *was my moment of weakness.* Except that it wasn't really a moment. It lasted all through that winter and into the following spring, which was when Richard stepped up to the counter one tedious morning—he was a regular, a middle-aged man with a neatly trimmed beard and an air of quiet authority—and asked if she was having as bad a day as he was, which for some reason felt like the first kind thing anyone had said to her in years. And that was how she'd ended up at this godforsaken playground.

Sarah knelt down and began slowly gathering up the vast assortment of crap that had been disgorged from the diaper bag. She knew she should have asked Lucy to help—at three, a child was old enough to begin taking responsibility for the messes she'd created—but asserting this principle was hardly worth the risk of provoking another tantrum.

Besides, the less help she got, the longer she could stay on the ground, away from the accusatory faces of the other mothers, letting the sharp edges of the wood chips dig even deeper into her kneecaps, inflicting a dull pain Sarah thought she probably deserved and might even begin to enjoy in a second or two.

Her copy of *The Handmaid's Tale* was lying cover down, on top of *The Berenstain Bears Visit the Dentist*, and the sight of the two books filled her with an odd sense of shame. She felt a sudden burst of kinship for those medieval flagellants who used to walk through town, publicly thrashing themselves to atone for their sins. Pretty soon she'd be packing a whip in the diaper bag.

"Maybe you should make a checklist," Mary Ann told her. "Tape it to the door so it's the last thing you see before leaving the house. That's what I do."

I am not long for this playground, Sarah thought. She looked up and forced herself to smile.

"Thank you," she said. "That's a really helpful suggestion."

THE SKATEBOARDERS

EIGHTY-ONE . . . EIGHTY-TWO . . .

Kathy called from the cell phone around four, when Aaron was napping, and Todd was nearing the end of his third and final set of push-ups.

Eighty-three . . .

"Hi," she said, the answering machine broadcasting her staticky voice throughout the downstairs. "How are my two favorite boys? Did you have fun at the pool?"

Eighty-five . . .

"Todd, I'm not going to be home until six-thirty. One of the POW interviews ran late, and I've been playing catch-up all afternoon. Sorry about that."

He groaned, trying not to break rhythm . . . *Eighty-seven . . .* he'd been hoping to get a run in before dinner . . . *Eighty-eight . . .* leaning to the left . . . *Eighty-nine . . .* better straighten out . . .

"The hamburgers and Smart Dogs are in the fridge, you just need to make the salad and marinate the peppers and eggplant in some of the good olive oil. All right, I guess that's it. Be a good boy for Daddy, Aaron. Mommy loves you. Bye."

Ninety-two . . . his arms were shaking . . . *Ninety-three* . . . really wanted to go for that run . . . *Ninety-four* . . . fucking POWs . . . *Ninety-five* . . . Smart Dogs, what a stupid name . . . *Ninety-six* . . . gonna be hell to pay in a few years . . . *Ninety-seven* . . . when all these kids wake up and realize that they've been eating these crappy vegetarian hot dogs . . . *Ninety-eight* . . . two to go . . . *Ninety-nine* . . . all you, baby . . . *One hundred* . . . Yes!

He sprang from the floor, his body humming from the surge of bliss that three sets of a hundred push-ups each never failed to inspire. Sure, there were lots of things in the world that sucked. Kathy working late, for instance, screwing up his exercise plans. How she was always so tired when she got home, and guilty about being away from Aaron all day. And the way she acted like it was all Todd's fault, which it was, to a certain extent, but what was the point of reminding him all the time?

On the other hand, lots of things didn't suck. Long summer days with nothing to do but hang out. Afternoons at the pool, surrounded by young mothers in their bathing suits. And the way his body felt right now, the blood pumping into the muscles, the excellent soreness in his triceps. And when Aaron called out for him just then, right on time, there was something beautiful about that, too, the way a little kid needed you for everything and wasn't afraid to say so.

"Hold on, little buddy," he said. "I'll be right there."

Most mornings Aaron woke up bright-eyed and affectionate, bursting with puppyish energy for the new day. Afternoon naps, necessary as they were, tended to produce the opposite effect. He emerged from his bedroom dazed and sullen as a teenager, his jester's cap flattened and comically askew, sodden diaper hanging halfway to his knees. Even the most innocent question—*Would you like a snack?*—could send him over the edge, into a screaming fit or bout of heart-broken sobbing. Months of trial and error had taught Todd not to say a word. He just set Mr. Crabby into a chair, handed him a sippy cup of milk and an Oreo, and cranked up *Raffi in Concert* on the boom box.

While Aaron zoned out at the table, Todd started his dinner preparations, drying the lettuce in a spinner and whipping up a fresh batch of balsamic vinaigrette. Then he got out the cutting board and set to work chopping the eggplant and peppers into grillable chunks.

"Tingalayo!" he absentmindedly sang. "Run, my little donkey, run!"

"Daaaddy." Unlike Raffi, Aaron was bitterly opposed to sing-alongs. "You stop."

"Sorry. I forgot."

If someone had told him ten years earlier that he would one day be a full-time househusband grooving to children's music while he fixed dinner, Todd wouldn't have been able to recognize himself in the image. He was a frat boy jock back then, a big fan of Pearl Jam and Buffalo Tom. Raffi wasn't even on his radar screen, and now the guy was the single biggest musical presence in Todd's life. He and Aaron listened to the live album at least twice a day. It was the sound track of their summer, no less central than *Nevermind* had been for Todd and his Deke brothers during the spring semester of sophomore year. It had gotten to the point where he knew Raffi's between-song patter word-for-word, and could recite it along with the CD.

"Boys and girls, do you know the song about the five little

ducks?" Pause, while the audience roars its assent. Then a mischievous chuckle. "Well, this is a different one."

Unlike a lot of parents he encountered, who claimed to despise the music their kids made them listen to, Todd wasn't afraid to own up: He *liked* Raffi. The music was infectious, the guy himself gentle and unassuming. There was no posturing, none of the bullshit theatrics that made rock stars so wearying once you reached a certain point in your life. Raffi wasn't going to get strung out on smack, abandon his wife and little daughter, then blow his brains out, just to make some sort of point about what a drag it was to be rich and famous.

"Daddy?" Aaron was holding his index finger in front of his nose and sniffing it with a dubious expression.

"Yeah?"

"Well . . ."

"What is it?"

"Somefing smells like poop."

"Oh, Aaron. How many times have I told you—"

"I didn't touch my diaper," he said, shaking his head in fervent denial. "I really, really didn't."

Train Wreck was an activity perfectly suited to the mentality of a three-year-old boy. This brutally simple game, which Aaron had devised himself, required nothing more than pushing two engines (Gordon and Percy from *Thomas the Tank Engine*) in opposite directions around a circular track set up on the living room floor, and making happy chugging noises right up to the moment when they met in an inevitable head-on collision.

"*Spdang!*" Aaron shouted. This was the sound effect that always accompanied the crash. "Take that, Gordon."

"Ouch," Todd groaned, as his engine tipped onto its side. "That hurt, Percy."

Aaron laughed uproariously at Todd's aggrieved tone and half-assed British accent. If they'd staged a hundred train wrecks, he would have shouted *Spdang!* a hundred times and cracked up with undiminished glee at Gordon's hundredth declaration of injury. (Todd was always Gordon, and Gordon was always the injured party.) That was one of the sweet, but slightly insane things about being three: Nothing ever got old. If it was good, it stayed good, at least until you turned four.

For whatever reason, Todd didn't mind the brainless repetition of Train Wreck half as much as he minded reading certain books five or six times in a row, or playing multiple rounds of some stupid game like Candyland. Maybe it was a guy thing, but there was an undeniable satisfaction to be found in the spectacle of two solid objects smashing into one another.

Spdang!

Ouch.

The game ended abruptly with the sound of a key turning in the lock. Aaron let go of Percy and scrambled to his feet, staring at the opening front door as if something too wonderful for words were about to be revealed.

And Kathy was wonderful, of course, even at the end of a long workday, releasing a tired sigh as she dropped her overloaded tote bag onto the floor. She was the kind of woman who always surprised you with the realization that she was just as lovely as you remembered, though it hardly seemed possible in her absence.

"Mommy!" Aaron gasped, ripping off his jester's cap and flinging it over his shoulder. "You're back!"

"My little boy," she said, dropping to one knee and holding her arms out wide, like a poster of Jesus Todd remembered seeing in a

Sunday school classroom many years before. "I missed my sweetie so so so so much."

Aaron sprinted across the floor into his mother's arms, burying his face against her chest. She stroked his fine hair so tenderly that Todd had to look away. He found himself staring at the engine in his hand, as if there were a personal message for him in Gordon's peevish expression.

That hurt, Percy.

"You got some color, didn't you?" Kathy shook her head unhappily as she examined Aaron's adoring face. "Did Daddy forget the sunscreen again?"

After dinner on weeknights, Todd studied for the bar exam at the municipal library. He could have easily done this at home—he and Kathy had set up a comfortable, relatively soundproof office in their small sunroom—but it had become a psychological necessity for him to get out of the house on his own for a couple hours a day. Walking briskly past the shops on Pleasant Street, Todd savored the sensation of being a free adult out and about on a warm summer evening, unencumbered by a stroller or the tyrannical demands of a three-year-old.

Besides, he had trouble concentrating in the home office. He was distracted by the knowledge that Aaron and Kathy were somewhere nearby, giggling or cuddling or whispering endearments to one another, not giving him a second thought. As touching as it was, there was also something alienating about the explosion of mother/son passion that lit up the apartment every night. It was as if Todd became a nobody once Kathy got home, just some stranger inexplicably taking up space in the house, rather than a loving parent who'd devoted his whole day—*his whole life*—to ensuring his son's safety and happiness.

The thing that always killed him was the jester's cap. All day long Aaron treated it like his prize possession—he ate, played, and napped in the cap, and would burst into tears if you so much as suggested he take it off to go in the pool—but the moment Kathy stepped into the house it came flying off like some worthless piece of trash. Todd was pretty sure it was Aaron's way of announcing that the entire day up to that point—the Daddy part—had been nothing more than a stupid joke. Now that Mommy was back, the real day could begin, the precious few hours before bedtime when he didn't feel the need to say a toddler's version of *Fuck You* to the world by walking around in a jingling pink-and-purple hat.

Todd knew he shouldn't take it so personally. It was ridiculous for a grown man to feel slighted by a little boy's attachment to his mother. He'd studied psychology in college and was well versed in the nuances of the Oedipus complex and the concept of developmental stages. He knew that Aaron would outgrow his all-consuming attachment to his mother in a few years; by adolescence he might even pretend not to know Kathy if she passed him in the mall. But all that was in the future. In the present, Todd felt jealous and excluded and even a little bit angry, and the only cure for it was to get the hell out of the house.

The skateboarders were out in front of the library, and Todd stopped in his usual spot to see what they were up to. There were four of them tonight, boys between the ages of ten and thirteen, dressed in knee-length shorts, baggy T-shirts, and fashionably retro sneakers. They wore helmets, but left the chin straps unbuckled or loosely dangling, rendering them more or less useless as protective gear. A few days earlier, Todd had pointed this out to the king of the skateboarders, a scrawny, loose-limbed daredevil known to the others as G., but the kid had responded with one of those blank looks they specialized in; he hadn't even bothered to shrug.

Graceful and fearless, G. was a natural athlete who seemed to possess an almost mystical connection with his board. He jumped stairs and curbs, surfed metal railings and retaining walls, and almost always landed on his feet. His more earthbound friends limited themselves to practicing the most basic maneuvers, though more often than not they ended up sprawled on the ground, moaning softly and rubbing their sore butts.

Todd wasn't sure what kept him coming back here night after night, watching the same group of kids performing the same small repertoire of stunts over and over again. Part of it was genuine interest, a kind of remedial education in what had become an essential boyhood skill. He had never learned to skateboard himself— as a kid, he'd been more focused on organized, competitive sports— and wanted to be able to instruct Aaron when the time came, the way Todd had been taught by his own father to ride a two-wheeler. About a week ago, he'd gone into Jock Heaven, intent on buying a board for himself, but he'd chickened out at the approach of the salesman, as though it were somehow unseemly for a thirty-year-old man to be purchasing a skateboard for his own use.

If Kathy had seen him loitering here beneath the beech tree, one arm resting on top of a green mail storage box, studying the skateboarders like some sort of self-appointed Olympic judge, she would have offered a simpler explanation—i.e., that he was procrastinating, jeopardizing his own professional future and his family's long-term financial prospects. And she would have had a point: The only thing worse than having to retake the bar exam was having to study for it again, like an actor memorizing lines he knew he'd forget the moment he stepped onstage. But if all Todd had wanted to do was waste time, there were a multitude of other ways to do it (he knew them all). He could read magazines in the library, surf the web, browse the stacks. He could buy an ice-cream cone and eat it with luxuriant slowness while sitting on a park bench, or feed a bagel to the bad-tempered ducks over at Greenview Pond. He could even wander over to the high school and watch the varsity cheerleaders practice their routines, which were a helluva lot sexier than they'd been back in Todd's day. But he didn't do any of that. He always just came here.

Todd had been watching G. and his friends for weeks, sometimes for as long as an hour at a stretch, but he'd never received the slightest acknowledgment from any of them, not the most grudging nod or muttered hello. They had a walled-off, wholly self-contained attitude toward the world, as if nothing of importance existed outside of their own severely limited circle of activity. They kept their eyes low and communicated in grunts and monosyllables, barely looking up when one of their number nailed a difficult landing or took a particularly nasty spill, or even when some cute girls their own age stopped to watch them for a while, whispering and giggling among themselves.

I must have been like this, Todd sometimes thought. *I must have been one of them.*

The afternoon his mother died, Todd and his friends had been throwing snowballs at cars. The roads were slick, and a station wagon that they ambushed skidded and jumped the curb across the street, plowing over some garbage cans and scattering trash all over the Andersons' front lawn. Most of Todd's buddies fled the scene, but he and Mark Tollan remained crouched behind some leafless bushes, snickering into their gloves as the middle-aged driver jumped out of his car and began shouting plaintively in the January twilight.

"Are you happy now? Is this what you wanted?"

When he got home an hour or so later, chilled and exhilarated and starving—he was always starving in those days—the first odd thing Todd noticed was that the house didn't smell like food. The second thing was the presence of his father, who usually returned from work later in the evening, sitting on the couch in a weirdly rigid posture, with what looked like an ominous expression on his face. Even before his father spoke, Todd knew for certain that he'd been busted, though he wasn't sure how. Had the driver recognized him somehow? Had one of his friends confessed? Had some neighborhood adult witnessed everything?

"Sit down, son. I need to talk to you."

"Is this about the car?" Todd asked.

His father was taken aback. "Did someone tell you?"

"No, I just had a feeling." Todd braced himself for a scolding, but his father fell into a peculiar silence, as if he'd forgotten they were having a conversation. "It was my fault, Dad. I should have known better."

"What are you talking about?" His father spoke softly, but there was tension in his voice, as if he were making an effort to remain calm. "It was an accident. It wasn't anyone's fault."

The powerful sense of reprieve Todd experienced quickly turned to confusion. For some reason, his father began talking about his mother in an awkward, almost mechanical monotone. Driving home from Sears. Treacherous conditions. Lost control on an exit ramp. Broke through a guardrail. Wrapped the car around a tree trunk. This was the phrase that had lodged itself in his memory, though in retrospect he couldn't believe that his father would have evoked such an awful image at that particular moment.

"I'm sorry, Todd. That's what happened. I just got back from the hospital. The doctors did everything they could."

"Does Janie know?"

"We're gonna pick her up at the airport in an hour."

We predicted it, Todd thought. Ever since he could remember, he and his sister Janie—she was seven years older, already a freshman in college—had been teasing their mother about what a bad driver she was. She was always checking her makeup while she drove, puckering her lips and appraising herself in the rearview mirror. She would take her eyes off the road for extended periods to rummage through her purse or change the station on the radio.

Look where you're going, they used to tell her. *You're gonna kill somebody.*

Probably just myself, their mother would say, in an oddly cheerful voice.

"What are we gonna do?" Todd asked.

His father seemed momentarily at a loss. He looked at his hand for a few seconds, as if hoping to find an answer scribbled on his palm, then softly patted Todd on the shoulder.

"We're going to keep moving forward," his father said, his voice regaining some of its normal authority. "Nothing's going to change. I want you to keep living your life as if this never happened. It's what your mother wants, too."

Todd was so relieved to find out there was a plan that it never occurred to him to question its wisdom. Two days after his mother's funeral he played in a youth league basketball playoff game and scored seventeen points. The day after that he was back in school. When a teacher asked how he was doing in that compassionate voice they used, Todd always said *Fine* so firmly and emphatically that no one ever pressed him to make sure if he was really okay, or maybe needed to talk to someone about what he was going through.

All through high school and college, Todd did exactly what his dead mother and quickly remarried father wanted from him, excelling in the classroom and on the playing field, impersonating a successful, well-adjusted kid who had somehow absorbed a terrible blow without missing a beat—starting quarterback, dean's list, social chair, lots of girlfriends, accepted into three of the five law schools he'd applied to.

It was only later, after he was married and the father of a newborn son, that he began to suspect that there was something not quite right, something unresolved or defective at the core of his being. And it must have been this something—this flaw or lack or whatever the hell it was—that kept his arm glued to the mailbox while he watched the skateboarders every night, desperately hoping that they'd notice him for once and say something nice, maybe even invite him to step out from the shadows and take his rightful place among them.

THE PROM KING

"HE SHOULD JUST BE CASTRATED."

Mary Ann made this declaration with magisterial calm, as if there were no possibility of another point of view on the subject. Cheryl and Theresa nodded in wholehearted agreement. The "he" in question was Ronald James McGorvey, a forty-three-year-old former Catholic school custodian and convicted sex offender, who had just moved in with his elderly mother at 44 Blueberry Court, a modest cul-de-sac Sarah and Lucy passed every day on their way to the playground.

Sarah studied McGorvey's shadowy face—he was a plump man with wiry, thinning hair and an anxious expression—on the badly photocopied handbill spread out on the picnic table. It was one of hundreds that had popped up all over town the past couple of days, stapled to telephone poles, tucked under windshield wipers, slipped beneath front doors. **DECENT PEOPLE BEWARE!!!** the headline blared. **THERE IS A PERVERT AMONG US!** The fine print explained that McGorvey had been charged repeatedly with indecent exposure and was "reputed to be a prime suspect in the still-unsolved disappearance of a nine-year-old Rhode Island girl in 1995."

"Quick and clean," Mary Ann continued. "Just chop it off. Then you wouldn't have to worry about notifying the neighbors."

"You know what else you should do?" Sarah suggested, employing the same take-no-prisoners tone as Mary Ann. "Nail his severed penis above the entrance to the elementary school. You know, as a warning to the other perverts."

Recognizing sarcasm when they heard it, Cheryl and Theresa chuckled politely. Mary Ann fixed Sarah with an icy glare.

"You think this is funny?"

"I just can't believe you want to castrate a man for indecent exposure."

"If that's what it takes to protect my children, then so be it," said Mary Ann. "And besides, he's probably a murderer."

"He's a suspect. In this country it means that he's innocent until proven guilty."

"He's *been* proven guilty. Why do you think he was in prison?"

"So? He did his time. He paid his debt to society."

Sarah was surprised to hear herself taking such a narrow, legalistic view of the situation. Back in college, she'd been an enthusiastic proponent of the hard-line antipornography position staked out by Andrea Dworkin and Catherine MacKinnon, and had written a well-received sociology term paper on "The Normalization of Abuse: Patriarchy and Marital Rape." She certainly wouldn't have objected if one of her Women's Studies professors had recommended the castration of incorrigible sex offenders. But her dislike of Mary Ann had become so strong that it trumped all other considerations. If Mary Ann had spoken out in favor of kindness to animals and small children, Sarah might have felt tempted to take up the cause of cruelty.

It wasn't her opinions per se that were so irritating, it was the smugness with which she expressed them. Underlying Mary Ann's every utterance was an obnoxious sense of certainty, of personal completeness, as if she'd gotten everything she'd ever wanted in the best of all possible worlds. *This?* Sarah always wanted to ask. *This is what you wanted? This playground? That SUV? Your stupid spandex shorts? Your weekly roll in the hay? Those well-behaved children who cower at the sound of your voice?*

"Snip, snip." Mary Ann made a scissoring motion with her index and middle fingers. "Problem solved."

"Some countries chop off the hands of shoplifters," Sarah pointed out. "Maybe we should do that, too."

"Probably cut down on shoplifting," Mary Ann said, drawing appreciative laughter from Cheryl and Theresa.

Sarah had no illusion that she'd gotten the better of the exchange, but it didn't matter. The important thing was that she was speaking up, no longer letting Mary Ann intimidate her into silence and implied agreement. After last week's incident with the rice cakes, Sarah had more or less decided to switch to a new play-ground—as soon as she located one within walking distance that offered some promise of reasonable human contact—and this deci-sion had liberated her from the thankless task of pretending to fit in with the other mothers.

"My brother used to expose himself," Theresa said suddenly. "When we were teenagers. He'd do it in my bedroom, or in the backseat of the car, even at the dinner table. He always figured out a way to do it so that no one could see what he was up to but me."

"Didn't you tell anyone?" Cheryl asked.

"No." Theresa shook her head, as if puzzled by her own answer, "I didn't want to get him in trouble. Or maybe I was scared someone was going to blame me. I don't know. It didn't stop until he went away to college."

"That's revolting," said Mary Ann. "Did you ever confront him?"

"Once," said Theresa. "About five years ago. We got a little drunk, and I asked him about it. He remembered it as a onetime thing, a stupid joke or something. But it happened a lot. Not every day or every week, but just enough that it always seemed like a possibility."

Sarah couldn't help herself. "He should have been castrated."

"It's not the same thing," Mary Ann snapped. "He wasn't doing it to strangers."

"Not that we know of," said Cheryl.

"He's married now," said Theresa. "His wife's pregnant with number three. And of all my siblings, he's the one I get along best with. Just goes to show."

Goes to show what? Sarah wanted to ask, but she didn't have a chance. Cheryl abruptly reached across the table and grabbed Theresa's hand.

"Look." She spoke the word softly, but with urgency.

"What?" Theresa glanced instinctively toward the play structure, where Courtney, Isabelle, and Lucy were taking turns on the baby slide. "Where?"

"Over there," said Cheryl. "The Prom King."

"Oh my God." Theresa smiled as if she'd just received good news. "He's back."

Sarah followed the other women's gazes over to the swing set, eager to finally get a glimpse of the Prom King, the handsome and mysterious young father who had been a regular at the Rayburn School

playground for several weeks this past spring before abruptly dropping out of sight. His departure had left a gaping hole in the emotional lives of Cheryl, Theresa, and Mary Ann. Barely a day went
by without one of them speculating wistfully about the reason for
his absence and the likelihood of his return.

"Maybe he got fired," Theresa said, lowering her voice the way
people did when discussing a shameful subject.

"You don't even know if he had a job," Mary Ann pointed out.

The Prom King knelt down to unbuckle his son, a slender little
boy wearing a pink-and-purple jester's cap, from the right side of a
double stroller. A large stuffed bear was strapped into the seat on
the left. With the ease of someone performing a familiar action, the
Prom King lifted his son into the air and dropped him into the
toddler swing, which resembled a black rubber diaper hanging from
two chains.

"Maybe he just needed a vacation," Cheryl said.

"A vacation from what?" Mary Ann sounded vaguely exasperated.

"From being Prom King," said Theresa.

"It's a dirty job," Cheryl added with a chuckle. "But someone's
got to do it."

As ridiculous as the nickname sounded, Sarah had to admit that
it seemed oddly appropriate. The Prom King was tall and well built,
with a shock of blond hair falling surfer-style across his forehead.
There was something generic about his good looks, a pleasantly
bland quality that reminded her of those cheerful men who modeled
jockey shorts in the Sunday supplements, smiling confidently with
their arms crossed on their chests, or pointing with fascination into
empty space.

In any case, it was easy to see why he'd made such an impression. Most of the men who showed up at the playground during

the workday were marginal types—middle-aged trolls with beards and potbellies, studiously whimsical academics who insisted on going down the slide with their kids, pinch-hitting grandfathers providing emergency day care, sheepish blue-collar guys who wouldn't meet anyone's eyes, the occasional cooler-than-thou hipster-with-a-flexible-schedule. But there was no one even remotely like the Prom King, who looked like he'd wandered off the set of a daytime soap to bring a little bit of glamour into the lives of bored young mothers.

"What's he do for a living?" Sarah asked.

No one had any idea.

"He must have had some kind of job," Sarah pressed on. "Before he got married."

"I'm sure he did," agreed Mary Ann. "He just didn't discuss it."

"What about his wife? What's she do?"

"We didn't really talk to him," Cheryl explained.

"We don't even know his name," Theresa added.

"Really?" All this time, Sarah had imagined herself as taking the Prom King's place at the picnic table. That was the way it had been presented to her by the others: *He left, and a few days later you showed up.* "I thought you said he was a regular."

"It was awkward," said Theresa. "It wasn't like he was one of the girls."

"He made us nervous," said Cheryl. "You had to think about what you were going to wear in the morning, put on makeup. It was exhausting."

"You went to all that trouble and you still didn't talk to him?" Sarah couldn't hide her amusement. "What is this, seventh grade?"

"We don't come here to flirt," Mary Ann said primly. "We come here to look after our children."

"My God," said Sarah. "What year is this? It's possible to talk to a man without flirting."

"He's kind of intimidating," Theresa insisted. "It's hard to explain."

Sarah glanced at the Prom King, who was having some trouble squeezing the stuffed bear into the swing next to his son's. Once he got it jammed in to his satisfaction, he began pushing both swings, as though the child and the stuffed animal held equal claims on his attention.

"What's with the double stroller?" Sarah asked. "Does he have another kid?"

"We've only seen the one," said Cheryl.

"He's a cutie," added Theresa. "That crazy hat."

Maybe they lost a child, Sarah thought, wondering if the Prom King might actually be a tragic figure. How thoughtless it would be, whispering and giggling about a man carrying a terrible weight of grief on his shoulders. On the other hand, he seemed fairly lighthearted at the moment, imitating a series of barnyard animals as he wove a figure eight between the two swings. The imitations were surprisingly realistic—he did an especially good chicken—and he performed them at high volume, with a lack of self-consciousness that was rare in an adult male. Lucy seemed to find this appealing, and she wandered over from the sandbox for a closer look.

"Mommy!" she called. "Swing me!"

Normally, Sarah tried to discourage Lucy from going on the swings. She tended to get hypnotized by the motion, and convincing her to stop invariably turned into a complex negotiation full of threats and bribery, and culminating in an inevitable tantrum. But right now that seemed like a small price to pay for the chance to show the other mothers that it was possible to treat a good-looking man as if he were an actual human being rather than some sort of two-dimensional sex object. She rose slowly from the bench, feigning weariness.

"Okay, sweetie. I'll be right there."

"Wait," Theresa whispered. She had her purse open and was groping for something inside.

"What?" said Sarah.

Theresa held up her wallet, smirking like a schoolgirl.

"Five bucks if you get his phone number."

The little boy observed Lucy with a certain amount of skepticism as she swung in near unison beside him. Then he turned to Sarah, his expression unexpectedly serious for someone wearing a floppy velour cap outfitted with real bells.

"Her how old?" he inquired.

"Lucy, honey?" Sarah coaxed. "Tell the nice boy how old you are."

Lucy shook her head, refusing as usual to do anything that might enable a social interaction to unfold smoothly, without awkwardness or unnecessary effort.

"I three!" the little jester shouted, undeterred by Lucy's silence. He jabbed the corresponding number of fingers into the air.

"His birthday was in February," the Prom King added, smiling pleasantly at Sarah. Up close his features were more distinctive than she had anticipated—the eyes set a bit too close together, two of his bottom teeth overlapping slightly—the imperfections adding a helpful touch of humanity to the package. "Still working on the potty training, though."

"Tell me about it." Sarah chuckled. "Lucy turned three in April. Isn't that right, honey?"

Lucy would neither confirm nor deny this assertion. She just stared at the boy, her expression composed of equal parts amazement and horror.

"She can be a bit shy," Sarah explained.

"Not Aaron," said the Prom King. "He's a real talker."

"My grandma lives in New Jersey!" the boy proclaimed, unable to contain this exciting fact a moment longer. But then his eyes narrowed and his mood turned somber. "She not have a swim pool."

"His grandmother in Florida has one," the Prom King reported.

"Do you like to swim?" Sarah asked the boy.

"I don't like sharks," he said. "They eat you up."

"Don't listen to him. He loves to swim. We go to the Town Pool almost every day." The Prom King held out his hand. "I'm Todd, by the way."

"Sarah."

"I haven't seen you here before."

"I've only been coming for a few weeks. I used to go to the playground with that old, creaky merry-go-round? The one by the ice-cream place?"

Todd knew it well. He and Aaron liked to rotate playgrounds every few weeks for the sake of variety. Though, he had to say, some places were friendlier than others.

"You're the first person who's ever talked to me here," he said, glancing in the direction of the other mothers, who were staring back with undisguised curiosity, as if Sarah and Todd were images flickering on a movie screen.

"I think you make them nervous," she said. "They're not used to running into good-looking men at the playground."

Oh my God, she thought. *I can't believe I'm flirting with him.*

Todd nodded thoughtfully at her analysis, neither blushing nor trying to deflect the compliment. When you were as handsome as he was, Sarah supposed, there wasn't much point in pretending to be surprised when other people noticed.

"I guess it is a little odd," he admitted. "There aren't as many stay-at-home fathers around here as I thought."

"What does your wife do?" Sarah asked.

"She's a filmmaker. She's doing a documentary on World War Two veterans. You know, the Greatest Generation, all that stuff."

"*Saving Private Ryan*," said Sarah.

"Tom Brokaw," agreed Todd.

"Anyway, I think it's great that you're here. There's no reason why men can't be primary caregivers."

"I finished law school two years ago," Todd volunteered, after only the briefest hesitation. "But I can't seem to pass the bar exam. Failed it twice now."

"That's a hard test." She shook her head. "I remember all the trouble John F. Kennedy, Jr. had with it."

Todd felt the twinge of sympathy he never failed to experience when people mentioned JFK, Jr. in an attempt to make him feel better, as they almost always did. It was bad enough that the poor guy had to lose his father and die in a tragic plane crash; did he have to go down in history as the patron saint of failed bar exams as well?

"I don't know," he said. "It's just whenever I think about it I'm filled with this unbelievable feeling of dread. It's like one of those bad dreams, where you suddenly realize that you forgot to go to math class all semester, and now it's time for the final."

"Maybe you just don't want to be a lawyer."

He seemed momentarily startled by this suggestion. "Well, maybe I'll get my wish. Kathy and I agreed that I'm going to take the test one more time. If I mess up, I'm going to have to find something else to do with my life."

He seemed so matter-of-fact while delivering this confession, not at all embarrassed by the fact of his failure. Most men weren't like that—Richard certainly wasn't. She wondered if Todd was always this forthcoming, or if he found her for some reason to be an unusually sympathetic listener. Either way, there was nothing the least bit intimidating about him. If anything, he seemed a little lonely, all too ready to open his heart at the slightest sign of interest, like a lot of the young mothers she knew.

"I couldn't help noticing your stroller," she told him. "Do you have another child?"

"Just Aaron. We got that at a yard sale. The extra seat comes in handy for carrying groceries and stuff. At least it used to, before Big Bear started joining us."

"Lucy won't even go in a stroller. We have to walk everywhere. It takes us half an hour to go three blocks."

They pushed their children and continued chatting for another fifteen minutes or so, until Todd glanced at his watch and discovered to his surprise that it was already past noon. Unlike Sarah, he had apparently developed an effective system for bringing swing time to a close. After issuing a five-minute warning, he loudly announced the passage of each successive minute, until the time came for the final ten pushes, which he and Aaron counted out together in enthusiastic voices. Then he left his son to swing slowly to a standstill while he removed Big Bear from the swing and returned him to the stroller. It was only then, while watching him kneel down to affix the safety belt around the bear's shapeless midsection, that Sarah found herself gripped by an unexpected pang of sadness.

Don't go, she thought. *Don't leave me here with the others.*

As if he'd heard her, Todd straightened up and gave her a curious smile, as if he were about to ask a personal question.

"Well," he said. "It was nice talking to you."

"Same here."

She watched in silence as he cupped Aaron by the armpits and attempted to lift him out of the swing. The boy's foot got caught in one of the apertures, and Sarah hurried over to free it before Todd even had a chance to ask for assistance.

"Thanks," he said.

"No problem. Happens to us all the time. Sometimes I think Lucy does it on purpose."

As Todd buckled Aaron into the stroller, Sarah found herself gazing at Big Bear, whose face was frozen in a look of wild alarm, as if he were witnessing something horrible but did not know how to cry for help. Todd stood up and shrugged, as if to say that was that. Sarah spoke without thinking.

"You know those women over there?" She gestured as discreetly as she could at the picnic table posse. "You know what they call you?"

"What?" Todd seemed intrigued.

"The Prom King."

"Ouch." He winced, as if this were a humiliating insult. "That's awful."

"They mean it as a compliment. You're a big character in their fantasy lives."

"I guess," he said dubiously. "I mean, you could easily come up with something worse."

"One of them bet me five dollars I couldn't get your phone number," Sarah said, once again shocked by her own boldness.

"Five bucks?" Todd smiled. "Could we split it fifty-fifty?"

"It could be arranged."

Todd patted himself down, then showed her his empty palms. "You got a pen?"

Sarah knew there was a pen in her diaper bag, but she didn't want to walk all the way over to the picnic table to retrieve it. And besides, she already had a better idea.

"You know what would really shock them? If you gave me a hug."

Neither one of them moved for a second or two, and Sarah's confidence began to falter. But then Todd began walking toward her, his Prom King face surrounded by the dazzling blue background of the summer sky. He smiled shyly and opened his arms.

Sarah was unaccustomed to the sensation of hugging someone so tall. She pressed her face against his collarbone, uncomfortably close to the sweat stain spreading out from beneath his arm. There was a sour odor radiating from his body that she found oddly reassuring.

"This feels pretty good," he whispered.

She nodded into his chest and held him a little tighter, as if they were slow-dancing at the prom. Her back was to the picnic table, so she could only imagine the consternation this embrace was causing among the other mothers. She pulled her head away from him and looked up.

"You know what would be really funny?"

In retrospect, she was never quite sure if he answered her question. Maybe he nodded or made some vague murmur of assent. In any case, he did exactly what she'd meant him to, as if she'd outlined the action in precise detail.

The first kiss was tentative, only half-serious, as if they were acting in a play, but the second one was for real—gentle, then forceful, and then completely electrifying, the kind of kiss that would have made perfect sense outside a dorm room at two in the morning. On a playground at noon, between near-total strangers, though, it was a kind of insanity. Luckily, one of them finally had the good sense to pull away from the other, though Sarah could not for the life of her remember which of them it was.

"My God," she murmured.

Todd wiped his bare forearm across his mouth. He was blushing now.

"Wow," he said.

"You better go," she told him.

He nodded and set off without another word, slowly pushing the stroller across the unreal green expanse of the soccer field. Sarah watched his broad back receding for as long as she could stand it, then turned to her daughter, who was sitting in her motionless swing, watching the same sight as her mother, her feet kicking dreamily at the air.

"Let's get going," Sarah told her.

For once, Lucy submitted without complaint as her mother lifted her out of the swing. The two of them walked back toward the picnic table in silence, holding hands. Sarah's legs felt unsteady as she approached the other mothers, her face burning with pride and shame. Cheryl and Theresa were staring at her in complete bewilderment. Mary Ann looked furious.

"I'm sure your daughter found that very educational," she said.

"His name's Todd," Sarah replied. "He's a lawyer. And he's really very nice."

THE COMMITTEE OF
CONCERNED PARENTS

AARON HAD DISCOVERED HIS PENIS. WHENEVER HE HAD A SPARE moment—when he was watching TV, say, or listening to a story—his hand would wander southward, and his face would go all soft and dreamy. This new hobby coincided with a sudden leap forward in his potty training that allowed him to wear big boy underpants at home during the day (at night, during naps, and in public he still needed the insurance of a diaper). Because he often had to sprint to the bathroom at the last possible moment, he preferred not to wear pants over the underwear, and this combination of easy access and an elastic waistband issued a sort of standing invitation that he found impossible to resist.

Having been reassured by parenting books that childhood masturbation was a common and harmless activity—and believing in any case that each individual has a sovereign right of ownership over his or her own body—Todd and Kathy had made a conscious decision not to interfere with Aaron's self-explorations. But sometimes they wondered.

"Did you do that as a kid?" Kathy asked. They were watching

from the hallway as Aaron absentmindedly stroked his tiny manhood while watching a video of *Clifford, the Big Red Dog*.

"I don't think so," said Todd. It was hard for him to remember the specifics of his early childhood. When he tried, the only image he could regularly produce was his mother's face hovering over him as she tucked him into bed at night, a luminous, looming, loving presence that he could still sometimes sense at the edges of his perception.

"I sure didn't," said Kathy. "My mother used to tell me it was dirty down there and to never ever touch it. Of course, she wouldn't let me suck my thumb, either. She painted that awful sticky stuff on it at night to make me stop."

"Eet ees puffeckly nawmal to zuck ze sum!" Todd exclaimed, doing the imitation of Dr. Ruth that Kathy used to get such a kick out of. He'd do it while they were making love, whenever he needed to get her to relax and experiment with something a little out of the ordinary. (*Eet ees puffeckly nawmal to vare ze handcuffs!*) That was one of her sweetest quirks (or at least it used to be): As long as you could convince her that the practice in question fell within the boundaries of "normal behavior," she was up for just about anything. "Und ees puffeckly nawmal to be aroused by big red dog!"

Kathy chuckled politely, but her mind had already shifted to another topic.

"By the way," she said. "Have you been doing the flash cards?"

"Not too much," Todd admitted.

Kathy had recently purchased a preschool "Fun with Math" kit. She wanted to get Aaron thinking about numbers—recognizing numerals, counting to a hundred, maybe doing some rudimentary addition—and had made a unilateral decision that Todd would be heavily involved, even though he had repeatedly expressed his lack of enthusiasm for the project. The kid was only three, for God's sake. His idea of a good time was smashing two trains together. He didn't need to be worrying about math.

"I wish you'd give it a try," she said. "I just want him to feel comfortable with the basic concepts. Just because you and I were bad at math doesn't mean he should be scared of it, too."

"I wasn't bad at math," Todd protested. "Except for calculus. I had some kind of mental block with that."

Kathy turned back to Aaron.

"Honey?" She had to repeat the word three times at increasing volume to get his attention. "When Clifford's over, we're going to do our flash cards, okay?"

Aaron nodded—Todd thought he would have agreed to just about anything right then—and turned back to the TV. Todd kissed Kathy on the cheek.

"Oh well," he said. "Better hit the books."

"So how's it going?" she said, making an unsuccessful attempt to sound casual.

"Fine," he said. "Why?"

"I don't know. I just worry about you sometimes," she said. "I worry about us."

He kissed her again, this time on the forehead.

"There's nothing to worry about."

Todd didn't understand the point of certain skateboarding maneuvers. They weren't always self-explanatory, like popping a wheelie or spinning a basketball on your fingertip. Sometimes it was hard to know what the boys were *trying* to do, let alone if they'd succeeded.

Tonight, for example, all of them were practicing a low-key move where they scootered along at a leisurely clip, crouched down like a surfer, and then hopped into the air for a split second. If the rider was skillful, the board clung to the soles of his sneakers as if by magnetism, and he continued rolling as before when the wheels reconnected with the ground. If not, the board slipped away from the rider's feet and plunged to the pavement, usually landing upside down or on its side, and making either a soft clattering noise or a decisive smack, depending upon whether the rider came down on top of it, in which case a fairly interesting fall could result.

A smooth landing was preferable to a painful tumble, of course, but was that it? Even when done properly, the maneuver seemed unassuming to a fault, barely worth the trouble. And yet, rider after rider kept gliding past him like figures in a dream, crouching and hopping, standing or falling, performing their pointless task with the stoic patience of early adolescence. *I don't know why I'm doing this*, each boy seemed to say, *but I'll keep doing it until I'm old enough to do something else.*

As he had so often in recent days, Todd closed his eyes and let out a low moan, mentally reenacting the kiss by the swing set. He still couldn't believe that it had really happened, right out in public like that, after only a brief conversation, with all those women and children looking on (Aaron had been particularly curious about what he'd seen, and had received Todd's explanation that it was just pretend, a game grown-ups sometimes played, with justifiable skepticism). But Sarah hadn't just kissed him. She had pressed her body against his with astonishing frankness, murmuring these sweet little noises of approval and encouragement right into his mouth. Todd had been *this close* to grabbing her ass when he remembered where they were. She looked dazed and disappointed when he pulled away, and he'd had to stop himself from inviting her back to his house for more right then and there, though what "more" might have meant with a pair of three-year-olds in tow, he couldn't have begun to say.

A week had passed, and Todd hadn't seen or heard from her since. He and Aaron had returned to the Rayburn School playground the following morning, but no one was there, not even the three bitchy women who supposedly called him "Prom King." They were back a few days after that, but played dumb when Todd asked about Sarah, as if they didn't know the first thing about her, not even her last name or where she lived.

"I'm surprised you have to ask," said the bossy one with the toothpick legs. "It looked like you knew each other pretty well."

Sarah hadn't shown up at the Town Pool, either, though Todd remembered telling her that he and Aaron could be found there most afternoons. So she was obviously in no big hurry to reconnect with him and explore phase two of the playground fantasy, whatever that might be. It was probably a good thing, Todd decided. It wasn't like he wanted to have an affair or anything. He just wanted to see her again, maybe talk a little about what had happened, find out if she felt as unsettled by their encounter as he did.

Because he couldn't get that damn kiss out of his mind. The whole thing was just so uncanny. Todd had been fantasizing about something like that for months, every time he found himself engaged in conversation with an attractive young mother—*Dear Penthouse Forum, I'm a 31-year-old stay-at-home dad, and you'll never believe what just happened to me at the playground*—and now it had really happened. It was like suddenly being a teenager again, returning to a time when sex wasn't a routine or predictable part of your life, but something mysterious and transforming that could pop up out of nowhere, sometimes when you weren't even looking, though usually you were. Walk into a party and Bang! There it was. The mall, McDonald's, even church! Some girl smiles at you, and it's a whole different day.

Losing that sense of omnipresent possibility was one of the

trade-offs of married life that Todd struggled with on a daily basis. Sure, he got to sleep with a great woman every night. He could kiss her whenever he wanted (well, almost). But sometimes it was nice to kiss someone else for a change, for the hell of it, just to prove it could still be done. It didn't seem to matter that Sarah wasn't his type, wasn't even that pretty, at least not compared to Kathy, who had long legs and lustrous hair, and knew how to make herself as glamorous as a model when you gave her a reason to. Sarah was short and boyish, slightly pop-eyed, and a little angry-looking when you got right down to it. She had coarse unruly hair and eyebrows that were thicker than Todd thought necessary. But so what? She'd read his mind and walked into his arms, as if she'd memorized a script he hadn't even remembered writing until he found himself standing in the middle of it, breathing hard and barely able to let go.

"Hey, pervert!"

Todd cringed at the word, flinging up his arms as if to deflect a blow. The minivan had crept up so slowly—or he had retreated so deeply into himself—that he didn't even notice it until it was idling right in front of him, blocking his view of the skateboarders.

"Like the little boys, do you?"

The teasing note was clearer now. Todd dropped his guard and squinted into the van in an effort to identify the driver, who was craning across the front seat to assist him in this task. It took a few seconds to pin a name on the broad, fleshy face grinning at him through the open passenger window.

"Jesus, Larry. Don't even joke about that."

Larry Moon was a father Todd had hung out with a couple of times at the Stuart Street sprinkler park during last summer's heat wave, and hadn't seen since. He was a stocky, thick-necked guy in his midthirties, an ex-cop who had recently retired on full disability, though there didn't appear to be anything physically wrong with him.

"You busy?" he asked.

"Actually, I'm, uh, supposed to be studying." Todd lifted his bookbag off the ground to bolster what sounded—even to himself— like an unlikely claim. "I'm taking the bar exam next month."

"Didn't you do that last year?"

"Yeah," said Todd. "See how good I did?"

Larry laughed, as if Todd had meant it as a joke. He popped the lock and the passenger door swung open.

"Get in," he said. "I got a better idea."

Larry cleared off the passenger seat, tossing a football and a pair of binoculars into the back of the van, and snatching up a fat stack of blue paper, which he dropped into Todd's lap a moment later.

"You mind?" he said. "I'm trying to keep 'em nice."

Todd recognized the pervert warning right away. He had received three of them in the past week alone—one in his mailbox, one folded into the Sunday paper, another slipped through his car window when he'd left it open a crack at the supermarket. A small footnote at the bottom of the flyer said, *Paid for by the Committee of Concerned Parents.*

"You part of the committee?" Todd asked.

"I *am* the committee. It just sounds better than *Paid for by Larry from Hazel Avenue.* A little more official."

"How'd you find out about this creep?"

"There's a web site. The state's required to disclose the whereabouts of convicted sex offenders." Larry shot him an inquiring glance. "Don't you check it?"

"Not on a regular basis," Todd confessed.

"I think decent people have a right to know if Chester the Molester's moving in next door, don't you?"

"McGorvey's not living next door to you, is he?"

"Not next door. But close enough." Larry's expression darkened. "They should just castrate the bastard and be done with it."

Todd nodded as noncommittally as he could, trying to acknowledge Larry's strong opinion on the subject without having to express his own more measured one. In the interval of silence that followed, Todd's attention latched on to the familiar music playing softly on the car stereo.

"You a Raffi fan?"

"What?" Larry seemed startled by the question.

"That's Raffi, right? 'Big, Beautiful Planet'?"

"Ah, shit." Larry punched EJECT. "After a while I don't even know what I'm listening to anymore."

"I actually like some of his stuff," Todd volunteered. "You know, just a song here and there. I'm not president of his fan club or anything."

Larry didn't respond, and Todd wondered if he'd been more forthcoming on the subject than he needed to be. His discomfort grew more acute at a red light just beyond the center of town, when Larry shifted in the driver's seat and examined Todd's body with disconcerting thoroughness, his gaze lingering on the legs and moving slowly upward.

"You look good," he said. "Been going to the gym?"

Oh shit, thought Todd.

He felt like an idiot, more embarrassed on Larry's behalf than his own. Because what was the guy supposed to think? He pulls up, calls you a pervert, and invites you into his van, and you climb in without even asking where you're going. The average five-year-old would have known better.

"I run a lot," Todd explained. "Lotsa push-ups and crunches and stuff."

"This is unbelievable." Larry grinned and gave Todd a hard but not unfriendly sock in the arm. "I've been searching for you for months, and when I finally give up, there you are, standing on the corner like some crack whore in the ghetto."

"Why were you looking?" Todd decided not to make an issue of the crack whore analogy, which did not strike him as auspicious. "Did you want to ask me something?"

"The guys are gonna love this," Larry said, more to himself than Todd.

The guys? Todd thought unhappily. *What guys?* But before he could pose the question, the minivan veered unexpectedly across two lanes of traffic, into the parking lot of the high school athletic complex, which was brightly lit and the scene of a reassuring amount of activity—senior citizens shuffling around the track, some teenage boys tossing a lacrosse ball, two Chinese women practicing Tai Chi near an equipment shed. Todd let go of his misgivings, despite the fact that Larry was staring at his legs again.

"Good thing you're wearing sneakers," he said.

As successful and satisfying as it had been, Todd's high school football career had unfolded on a field so incurably dingy that not even the most nostalgic glow of memory could improve it. The grass of Arthur "Biff" Ryan Stadium was coarse and mottled with permanent bald spots between the thirty yard lines that the long-suffering groundskeeper tried to mask with some kind of vegetable-based spray paint for big games and graduation ceremonies. This organic ground cover held up to the rough-and-tumble of twenty-two pairs of stampeding feet about as well as the white powder they used to mark the field, a highly volatile substance that rarely survived the first quarter, rendering the out-of-bounds and goal lines more or less hypothetical for the players, referees, and spectators. On top of everything else, the soil didn't drain well; an hour of hard rain could transform the field into an evil swamp capable of sucking a shoe right off your foot as you tried to duck out of the grasp of a blitzing linebacker.

How much better it would have been to scramble around on this, Todd thought, the moment he and Larry stepped onto the Bellington Bombers' state-of-the-art field, the taut blue-green skin of the artificial turf glowing with Caribbean purity beneath the dazzling night game lights, the crisp white lines and numbers marching with precision from one yellow end zone to the other. Even with the bleachers empty and only a half dozen men tossing balls and doing warm-ups at midfield, the stadium communicated a powerful sense of occasion and romance that Todd felt immediately in the pit of his stomach.

"Wow," he said. "This is something."

"It's pretty," Larry agreed. "But it doesn't have a lot of give. It's like playing on cement."

The men at midfield stopped what they were doing and assembled themselves into an impromptu welcoming committee. Like Larry, all of them were wearing gray athletic shorts and T-shirts with GUARDIANS written across the front. They stared openly at Todd as he approached, but their collective scrutiny felt less intimate than Larry's had in the close quarters of the van.

"Who's he?" grunted a barrel-chested man with a drill-sergeant crew cut and a nose that looked like it had been broken more than once.

Larry draped his arm around Todd's shoulder. "He's that quarterback I was telling you about."

Todd was startled to hear himself referred to in this manner. He had a vague memory of swapping football stories with Larry at the sprinkler park, but he must have made it clear that he hadn't played the game in a serious way for almost a decade. At this point in his life, he was no more a quarterback than he was a seventh grader.

"You told us he moved," said a bald-headed black guy who was maybe five-six, but had a build like Mike Tyson's. He had cut off his shirt so it hung well above his navel, exposing an abdominal six-pack that belonged on the cover of a fitness magazine.

"I just ran into him," Larry explained. "Outside the library."

"I hope he's as good as you said," said a lanky guy with an orthopedic brace on one knee.

"He played in college," said Larry. "How bad could he be?"

Todd didn't think this was the right time to explain that he hadn't been a starter and that it was a very small college. He already felt like enough of a civilian in his cargo shorts and polo shirt.

"I'm a little behind the curve here," he said. "Who are you guys?"

"We're the Guardians," said the drill sergeant.

"We're cops," said the black guy.

"We play in the Tri-County Midnight Touch Football League," Larry added. "A lot of towns have teams."

"Our quarterback's wife made him quit," said the guy with the knee brace. "He got too many concussions."

The other Guardians glared at the speaker, as if he'd divulged top secret information.

"Concussions?" said Todd. "I thought you said it was touch."

"Rough touch," said Larry. His teammates seemed to find this amusing.

"It's basically tackle." The drill sergeant spoke in a comically nasal voice. If Todd hadn't been looking straight at him, he would have sworn the guy had clamped a clothespin on his nostrils. "We just call it touch for insurance purposes."

"We really need a quarterback," said a cherubic-looking behemoth who'd been silent up to that point.

"Why don't we work on some simple pass patterns?" Larry suggested.

Todd waited for his good sense to kick in. There were lots of excuses available to him. *My wife works nights. I have to study for the big exam. I can't keep my eyes open at midnight, let alone play football. I don't like concussions.* But it felt so good to be standing there beneath the bright lights on that vast turquoise carpet, surrounded by men who called themselves the Guardians. Way better than standing in front of the library watching twelve-year-olds ride their skateboards. He had a feeling similar to the one he'd had right before kissing Sarah, like his world had cracked open to reveal a thrilling new possibility.

"Just let me warm up a little," he told them.

After practice, Larry invited Todd out for a beer to celebrate their new alliance. Todd started to say no—it was already ten o'clock—but then figured, what the hell. It wasn't like he went out drinking every night of the week.

"Cheers." Larry lifted his mug. "You looked good out there."

"You think?" Todd checked his face for signs of insincerity. "Some of the other guys weren't so sure."

"Who, Tony Correnti?" Larry waved away Todd's concern. "He's a pussycat. Give you the shirt off his back."

Todd's altercation with Correnti—he was the drill sergeant with the off-kilter nose—had taken place during a scrimmage at the end of practice. He'd just let go of a pass, a sweet spiral that floated right into the hands of DeWayne Rogers, the short black guy he already thought of as his go-to receiver, when Correnti nailed him with a cheap shot, knocking him flat onto the artificial turf, which, true to Larry's description, was about as forgiving as freshly paved blacktop.

Except for having the wind knocked out of him, Todd was unhurt. He struggled to his feet and glared at his assailant, arms spread, mouth open, his whole body a tacit *what the fuck?* Correnti stepped up, getting right in Todd's face like he was spoiling for a fight.

"You got a problem?" he honked.

"That was a late hit."

"Poor baby."

"Roughing the passer. Any ref woulda called it."

"No refs in this league, pretty boy."

Todd didn't know what to say to that.

"Well, take it easy, okay? It's just a friggin' scrimmage."

Correnti laughed in his face. "You think the Auditors are gonna take it easy? You think the Supervisors are gonna ask permission before cleaning your clock?"

"You're supposed to be my teammate."

"This isn't Pop Warner, Ace. You either suck it up and play ball, or you get the fuck off the field, okay?"

Larry told Todd not to worry about it. He said Correnti was just testing him, making sure he was a good fit with the team.

"He's an ex-Marine," Larry explained. "A jarhead of the old school."

Todd shook his head, reminding himself to take shallow breaths. Every time he inhaled past a certain point, he felt a sharp stitch in his rib cage.

"No wonder your last quarterback quit."

"Little Scotty Morris." Larry spoke the name with contempt. "What a pussy. He wouldn't have even gotten up after a hit like you took."

Todd nodded, acknowledging the compliment. Aside from Correnti's cheap shot, practice had gone pretty well. He threw the ball better than he expected—all those push-ups had paid off—and had been surprised to find his football instincts intact after the long hiatus.

"There aren't too many guys who can throw on the run," Larry continued. "You looked like John Elway out there."

"Thanks." Todd was flattered. "I always kind of modeled my game on Elway's."

"Well, it shows." Larry signaled the bartender. "Hey, Willie, how about another round for me and my new QB?"

Larry's mood darkened suddenly, somewhere between the second and third beer, when Todd asked how his boys were doing. He remembered the twins from the sprinkler park, beefy kids with enormous heads, dead ringers for their dad.

"The boys are fine," Larry said. "But my marriage is in trouble."

Todd didn't press for details. He didn't know Larry that well— had never even laid eyes on his wife—and didn't think it was any of his business. But Larry felt like talking.

"Joanie thinks I should get a job. She thinks I'm too young and healthy to be hanging around the house all day."

He looked expectantly at Todd, as if asking for his opinion on the matter. Todd didn't think he understood the matter well enough to have one.

"Why did you retire? If you don't mind my asking."

Larry seemed genuinely surprised by the question.

"You don't know?"

"You never told me."

"Huh," said Larry. "I thought everybody knew."

Todd shook his head and waited. Larry took a thoughtful slug of beer and inclined his head in Todd's direction. He kept his voice low, even though there was no one within eavesdropping distance.

"I was the one who shot that kid," he said. "At the mall."

Todd understood immediately. It had happened a few years ago, around the time Aaron was born. A local cop had been dispatched to the Bellington Mall to investigate a report of a black teenager carrying a gun. The cop had entered the mall with his own gun drawn, just in time to see the suspect heading up the escalator to the food court. The cop gave chase, cornering the suspect in front of the Taco Bell kiosk. The kid reached for his gun, and that was that. It was only after firing the fatal shots that the officer discovered that the kid was packing a toy, a cheap plastic six-shooter purchased at the Dollar Store.

There were some protests from civil rights groups, who insisted that the kid—he turned out to be only thirteen, though already over six feet tall—never would have been shot if he'd been white, but a departmental investigation determined that the cop had acted in accordance with legal guidelines for the use of deadly force. After that the story pretty much faded from the local news.

"Jesus," said Todd. "That's terrible."

"I still have nightmares about it," Larry confessed. "Antoine Harris was his name. Turns out he was a good kid. Real skinny, class clown. Thought it was a big joke, waving around his cowboy gun."

"You didn't know. It could have been real."

"I was diagnosed with post-traumatic stress syndrome," said

Larry. "By three different psychiatrists. That's why I retired. I couldn't do the job anymore."

"Not after that."

"For a year or two, Joanie was okay with me hanging around the house. But now she thinks I'm getting lazy."

"Maybe you could do something else," Todd suggested.

"Like what?" Larry snapped. "Drive a forklift at Costco?"

"Maybe go back to school."

"You sound like Joanie." Larry looked like he was trying to control himself. "I loved my job. I don't want to do anything else."

Todd had given clear directions to his house, but Larry must have misheard them. He turned off Pleasant a mile too soon, onto a network of curving streets near the Rayburn School.

"This isn't it," Todd told him. "I'm farther down toward the park."

Larry ignored him. They were moving at a crawl through a sleepy enclave of Cape Cods and garrison colonials, a modest family neighborhood a lot like Todd's own—tricycles abandoned on lawns, hockey nets tipped over in driveways, soccer ball flags flying proudly over front doors.

"Can you believe they let the bastard live in a place like this?"

"Oh shit," said Todd. "This is Blueberry Court."

Larry released a bitter chuckle.

"Why not give the pervert his own day-care center, too?"

Larry pulled to a stop in front of a small white house, Number 44. An old-fashioned lamppost cast its light over a well-kept square of lawn outlined by a border of scalloped bricks. The flower boxes beneath the picture window and the horse-and-buggy cutouts on the shutters gave the place the quaint, frozen-in-time look of an old photograph. Larry pressed three times on his horn, shattering the late-night silence. It was almost like he was summoning the pervert, like he expected McGorvey to come out and join them in the car.

"Why'd you do that?" Todd asked.

"Just to let him know I'm out here."

Larry reached into the backseat for his binoculars and trained them on the picture window. This seemed like overkill to Todd; the backs of two heads were clearly visible through the glass, silhouetted against the throbbing blue light of the TV.

"I want this scumbag to know I'm keeping an eye on him."

Time clicked by on the dashboard clock—five, ten, fifteen minutes. Todd just wanted to go home. Kathy would be worried; he had to take a wicked piss. But Larry seemed in no hurry to end his vigil.

"Unbelievable," he muttered. "Just sitting there watching Leno like a normal human being."

Todd could have spoken up, of course. But something held him back, the passenger's code of conduct. He felt like he'd surrendered his control of the night the moment he'd stepped into the van. For better or worse, the driver called the shots.

"You know that Girl Scout he exposed himself to?" Larry asked. "She was my buddy's daughter. Still hasn't gotten over it."

"He exposed himself to a Girl Scout?"

"Sweet little kid. She was just selling cookies." Larry lowered the binoculars. "Joanie thinks I'm obsessed with this creep. She thinks if I had a job, I wouldn't be driving by his house five or six times a day."

Larry tossed his binoculars into the backseat and grabbed a handful of flyers off the stack that was resting on Todd's lap.

"But I kinda feel like this *is* my job," he said. "There's a roll of tape in the glove compartment. Could you grab it for me?"

———

Kathy was still awake, hiding behind a fat biography of Eisenhower when Todd entered the bedroom. Aaron was asleep beside his mother.

"Where were you?" she asked, striking a tone of profound indifference.

For an instant, Todd actually considered telling her the truth—i.e., that instead of studying he'd spent the night playing tackle football with a bunch of cops—but then he saw a better way.

"I joined the Committee of Concerned Parents," he told her. "We're distributing the flyers about that creep on Blueberry Court."

It was not technically a lie, at least not the second part. They *had* distributed flyers—Larry had taped about a dozen on the pervert's front door, and then he and Todd had tossed handfuls out of the car windows as they drove away, littering the neighborhood with warnings. It was actually kind of fun, letting the wind pull the papers out of his hand, watching the individual sheets flutter and dive to the ground.

Kathy put down her book and studied him with a quality of attention he rarely received from her these days. He was delighted to see that she was wearing her black camisole, the semisheer one that offered a shadowy glimpse of her nipples, but his pleasure was diluted somewhat by the thought—not the first time it had passed through his head—that she was a lot more likely to wear something sexy to bed on nights when she was home alone with Aaron. When Todd was around she favored extra-large sweatpants in weird colors and T-shirts that hung to her knees.

"You remember Larry Moon?" he continued. "That retired cop from the sprinkler park?"

"The guy with the twins?"

"Yeah, it's his organization."

"I thought you didn't like him."

"I can take him or leave him. But this committee makes a lot of sense. It's pretty scary having a guy like that living right in town."

Kathy glanced at Aaron, who was sprawled out on his back, one arm bent at a right angle, the other sticking out straight. There were bunnies and carrots on his pajamas.

"I know," she said, touching him tenderly on the forehead. "I hate to even think about it."

Todd showered with the efficiency of a man who believes he has a fairly decent chance of getting laid if he hurries. All the stars were in alignment—Kathy was awake and wearing black underwear; Aaron was far away in dreamland. What was there to stop them, aside from a little soreness in his ribs?

This is what we need, he thought, brushing his teeth at twice the normal speed. *Something to take my mind off that kiss.*

Todd was painfully aware of the fact that he and Kathy had not made love for over three weeks. First, she'd had her period, then she'd been stressed out at work. One or the other of them was usually too tired at night, and Aaron was always hanging around in the morning, ready to intervene at the slightest sign of physical contact that didn't involve him. About six months earlier, they'd somehow managed to plop him in front of the TV by himself while they shared a precious—if somewhat distracted—half hour upstairs. Todd still remembered how good it felt afterward, lounging around like royalty in his bathrobe, sipping coffee and exchanging significant glances with his wife, but it was a one-shot deal. Now, whenever Todd—it was always Todd—suggested that Aaron go downstairs and watch PBS while he and Mommy "rested" for a little while longer, their little chaperone immediately smelled a rat and insisted that one of them join him on the living room couch.

Deciding that this was no time for subtlety, Todd emerged from the bathroom wearing only a towel, his manly intentions on full display. All he had to do was successfully transfer Aaron to his own bed without waking him, and they'd be home free. But when he pulled back the covers and slipped his hands under his son's knees and shoulders, Kathy released a barely audible whimper of protest.

"Please don't."

Todd straightened up, his high hopes already wilting.

"Come on, Kathy. How many times do we have to argue about this? He's three years old. He needs to start sleeping by himself."

"I know," she said, in the melancholy tone of someone fighting a battle she knew she'd someday have to lose. "But he just looks so comfy."

"He'll be just as comfy in his own bed."

"I just like to have him next to me." She gazed down at her son with a look of profound adoration and shook her head, as if to say that she knew Todd was right but was helpless in the face of her own feelings. "Don't you love his warm little body?"

What about me? Todd wanted to ask. *What about my big warm body?*

"Look, Kathy, I'm just getting a little tired of waking up with his foot in my face."

"But isn't he just so perfect? Was there ever a more perfect face in the entire history of the world?"

There was only one right answer to a question like that. And besides, for the most part Todd did like having Aaron in bed with them, especially when he was all warm and soapy-smelling from his bath. He'd wake up happy at the first light of morning and beg his parents to tickle him until he couldn't take it anymore, at which point he'd beg them to stop.

"He is a handsome devil," Todd had to admit.

"I know," said Kathy. "He's my perfect little man."

So Todd cast off his towel, put on a pair of boxers, and climbed into bed with his wife and sleeping child. Just before she turned off the light, Kathy leaned over Aaron to give Todd a kiss. He pushed himself up on his elbows, just high enough to get a quick peek at her breasts. Even after five years of marriage, it still gave him a little thrill.

"Night, night," she told him.

"Night, night," he said.

BLUEBERRY COURT

RONNIE WASN'T COOPERATING.

"Okay," he said. "How about this? Overweight ex-con with receding hairline, bites nails and smokes like chimney. Likes kiddie porn and quiet nights in front of the television."

"That's not funny," said May.

"It wasn't a joke."

"Come on, Ronnie. This isn't going to work if you don't try. We've got to look on the bright side."

"The bright side? Why didn't you say so? Let's see . . . I have no job, no friends, and everyone hates me. I think that about covers it."

"You have friends," May insisted, but she regretted the remark as soon as it came out of her mouth.

"Yeah? Like who?"

She thought it over. "What about Eddie Colonna?"

"That was tenth grade, Ma. If Eddie saw me now, he'd probably spit in my face."

"You must have had friends in . . . in . . ." May's voice trailed off. She had a hard time saying the word *prison* out loud. "You lived there for three years."

"Oh yeah," said Ronnie. "I was extremely popular."

"Dr. Linton liked you," she continued, not knowing why she felt a need to press on with such an upsetting subject.

"She was paid to like me. If the state stopped sending her checks, I don't think we'd have been hanging out together too much."

"Didn't she say you were highly intelligent?"

"She also said I was unusually devious and not to be trusted around children."

"Well, I know Bertha likes you." This wasn't precisely true, but May was determined not to come up empty-handed. "She said so the other day."

"Oh, that makes me feel much better. It's nice to have a nasty old wino in my corner."

"Bertha's my best friend. And I won't have you talking about her like that."

"You know why she likes you, Ma?" Ronnie was giving her that hard, pitiless look, the one that scared her sometimes. Like he saw right through everything and everyone, to the worst truths you could imagine. "Did you ever think about that?"

"Don't," said May. "Don't do this to me."

Ronnie let out a long, weary breath and buried his face in his hands. Then he smiled meekly, doing his best to be a good boy.

"I'm sorry, Ma. I know you're trying. But sometimes that just makes it worse."

May couldn't really blame him for being discouraged. It was bad enough that his own sister refused to talk to him or let him anywhere near her kids, and even worse that he couldn't find a job, not even collecting garbage, or delivering pizza, or bagging groceries. All the applications had a question about your criminal record; you got in trouble with your parole officer if you lied, and nobody would hire you if you told the truth. And then those posters started showing up with his picture on them, spreading the ugly rumor that he'd been involved in that poor girl's disappearance five years ago. But the police had looked into all that. He'd been called in for questioning three times—once by the FBI—and nothing had happened. If Ronnie had had something to do with that, they would have arrested him, wouldn't they?

"Come on," said May. She held up the personal ads page of *The Bellington Register*. "There are two whole columns of lonely women here, and only a handful of men. The odds are on your side."

Ronnie lit a cigarette and gave May the same incredulous look he'd been giving her since he was a teenager, as though she were some sort of fantastical creature never before seen on earth.

"Don't look at me like that," she said. "Why wouldn't one of these women want to meet a nice person like you?"

"I'm not a nice person," Ronnie said. "I'm the scum of the earth."

"You did a bad thing," May admitted. "But that doesn't mean you're a bad person."

"I have a psychosexual disorder, Ma."

"You're better now," said May. "They wouldn't have let you out if you weren't."

"They let me out because they had to."

Ronnie lit a fresh cigarette, sucking on it like a kid drinking out of a straw. May felt panicky, like maybe one of her breathing attacks was coming on. Her inhaler was upstairs by her bed, next to her denture glass. She wished she'd thought to bring it down.

"Well, maybe if you found a girlfriend"—she paused for breath—"closer to your own age, you wouldn't have the bad urges so often."

"I don't want a girlfriend my own age," said Ronnie. "I wish I did."

"Look at this one," said May, choosing an ad at random. Even with her reading glasses on, the print was painfully small. " *'Lovely green eyes. Kindhearted DWF, 33, looking for friendship and maybe more. Nonsmoker preferred.'* Whoops, forget her. How about this one? *'Full-figured mama, midforties. Likes swing dancing,* Everybody Loves Raymond, *and lazy Sunday mornings.'* "

"Full-figured," chuckled Ronnie. "She's probably three hundred pounds. The black guys in jail would go for her."

"So what if she is? Maybe she's a nice person inside. Maybe she'd appreciate it if someone gave her a chance and didn't make her feel bad about the way she looked. Maybe she'd be willing to overlook another person's faults as well."

Ronnie took another drag and exhaled two neat jets of smoke from his nose, just the way his father used to do. If Pete had been kinder and more reliable, May had a feeling Ronnie would have been a happier child. Maybe the other boys wouldn't have picked on him so much, or maybe he'd have known how to defend himself when they did. But her ex-husband was a liar, and a cheater, and a mean drunk who enjoyed making other people feel small and stupid, and Ronnie was always his favorite target. When he finally left it had seemed like the end of the world to May, but now she saw that it was for the best. Ronnie gave a small shrug of surrender.

"All right, Ma. If it'll make you happy, I'll give it a shot. But just one date, all right? I'm not gonna make a career of it."

He was humoring her, but that was better than nothing. It wasn't natural for a grown man to be living with his mother, no hobbies and diversions, just reading the paper and watching TV all day. It was almost like he was still in prison, except for the long rides he took on his old bike, which made her nervous, since he refused to tell her where he went or what he was doing. But a bike was better than a car, wasn't it? She wouldn't want him going around in a car, or in a van, God forbid. Plus, he could use the exercise. He was always complaining about the prison food, but he'd come home fifteen pounds heavier than when he'd gone in.

What he needed was a girlfriend, and May intended to help him find one. If he had a nice girl in his life, maybe he wouldn't spend so much time alone in his room, spying on the neighborhood kids through his binoculars. He always denied it, but she knew what he was up to. And if he got married someday—Why not? Didn't all sorts of people get married: midgets, retarded people, people with missing limbs, whatever?—then she could die in peace, without worrying about what would become of her boy if she wasn't around to keep him out of trouble. Because she got so tired sometimes and just wanted a little rest, some time to put her feet up. Didn't she deserve that much, after a long life with so much trouble in it, and so little happiness? She often found herself thinking about the cemetery as she drifted off to sleep at night, and it seemed like a nice, welcoming place, all that grass and those beautiful trees, and neighbors who didn't make you feel like you had some sort of disease. She flipped open her steno pad and started writing.

"You have a nice smile," she said. "Why don't we start with that?"

As usual, Bertha arrived just in time for lunch, carrying a small brown grocery bag.

"Here's the fruit juice," she said in a loud voice, winking slyly as she handed the bag to May. "I brought the fruit juice like you told me, Mrs. McGorvey."

For some reason or other, Bertha insisted on calling the wine coolers "fruit juice." At first, May had assumed that she did it for the benefit of any neighbors who might be within earshot—not that it was any of their damn business—but it turned out just to be another of Bertha's private jokes. She had a whole storehouse of them—most were tiresome rather than funny—but May accepted them as the price of her company. God knows she'd put up with worse in her day.

"Where's the Prince?" Bertha asked, peering into the living room. "Out gallivanting on his tricycle?"

Almost as soon as Ronnie had come home, Bertha had nicknamed him "the Prince" in honor of his alleged freeloading tendencies, even though May had explained repeatedly that her son was not unemployed by choice. Bertha scoffed at this claim. In her view, Ronnie had an enviable setup: a grown man with no responsibilities whatsoever, boarding at his mother's expense, eating chips and watching cable all day, and generally carrying on like a member of the royal family.

"He's getting some exercise," said May, though both women understood that Ronnie despised Bertha and timed his bike rides to coincide with her visits.

"Something smells delicious." Bertha sniffed the air as though it were a flower. "What's on the grill?"

"Nothing," said May. "We're having tuna sandwiches."

"And fruit juice," said Bertha. "Don't forget the fruit juice."

Until she'd struck up her friendship with Bertha, May hadn't been in the habit of drinking in the daytime hours—in fact, she rarely drank at all—but she'd learned to make an exception for her wine cooler at lunch. Partly she did it to be sociable—Bertha didn't like to drink alone—but she'd come to rely on the pleasantly fuzzy mental state induced by the beverage, even if it sometimes left her headachy and tired later in the afternoon. It was a small indulgence, and May felt like she'd earned the right.

May had first seen Bertha four years earlier in the visiting area of the county jail, where they each had a son awaiting trial. It was hard for them not to notice each other, two old white women in a sea of mostly younger, mostly darker faces. May would offer a shy smile of commiseration whenever they made eye contact, but she was reluctant to introduce herself or otherwise invite conversation. Ronnie's case had attracted a fair amount of lurid publicity—the Girl Scout cookie angle made it irresistible to the newspapers—and May had felt a distinct chill fall over most of her encounters with other people. Friends stopped calling. Neighbors no longer smiled and waved hello. Her own daughter said terrible things about Ronnie that were probably true, but that May didn't think should be spoken out loud by members of his own family. Father Ortega even suggested that she take a short break from volunteering on bingo night until "things settled down." May was in no hurry to meet anyone new, or put herself in any kind of situation where she'd have to explain who she was and what she was doing at the county jail.

It was Bertha who finally broke the ice. She followed May out to the parking lot one breezy spring afternoon and began chatting as naturally as if they were old friends, making a series of statements to which May could only say *Amen*, about how mortifying it was to see your own child under lock and key, and how he was still your little boy, no matter what he'd done, and how you had no choice but to keep loving him, no matter what he'd done, and how impossible it was for other people who hadn't had this experience to understand the strength of the bond between a mother and her child, no matter what he'd done. Then she started moaning about the long and difficult trip from the courthouse back home to Bellington on Sunday, when the buses ran so infrequently, and before May had a chance to think it through, she blurted out that she lived in Bellington, too, and would be happy to give her a ride home.

For the next few weeks May shuttled her new friend back and forth on visiting days, until Bertha's son, Allen, was sentenced to six months—it was not his first offense—for stealing a welding machine from a construction site and trying to sell it to a man who turned out to be a cousin of the original owner. By that point, though, Bertha had already begun stopping by May's house at lunchtime, first by invitation, then on impulse, and finally, on a more or less daily basis. During the school year, Bertha worked as a crossing guard outside the Rayburn School, and she had a couple of hours to kill between lunchtime and dismissal, so why not spend them with May?

And the truth was, May appreciated the company. Not because she liked Bertha, exactly—Bertha was hard to like in any simple way—but because a person needed company. Something went sour inside if you didn't have someone to talk to every day. So what if Bertha dyed her hair a brassy red and drank too much (though May couldn't say she approved of her drinking on school days), or made mean jokes, and rarely had a good word to say about anyone? No one else was visiting May these days, except her daughter, Carol, who came by maybe once a month to complain about Ronnie and insist that May acknowledge what a repulsive person he was. Diane Thuringer from down the street, whom May had once considered a good friend, pretended not to notice her even after their carts almost collided in the supermarket. So that was May's choice: not between

Bertha and family, or between Bertha and someone nicer, but between Bertha and no one.

It wasn't that hard to choose.

"He knows where the body is," Bertha insisted. "You can tell by the way he blinks those shifty little eyes."

May didn't even like thinking about Gary Condit, let alone talking about him. The missing girl, the grieving parents, the murderer walking around unpunished—it was just too horrible. Bertha, on the other hand, couldn't get enough.

"He might as well have had the word *guilty* stamped across his forehead. And sweet little wifey standing by his side."

What else can she do? May wanted to ask. *What else can she do if she loves him?*

"I got news for Congressman Howdy Doody." Bertha twisted off the cap on wine cooler number two. She could polish off three or four during the average lunch. "His shit stinks like everyone else's."

"Please," said May. "Language."

"I hope she gets to visit him in prison. I'm sure he'll look very distinguished in his jumpsuit." Bertha cackled at the thought. "So who spray-painted your driveway?"

She asked this question so abruptly and matter-of-factly that it took May a couple of seconds to realize that they weren't talking about Congressman Howdy Doody anymore.

"Spray paint?"

"You didn't know?" Bertha couldn't quite conceal her pleasure at being the bearer of bad news. "You got some new graffiti last night."

"Oh no. Is it disgusting?"

"Just one word," said Bertha. "But it's not a very nice one."

May started to rise from her chair, then thought better of it. The word—she could imagine which one it was without too much trouble—could wait. There was no sense spoiling her lunch, getting herself all worked up for nothing.

"The nerve of these people," she muttered.

"The tuna's good today," said Bertha, though she'd only taken a few tiny nibbles of her sandwich. "Is it StarKist?"

"The store brand," May replied distractedly.

"I don't buy the store brands." Bertha shook her head with great vehemence, as if she'd learned this lesson the hard way. "You save a couple pennies, but I'd rather have the peace of mind."

"It's the same product," said May. Her heart wasn't in the argument, which she and Bertha revisited every time they ate tuna fish. "They just slap different labels on the cans."

"Don't be naive," said Bertha, but her attention shifted suddenly to the steno pad in the center of the table with the red pen resting on top. She picked up the pad and examined it. "What's this?"

"Ronnie's personal ad. I need to find him a girlfriend."

"Hmmm." Bertha seemed impressed. She squinted at the page and read aloud. " '*SWM, 43, nice eyes and smile. Likes biking and long walks on beach. I'm not perfect and don't expect you to be, either.*' "

"What do you think?" May asked. It sounded pretty good to her.

Bertha pondered the matter for a few seconds before shaking her head.

"It's not gonna work. You need to say *handsome*."

"I wanted to. Ronnie wouldn't let me."

"Trust me," said Bertha. "If you don't, they're just gonna think he's ugly."

"That's what I said. But you know how stubborn he can be."

Bertha uncapped the pen and scrawled a quick correction to the ad.

"There," she said. "He'll have to beat them off with a stick."

May stood in the midday sun and stared at the awful word painted on her driveway. It wasn't the one she'd expected. Her legs felt weak.

"Where do people learn their manners?" she wondered. "This used to be a nice town."

"It was never that nice," Bertha told her. "It just liked to pretend it was."

"But vandalizing someone's driveway?"

"Probably teenagers," said Bertha. "They go drinking in the woods, and then they run amuck."

"No," said May. "It's that creep in the van. He's always driving past, honking the horn, stapling those damn posters everywhere."

May knew that Ronnie had seen the word on his way out of the garage. He must have ridden right over it on his bike. She hoped it wouldn't spoil his day or make him any more depressed than he already was.

"I'll go to the hardware store," she said. "I can spray right over this with some black paint."

"I can loan you a gun if you want," said Bertha. "Allen has three of them."

"I wouldn't even know how to hold it," said May.

"It's easy," said Bertha. "I could teach you in a few minutes."

May shook her head. She didn't want to think about guns. She wanted to think about the day she moved into this house. It was a long time ago—over thirty-five years. She was pregnant with Carol; Ronnie had just started school. It was the first house she'd ever owned.

It wasn't like she had any illusions about her life even then. She already knew that she'd married the wrong man—at the beginning he'd at least been a charming drunk, but by then the charm was all used up—and that her son wasn't going to have an easy time of it in school. There was something about him that people didn't like.

But in spite of everything, she'd felt hope. They were moving into a place of their own in a nice neighborhood near a good school. Maybe things would be different there; maybe they would be happy. She stood on the front lawn in the early evening and whispered a prayer that her family would thrive on Blueberry Court, that her marriage would improve, that her children would grow up into healthy, successful adults.

And this is what her prayer had come to: the word *EVIL* spray-painted in gigantic Day-Glo orange letters at the foot of her drive-way, along with an arrow pointing straight to her house.

"God help us," she said, reaching for Bertha's arm so she could steady herself for whatever was coming next.

RED BIKINI

JEAN MCGINNISS, THE NEWLY RETIRED SECOND-GRADE TEACHER who lived next door, was marching in place on Sarah's welcome mat, pumping her knees and elbows like a majorette for the AARP band.

"Ready to roll?" Jean was an energetic dumpling of a woman with a relentlessly upbeat personality that must have gone over well with the seven-year-olds. For the past several months, the two women had been going on brisk after-dinner fitness walks that had rapidly become the highlight of Sarah's day, even if Jean's chattiness sometimes got to her. "There's a supernice breeze out."

"Could you wait a few minutes?" Sarah asked. "Richard's in his office again."

By this point in the summer, both of them knew to factor in a half hour delay to accommodate Richard, who had recently begun exhibiting strange workaholic tendencies after years of pontificating about the sacred importance of leisure time and contemplative space in a fast-paced, moneygrubbing culture. Even so, Jean kept showing up on Sarah's doorstep at seven on the dot. Her husband Tim, a retired shop teacher, was one of those *we're-going-to-hell-in-a-handbasket* types who worked himself into a lather watching the TV news, and Jean preferred to be out of the house when he started muttering about politicians and minorities. She set her one-and-a-half-pound dumbbells on the porch and followed Sarah inside.

"Helloo?" Jean called out in a warbly singsong. "Is there a cute little girl in the house?"

"She's a terror tonight," Sarah warned her. "I couldn't get her to nap again."

"Oh dear." Jean couldn't have looked more sympathetic if she'd just found out that Lucy needed a kidney transplant. "Poor thing."

"Poor Mommy," Sarah corrected her. "I'm the one who suffers. She's completely unhinged. Like a character out of Dostoevsky."

But the little girl who poked her head out of the living room just then seemed more like a creation of Norman Rockwell than a brooding Russian epileptic. Her face blossomed into a bright smile at the sight of the visitor; she scampered down the hallway and flung herself into the older woman's arms as if they were lovers meeting in an airport. Jean sniffed Lucy's hair, then dropped to one knee and gave her a long, searching look.

"Did you nap today?"

Lucy shook her head sadly.

"Are you sleepy?"

Lucy shook her head again, this time in fervent denial. Except for a ring of grape juice staining her mouth like a drunk's lipstick, she looked adorable, a wide-eyed waif in a sleeveless Barbie night-gown (a gift from Richard's mother that Sarah strongly disapproved of, and that Lucy, naturally, cherished beyond reason).

"She must have gotten a second wind," Sarah observed.

"I'm glad to hear it," said Jean. "Because if you were tired, I couldn't give you your present."

Lucy snapped to attention. "What present?"

Jean cupped one hand around her ear, as if she were listening to far-off voices.

"Do you hear barking? Is there a dog in your house?"

Lucy checked with her mother, just in case there was a dog she hadn't been told about.

"Not that I know of," said Sarah.

"Maybe it's coming from in here." Jean rotated her extra-large fanny pack—it was an elaborate contraption, with multiple compartments and attachments for carrying two water bottles and a flashlight—so the main storage pouch was facing forward. Sarah didn't know what possessed her to wear something big and lumpy like that on her ass.

"Oh my." Jean tugged slowly on the zipper. With a flourish, she reached in and removed a cute little husky with a heart-shaped tag dangling from one ear. "Look what I found."

"A Beanie!" Lucy shouted, as if she needed to notify the whole neighborhood.

"His name's Nanook," said Jean. Lucy released a small whimper of joy as Jean placed the dog in her cupped hands.

"You didn't have to do that," said Sarah.

"I got one for Tyler," Jean explained. Tyler was her four-year-old grandson who lived in Seattle. She only got to see him twice a year, but she talked about him every day, and began Christmas shopping for him in April. "And I know Lucy collects them, too."

"Well, that was really thoughtful." Sarah turned to her daughter. "Say thank you to Jean."

"Fank you, Jean," said Lucy, in her softest, sweetest voice. There was a look of ecstatic gratitude on her face that made Sarah cringe. You would have thought she'd never received a gift before in her life.

————

What the hell is he doing up there? Sarah wondered, as seven-thirty came and went. She didn't care how busy he was, it was a simple matter of equity. He'd been out of the house all day, being an adult, talking to people, lunching with clients in a nice restaurant. Couldn't he just turn off his computer and let her go for her goddam walk, the one thing she looked forward to all day? Couldn't he spend an hour a day with his three-year-old daughter? Was that too much to ask?

At least Jean didn't mind. She'd been kneeling on the rug for the past half hour, helping Lucy introduce Nanook to the rest of her twenty-seven Beanies. (How had she managed to accumulate twenty-seven Beanies, anyway?) Now they were arranging the animals in chronological order, according to the "birthdays" printed on their name tags. No, Jean actually *liked* Lucy, a fact that struck Sarah as a fresh surprise every time she saw them together. It wasn't that there was anything wrong with Lucy, it was just that Sarah wasn't in the habit of thinking of her daughter as a particularly lovable child.

It wasn't Lucy's fault. She and Sarah just spent too much time together. Of course they got on each other's nerves. Today, for instance, they'd been stuck together like Siamese twins since 6:13 in the morning. Three meals, two snacks, five diapers, a trip to the supermarket (tantrum on the checkout line), some unproductive time on the potty, a visit to the merry-go-round playground (which Sarah despised, but had no choice but to frequent now that Mary Ann had declared her *persona non grata* at the Rayburn School), a dozen Berenstain Bears books with their suffocating platitudes and hideous illustrations (Lucy adored them and would read nothing else), some finger-painting, a bath, no nap, and a late-afternoon meltdown (Lucy dumped a box of crayons in the toilet; Sarah had to fish them out)—that was the sum total of Mommy's day.

What the hell is he doing up there?

A half hour of *Blue's Clues* after lunch was the only time Sarah could have plausibly gotten to herself—a little time to read the paper, call an old friend, maybe practice some yoga stretches—but instead she'd sat beside Lucy on the couch and watched the show, fantasizing the whole time about Steve, the boyish host, who seemed like a guy she might actually hit it off with if they ever got a chance to meet. He reminded her of herself: a smart, somewhat passive person who'd somehow gotten trapped in Kidworld. He pronounced his words a little too clearly and made big exaggerated faces as he dished out halfhearted compliments to his viewers (*Wow! You're really smart!*). A rumor had recently gone around the playground that Steve had a drug problem, and who could blame him? *Oh, Steve, run away with me! We can hole up in a flophouse and smoke crack for a couple of days.*

How pathetic was that, fantasizing about a lost weekend with a guy in a rugby shirt who interacted with a cartoon dog? But at least it was better than thinking about Todd all the time, the way she had for days and days after that ridiculous kiss. Mr. Big Handsome Frat Boy. Who the hell was she kidding? Jean looked up from the Beanies, which she and Lucy were now arranging by color.

"I saw the UPS truck this afternoon," she said. "Did you get the bathing suits?"

"Finally," said Sarah.

"Well?" Jean seemed a little too interested. "What's the verdict?"

"I haven't had a minute to try them on."

"Do it now. I'd love to see how they look."

"I don't think so," said Sarah.

"Come on." Jean frowned and patted her hips. "I graduated a

long time ago to the ruffled skirt club. I like to see what a real bathing suit looks like once in a while."

There was really no way out of it, so Sarah carried the J. Crew box into the bathroom and began to undress, wishing she'd never mentioned her bathing suit quest to Jean in the first place. She hadn't been able to stop herself, though. At the time—not even two weeks ago—her mind was consumed with thoughts of Todd, and talking about bathing suits was the closest she could come to talking about him, without having to mention his name or explain the circumstances that triggered her sudden and desperate desire to visit the Town Pool.

The only thing that was holding her back was her five-year-old Speedo, which had seemed perfectly satisfactory and even reasonably sleek right up until the morning after the kiss, when she tried it on in front of the mirror and saw how hopelessly ugly it was. After the moment they'd shared, it would be insulting to present herself to Todd in a frumpy blue one-piece with tufts of unruly pubic hair curling out around the crotch (the hair was a separate matter from the bathing suit, of course, but it wasn't helping any). She considered showing up at the pool in street clothes, or wearing some kind of dress or baggy T-shirt over the Speedo, but she didn't think the fantasy she was envisioning permitted half measures. The thing was to wear a bathing suit and look good in it, to somehow make yourself worthy of the scenario you were volunteering for.

She took Lucy to Filene's the following morning, but it was a disaster. Lucy hated shopping, and Sarah spent more time making sure she wasn't losing visual contact with her daughter than she did looking at swimwear. When she finally made her selections, she dragged Lucy into the fitting room and told her to stay put while she tried the suits on over her generously cut gray cotton panties, which kept poking out and spoiling the effect, not that there was much to spoil. The first suit hugged her hips and waist perfectly, but looked about three sizes too big on top. The second fit nicely across her chest, but drooped off her ass like a tote bag. She thought the third suit looked okay—it was a black one-piece, daringly low-cut with a series of oval cutouts traveling up the side—but when she left the fitting room to consult with the saleslady in front of the three-way mirror, the woman hesitated for a long time before answering.

"I wouldn't," she said finally.

Sarah returned to the fitting room in a funk, only to find that Lucy had disappeared. Trying not to panic, she began calling out her daughter's name in a loud voice. When she got no response, she checked all the nearby fitting rooms, pulling open doors and peering under the ones that were locked, drawing indignant stares from women in various states of undress.

"Have you seen a little girl?" she asked. "She's got a Band-Aid on her knee."

Then, out of nowhere, she remembered the posters—*There is a pervert among us!*—and panicked. Still wearing the bathing suit, its price tag bouncing off her right thigh, she burst out of the dressing room and began running up and down the aisles of the store in her bare feet, calling out, "Lucy? Where are you?" Whenever her fellow shoppers looked at her with the puzzlement she deserved, she'd clutch her head and wail, "I've lost my daughter!" She imagined Ronald James McGorvey patting her on the head and offering to buy her an ice-cream cone. Lucy loved ice cream.

"Lucy? Where are you?"

In the electronics section, she was accosted by a young black security guard who took her by the shoulders and told her to please calm down. He explained that her daughter was safe, and waiting by the cash registers.

"We're watching her," he said. "So why don't you just go back to the dressing room and put your clothes on."

When she told the story to Jean that night, she left out the part about Lucy getting lost. She just talked about how hard it was to buy a bathing suit under the best of circumstances, let alone with a little kid in tow.

"I really need a new one," she said, startled by the level of emotion in her voice. "The old one doesn't look right."

"Why don't you just order a bunch from a catalogue?" Jean suggested. "That's what my daughter-in-law does. You can try them on at home when Lucy's asleep, and send back the ones that don't fit. Save you a lot of trouble."

Having worn solid color tank suits for most of her adult life, Sarah was bewildered by the cornucopia of styles and colors featured in the catalogue. Bikinis were back, apparently, with numerous variations on the basic theme—bandeaus, tank tops, underwires, plus a variety of bottoms, each offering more or less in the crucial area of "rear coverage." Once she wrapped her mind around the options, though, she found it liberating not to be restricted by the limited inventory available in a particular store, or inhibited by the scrutiny of her fellow shoppers or the salesclerks, who never failed to raise a disapproving eyebrow if you lingered too long in front of an item they considered inappropriate for a woman of your age or body type.

Her selections were bolder and sexier than anything she would have dreamed of trying on in a department store (or actually wearing in public for that matter). Her mental audience as she flipped through the catalogue was Todd and Todd alone. He was sitting shirtless on a towel in the grassy area adjacent to the Town Pool—the whole complex was mysteriously deserted except for the two of them—watching with unconcealed pleasure as she emerged, dripping, from the deep end, Aphrodite in a black underwire bikini with hipster briefs, size medium or maybe small. She placed her order over the phone with a feeling of almost shameful excitement, her voice trembling as she recited the numbers on her VISA card.

But the suits took six business days to arrive—she should have sprung for the expedited shipping—and by then her fever had broken. The farther away she got from the kiss itself, the more bizarre and inexplicable it seemed. How could she have let something like that happen? What was wrong with her that she allowed a stranger to do that to her in front of the other mothers, and more importantly, in front of her own child? Luckily, Lucy seemed strangely unfazed by the kiss, had never even mentioned it, but even so, there were times when Sarah actually found herself sympathizing with Mary Ann and Cheryl and Theresa. Why *should* they talk to her after what she'd done? How had they explained it to their own children?

And who was she to assume that a guy like Todd actually wanted to see her in a bikini, if she ever found the courage to wear one to the Town Pool? She imagined him wincing as she approached, disappointed by her small breasts, repulsed by that little roll of fat below her navel. What if he treated her the way Arthur Maloney had? What would she do then?

Arthur Maloney was a scrawny high school theater nerd with bad skin and a habit of laughing nervously at his own jokes. But Sarah had seen him in a student production of *Death of a Salesman* in the fall of their junior year—he was an oddly convincing Willy Loman at age sixteen—and decided that he needed to be her boyfriend. Having had little experience in this area, she tried to follow the rules of flirtation to the best of her limited understanding. She stared at him obsessively in English—the one class they shared—and memorized the rest of his schedule, so she could arrange to "accidentally" bump into him several times a day. On the rare occasions when she managed to exchange a few words with him, she made sure to compliment an article of his clothing or remind him of something clever he'd said. Sometimes she'd ask if he had plans for the weekend, or had seen a certain movie; but her signals just bounced right off him, as though he were encased in some sort of invisible protective shield.

After enduring several months of these vaguely humiliating encounters, Sarah's luck finally changed at the Spring Dance-a-Thon for Muscular Dystrophy. The event had a Fifties Sock Hop theme, and Sarah showed up in a pleated skirt, fuzzy sweater, and saddle shoes. Arthur was there, too, looking like James Dean's not-so-cool cousin—he had an empty cigarette pack rolled up in the sleeve of his T-shirt—but he spent the whole night hitting on Beth D'Addario, a sophomore with a big chest and an even bigger laugh, so the whole world could know just how much fun she was having at any given moment. But when Beth blew off Arthur for a soccer player, Sarah saw her chance. She hurried over—Arthur was shrugging on his jean jacket at the edge of the bleachers, looking angry and rejected—and volunteered to walk him home. He said okay, but without even pretending to be enthusiastic about the idea.

He cheered up on the way, though, probably because she kept brushing against him as she talked about what a big famous movie star he was going to be and how the town would throw him a parade down Main Street when he won his first Academy Award. Finally, when she figured she'd softened him up to the appropriate degree, she asked the question she'd been choking on all night.

"Why don't you like me?"

"I like you," he protested.

"Don't lie," she told him. "You think I'm okay. But you don't *like me* like me, not like you like Beth."

"I don't like *Beth*," he said angrily. With his hair slicked back, Arthur looked even more weaselly than usual, but at least his pimples weren't so conspicuous in the dark. "She's such an airhead."

"You talked to her all night. You didn't talk to me."

"I didn't even know you were there."

"See?" she said. "If you liked me, you would have known. I was watching you all night. I didn't dance, I didn't do anything. I was just waiting for you to look at me."

Arthur seemed startled, and even moved, by this declaration.

"I'm sorry," he said, and to her amazement, he hugged her, right there on Summer Street (no one was around, but still). It was all she could do to keep from bursting into sobs.

"Let me make it up to you," he said.

He made it up to her on a cold metal bench inside a Plexiglas shelter at the commuter rail station, which was closed for the night. The intimacy of their first kiss—she could taste the broccoli he'd eaten for dinner—was one of the few genuinely shocking revelations of her life. *My God*, she thought, *I'm sucking on Arthur Maloney's tongue . . . And I like it!* It was disgusting and thrilling at the same time, a combination so overwhelming that it didn't even occur to her to object when he slipped an icy hand inside her sweater and squeezed her right breast, a little less tenderly than she would have liked.

"I'm sorry," she whispered.

"For what?"

"They're so small. Beth's are so much bigger."

"Would you shut up about Beth?"

When he got tired of examining her breasts, he tried to reach up her skirt. She stopped him, not because she didn't want him to—she wasn't sure *what* she wanted in that respect—but because it was all starting to feel like so much so soon, more than either of them really needed.

"Sorry," she said again.

"It's okay." He sighed. "I better get going anyway. Gotta rest up for the SATs."

"Oh my God," said Sarah. "I forgot all about them."

"It's the most important test of our lives," he said. "How could you forget?"

"You made me," she told him.

Arthur looked troubled by this statement, as if it were a dubious honor at best to distract someone from the Scholastic Aptitude Test. But he walked her home, holding her hand all the way, and kissed her good night at the edge of her lawn.

Of course she couldn't sleep after that, couldn't even look at her breakfast in the morning. She felt weak, nearly delirious in the car with her father, who kept rattling off test-taking advice she'd heard a thousand times—answer the easy ones first, eliminate the obviously wrong answers, never leave anything blank—while she had to restrain herself from sticking her head out the window and screaming her new boyfriend's name to the sleeping town.

Dozens of her classmates were lined up outside the main entrance to the high school, but her eyes went straight to Arthur without even trying, the connection between them was that strong. He was standing near the front of the line, involved in what looked like a serious conversation with his best friend, Matt. *He's talking about me*, Sarah thought proudly, and she walked right up to them without having to ask permission, the way a girlfriend could.

"Lugubrious," said Matt.

"Mournful," replied Arthur. "Melancholy."

She chose that moment to tap him on the shoulder blade.

"I'm so happy," she announced. "I can't stop smiling."

Arthur stared at her for a few seconds, as if he were having trouble remembering her name. He had shaved that morning, and his skin was freckled with blood.

"Can we talk about it later?" he asked. "I'm kinda busy right now."

He turned his back on her—he was wearing the same jean jacket as last night—and she understood, as clearly as if he'd punched her in the stomach, that she didn't have a new boyfriend anymore.

The doors opened, and Sarah followed the rest of the sheep inside. But all she could think about as she filled in the blanks with her Number 2 pencil was what had gone wrong. *Wasn't I pretty enough? Was I a bad kisser? Should I have let him touch me down there? All of the above?*

Oddly enough, it all worked out okay. She did fine on her SATs, way better than she expected. And Arthur got his heart broken by Beth, after which he came crawling back to Sarah, who went out with him for the whole summer between junior and senior year, and then had the vengeful pleasure of breaking up with him on the day before school resumed in September.

That was what baffled her. Arthur Maloney was not an important person in her life. At best, he was a minor footnote in her romantic history, a teenage boy—not even a cute one—who'd kissed her one day and regretted it the next. She'd barely given him a thought since the day she graduated from high school. So why, she had wondered, in those strange days while she awaited the delivery of her bathing suits, was she suddenly thinking about him all the time?

―――――――

The floral bandeau was a bad idea, that much was obvious. It squeezed her chest like a tourniquet and possessed none of the "bust-enhancing" qualities boasted of in the catalogue. Not to mention the fact that Sarah always felt extremely self-conscious in flowered clothing, as though she were surrounded by quotation marks. *Hello, I'm wearing "flowers."*

The black underwire top was more flattering—and less embarrassing—but she must have ordered it a size too small. The supports dug into her ribs without mercy, mortifying her flesh like a whalebone corset. How odd to be reminded of bustles and hoop skirts while wearing such an un-Victorian article of clothing.

She did like the tank top. It was casual and alluring at the same time, revealing a modest but still provocative glimpse of midriff. Unfortunately, the color was all wrong. They could call it "blush sunset" if they wanted to, but it was really just pink. And Sarah didn't wear pink.

My God, she thought, *what is wrong with me? I don't wear flowers, I don't wear pink.* She recognized the debilitating voice in her head, the one that said no to everything. It had been lurking there all her life, holding her back, keeping her from taking chances and breaking free of unproductive patterns.

In grad school, Sarah had written a paper criticizing Camille Paglia as a "false feminist" for celebrating the sexual power of a few extraordinary women instead of focusing on the patriarchal oppression of women in general. She was especially irritated by Paglia's worshipful take on Madonna. What did ordinary women—secretaries, waitresses, housewives, prostitutes—have to learn from a rich, famous, beautiful, egomaniac who'd gotten everything she'd ever wanted?

But lately Sarah had come to the conclusion that they—or at least she—had a lot to learn. Madonna didn't say, *Oh no, I couldn't possibly wear those cones on my chest. Oh no, I couldn't pose as a nude hitchhiker.* She just said yes to everything. *Cowboy hats—sure! Sex with Jesus—why not? Motherhood—that's cool, too.* When one role got old, she just moved on to the next one. That was a form of liberation in itself, Sarah realized. Only temporary, and not for everyone, but real enough for the lucky few who had the imagination to pull it off. And the fact was, women in general weren't about to get released from patriarchal control anytime soon, so in the meantime, it was every girl for herself.

The fourth suit she tried on was a red bikini, the color of a candy apple. The top was skimpy—"unconstructed," according to the catalogue—but her breasts fit nicely inside the two cloth triangles. The bottoms came in a style called "boy shorts," which promised "ample coverage." Somehow the boyishness of the shorts brought out the womanliness of her body, accentuating the curves of her hips and ass, while concealing the problem area at the top of her thighs. Amazingly enough, she looked okay. Maybe even better than okay, at least for a woman pushing thirty who'd gone through childbirth.

I should wear red more often, she thought, pondering herself in the full-length mirror on the back of the bathroom door.

Jean and Lucy looked up together as she stepped into the living room and struck a model pose, one hand on her hip, the other behind her head. Lucy squinted. Jean's mouth dropped open.

"Wow," she said to Lucy. "Doesn't Mommy look sexy?"

Lucy mulled this over for a moment or two, with an oddly reflective air. Then she nodded, but there was something tentative in her assent, as if she wasn't quite sure she'd understood the question.

Exhaling sharply, Jean raised her dumbbells overhead.

"Funny you should mention Dostoevsky," she said. "We're reading *Crime and Punishment* in our book group."

"Crime and Punishment?" Sarah huffed, struggling to keep pace. "That's pretty highbrow for a book group."

"Not for us." Jean pressed the weights straight out from her chest. "We only read the classics. Last month we did *Sister Carrie.*"

"Good for you," said Sarah. "Some mothers from the playground tried to get me to join a group last year, but all they ever read were those Oprah novels."

"We're schoolteachers," said Jean, as if that accounted for the difference.

"I went to one meeting, and half the women hadn't even done the reading. They just wanted to sit around and talk about their kids. I mean, I went to graduate school. Don't call it a book group if you're not gonna talk about books."

"We have some very stimulating discussions," said Jean. "You should come next month. We're doing *Madame Bovary.* You could be my little sister."

"Little sister?"

"We're trying to get younger women involved. We call them our little sisters." She waved her hand, as if it wasn't worth discussing. "I'd love it if you'd be my guest."

"I'll think about it," Sarah said, groaning inwardly. The last thing she wanted was to spend a night talking about Flaubert with a bunch of retired schoolteachers. "I'm sure I have a slightly different critical perspective from the rest of you."

"That's the whole point," said Jean. "We could use some fresh blood."

They did their usual three-mile loop, through the park and around the new developments, Jean pumping iron and talking about the book group the whole time. She described the other members in unnecessary detail, sketching in their educational and family backgrounds, and making sure not to neglect their charming personality quirks. Bridget spoke three languages and had traveled *everywhere*. Alice, attractive but very demanding, was working on hubby number three. Regina's son—he was always a high achiever—was CFO of a Fortune 500 company. Josephine was funny and very opinionated, but her memory wasn't what it used to be. Laurel only attended during summer and fall. The rest of the year she was a golf widow in Boca.

"I tried to get Tim to take up golf," she said, as they turned back onto their street, "but he wouldn't do it. He's too busy sitting around the house all day letting his brain turn to mush. It's hard to believe, but twenty years ago, he was considered to be a charming and intelligent man."

Once Jean got started on the subject of her husband, it was hard to get her to stop. A lot of their walks ended with Sarah inviting Jean inside for a glass of ice water, then having to listen like a therapist to an hour's worth of complaints about Tim's failure to cope with retirement. That night, though, Sarah was saved from this ordeal by a surprising development: Theresa from the playground was sitting on her front stoop, obviously waiting to speak to her.

"You'll have to excuse me," said Sarah. "I think I have a visitor."

Sarah hadn't seen any of the other mothers since the day she kissed Todd. She'd gone back to the Rayburn School playground the following morning, and for the next two mornings after that, but each time the regulars were absent, the picnic table empty and reproachful. They couldn't have made themselves clearer if they'd sent her a registered letter.

She didn't care about Mary Ann or Cheryl; she was happier with them out of her life. But she missed Theresa—they'd always had a special connection—and had been thinking about giving her a call and trying to explain herself. And now here she was, her very presence a kind of implied forgiveness. Sarah felt her face breaking into a helpless grin as she headed up the front walk.

"Wow," she said. "Look who's here."

"I hope you don't mind," said Theresa. "Your husband said you'd be back any minute."

"It's good to see you. Can I make you a cup of tea or something?"

Theresa shook her head. "I can only stay a minute. I just wanted to warn you. You know that guy, the pervert? He's been riding his bike near the playground, checking out the kids."

"Oh God," said Sarah. "Do the police know?"

"Nothing they can do. He's not breaking any laws." She laughed bitterly. "I guess they're waiting for him to kill someone. I just thought you should know. I think we all need to be extra careful."

"Thanks. That's nice of you." Sarah hesitated for a moment. "You sure you don't want some tea?"

"I don't think so."

"Come on, just for a minute?"

Theresa stood up. "I'm sorry, Sarah. I don't think it's a good idea."

"I didn't mean to kiss him," Sarah blurted out. "I don't even know how it happened."

Theresa shrugged, as if all that were ancient history.

"I better get home," she said, patting Sarah gently on the arm as she passed. "Mike's gonna worry."

After she left, Sarah sat on the porch for a while, watching the lightning bugs rise from the lawn and feeling like a fool. She'd thought that Theresa had come to apologize, or to laugh with Sarah about what a bitch Mary Ann could be. She'd thought that they were going to make up, drink some tea, figure out a way to be friends again. But she'd just come to tell her about a pervert on a bicycle.

She wished she'd thought to bum a cigarette when she had the chance, because right now there was nothing left to do but get up and go inside to Richard, and she wasn't quite ready for that yet. She still hadn't forgiven him for the way he'd treated her when he finally came down from his office. He just walked into the living room, with his shirt untucked and that glazed expression he got when he spent too much time on the computer, and told her she could go for her walk. He was looking right at her as he said it, but it was as if he didn't even see her, as if she weren't actually standing two feet in front of him in a red bikini that fit her like a dream.

WHERE THE HELL HAVE YOU BEEN?

LARRY'S FLYERS DID THEIR JOB. WITHIN WEEKS, RONALD JAMES McGorvey's presence in Bellington had become the focus of a civic uproar. Numerous articles on the subject appeared in the local and regional papers; there was even a brief segment on *Eyewitness News* about "grassroots resistance to sex offenders in an otherwise sleepy suburban community."

The more Todd learned about McGorvey from these reports, the more he came to understand and share Larry's anger. McGorvey had been arrested three times for exposing himself to a minor, and once for indecent sexual assault (this charge had been dropped for an unspecified reason). But the really troubling part of the story was the crime he hadn't been arrested for.

Holly Colapinto was a nine-year-old girl from Green Valley who'd disappeared while walking home from school on a spring day in 1995. What happened to her was a matter of pure conjecture. No one saw her getting into a car or talking to anyone. Her body had not been found. She had, as the journalists liked to put it, "simply vanished."

The custodian at her school, Ronald James McGorvey, was quickly identified as the prime suspect on a tip from Holly's mother. Mrs. Colapinto said that the girl had complained to her several times about "the creepy way" the janitor looked at her. She said he also had a habit of barging into the Girls' Room, supposedly to mop the floor or replenish the paper towels, while Holly was going to the bathroom. Mrs. Colapinto reported her concerns to the school authorities, who said they'd issued a stern warning to McGorvey to be more careful.

Investigators who questioned the custodian said he had no alibi for the time of the girl's disappearance. He lived alone and called in sick to work that day. He claimed to have been napping in his apartment all afternoon, but no witnesses could vouch for his whereabouts until the following morning, when he arrived for work at Blessed Redeemer Elementary School at the usual time.

McGorvey steadfastly insisted on his innocence. He cooperated with the police, and later with the FBI, submitting to repeated interrogations without a lawyer present, and even taking a lie detector test, the results of which were described by a law enforcement source as "ambiguous." But in the end, there was nothing anybody could do: Without a body there wasn't a crime, technically speaking, just an unsolved missing persons case. Eventually the story ran out of steam and faded from view.

But people in Green Valley never stopped believing that McGorvey was guilty of murder, and they set out to make life as unpleasant for him as possible. The sources interviewed for this chapter of the saga failed to provide much in the way of concrete details.

"It wasn't one big thing," a man explained. "It was more like lots of little things. To remind him that he wasn't welcome here."

"People called him on the phone and told him what they thought of him," a woman remembered.

"I don't think anyone out-and-out threatened him," said the police chief. "At least not to my knowledge."

Within six months of Holly's disappearance, McGorvey quit his job at the elementary school and moved back to Bellington to live with his mother. Two years later, he was arrested for the Girl Scout incident, and sentenced to three years in state prison. And now he was back.

As a result of all the attention, the mayor of Bellington called for an emergency town meeting. It was a bigger deal than Todd realized; the streets leading to the school were as packed with parents that warm summer evening as they were with schoolchildren on a September morning.

Larry had explicitly requested that Todd wear his Guardian T-shirt and shorts to the meeting—it was practice night anyway—so he wasn't too surprised to find his teammates gathered outside the main entrance, all of them dressed exactly as he was. He was a little surprised, though, when Larry had them march into the auditorium in single file, and then lined them up in the orchestra pit, all eight of them evenly spaced from one end of the stage to the other, like Secret Service men protecting the president. Larry instructed them to cross their arms in front of their chests, and not to smile, even in the unlikely event that someone said something funny.

Todd was stationed off to the far right, between Tony Correnti and DeWayne Rogers, both of whom had adopted wide-legged stances and expressions that somehow combined alertness and serenity. He tried to follow their lead, but it wasn't easy. He was plagued by the self-consciousness of the impostor, an adult playing dress-up.

In the past couple of weeks, Todd's membership in the Guardians had solidified into an established fact, though he still didn't feel like he'd earned the full trust of his teammates. He'd gone to two more practices and both had been grueling affairs—lots of drills and conditioning work, followed by a ferocious intrasquad scrimmage. When practice was over, though, no one except Larry patted him on the back or suggested going out for a beer. The most he got from the other guys was a polite nod or a grudging wave. They were cops, and he wasn't; it was as simple as that.

Todd leaned toward DeWayne, whom he considered a potential ally.

"Why are we up here?" he whispered.

DeWayne shrugged, like he didn't know and didn't care.

"Gotta be somewhere," he replied.

The auditorium was packed—Todd recognized a lot of faces from the various playgrounds he and Aaron had visited over the past year and a half—and there seemed to be a general sentiment among the crowd that you weren't doing your duty as a citizen and parent if you didn't stand up to express your strenuous disapproval of sex offenders and demand to know what the town was going to do to ensure the safety of Bellington's children and prevent any further erosion of property values.

"Maybe you should put up a new sign," one angry man suggested to enthusiastic applause. "Entering Bellington. A Pervert-Friendly Town!"

The officials on stage—the mayor, the chief of police, and the school psychologist—kept patiently dispensing the same advice over and over. We can protect our children by making sure we know exactly where they are and who they're with at every moment in the day. Don't send a young child to the store, or even down the street to a neighbor's house, without an escort. But take these precautions calmly, without creating an atmosphere of panic. Childhood should be a time of innocence, not anxiety. For its part, the police department was stepping up its surveillance of parks and playgrounds, and closely monitoring McGorvey's activities.

After about a half hour of this, Todd's mind started to wander. He found himself thinking about Kathy and her strangely muted reaction to the news—he felt the time had come to tell her the truth—that he was going to football practice after the town meeting.

"Football practice?" she said. "What are you talking about?"

"The Guardians." He pointed to his T-shirt, which Larry had dropped off that afternoon. "I'm the new quarterback. That's why I've been staying out so late on Thursday night."

"I thought you joined that parents' committee."

"I did. It's the same guys. We're a sort of watchdog group slash football team. I guess I should have explained it a little more clearly."

Kathy didn't get upset. She just nodded for a little longer than necessary, as if he'd confirmed something that she'd been wondering about.

"I need something . . . *physical* in my life right now," he continued, in response to a question she hadn't asked. "I've been feeling kinda depressed."

"Fine," she said. "Whatever."

Maybe she's just tired, he thought. She'd been working late at the VA Hospital, interviewing elderly survivors of the brutal island-hopping campaign in the Pacific, and she'd been deeply affected by their stories. What these stories *were*, Todd had no idea, because she didn't talk to him about it. These days she hardly talked to him about anything except Aaron. Aaron and the bar exam.

They were heading for trouble, Todd understood that, driving toward a high cliff at very low speed in a car with no brakes. Kathy seemed to have developed the idea that everything would be fine once Todd passed the bar exam. He would get high-paying work as an associate at a big firm in a major city; they would finally be able to buy a house. She would finish up her documentary, then take some time off to be with Aaron. After a while, they could start thinking about getting pregnant again.

It was a pleasant scenario, except for the fact that it relied so explicitly and relentlessly on Todd's passing the bar exam. It wasn't that he *couldn't* pass the test. He'd made it through law school, hadn't he? It was just that he was having a little trouble concentrating these days.

Maybe I could be a cop, he thought, casting a sidelong glance at DeWayne. There was something tangible and exciting about the job that appealed to him, chasing crooks and tackling them in the middle of a busy street. *Or maybe a fireman.* That would be cool. What an adrenaline rush it would be, charging into a burning building, or climbing down a ladder with a baby in your arms. But why hadn't he thought of it a long time ago? Why had it ever seemed like a good idea to put on a suit every morning and spend his day researching copyrights or figuring out ways to exploit loopholes in the tax code? What kind of life was that for a grown man?

He thought about Sarah, too, but only fleetingly, just long enough to note her absence when he saw her three friends from the playground moving down the center aisle of the auditorium in triangular formation, the spandex queen leading the way, her two sidekicks following at a respectful distance.

Almost a month had passed since the kiss at the playground, and it no longer occupied such a central place in his mental universe. He still kept an eye out for Sarah at the pool and the supermarket, but he did so more out of habit than urgency, and without any real expectation of seeing her again. When he remembered her at this remove, it was with a hopeless but still somehow pleasant twinge of melancholy, as if she were someone he'd known briefly a long time ago—a one-night stand from college, say—who'd drifted in and out

of his life in the natural course of events, without saying good-bye
or making an insincere promise to keep in touch.

Which is probably why it took him so long to recognize her
when she poked her head into the auditorium midway through the
meeting. He registered a new arrival, but only in the most general
way: a break in the monotony, a youngish, semiattractive woman
lingering in the doorway, studying the scene with an uncertain expression, as if she'd wandered in by mistake.

When he finally realized who she was—it hit him when she
stepped into the room, something familiar in her walk, or maybe
just the proportions of her body—it was with the inevitable sense
of letdown you feel seeing someone in the flesh after spending a
little too much time visualizing them in your head. Mainly, he decided later, it was her clothes that threw him off. She was dressed
all wrong. At the playground she'd been girlish and sloppy in her
clamdiggers and ratty T-shirt, her hair frizzing crazily, like she'd
jammed her finger in a light socket before leaving the house. And
now here she was, all put together like a grown woman on a date,
long black skirt, tight white top, hair pulled back, and maybe—he
couldn't quite tell from this distance—even some lipstick.

There were some seats open in the first few rows, but she either
didn't see them or didn't want to call attention to herself by walking
down the center aisle in the middle of the meeting, so she settled
for standing room along the back wall, where a handful of latecom-
ers had established a kind of mirror image to the Guardians. She
looked at the stage for a few seconds, then whispered something to
the man standing next to her. He answered; she nodded and shifted
her gaze back to the front.

He felt a palpable connection when their eyes met, a sensation
somewhere between jolt and thrill, and she must have felt it, too,
because her body suddenly recoiled, almost as if a pair of invisible

hands had shoved her against the wall. And then she gave him this look, this wounded, searching *Where-the-hell-have-you-been?* look. Todd felt a momentary surge of guilt, as if their separation the past few weeks had been all his fault, as if he'd known where to find her and had deliberately avoided going there. The only answer he could give her was a small, apologetic shrug, though he had no idea what he was apologizing for.

The spandex queen rose to speak just then. She, too, was dressed for a night out, in black tights and an oversize silk shirt. Her posture was ramrod straight, but her public voice seemed incongruously sweet, cleansed of the harsh note of command she often struck at the playground.

"My name is Mary Ann Moser," she said, reading off an index card. "What I'd like to know is whether anyone in city hall is looking into specific legal strategies for forcing Mr. McGorvey out of Bellington. For example, couldn't the building inspector find some code violations and condemn his house? Couldn't the town find a way to seize the property through eminent domain?" She hesitated, and Todd could see her trying unsuccessfully to suppress a smile. "If not, couldn't we just run him out on a rail?"

The crowd erupted in rowdy applause, to Mary Ann Moser's obvious gratification. Todd turned back to Sarah, with an expression of eye-rolling disdain he hoped would mirror her own, only to discover that she had vanished, her body replaced by a highly charged patch of empty space on the wall. His eyes darted to the door, just in time to see it clicking shut.

He hesitated only a second before deciding to pursue her. He didn't want to go another month without seeing her again, without being able to ask her why she'd looked at him with such anguish, as if he'd done something to hurt her. He thought he could slip quietly out the side door without calling too much attention to himself, but he'd only gone a step or two in that direction when Tony Correnti grabbed him from behind by the collar of his T-shirt, the way a parent might restrain a child who's about to run into a busy street.

"Hey," Correnti whispered. "Whaddaya doing? You can't leave now."

Todd started to explain, but the look on Correnti's face made him stop. Stepping back into formation, he crossed his arms on his chest and stared blankly into space, just the way he'd been instructed.

Todd noticed the odor the moment he stepped into Larry's van. It wasn't the kind of thing you could miss. He checked the soles of his sneakers, but they were clean.

"That was a good meeting," Larry proclaimed, as he slipped into the driver's seat. He held up one hand so Todd could give him a high five. "We finally got their attention."

"Ran a little long, though," Todd observed, speaking in the head cold voice of someone who's either unable or unwilling to breathe through his nose. "Thought it would never end."

The Q&A had continued for a full hour after Sarah left, and Todd still couldn't believe he'd stood in front of the stage like a good little soldier the whole time. He should have just told Correnti to mind his own business and gone after her, but instead he'd surrendered without a word of protest, as if the stupid football team were more important to him than a woman he'd kissed and needed to talk to. Where had he learned to be such a sheep? The smell in the van intensified until it seemed like an accusation of cowardice, a cosmic commentary on his failure to seize the moment.

"It was a step," Larry said cheerfully. "A really good first step. Now we just gotta keep up the pressure."

Todd rolled down his window as soon as Larry started the engine, but it didn't do much good.

"I hate to say this, Larry, but something doesn't smell too good in here."

"No kidding," Larry replied.

"I checked my shoes," said Todd. "It's not me."

"It's not me, either," Larry assured him. "It's that bag of dog shit I got in the back."

On the way home from practice, Larry took the usual detour to Blueberry Court. A week ago he'd spray-painted Child Molester in Day-Glo letters on the McGorvey's driveway. The week before that he'd planted himself in the middle of the front lawn and lobbed a dozen eggs at the house, including two that exploded against the picture window. Todd had sat in the van both times—Larry didn't ask him to join him in the dirty work—watching the vandalism in silent disapproval. It reminded him of his fraternity days, when his Deke brothers would pull stupid pranks in his presence without expecting him to participate or even approve. It just seemed important to them that he provide an audience while they Krazy-glued a flowerpot to a dog's head or threw darts at a drunk guy's ass.

Todd didn't have to be here, he understood that. He could have walked home, or driven himself back and forth from practice. But instead he continued on as Larry's passenger and supposedly reluctant sidekick. Sometimes he told himself that he was keeping an eye on his teammate, making sure he didn't do anything *really* crazy. Other times he wondered if he wasn't just a coward, if his real feelings toward Larry involved a little more admiration than he wanted to admit.

"Could you grab that bag for me?" Larry asked. "It's on the floor behind you."

The dog shit was in a plastic supermarket bag, knotted at the top. It felt bottom heavy, overfilled, like a sack full of mud.

"Jesus, Larry. This thing weighs a ton."

"I got a friend at the Humane Society. There's some lighter fluid in the glove compartment."

Larry didn't hurry, didn't act like a man on a furtive or illegal mission. He walked up to McGorvey's front stoop like a mail carrier making a delivery. He dropped the sack, calmly doused it with lighter fluid, and then set in on fire with a match. He sprayed a little more fluid on the bag for insurance—the flames spiking and subsiding, just like on a barbecue grill—and then rang the doorbell several times before walking back to the van and climbing inside. They stayed right where they were, watching from the curb as the front door swung open.

It wasn't McGorvey, though, who appeared in the doorway, illuminated by the dying, but still noxious, flames. It was an old woman in a nightgown, holding a coffee cup in one hand. She stood there for a couple of seconds, taking stock of the situation, and then calmly shut the door, as if a shit fire on your welcome mat was just something you had to live with, something that happened every day.

PART TWO

MADAME BOVARY

SEX LOG

RICHARD WAS PAST THE GUILT. EVEN THE EXCITEMENT—THE aching indecision and wild anticipation of the past few weeks—had pretty much run its course. What was left, now that he'd taken what only a short time ago had seemed like an unimaginable step, was a calm sense of detachment, as if he were watching himself from a great distance, wondering if there was any chance he could stop before he did something he might regret.

But he also knew that it was beyond his power to stop, now that he'd come this far. Besides, if there was one thing life had taught him, it was that it was ridiculous to be at war with your own desires. You always lost in the end, so the interlude of struggle never amounted to anything but so much wasted time. It was much more efficient to give in right away, make your mistakes, and get on with the rest of your life.

The irony, of course, was that he had so strenuously resisted his own inclinations in the present case. He'd agonized over his decision for weeks, mainly because he couldn't accept the reality of his desires. Day after day he'd laughed at himself, and said, *You don't want this. You can't want this. You're not the kind of creep who orders a pair of used panties over the Internet.*

He was a married man, after all. If he wanted to get his hands on a pair of unwashed panties, he didn't have to look any farther than the bathroom hamper. But the panties within easy reach held no erotic interest for him whatsoever. They were just his wife's dirty underwear. The thong he'd received in the mail that afternoon—a wisp of white silk decorated with lime green polka dots, to be exact—was a different sort of garment, worn by a different sort of woman, and Richard could not have found it more fascinating.

At the moment, the thong was still enclosed in a Ziploc freezer bag—he was unaccountably delighted by this odd domestic touch— the kind that had a white bar running beneath the seal. On this bar, where the user was meant to identify the food in the bag and the date it was frozen, was the following message, written in big, flirty cursive: "Worn by Slutty Kay, 6/02/01. Enjoy!!!" Inside, along with his purchase, was an envelope containing a photo of Slutty Kay wearing the thong, and a detailed log of her sexual activity for the day on which she'd worn it. Richard knew all this without opening the bag or the envelope; he'd had a long e-mail correspondence with Kay before placing his order, and she'd walked him step by step through the process. The only thing she hadn't told him was the thing that couldn't be put into words, the mystery that was about to be revealed to him.

He could easily imagine what people would say if they could see him now: exactly the same thing they'd say if someone had told them that Ray from work was a transvestite or that Ted from next door had anonymous gay sex at highway rest stops. They'd shake their heads with the standard combination of amusement, pity, and smug superiority, and say, *Ha-ha-ha, poor Ray. Ho-ho-ho, poor Ted.*

At least I'm not like that. But we want what we want, Richard thought, *and there's not much we can do about it.*

He took one last glance at his computer screen. In a rectangular box that took up a little less than half of the available space, was one of his favorite images of Slutty Kay. She was sitting naked in front of her own computer—if you looked closely you could see that the picture on her screen was identical to the one on yours—and smiling over her shoulder with that look of friendly complicity that always undid him. *Hey,* she seemed to be saying, *isn't this fun?* Richard's hands, he was pleased to note, were almost completely steady as he peeled open the bag and pressed his face into the aperture.

He had stumbled upon sluttykay.com nearly two years earlier, while doing research for a client. Richard worked for a consulting firm that specialized in marketing and branding—his own area of expertise was in company and product names—and was trying to devise a clever take on "Y2K," a phrase that had worn out its welcome well before the arrival of the new millennium. In the course of compiling a list of domain names that utilized some combination of the three constituent parts, he found himself staring at a digital photo of a woman, neither particularly young nor particularly beautiful, standing on the beach at sunset, her back to the ocean. With her hair scraped back and her long, almost horsey face, she might not have even seemed sexy, except for the fact that she was lifting her tank top to flash her decidedly natural and—or so he thought at the time—none-too-fetching breasts. *Hi,* said the caption, bright pink letters on a pale blue background, *I'm Slutty Kay, a 36-year-old married bisexual exhibitionist actively pursuing a swinging lifestyle. To read*

*more about me and the unique ways I've chose to explore my God-given
sexuality, Click Here.*

Richard was at work at the time, his office door wide-open, lots
of activity in the hallway, but he clicked on the link anyway. There
was something in Kay's voice, some combination of the brazen (calling herself "slutty") and the banal ("actively pursuing a swinging
lifestyle"; "my God-given sexuality") that threw him into a state of
high alert. In some dim intuitive way, he sensed the presence of a
real, possibly somewhat confused person speaking directly to him. It
couldn't have been more different from the boilerplate you came
across at most porn sites, greedy male businessmen speaking through
the mouths of young women with big fake tits: "Hi, I'm Amanda,
and I love to suck cock!"

On the "Read More About Me" page, Richard found a series
of questions and answers from Kay, the terseness of which reminded
him of the catechism he'd had to memorize some thirty-odd years
ago, back when he'd made his confirmation.

Q: *Are you married?*
A: Yes.

Q: *Does your husband approve of your lifestyle?*
A: Absolutely. He's a swinger, too, but not bi (sorry,
    guys!).

Q: *Is this your only job?*
A: No, I'm a corporate professional with advanced tech-
    nical and business degrees.

Q: *Are you worried that your business associates will see
    this web site?*

A: What I do on my own time (and on this web site) is my own business and has no connection whatsoever with my professional life.

Q: *What kinds of sex do you like?*
A: All kinds! Straight, bi, group, phone, solo. I also like integrating toys, vegetables, and household objects (bottles, utensils, etc.) into my sex play.

Q: *Are you doing this for fun or money?*
A: Both! Isn't that the American Dream?

He was halfway through this catechism when Ray knocked on his door, taking orders for a lunch run. Casually, but with great haste, Richard banished Slutty Kay from his screen, told Ray that he'd like a small chicken caesar, and reentered the flow of an ordinary day. He didn't think about Kay or revisit her web site for several months, but a seed had been planted in his brain. She was out there, and he knew where to find her.

Like a lot of men, Richard was of two minds on the subject of pornography. Part of him was a responsible adult who disapproved on moral grounds and understood quite clearly that the porn industry exploited and violated young women, and part of him was a horny teenager who just thought it was incredibly cool to see pictures of naked ladies doing crazy stuff.

After his first marriage collapsed, Richard had gone through a period when he was more or less addicted to pornographic videos. Alone at night in his grim little townhouse, he'd jam *Dirty Debutantes 3* into his VCR the way someone else might pop a bag of

Orville Redenbacher's into the microwave. Hours upon hours of his life were devoted to the activity of watching people he didn't know have sex. He was a fan, fully capable of conducting an intelligent water cooler conversation on the respective ouevres of Nina Hartley and Heather Hunter, had he known anyone who would've been interested in hearing his opinions.

At some point he just got tired of it—the sameness of the acts, the histrionic moaning, the god-awful music. *What am I doing?* he asked himself. *Is this why I was put on the earth?* Fueled by a sudden burst of moral fervor, he tossed all his tapes into a garbage bag, drove to a construction site a few blocks away, and flung the bag into a Dumpster. This act of self-purifying rebellion left him feeling righteous and exhilarated.

A period of unusual physical and mental health ensued. Richard joined a gym, took some yoga classes, started reading books again. No longer distracted by the fantasy women on his TV screen, he began paying closer attention to the flesh-and-blood women he encountered as he went about his day, including the sullen, but obviously very intelligent young woman who took his orders at Starbucks, and who, to his amazement, agreed to go out with him the very first time he asked.

Lately, though, Slutty Kay had become a problem. He thought about her far too often, and visited her web site several times a day. He was neglecting his work and his family, and staying up until ungodly hours composing lyrical e-mails in her honor that he couldn't quite bring himself to send. It was as if he were back in high school, pining after some girl in chemistry class, knowing he'd never find the nerve to talk to her. Only this time he didn't have to go to the trouble of fabricating his own fantasies. They were all right there for him on his computer screen, thumbnailed and neatly archived.

Some of Kay's practices struck him as bizarre, even off-putting (she had a thing about kitchen utensils, spatulas, barbecue forks, and the like), and some were inexplicable (dressing up like a little girl and playing with balloons), but who was Richard to judge? She traveled to national parks and sites of historical interest—the Redwood Forest, Civil War battlegrounds—where she would invariably be photographed in front of some monument or marker, sans underwear, with her skirt hiked up to her waist. She had a vast collection of sex toys and used them in every possible permutation. The web site contained literally thousands of still photos of Kay alone and with various admirers, including a voluminous series memorializing a "hot tub encounter" she had with eight male members of the Slutty Kay Fan Club. The youngest guy looked like he'd just finished final exams; the oldest looked like he'd slipped out of the nursing home for the day. Kay didn't mind; she took care of everyone with the same no-nonsense air of friendliness and good cheer that made her seem so paradoxically wholesome, as if she were convinced that being a slut and being a really nice person were just two things that naturally went together.

The niceness—it verged on a kind of innocence, Richard thought—just radiated from her face. When people were mean or selfish you could see it even when they smiled. By the same token, Kay's sweet nature was unmistakable, even when she was performing unspeakable acts with a champagne bottle. She just did what she wanted, sharing her pleasure with the world without shame or apology. Richard wished he'd attained her level of moral and intellectual clarity; it would have saved him a lot of mistakes and would have kept his face from looking so tense and furtive all the time. If he'd been more honest, he would have had a smile like Kay's, joyful, self-assured, and full of kindness.

But as close as he sometimes felt to her—as much as he believed that he *knew* her—he could never get past the uncomfortable fact that she existed for him solely as a digital image. He'd never heard her voice, never touched her skin, never made her laugh. The more he dwelled upon this inequality, the less satisfied he was by her pictures. Sometimes he'd have to click through dozens or even hundreds of images before finding one that brought him to the state of arousal that a single picture used to inspire. It had gotten to the point where she was just taking up too much of his time.

The panties were an attempt to solve this problem. He thought they might provide a connection to the actual woman and her physical body, liberating him from the sanitized stillness of a photograph. Maybe a sniff or two would hurry things along, so he could get back downstairs to his real life, where his wife and daughter were waiting for him, their impatience increasing by the minute.

Though it had lasted for almost twenty years, Richard's first marriage had been wrong from the start, based as it was on a serious misunderstanding. Peggy had become pregnant during their final semester of college—this was in 1975, two years after Roe *v.* Wade—but they'd decided, in a fit of self-defeating undergraduate bravado, to do "the difficult and honorable thing rather than the shameful, easy one." Actually, this was Peggy's formulation; Richard just wanted her to get an abortion, though he never quite got around to stating this preference in so many words.

His silence and passivity in the face of an event that so profoundly transformed his life was something that still baffled him. He didn't love Peggy, didn't want to become a father. And yet he married her and accepted the burden of parenthood without a squeak of protest. To make matters worse, "the baby" turned out to be twins, a much more difficult and honorable project than even Peggy had bargained for. Their domestic circumstances were so chaotic and relentless for so long that Richard was in his midthirties before he realized how badly he resented his wife and children for imprisoning him in a suburban cage and forcing him onto the hamster wheel of corporate drudgery while his college buddies were off backpacking through Asia and snorting coke in trendy discos with high school girls who looked much older than they actually were.

By this point in his life, Richard had a night school MBA and a series of professional triumphs under his belt, mostly in the fast-food sector—The Cheese-Bomb Mini-Pizza™ and The Double-Wide Burger™ were two of his notable achievements. He traveled a fair amount on business and consoled himself with a string of hotel flings, as well as a long-term affair with a client's receptionist in Chicago that went sour after he forgot her birthday for the second year in a row. She retaliated with a long, informative letter to Peggy, complete with surprisingly well-written excerpts from her diary.

His daughters were sophomores in high school when this bombshell struck; Richard and Peggy agreed to stay together until they graduated. Oddly, those last two years were their happiest as a couple, though they rarely slept in the same bed and kept their social calendars as separate as possible. Something about the expiration date on the marriage made each of them more generous than they'd been in the past—your spouse's annoying habit becomes a lot less oppressive if you don't have to imagine putting up with it until the day one of you dies. By the time they split, he'd developed a real affection for her, and still called once or twice a week to see how she was doing.

The envelope in the bag contained not one but three Polaroids of Slutty Kay wearing the polka-dot thong, each of them bearing a scrawled inscription. In the first one (*Hi, Richard!*), she was standing otherwise naked in front of what must have been her bedroom closet, looking unusually contemplative as she brushed her hair. In the second, she was wearing a sleeveless turquoise minidress and sitting in a car in such a way—open door, one leg in, one leg out— that you got a very clear glimpse of her crotch (*Hope this gets you hot!*). The trio concluded with a rearview shot of Kay bending over and smiling up at the camera from between her knees (*Love and Kisses, S.K.*). The enclosed sex log was written in the same girlish cursive on a sheet of plain yellow legal paper:

> *7 A.M. — Up and at 'em . . . first orgasm of the day (silver bullet vibrator) . . . mmmm . . . quick shower*

> *7:30 A.M. — Put on Richard's thong*

> *8 A.M. — Coffee at Java House . . . Window seat so I can flash the businessmen . . . Hope they like polka dots!*

> *8:30 A.M. — Stuck in traffic again . . . Why not masturbate? (Wow, these panties are getting moist!)*

> *9 A.M.-12 Noon — Work* (illustration of frowny face)

> *12:14 — Lunchtime sex with girlfriend Trudy from Personnel Dept.—all she can eat! (Ha-Ha)*

12:46 — Tuna sandwich, light mayo, Diet Coke

1-5 P.M. — Work (frowny face)

6 P.M. — Masturbate while cooking dinner (roast slightly burned)

8-11 P.M. — Hotel room orgy with members of Slutty Kay Fan Club—and I do mean members! (panties off for most of this time, but back on for drive home)

12 Midnight — too tired to remove panties before falling asleep . . . but NOT too tired for one last orgasm (trusty blue dildo)

7 A.M. — Up and at 'em . . . remove yesterday's thong, still wet and very fragrant, and seal them in bag for my good friend, RICHARD.

p.s.—They're autographed too!

Richard had been divorced for almost two years when he started seeing Sarah. They hit it off right away, though he suspected later that this instant intimacy had less to do with any real connection between them than it did with the fact that they were both desperately lonely and waiting for someone to rescue them. At the time he'd been drawn to her bitter sense of humor, her youthful body, and her enigmatic sexuality (she claimed to be "basically straight," but spoke frequently about the Korean woman she'd been in love with in college). She seemed to appreciate his social ease, his liberal politics, and, though she never actually said so, the promise he held out of liberation from Starbucks and long-term financial security, at least once his daughters graduated from college.

They'd been married for less than a year when she got pregnant. This time around Richard had no mixed feelings—he was thrilled with the idea of bringing a child into the world, consciously and without regret, correcting the mistakes he'd made with the twins (they blamed him for the divorce and were no longer speaking to him, though they were happy to accept buckets of his money). He vowed to himself and to Sarah that he would be involved and available in this new child's life. He would work less, spend more time at home. He would coach soccer, sing songs in the car, organize memorable birthday parties. He attended Lamaze classes, read a slew of child care books, and coached Sarah successfully through labor and delivery, a miraculous (but also disturbing and horrible and nearly endless) event that he had completely missed out on with the twins, whose birth he'd spent pacing the hospital waiting room like Ricky Ricardo, and then passing out cigars to the other expectant fathers when the doctor gave him the thumbs-up.

He tried, he really did, at least for the first year. He said all those things new fathers are supposed to say and changed his share of diapers. But sometimes he found himself wishing that Lucy was a boy. He'd had two girls already, why did he need a third? And sometimes, when he was stuck at home with the baby on a rainy weekend, he found himself overcome by a familiar sense of claustrophobia and resentment, as if he were once again a young man throwing away the best years of his youth.

His sex life suffered, too, of course. How had he forgotten about that? Sarah was too tired, her nipples were sore, she couldn't even think about it. When he suggested leaving the baby with her mother for a few days so they could take a quick getaway to the Caribbean, she looked at him like he was crazy.

"My mother can barely take of herself," she said. "How's she going to care for an infant?"

It was around that time that he started logging onto swingers' web sites and thinking, *Why not? It looks like fun.* He printed out a list of "house parties" in their area and decided to approach Sarah about the possibility of attending one, just to see what it was like. *They love bisexual women,* he would tell her. *You don't have to do anything you don't want.* But when he went downstairs to talk to her, she was sitting at the kitchen table, expressing milk from her engorged left breast with a loud electric pump, looking pale and haggard as she flipped through the newspaper, and for a second or two, he felt an emotion toward her that was a little like contempt.

He still hadn't gotten over how completely he'd misread his own needs. He'd assumed he was evolving and improving as a person, but all he'd really done was repeat his own failure, this time with his eyes wide-open and no one to blame but himself.

The panties weren't working as well as he'd hoped. It wasn't that the thong wasn't as fragrant as Kay had promised—that was definitely *not* the problem—it was just that the fragrance wasn't as distinctive or evocative of Kay's unique sexuality as he'd expected. For all he knew, it could have been worn by any woman in the world, including Sarah.

Which got him thinking, at a very inconvenient time, about a troubling possibility: What if Kay *hadn't* worn it? On her web site, she claimed to provide the panties to her devoted customers as a labor of love, but Richard wasn't sure he believed her. After all, didn't Kay have an advanced degree in business? For the panties to be really profitable, she would have to deal in bulk. She couldn't just wear one pair per day, as the sex log suggested.

If I were Kay, he thought, *I'd subcontract the panty-wearing.* It was all too easy to imagine a sweatshop full of bored women—Chinese and Latina seamstresses—all of them wearing polka-dotted thongs as they worked their sewing machines, then wearily slipping them into plastic bags at the end of the day, along with a completely fictional "sex log." What kind of fool would that make Richard?

He pressed the thong over his mouth and nose and inhaled deeply, trying to banish these inappropriately commercial considerations. This was no time to be thinking about business, his pants around his ankles, his palm slick with Vaseline Intensive Care. *These are Kay's panties*, he chanted to himself. *These panties belong to Kay.* But then, just when he got himself going, he'd think, *Maybe they're not. Maybe they're outsourced.*

It was hard to know how long he'd hosted this dialogue in his mind before the whole issue of authenticity suddenly became moot. His eyes were darting in a regular pattern from the sex log to the Polaroids to an image on his computer screen of Kay leaning on a guardrail overlooking Niagara Falls, discreetly lifting her dress to give the camera a glimpse of her bare ass. He was breathing deeply, taking her essence deep into his lungs, into his bloodstream—

"Ahem."

He whipped his head around, the panties still pressed over the lower half of his face. Sarah was standing in the doorway, her expression wavering between revulsion and amazement.

"Is this going to take much longer?" she asked. "I'd really like to go for my walk."

Richard understood that something terribly embarrassing had occurred, but all he felt just then was a profound annoyance at the interruption.

"You could have knocked," he said, his words disappearing into the undergarment.

"I did."

It took an effort of will for him to remove the thong.

"I'm sorry," he said. "This will just take a minute."

"I think we need to talk," she said, but to his immense relief she backed out of the room without another word, pressing the door shut with the gentlest of clicks, not unlike the sound your tongue makes against the roof of your mouth when you think something's a shame.

ELECTRICAL STORM

SARAH AND TODD MADE LOVE FOR THE FIRST TIME DURING A LATE-afternoon thundershower on the scratchy rug in her living room, the bed upstairs being occupied just then by Lucy and Aaron, both of whom had conveniently dozed off on the way home from the pool.

"This is incredible," Todd whispered as he thrust himself into her with a vigorous yet artful corkscrewing motion that she would soon come to recognize as his trademark sexual maneuver.

"We smell like chlorine," she replied. Despite her fervent wish to remain in the moment, to block out all extraneous information and sensation, she found herself thinking sadly of her husband as she gripped the taut muscles of Todd's ass. At forty-seven, Richard was still reasonably thin, but his butt had gone flabby. Even when they'd had a halfway decent sex life, Sarah had preferred not to think too much about that part of his anatomy and only touched it by accident.

"I love your red bikini," he told her.

"Thank you," she murmured.

He stopped, mid-spiral. A vaguely pained expression passed

across his sun-burnished face, as if he were trying hard to remember the name of his congressman. *My first handsome boyfriend*, Sarah thought proudly. She wished Arthur Maloney and Amelia and Ryan and everyone else who'd ever hurt her could be watching right now on closed circuit television. Todd peered down at her, his face enormous above hers, a lovely eclipse.

"Do you feel guilty about this?" he asked.

Sarah hesitated. She would have liked to explain that her husband had become some sort of panty fetishist, but it didn't seem like the right time to broach such an awkward subject. It had been hard enough to discuss it with Richard, to keep a straight face while he attempted to convince her that he'd mail-ordered the panties for professional purposes—some sort of research he was conducting on web-based sales and marketing models, blah blah blah—and had inadvertently let his curiosity get the best of him. Sarah had accepted his pathetic alibi with a polite expression, feeling both sorry for him and oddly liberated, as if she'd been formally released from her marriage by the sight of her husband huffing another woman's underpants.

"No," she told Todd. "I thought I might, but I don't."

"I do," he said.

Oh God, she thought, *here it comes*. Some primitive high-school-era defense mechanism kicked in, and she managed to accept this confession with a calm, curious expression, while at the same time bracing herself for a sudden descent into misery. *This is where he rolls off me and buries his face in his hands.*

"I feel really bad," he continued. But then he shrugged, as if this were a minor nuisance at best. "What can you do?"

Sarah forced herself not to smile.

"You better pick up the pace," she said, slapping him lightly on the thigh. "They could wake up any minute."

With admirable haste, he started up the corkscrew again. Sarah couldn't help laughing.

"Who are you?" she asked in not-quite-mock bewilderment. "The Roto-Rooter Man?"

Before he could respond, a ferocious crack of thunder shook the house, as if the sky had exploded directly above them. The lovers froze in place, their faces turned toward the stairs, waiting for a cry to erupt from the bedroom.

"Keep going," she said, after a few seconds had passed. "It's okay."

He sprang back into action, but then abruptly checked himself.

"Did you just call me the Roto-Rooter Man?"

"It's a compliment," she assured him.

Sarah had come to the Town Pool the previous week in the full knowledge that she was offering herself to Todd. There was nothing coy, or even subtle, about her methods. She had spotted him from a distance before she'd even shown her badge to the gate attendant— he and Aaron had staked out a prime piece of poolside real estate, a shady patch of grass near the shallow end, neither too close nor too far from the rest rooms—and once inside, she led Lucy over to this spot with the confidence of someone who holds an equal claim on the property. She spread her towel on the grass just inches from his, sat down without a word of greeting, and began rummaging in her straw bag for a container of sunscreen. Only after she'd found it did she deign to acknowledge the neighbors whose space they'd so blithely invaded—the father shirtless and reading *Men's Health* magazine, the son in Rugrats swim trunks and his jester's cap, and Big Bear, still buckled into the double stroller, watching the scene with his perpetually horrified expression, as if he could foresee a calamity he felt helpless to prevent.

"Oh, look, honey, it's that nice little boy from the playground."

"He's a bad boy," Lucy said darkly.

Aaron didn't take the bait. He was busy staging a head-on collision between a garbage truck and an oil tanker, an act he choreographed with peculiar sound effects and an air of grave concentration.

"Don't you like his hat?"

"It's stupid."

This got Aaron's attention. He glared at Lucy.

"You stupid," he informed her.

"Aaron," said Todd. "That's not nice."

"Stupid, stupid, stupid," the boy muttered, in a barely audible voice.

Sarah smiled, offering Todd a small shrug of apology.

"I hope you don't mind. Lucy has sensitive skin. She's better off in the shade."

"Not at all," he said, swatting the magazine at a fly that was dive-bombing his head. "It's nice to see you again."

Sarah made Lucy stand at attention for a thorough slathering of water-resistant SPF 45 sunscreen that included the tips of her toes and the rims of her ears. After getting her daughter settled with a coloring book and a box of crayons, she shed her baggy T-shirt and began applying the protective goop to her own body, wishing she had something a little sexier to caress into her skin, baby oil or one of those coconut-scented lotions so popular during her adolescence, back when a lobstery sunburn was seen as a necessary first stage in the tanning process. Then she turned to him, as casually as if he were her cousin or brother, and said, "Could you do my back?"

"Sure."

She wriggled toward him, passing the plastic bottle over her shoulder. Bending forward, she lifted her hair away from the nape of her neck—she knew it was one of her finest features—with a languid gesture that made her feel momentarily glamorous, a model posing for a cover shoot.

He didn't overdo it. He rubbed the sunscreen onto her back and shoulders in a polite and businesslike manner. He didn't linger unnecessarily in her lumbar region or take any other liberties.

And yet.

It felt illicit.

She might as well have been naked.

"Oh my God," she whispered.

"Tell me about it," he said.

She knew, at that moment, as clearly as she knew her own name, that they were going to be lovers, and that it would happen sooner rather than later. They didn't really have a choice; there was some kind of raw sexual connection between them that she'd never experienced with anyone in her life.

That was Monday. By Friday her opinion on the matter had taken a 180-degree turn. *It's not going to happen,* she told herself. *And maybe that's okay.*

It wasn't that her attraction to him had faded as they spent more time together; if anything, it had increased. He looked like some kind of blond American god stretched out on his rainbow-striped towel, baseball cap pulled low over his forehead, bronzed torso rising and falling with each lazy breath. Lying beside him without being able to touch his hand or lick his skin was a fresh erotic torment to her every day.

But there were compensations. She'd been so focused for so long

on the memory of their unexpected kiss at the playground that she'd
forgotten how easy it was to talk to him, the way they'd just plunged
into conversation as they pushed their kids on the swings, his dis-
arming honesty about himself, a quality he had of accepting people
for who they were, of simply enjoying their company for however
long he was allowed to share it.

Day after day, they sat in the shade, distributing snacks and
brokering occasional disputes—having little choice in the matter,
Aaron and Lucy had formed a fragile friendship—talking all the
while about their own childhoods, things they'd read in the paper
or heard on the radio, household matters, the people around them.
When the kids got too hot or bored, they took them in the pool,
continuing their conversation in waist-high water. Sometimes they
traded offspring. Todd taught Lucy to doggie paddle while Sarah
played rough with Aaron, lifting the feathery boy in and out of the
water, the jingling of his bells mingling with his giddy laughter as
he windmilled his arms wildly at the air.

It was the most fun she'd had in years. On three separate occasions strangers complimented Sarah on her beautiful family, and
she neglected to correct them. One afternoon, when she and Todd
were snacking on a huge bunch of grapes, Sarah saw Mary Ann and
gave her a big wave. Mary Ann hesitated for a moment—she was
wearing sunglasses, a gigantic straw hat, and some kind of gauzy
yellow cover-up—before putting on the fakest smile Sarah had ever
seen on the face of another human being. She raised her arm slowly,
as if it were made of lead, and waved like it hurt.

As badly as Sarah sometimes wanted to just grab Todd by the
face and kiss him, to crawl onto his towel and blast away the pretense
that they were just a couple of pals killing time together, she wanted
just as badly to hold on to the innocent public life they'd made for
themselves out in the sunshine with the other parents and children.

If they had an affair, all this would have to head underground, into a sadder and darker and more complicated place. So she accepted the trade: the melancholy handshake at four o'clock in exchange for this little patch of grass, some sunscreen and conversation, one more happy day at the pool.

So much depends on the weather, she thought later. Maybe that first week felt idyllic not only because of the supercharged current running between her and Todd, but also because every day of it was sunny and dry and in the mid-eighties, a cosmic smile of approval, one blessing piled on top of another.

The idyll ended over the unspeakably dreary weekend that followed, when a stubborn heat wave pushed into the area and refused to budge. Monday and Tuesday were brutal, in the nineties, with the kind of humidity that turned Sarah's already frizzy hair into a freak show, the air quality index edging from "bad" to "unhealthy." The pool was packed, the patch of shade she'd come to think of as "our spot" overrun by early birds. Lucy was cranky, Aaron lethargic; Todd couldn't think of anything to talk about but how damn hot it was, which at least gave him a one-topic advantage over Sarah, who didn't want to talk about anything at all.

By Wednesday the whole world was in a rotten mood. The sky loomed low and heavy, promising rain but not delivering. The pool was tepid, barely any relief at all. Todd squeegeed the sweat off his forehead with an index finger.

"It's funny," he said. "In the middle of winter you can't even imagine a day like this. And if you could, it would probably seem okay."

Sarah could barely muster the energy to nod. *We should just go to the movies,* she thought. They could see *Spy Kids* at the mall, hide out in the air-conditioning for a couple of hours. But she kept this idea to herself. It seemed dangerous somehow, too much like a date.

"It works the other way, too," he went on. "On a day like this, it's hard to believe in February. You know, that week around Valentine's Day, when you don't even want to walk out to your car." He shook his head. "Remember those vinyl seats they used to have? Might as well sit naked on a block of ice."

"I wish," Sarah muttered.

"It's a little like being dead," he added, after a moment's thought.

"Vinyl seats?"

"No, it's just like when you're dead and you try to remember being alive, it'll be like thinking of winter on the hottest day of the year. You'll know it's true, but you won't really believe it."

"That's actually sort of comforting," Sarah pointed out. "I always figured that when you're dead, you wouldn't be able to think of anything. There wouldn't be any *you* to do the thinking."

"That's a depressing thought."

"Only if you're alive," she said. "If you're dead, it doesn't matter."

Todd looked at the sky. There was a whiny note in his voice that Sarah didn't like.

"They said scattered showers. I don't see any scattered showers."

Oh, what the hell, she thought. *I'll just ask him to the movies. We don't even have to sit next to each other.* But then something distracted her. A disturbance in the air, maybe. A low murmur of warning. Some kind of collective shift of attention. One of those moments when you and a lot of other people are suddenly looking in a certain direction, though most of you have no idea why.

The Bellington Town Pool was set at the bottom of a grassy hill, an enormous, but still somehow jewel-like circle of water ringed by a concrete walkway. A group of coltish adolescent girls, awkward and lovely in their tiny bikinis, did their sunbathing on the walkway, but everyone else pitched camp on the hillside, which undulated upward in a series of gentle plateaus that gave the whole facility the feel of a natural amphitheater.

Sarah and Todd and the kids were sitting maybe a third of the way up the hill on that sweltering Wednesday afternoon, much closer to the center of the pool than if they'd been able to claim their usual spot under the spreading oak tree. They had an unobstructed fifty-yard-line view of the water, from the toddlers sitting in the shallow end to their left, to the junior high kids batting around a beach ball in the middle, to the teenage daredevils doing backflips off the deep end diving board to their right.

But like most of the people around her, Sarah wasn't looking at the water just then. Her gaze was drawn—irresistibly, it seemed—to the nearside walkway, to the man standing near the lifeguard chair and glancing around with a worried expression, apparently searching for a clear patch of grass on which to spread the rolled-up pink towel that was draped around his neck.

At first she thought she was looking at him because he was holding a bright orange scuba flipper in each hand and had a diving mask of the same color perched high on his forehead. People didn't often wear that sort of gear to the Town Pool, and even if they did, this guy wouldn't have seemed the type. He was a pasty, overweight man who had made one mistake by going shirtless and another by wearing a ridiculously loud pair of swim trunks, lurid tropical flowers throbbing against a flat gray background, a combination of errors that somehow made him seem overdressed and underdressed at the same time. But then Sarah took a second look at his oddly familiar face and realized that she was staring at him for an entirely different reason.

"Oh my God," she said.

"What?"

"It's him." She lowered her voice and pointed. "You know who."

Todd squinted. "Oh, Jesus. He shouldn't be here. I don't care how hot it is."

As if by reflex, Sarah turned to check on the kids, who were engrossed in a game of Car Doctor. Lucy was the doctor. After Aaron staged one of his crashes, she examined the injured vehicles, listening to them with a toy stethoscope and then kissing them to make them feel better, at which point they were eligible to participate in another collision. Sarah reached out, in a rush of tenderness, and pressed her hand against her daughter's sweat-sticky cheek. Lucy brushed it away, annoyed by the interruption.

When Sarah turned back around, Ronald James McGorvey was sitting on the edge of the pool, tugging his flippers onto his feet, the towel resting in a heap beside him. Then he lowered the mask over his eyes and nose and wiggled it into position. He slid feetfirst into the pool, breaking the surface with only the barest hint of a splash.

No one minded at first. The beach ball kept popping into the air as McGorvey cut through the game with the heavy grace of a seal, the flippers beating a frothy trail in his wake. The divers kept cannonballing and somersaulting and bellyflopping off the springboard as he moved into the deeper water. But then a woman's panicky voice cried out from the base of the hill.

"Jimmy! Jimmy Mancino! Get out of the pool this instant!"

A skinny kid, maybe ten years old, started paddling uncertainly toward the voice.

"Jimmy, now!"

Another voice rang out.

"Randall, Juliette. You too!"

"Sheila!"

"Pablo!"

"Mark! Mark Stepanek!"

Once the exodus began, it happened quickly. The shallow end emptied first, anxious mothers wading out with frightened-looking toddlers in their arms. The older kids were slower to leave, but before long they were climbing out, too, standing in sullen confusion on the walkway, water streaming off their bodies, puddling at their feet. All over the hillside, adults were whipping out cell phones, dialing 911.

For maybe five minutes, McGorvey had the whole gigantic pool to himself. He dove to the bottom of the deep end, then rose slowly, breaking the surface just long enough to catch his breath before heading back down. When he got tired of that he floated on his back for a while, his gaudy shorts billowing around his waist, the pale mound of his belly rising out of the water like a deserted island. He kept his mask over his face the whole time, so Sarah couldn't tell if he was defiant or embarrassed or simply oblivious of the fact that he'd cleared the pool as effectively as if he'd been a shark.

By the time the police cruiser pulled into the parking lot—it was located near the deep end, behind a tall chain-link fence—Aaron and Lucy had caught on to the fact that something momentous was going on. They suspended Car Doctor and wriggled into the laps of their respective parents.

"Kids not swimming," said Lucy.

"Why police?" Aaron wondered.

Sarah checked with Todd, uncertain how to explain the situation. But before she could begin to answer, a busybody with pink cheeks sitting directly in front of them turned around.

"There's a bad man in the pool," she said. "The police are coming to get him."

"Why he bad?" Lucy asked.

"He's not nice to children," said Sarah. "But you don't have to worry about it."

By then, the cops—there were two of them, an older white guy and a younger black guy—had entered the pool area through a padlocked gate that had been opened by one of the lifeguards. Looking hot and miserable in their uniforms, they trudged down the walkway, stopping near McGorvey's pink towel and gazing at the lonely swimmer with what seemed more like envy than professional interest. Sarah didn't hear them say anything, but McGorvey swam toward them as if they had. He had a little trouble hoisting himself out of the pool, so the black cop reached down and gave him a hand. The white cop handed him his towel.

"What's those?" Aaron asked. "On the feet."

"Flippers," said Todd. "They help you swim better."

The cops talked, and McGorvey nodded as he toweled off, the mask still concealing most of his face. The white cop shrugged. The black cop touched McGorvey, almost gently, on the shoulder. They didn't seem to be arresting him. If you didn't know better, you would have thought they were all friends. The cops stood motionless as McGorvey turned on his heels and began trudging toward the exit, his flippers slapping wetly against the concrete of the walkway. After just a few steps, though, he stopped to pull them off, balancing unsteadily on one leg, then the other. He did the same with the mask. Then he turned toward the hillside, spreading his arms wide, like an actor addressing his public. His voice was loud and plaintive, as if he wanted everybody to hear.

"I was only trying to cool off!"

After McGorvey left, the swimmers returned with a vengeance. It was a massive invasion of the Town Pool, the decent people of Bellington reclaiming it for their own. Grabbing their children by the wrists, Sarah and Todd joined the stampede, stumbling downhill with their fellow citizens, then waiting in an orderly line for their turn to walk down the safety ramp into what felt just then like the world's largest bathtub.

Despite the overcrowding and disconcerting warmth of the water, there was a giddiness in the air, as if the collective funk of the past few days had finally broken. Adults got into giggly splashing fights. They bumped into one another and smiled. A beach ball appeared, and everyone understood that the point was to keep it aloft for as long as possible. When it finally touched the water, what sounded like a hundred voices said *Oooh* in unison.

The fun was only a few minutes old when the clouds abruptly darkened. A breeze stirred for the first time in recent memory, and faces turned skyward in surprised gratitude as fat, widely spaced raindrops began plummeting into the pool with the force of small pebbles. Kids staggered around with their tongues out, the way they did during the first snow of the year. Then it thundered. Nothing too scary, a sustained bass rumble off to the right.

"Clear the pool, please," said a voice over the PA. "Everybody out! No swimming during an electrical storm."

The swimmers groaned but obeyed. Once again Sarah and Todd were part of the herd, this time tugging their children uphill. As soon as they reached their towels they began gathering up their stuff with a sense of urgency that was intensified by another boom of thunder, this one considerably louder than the first, and followed seconds later by a crackling spike of lightning. Lucy whimpered and latched on to her mother's leg.

"It's okay, honey." Sarah squatted to lift her daughter. "We better get going."

"You're gonna carry her?" Todd asked.

"It'll be faster this way. She's scared of the you-know-what."

"That's crazy," he said. "Put her in the stroller. We'll walk you home."

The next thunderclap made Lucy squirm in her mother's arms, her grip tightening uncomfortably around Sarah's neck. Lightning flashed right on top of it, a yellow exclamation mark in the greenish sky.

"But that's out of your way."

"We don't mind, do we, Aaron?"

Aaron looked skeptically at the stroller.

"What about Big Bear?"

"He won't mind a little rain."

To Sarah's surprise, Lucy agreed to ride in the stroller, her usual disdain for that childish mode of transportation trumped by a desire to get home as quickly as possible, not to mention the novelty of riding with a friend. She switched places with the stuffed animal, whose synthetic fur felt no better against Sarah's body than her daughter's clammy skin.

The rain remained light during their journey across town, Todd pushing the stroller at a brisk clip, Sarah lagging a few feet behind, trying to figure out a good way to hold the unwieldy bear that didn't require her to look at his creepy, disapproving face.

"Here we are," she said, amazed to be standing in front of her house after only a ten-minute walk. It usually took her a half hour to cover the same distance with Lucy.

She handed Big Bear to Todd with a sense of relief and walked around to the front of the stroller. Kneeling to unbuckle her daughter, she suddenly understood why the kids had been so quiet on the way home.

"This is amazing," Sarah whispered. "She never naps."

It was a sweet sight, Aaron's hand resting on Lucy's thigh, her head leaning against his shoulder. She was sucking her thumb, making happy smacking noises with her lips.

"Aaron'll be out for the next two hours."

The wind rushed through the treetops, spinning the leaves upside down, signaling the true arrival of the storm. A faucet opened in the sky, releasing a sudden deluge.

"You better come in," Sarah said, tugging Todd toward the house. "I can't let you walk home in this."

Dripping wet, they carried their sleeping children upstairs and laid them down on Sarah's bed, which she was glad she'd made before leaving the house. Still sucking her thumb, Lucy rolled onto her stomach, sticking her plump little butt in the air. She was wearing an orange-and-yellow bathing suit with a little ruffled skirt that had flipped up, exposing the dimpled baby fat at the top of her thighs. Aaron was sprawled out on his back, the pink-and-purple tentacles of his jester's hat spreading wide along with his arms and legs. He had delicate features, and those miraculously long eyelashes you only saw on little boys, never on grown men.

Sarah and Todd stood at the edge of the bed for what felt like a long time, watching their children sleep, and listening to the rain drumming against the house, afraid to even look at one another. Sarah's mouth was dry, her bathing suit unpleasantly tight around the waist. When Todd finally spoke, there was an audible tremor in his voice.

"We're not gonna do anything crazy, are we?"

Sarah thought it over for a moment. She felt light-headed, almost weightless, as if she were about to rise off the floor.

"I don't know," she whispered, reaching for his hand, threading her fingers through his. "You'll have to define crazy."

NIGHT GAME

TODD WAS A NERVOUS WRECK ON THE DAY OF THE GUARDIANS' season opener against the Auditors, a team of CPAs who were the reigning champs of the Midnight Touch Football League. Even though the kickoff wasn't scheduled to take place until the ungodly hour of 10 P.M., he woke at six in the morning with a full-blown case of game-day jitters, and couldn't manage more than two bites of the frozen waffle Kathy slid in front of him at the breakfast table.

"Sorry," he said. "I'm not really hungry."

She looked at him a little more closely.

"Are you sick?"

"I'm fine. Just a little keyed up about the game tonight."

Kathy's eyes went dead, the way they always did when he tried to tell her about the Guardians. He didn't blame her, exactly; he understood that she saw his return to organized football as pure self-indulgence, some kind of premature midlife crisis, and even a potential threat to their family, at least to the extent he allowed it to interfere with his preparation for the bar exam (she had no way of knowing that his preparation had diminished to the point where it could no longer be interfered with). Even so, he would have appreciated a smile or a word of encouragement, some miniscule signal of support. When he was in high school, the cheerleaders used to visit his house while he slept, festooning the trees with toilet paper and writing inspirational messages on his driveway in colored chalk— *Go, Todd! We Love #12! Let's Get Rowdy!* During his senior year, Amanda Morrissey, a wispy little junior with bleached hair and a sexy overbite—she was always the pinnacle of the human pyramid— snuck into his bedroom on the night before the big Thanksgiving Day game and woke him up with what she called "a good luck blowjob." Back then, the whole world noticed when Todd had a game.

"I'm running low on underwear," Kathy reported. "Think you could do some laundry today?"

Todd said he would. He smiled at her across the table, glad to be able to resent her a little for a change. In some very small way, it helped counteract the massive amount of guilt he'd been feeling for the past couple of weeks.

"What about dinner?" she said. "Any ideas?"

"I can't even get my mind around breakfast."

"Anything but pasta," she told him. "We eat way too much pasta around here."

"I thought you liked pasta."

"I do," she said, gathering up the breakfast dishes and carrying them to the sink. "That's the problem. Pretty soon I'll be able to sell advertising space on my ass."

Todd studied her back as she rinsed the cups and plates and stuck them in the dishwasher. She was dressed for work, summer casual in a blue tank top and a silvery gray skirt that fit snugly enough that you could see what a great body she had, but not so snugly that you thought she was showing off. Her legs were lean and athletic, the graceful bulge of her calf muscles somehow accentuated by the flatness and practicality of her sandals. It would have been nice to notice that she'd put on some weight—as if that would have supplied him with some sort of excuse for fucking another woman—but no one was going to be using Kathy's ass for a billboard anytime soon.

Am I angry with her? Todd wondered. If he was, that would help to explain his otherwise inexplicable behavior. But he didn't really have a lot to be angry about. She loved him and treated him well. He couldn't have asked for a better mother for his child or a more patient and considerate life partner. He had disappointed her, of course—he had disappointed himself, for that matter—but most of the time she kept it to herself. Their sex life wasn't what it used to be, but that was only because they had so little time to themselves. If they'd been able to sneak off for a weekend, he had no doubt that they'd be going at it like they had the summer after graduation, when they lived together for the first time and sometimes didn't stagger out of the apartment until four or five o'clock on a Sunday afternoon. Kathy shut the dishwasher and turned around.

"I'm dreading work today," she informed him.

Todd was tempted to ignore her, to mirror the indifference with which she'd greeted his mention of the game, but he didn't want to stoop to that petty level of payback.

"Why's that?"

"I'm interviewing this vet at the hospital." She glanced at Aaron before continuing. He was sitting on the floor in front of the refrigerator, staging a battle between magnets. Just then, a strawberry was inflicting serious damage on a local realtor. "He lost both legs at Iwo Jima."

"Jesus."

"But that's not the worst of it." She smiled, the way people sometimes do when every expression seems equally inappropriate. "He's in this state of like permanent denial. He still believes it's 1944, and that he's the same person he was back then. Basically, he's a seventy-five-year-old man with no legs who thinks he's a healthy teenager."

"Maybe that's not so bad," Todd speculated.

"I know what you mean," she said. "But it doesn't really work like that. He can't understand why his parents don't visit, and he's furious with his girlfriend for not answering his letters."

Todd sipped his coffee, marveling as he did almost every day at the way he'd underestimated his wife. When they met in college, he'd mistaken her for a bit of a phony, a pretty girl dabbling in poetry and painting, trying to look more artsy than she actually was. Even when she got accepted into film school, he figured that she was just killing time until they could begin a conventional upper-middle-class life in the suburbs: i.e., he'd work his ass off every day for a big law firm, while she went to the gym and Starbucks before picking up the kids at day care. And now here she was, ten years down the road, spending her summer with shell-shocked amputees at the VA Hospital while he lounged at the pool all afternoon, fine-tuning his tan and getting into trouble.

"You know what else? He keeps asking me out. He wants to take me dancing."

"You're joking, right?"

"It's breaking my heart." Kathy glanced at Aaron again, and then back at Todd. She kept her voice soft, so only he could hear. "And we think we have problems."

No matter what time Todd and Aaron arrived at the Town Pool, Sarah and Lucy always managed to show up a good ten or fifte minutes later. He wasn't sure how she made it work out that way, but it happened too consistently for him to imagine it was an accident. It must have been a point of pride for her not to be first, not to look too eager.

Every day Todd waited for her in the shade and tried to convince himself that the spell was broken, that he'd finally come to his senses and realized that it just wasn't worth it, risking his marriage for a woman he barely knew and who wasn't even his type, and what was worse, implicating his own child in the deception. Sometimes he practiced break-up speeches in his head, a series of disconnected utterances—song and movie clichés, mostly—strung together in a momentarily plausible chain: *We must be out of our minds, Sarah, let's put a stop to this before someone gets hurt, maybe if there weren't kids involved, this is really hard for me, Sarah, I still want us to be friends . . .*

But then he'd see her, bopping down the concrete walkway with Lucy, a big smile on her face, straw bag swinging jauntily at her side, and all these shopworn phrases popped like soap bubbles in the air around his head. *She's here! Right on time!* He'd watch with indiscreet pleasure as she spread her towel out next to him and untied her navy blue beach robe—she'd gotten the robe a few days after they'd begun their affair—to reveal the red bikini underneath, and all he could do was shake his head and sheepishly admit that he'd been kidding himself again, that the spell was nowhere near being broken, that he was just as startled by the force of his desire for her today as he had been yesterday.

Startled, because at any other time in his life, he wouldn't have even looked twice at her, wouldn't have had the imagination to see past her sharp-featured, not-quite-pretty face, her less-than-stunning body. Why would he? He'd always been the kind of guy who could get the obvious girls, the pretty ones with haughty expressions and legs-up-to-here, the short sexy ones with the big brown eyes and the improbably large breasts, the would-be models, the willowy Asians, the hotties who caused a stir walking down the beach or past a row of lockers, the ones who'd never been without a boyfriend since the day they turned eleven, the girls most other guys knew better than to even make a play for. He'd never had to make the adjustments and compromises other people accepted early in their romantic careers, never had a chance to learn the lesson that Sarah taught him every day: that beauty was only part of it, and not even the most important part, that there were transactions between people that occurred on some mysterious level beneath the skin, or maybe even beyond the body. He was proud of himself for wanting her so badly. It made him feel like he'd grown up a little, expanded his vision, like he'd traveled to a faraway place or learned to appreciate an exotic food.

Todd had always been disturbed by the idea of elderly people making love, their droopy, liver-spotted bodies, the hair sprouting from where it shouldn't, the wayward odors, the unpleasant proximity to death. Sometimes Kathy joked about it, asking if he'd still find her attractive when her gums receded and her tits were hanging halfway to the floor. Of course he said yes; what else was he supposed to say? But the truth was, he couldn't even imagine Kathy as an old woman, or himself as an old man hoisting himself aboard her creaky bones. Kathy not beautiful wasn't really Kathy. But sometimes, when he was making love with Sarah, a weird sense of exhilaration would wash over him, and he'd believe for a moment or two that he could happily fuck her when they were both eighty-five and toothless, that the way their bodies looked was somehow beside the point. But he kept this thought to himself, suspecting that she wouldn't take it as a compliment.

No matter how often he reassured her, she remained insecure

about her appearance, nervous that she didn't measure up. She talked all the time about how handsome he was—square jaw, broad shoulders, etc.—and complained in the next breath about her own shortcomings: damaged hair, stubborn little potbelly, the surprising darkness of her nipples. *I love your mouth,* she'd say. *I hate my earlobes.* She praised the blondish down on his forearms and his crooked bottom teeth, then lamented a tiny mole on her lower back. *You have such slender fingers. Mine look like sausages.*

She did her best to make herself pretty for him, and he was touched by her efforts. Lipstick one day, earrings the next. She tweezed her eyebrows, got an expensive haircut. The robe. Platform sandals. On the afternoon of Todd's football game she showed up with a pedicure. She didn't announce it, just stretched her legs out in front of her and wiggled her squat little toes, the startling drops of fresh metallic blue lacquer turning them into a series of oddly shaped, upside-down exclamation points.

Just the day before, she'd reacted badly when he tried to suck her toes. "No," she snapped, yanking her foot away from his mouth. It was the first time the word had been uttered between them in two weeks of fairly comprehensive sexual exploration, all of which transpired during Aaron and Lucy's now-habitual late-afternoon nap.

"What's wrong?"

"My feet are disgusting. You don't want them in your mouth."

"I don't mind," he insisted.

"Well, I do."

It was true that Sarah's feet were not her finest feature. They were short and broad, almost primitive-looking. She was especially ashamed of her toenails, several of which had been thickened and discolored by fungus. Even now, after they'd been professionally clipped and polished, they still didn't look quite right.

"You didn't have to do that," he told her.

"I wanted to," she said. "Do you like it?"

He checked quickly on the kids. Aaron was showing Lucy his plastic dinosaur collection, letting her hold the less important ones. Todd slid his own foot across the grass and caressed Sarah's instep with his big toe.

"I love it," he whispered. "Ten little lollipops."

That afternoon, for the first time, Todd had trouble maintaining his erection. It was nothing personal; the voice of his high school football coach just kept echoing in his head, reminding him that it was a bad idea to have sex before a game.

"Men," Coach Breeden would say at the conclusion of Friday practice, "from now until this time tomorrow, you need to keep Little Willy under wraps. Those lucky few of you who have good-hearted girlfriends, please instruct them that a strict no-touchie policy is in effect. Those of you who are going steady with Sally Palm and her Five Sisters, I'd advise you to give those hardworking ladies the night off. God knows they deserve it. I want mean, hungry warriors out there on the field tomorrow, not a bunch of dreamy, weak-kneed lover-boys in velvet smoking jackets." Coach would grin his cockeyed, unsavory grin. "To express my own solidarity with your ordeal, I hereby pledge to avoid any and all physical contact with Mrs. Breeden during the next twenty-four hours. Of course, those of you who have had the misfortune of laying eyes on Mrs. Breeden will understand that this does not technically qualify as a sacrifice."

Coach Breeden was hardly a reliable source. He was a taskmaster from the old school, a short, thick-necked man who had a way with words and a host of dubious ideas about the human body—stretching causes injury, never swallow water during a game, pain is good— that were later debunked by younger, better-informed coaches. On some level, Todd understood that the prohibition against pre-game sex was pure superstition, like not walking under ladders or not swimming for an hour after a meal, but he didn't do those things either, at least not if he could avoid them.

"What's the matter?" Sarah asked. She was on her hands and knees, addressing him over her shoulder. "Am I doing something wrong?"

"No, it's not you. I'm just a little distracted."

She tried to help him out, coaxing him onto his back, telling him to just close his eyes and relax. She began licking his chest, moving slowly downward, past his rib cage to his navel, and then even lower. It felt good, until Todd remembered how badly he'd played on Thanksgiving Day of his senior year—a miserable five for sixteen passing, with three interceptions—after Amanda Morrissey's surprise blowjob. He opened his eyes in alarm.

"It's okay," he said, grimacing from the effort of self-discipline. "You don't have to do that."

"But I want to."

He raised himself up on his elbows.

"Could we just take a break for today?"

She lifted her head, wiped the back of her hand across her mouth.

"If that's what you want."

She looked so crestfallen—they had never "taken a break" before—that Todd felt he owed her an explanation. A bit sheepishly, he told her it was opening day for the Guardians, and that his place on the team still wasn't secure. Some of the guys—they were cops, men who'd been tested by fire—suspected him of being a pretty boy who'd crumble under pressure, and he was determined to prove them wrong, to show that he belonged.

"I always get nervous before games," he added. "In high school

I used to throw up in the locker room. It was my body's way of relieving tension."

"I used to throw up in high school, too," she confessed. "It was my body's way of purging a big meal."

He wasn't sure if she was kidding, so he limited his response to a polite chuckle.

"I'm sure it sounds ridiculous," he said. "I'm a grown man. I should have more important things on my mind than a football game."

"It's not ridiculous," she told him. "No more ridiculous than me worrying about my ugly toes."

"You have beautiful toes."

She leaned over and kissed him on the forehead.

"You're gonna be great tonight."

"I don't know," he said. "I haven't played for ten years. It used to be such a big part of my life. That's who I was in high school, even in college—Superjock, Mr. Quarterback. Then when I stopped, I just stopped. I didn't even miss it. But now that I'm doing it again, I can't help feeling like something important's on the line."

This whole time he'd been lying on his back with his hands behind his head, looking up at her bare breasts and sympathetic face. It was a nice way to look at a woman.

"I envy you," she said. Almost absentmindedly, she threw one leg over his waist and straddled him. She began slowly rocking her hips, pressing herself against him, a moist groove engulfing his softness. "I missed out on all that. I was a smart girl. Drama Club. AP English. I pretended to look down on the cheerleaders, but I was really just jealous of them."

"Why?"

Her breath was warm against his ear, her voice husky.

"Because they had you."

He was hard again; it hadn't taken much. She leaned forward, reaching back between her legs, guiding him inside. He arched his back, lifting her up. She pressed down against the movement.

"You have me now," he said.

Ever since his first practice with the Guardians, Todd had been hearing ominous rumors about their opening night opponents, who were widely considered to be the nastiest team in the league, as well as the best. He didn't give it a second thought until he saw the Auditors file onto the field, one guy bigger and meaner-looking than the next, like finalists in a Mr. Steroid contest. Five were white, two black; all of them wore nylon rags knotted gangsta-style on their heads.

"Jesus," said Todd. "Are these guys really accountants?"

The teams shook hands at midfield; with only seven on a side, there wasn't any need for captains. The Auditors were stone-faced and utterly silent during the ritual, like heavyweight boxers trying to intimidate a challenger during the weigh-in. Todd thought the tough-guy act was ridiculous, but also felt a cold splinter of fear enter his lower abdomen, a sudden inkling that maybe he was in over his head. He wished he hadn't let Sarah talk him into having sex. *Oh no*, he thought. *I'm a dreamy, weak-kneed lover-boy in a velvet smoking jacket.*

The Guardians won the coin toss and elected to receive. Todd and DeWayne Rogers dropped back to return the kick. Right on time, Todd felt a welcome jolt of adrenaline rush through his system, a biological response to the bright lights, the goalposts and yard markers, the knowledge that large men intent on mayhem would soon be charging in his direction. It no longer mattered that the bleachers were empty, that no one except the players themselves gave a damn about what was going to happen on the field. From where Todd was standing on the twelve yard line, it felt as real as any game he'd ever played.

There was no ref, no whistle. The Auditors' kicker just raised his right hand and brought it down in a chopping motion to signal the beginning of play. He jogged toward the ball, his teammates moving in unison on either side of him, and booted it high into the sky. Todd lost it for a moment in the glare of the stadium lights, then found it again, a little chocolate egg spinning end over end, growing larger with each revolution. He was relieved—and immediately embarrassed by his relief—to see that it was plummeting toward DeWayne, that it wasn't his responsibility.

By the time Todd started moving forward, looking for someone to block, the Auditors were stampeding down the field, shrieking out a weird, ululating battle cry, as if they were a tribe of ferocious native warriors bent on avenging some ancient insult. It was a chilling sound; Todd felt naked and defenseless in the face of it, suddenly amazed to find himself standing on a football field without pads or a helmet, but he wasn't standing for long. One of the Auditors clotheslined him as he rushed past—a rock-hard forearm to the face—and the next thing Todd knew he was scrutinizing the cosmos, his head humming emptily, as if every last thought had been knocked right out of it, his body blessedly free of sensation, at least until a very large sneaker descended upon his left hand, grinding it into the turf as though it were a lit cigarette that needed to be extinguished. Todd's gaze traveled north from the sneaker. A cheerful-looking black man with massive thighs was attached.

"Yo," said Todd. "Could you get off my hand?"

"I could." The big man smiled, revealing a golden tooth. "What's the magic word?"

———

After Aaron fell asleep, Kathy surprised herself by calling her mother. Normally, when she was feeling stressed out about her marriage, she turned to her older sister, Claire, or her college roommate, Amy, for advice and encouragement. Both were sympathetic, highly intuitive listeners who also happened to be big fans of Todd. The bottom line, as they often reminded Kathy, was she'd been lucky enough to marry a good-looking, intelligent, and kindhearted man who was willing to stay home and care for a small child while she pursued her dream of making documentary films. So what if he had a little trouble passing a test? JFK, Jr. didn't ace it on *his* first try either, right?

"Hi, Mom."

"Oh, hi, honey." Marjorie sounded flustered, raising her voice to make herself heard over the blaring TV. "It's late. Is everything okay?"

"I'm fine."

"You don't sound fine."

"There's nothing wrong," Kathy insisted. "I just wanted to say hi."

"Hold on. I had it in my hand a second ago."

"What?"

"The stupid remote. Where the heck did it go?"

For the same reasons that she sought out Claire and Amy, Kathy tended not to confide in her mother when she was feeling angry or exasperated with Todd. Marjorie's first impulse was not to defend her son-in-law or to reassure her daughter about the choices she made. Her inclination, conscious or not, was precisely the opposite:

to sow discord, to exaggerate the significance of whatever it was that was bothering you, and ultimately, if she could manage it, to pull you down into the swamp of her own unhappiness, just so she could have a little company.

Kathy's father, Rick, had jumped ship after three kids and sixteen years of wedlock, not for a younger, sexier woman—which would have at least been understandable on some pathetic, totally clichéd level—but for a sickly neighbor five years Marjorie's senior. The humiliation of *that*—of being traded in for Gail Roberts, a middle-aged divorcee with a smoker's hack and orthopedic shoes—had done permanent damage to Marjorie's psyche, scarring her with the bone-deep conviction that men were liars and marriage a cruel joke, the punch line of which always came at the expense of the unsuspecting wife.

"There," said Marjorie, as the TV went mute in the background. "That's better. So how's my little guy?"

"Great. He's sleeping right next to me. What a cutie." Kathy gazed down at Aaron, who was shirtless, wearing only a pull-up. His rib cage looked frail beneath the taut skin, his limbs scrawny and delicate. And yet it was oddly easy to imagine him stretched out and bulked up, a fully grown man, as strong and handsome as his father. "What are you watching?"

"*E.R.* just started. School bus went into a ditch." Marjorie clucked her tongue, as if reacting to an actual disaster. "What a mess."

"I can call you back when it's over."

"That's okay. I saw this one already."

Kathy kept quiet, waiting for her mother to pose the inevitable next question.

"So where's Todd?"

"Out."

"I'm surprised the library stays open this late."

"Oh, he's not at the library," Kathy reported. "He's playing football with his buddies."

"Football?"

"He joined some kind of team. They play tackle without pads."

"But it's ten o'clock."

"You should have seen him before he left the house. Couldn't eat dinner, couldn't carry on a normal conversation. All worked up, like he's playing in the Super Bowl."

"Did you say tackle?"

"No helmets or anything."

"He'll be lucky if he doesn't break his neck."

"If he does," Kathy said, "he better not come crying to me."

In the pause that followed, Kathy flashed on a strangely vivid image of Todd in a wheelchair, his mouth open wide, waiting for Kathy to feed him another spoonful of baby food.

"Can I ask you something?" Marjorie said. "Do you think he's having an affair?"

"An affair?" Kathy scoffed. "He joined a football team."

"Honey," Marjorie said, affecting a tone of world-weary patience. "It's just a smoke screen. Nobody plays football at this time of night."

"These idiots do. He comes home drenched in sweat, scrapes, and bruises all over his body."

"If you say so. But do you remember when your father took up golf? He bought a new set of clubs and started getting up at the crack of dawn on Saturday mornings? Well, it turned out he wasn't spending much time on the golf course."

"It's not an affair I'm worried about, Mom. Something's wrong with Todd. He doesn't talk about the future anymore, doesn't even like to think about it. It's like he's stuck in place, like he doesn't even realize that his life is slipping away from him."

"Do you want me to come up for a visit? I could keep an eye on him while you're at work, make sure he's staying out of trouble."

Kathy scrunched up her face and raised her middle finger to the phone. She should've known it was hopeless to try and have a serious conversation with her mother, one that would require her to imagine a world in which not every man was as heartless and deceitful as her ex-husband. And even *he* was hardly the monster Marjorie made him out to be. For all his faults, her father had built a loving and long-lasting relationship with Gail, nursing her through the twin afflictions of emphysema and chronic arthritis. Whenever she visited them, Kathy was touched to see how he fussed over that poor woman, fiddling with the pressure on her oxygen tank, making sure the plastic tubes were properly situated in her nostrils, holding her hand as she sat gasping for breath on the couch.

"You know what, Mom? I shouldn't burden you with this stuff. It's not like you don't have troubles of your own."

"That's okay," Marjorie said cheerfully. "It's no burden. I'm happy to help."

————

The Auditors' middle linebacker started talking trash during the very first series of the game. He was an angry slab of muscle—five-ten or so, maybe two-twenty—with a buzz cut and a demonic-looking goatee.

"Sweetheart." The linebacker waved to Todd as the Guardians broke their huddle and approached the line of scrimmage. "Over here."

Todd ignored him, glancing left and right to make sure his teammates were set. It was third and eight. The linebacker amplified his wave, crossing his arms overhead, as though signaling to a rescue helicopter. The sleeves of his T-shirt had been ripped off to expose the barbed-wire tattoos encircling his grotesquely pumped biceps.

"Did you shave your pussy for me?"

Todd gestured to DeWayne, moving him farther toward the sideline. With fourteen players on a regulation field, there was a lot of open space to work with.

"You know I like my bitches smooth."

"Green 42! Green 42!" Todd shoved his hands up against Larry's ass in anticipation of the snap. "Hut! Hut!"

He faked a handoff to Bart Williams, then bootlegged to his right, glancing around the secondary while waiting for DeWayne to make his cut to the middle. Out of the corner of his eye, he saw the linebacker slice past Larry, who was no match for his speed and strength. Hearing footsteps, Todd rushed his throw, releasing an off-balance wobbler that he knew would fall short. He didn't actually see it land; the linebacker crashed into him while the ball was still in midair. Todd heard himself whimper as he slammed into the turf.

"You're cute," the linebacker said, using Todd's skull for support as he stood up. "Wanna have my baby?"

Todd was still lying on the ground, gasping for air when Larry came rushing over to help him to his feet. Blushing with embarrassment, he squeezed Todd's shoulder and brushed off the front of his shirt with the brisk efficiency of a valet.

"My fault. I missed my block. It's not gonna happen again."

It went downhill from there. Sometimes you were simply overmatched, dominated by the opposition. Todd remembered the feeling well from his high school and college days; it was like a waking dream where nothing your team did seemed to have any effect. Your guys hit the other guys, but the other guys don't fall down. Perfectly thrown passes squirt through the hands of your butterfingered receivers; your opponents make impossible catches, as if their palms are covered in Velcro. The Guardians fumbled pitchouts, shanked punts, blew their coverage. The Auditors just kept marching up and down the field at will, methodically eating up the clock.

After a while you stop worrying about the score and start worrying about your dignity. For Todd, this meant defending himself against the linebacker, who seemed to be everywhere on the field and had begun pushing the prison bitch motif to unpleasant extremes. He complimented Todd's pretty mouth, groped his ass in the pileups, and repeatedly offered to show him a good time under the bleachers after the game.

"I'll love you nice and slow, honey. Not like those other slobs."

Because each team had so few members, there were no subs, not even for injuries; everyone had to play both ways. On defense, Todd was the free safety, a position that gave him lots of good opportunities to tackle the linebacker—he doubled as fullback for the Auditors—or at least take a crack at him after someone else had brought him down. A knuckle in the nose here. A knee in the spine there. Was that my elbow in your gut? The more shots he took, the looser he started to feel, until he got to the point where he was throwing his body around without reservation, as if hurting the other guy were more important than not hurting himself, which was, of course, the secret to playing good football.

And then he got it: the play the safety dreams about. His enemy cutting across the secondary, leaping for a badly thrown pass, arms stretched overhead, midsection exposed, defenseless. Todd leapt too, going for the man, not the ball, two large bodies smashing together at high speed, like atoms in a collider, his shoulder catching the other man right in the breadbasket, just below the rib cage. *Ooof!*

The sound of air escaping a container, a bag squeezed flat. They both went down; only Todd got up.

The loudmouth linebacker lay flat on his back, gulping like a fish on the thirty yard line. Todd didn't do a celebratory dance or anything like that. He just bent down, until his face was a couple of inches from the linebacker's, and gave the man's cheek an affectionate pinch.

Todd had played football long enough to know that there'd be a price to pay for such a sweet moment, and he paid it two series later, when the enraged linebacker blindsided him on second and long, wrapping him in a bear hug, lifting him off his feet, and slamming him into the earth with a savage pile-driver tackle worthy of World Wrestling Federation. Arms pinned uselessly to his sides, Todd had no choice but to break the fall with his face. He left a fair amount of skin on the artificial turf—it felt like granite covered with sandpaper—and was surprised to discover that his teeth were still planted in his mouth.

He was lying in a fetal position, whimpering like a little dog as the linebacker squatted above him, beating his chest and roaring like Tarzan. Todd kept his eyes open, hoping to fend off whatever cheap shot was coming next, so he got a good view of Larry Moon calmly walking up to the linebacker and delivering a right hook to the side of his head, a good solid sucker punch that knocked the King of the Jungle right off his feet. The game was called on account of the brief brawl that ensued, the victory going to the Auditors, 26–0.

———

Kathy lay wide-awake in the dark, her hand resting on Aaron's shoulder, rising and falling with the gentle rhythm of his breath. She still felt guilty about going behind Todd's back, complaining about him to her mother, of all people. Marjorie had never come out and said it in so many words, but she'd never really liked Todd or accepted him as a member of the family. She was suspicious of his good looks and winning personality, both of which she considered to be serious liabilities in a husband—the average-looking dullards were enough trouble, as she'd learned from bitter experience—and weirdly gratified by his inability to pass the bar exam, as if she had known all along that he wasn't quite up to snuff. Kathy must have been angrier with him than she'd realized, to betray him to his enemy like that.

What made it even more self-defeating was the fact that she hadn't even told her mother the truth. She'd made it sound like it was the football that was bothering her, the sheer physical recklessness of the game, the possibility that Todd might be seriously injured on the playing field, throwing their already complicated domestic arrangements into complete disarray.

But that wasn't the issue. Kathy wasn't one of those timid people who believed that a life worth living could—or even should—be risk-free, purged of any chance of a bad outcome. She understood that sometimes you needed to do something crazy, even potentially self-destructive—ride a motorcycle, jump out of an airplane, play tackle football without a helmet—to remind yourself that you were alive and not just cowering in the basement, waiting for the storm to blow over. She had compiled a substantial list of foolhardy things she was planning to do the moment her last child went off to college—traveling to a war zone was right at the top of it—and she wasn't about to condemn the thrill-seeking urge in anyone else, especially the man she loved.

No, the thing that really annoyed her about Todd joining the football team was how transparently *happy* it made him. The past couple of weeks he'd been a different person, as if he'd finally served eviction papers to the grim stranger who'd been living in his skin all spring, trudging dutifully off to the library every night, trudging dutifully back home. Ever since he'd hooked up with the Guardians, he'd been smiling more, listening when she talked, asking about her work. She could even see it in the way he moved—he was energized, lighter on his feet, as if he'd been magically reunited with his younger self, the carefree boy she'd fallen in love with in college. It should have pleased her to witness this transformation, but instead it filled her with shame and sadness, made her realize how much pressure he must have been feeling to live up to a vision of himself that had never really been his own.

I did that to him, she thought. *I sucked the life right out of him.*

She was the one who'd encouraged him to go to law school, despite his grave and frequently expressed doubts about his fitness for the profession, and *she* was the one who'd insisted that he give the bar exam one final shot, make one last good faith effort to pass the test before giving up on a career into which he'd put so much time and effort. At any point in the past six months she could have set him free with a single word, released him from his private hell of failure, but she hadn't done it.

She hadn't said the word.

It was because she was a coward, Kathy understood that, a selfish person who wanted to have it both ways—wanted to live the interesting life of an artist without accepting the unpleasant financial sacrifices that usually came along with the package. She had friends from film school, people in their thirties, who were still living in run-down apartments in Brooklyn and Somerville—*with room-mates!*—deferring marriage and children, scraping by without health insurance or dependable cars, still trying to nurse their youthful dreams of making honest, noncommercial, socially conscious movies, dreams that were becoming more and more unlikely with each passing year.

Kathy, by contrast, had chosen the path of compromise and accommodation, working her way up the public television food chain, from lowly PA to sound technician to editor to assistant director, putting in impossibly long hours on remarkably dull projects ("Part Four of *A-Pickin' and A-Grinnin'*, Our Comprehensive Five-Part History of the Banjo"), finally arriving at a point where she was able to direct a project of her own. *Wounded Survivors: Forgotten Heroes of the Pacific War* wasn't a particularly original piece of documentary filmmaking, or even a subject in which she had a great deal of interest—she had consciously, if not cynically, designed her grant proposal to piggyback on the wave of World War II nostalgia that was sweeping the nation in the late nineties—but she knew it was an important landmark in her own career, a stepping-stone to bigger and better things.

All along, her ace in the hole, the one thought that saved her from the tedium and petty politicking of public television and the bourgeois economic despair that was always gnawing at her—*How will we ever be able to buy a house, take a nice vacation, send our kids to a decent college, etc., etc.?*—was the prospect of Todd becoming a successful lawyer, making enough money to support the family in the style she believed they deserved to live, while at the same time freeing her to have more children (and more child care), and to work only when she wanted, and only on projects she believed in. All that was standing in their way was one stupid test.

Her plan—it was so humble, so eminently *doable*—made so much sense that she couldn't quite bring herself to let go of it even now, when she had no choice but to admit to herself how miserable it had made her husband. Maybe the football would help.

Maybe it would wake Todd up from his funk, give him the energy and confidence to rise to the occasion and pass the test on his third try. If it happened that way, it would all be okay: They'd be able to look back on the past two years as a blip on the screen of their happy life together, a necessary interlude of struggle, rather than a grim period of anxiety and stagnation, the time when it all went to hell.

He can do it, she told herself, rolling onto her back and gazing up at the gray blankness of the ceiling. *He can do it if he wants to.*

―――――

Despite the loss, and despite the searing pain in his face—his right cheek felt like it had been pressed against a hot skillet—Todd felt oddly exhilarated in the bar after the game. It wasn't that he'd given a superstar performance—he'd made his share of mistakes on the field—it was that he'd refused to be intimidated. He'd taken his lumps without complaining, and then he'd hit back with everything he had. He could feel a new respect in the way the cops looked at him, slapped him on the back, included him in the conversation. *Big Todd! What are you drinking, buddy?* He wasn't on probation anymore; he was a member of the team.

"Oh man." Tony Correnti stood behind him like an old-time boxing trainer, massaging his trapezius muscles. "You are gonna be one sore puppy tomorrow morning."

"Advil," advised DeWayne. "Advil and ice. Ice and Advil."

"Don't forget the Ben-Gay," said Pete Olaffson.

"And if all else fails," said Bart Williams, "you can always consult our team physician." Bart grabbed a shot glass from the cork-lined tray in the center of the table and offered it to Todd. "Dr. Daniels. His friends call him Jack."

"To the good doctor." Todd saluted his teammates with the glass, then threw back the shot. "I feel better already."

One by one the Guardians took their leave until only Todd and Larry Moon remained at the table. Larry was in a funk; Todd had noticed it the moment they sat down. He'd been drinking steadily for the past hour and a half, but he'd held himself aloof from the conversation, only joining in if someone asked him a direct question.

"Thanks for punching that guy," Todd told him. "I think he was about to dance on my head."

Larry looked up in pained surprise. He lifted a small bag of ice away from his left eye, which was pretty much swollen shut. The Auditors had made him their primary target during the game-ending fisticuffs.

"You shouldn't thank me. You should spit in my face."

"What are you talking about?"

"I couldn't block that guy. He was killing me all night." Larry hung his head like a little boy caught misbehaving. "I let you down. I let the whole team down."

"Bullshit. You played your heart out."

"I'm slow and I'm fat and I let that dirtbag piss all over me."

"It's over," said Todd. "Just forget about it."

Larry pressed the ice bag against his eye and glared at Todd for a few uncomfortable seconds.

"Don't fucking tell me to forget it, okay?"

Todd glanced at his wrist, where his watch would have been if he'd been wearing it.

"You know what?" he said. "I think I better get going."

———

Todd didn't think Larry was in any condition to operate a motor vehicle, but he didn't want to upset him by raising the issue. It was just a short drive home, and the streets were pretty clear at this time of night.

"I let you down," Larry repeated morosely, jabbing his key in the general direction of the ignition switch. "That's what I do. I let people down."

Larry handed Todd the ice pack. Without thinking, Todd pressed it to his own injured cheek. It felt good, better than he expected.

"My family, my teammates, the guys I worked with." Larry successfully inserted the key and started the van. "Don't count on me, 'cause I'm gonna let you down."

"You're overreacting," Todd told him. "Anyone can have a bad game."

Larry hesitated before leaving the parking lot. He looked both ways several times, then inched out into the empty street as if merging with rush-hour traffic.

"Joanie left me," he announced. "Took the kids and went to her mother's."

"Jesus, Larry. That's a tough break."

"I deserved it. Me and my big mouth." Todd didn't ask for elaboration, but Larry provided it anyway. "I called her a fucking whore. Right in front of the kids."

"Why would you do that?"

"I was in a bad mood or something."

Larry punched the gas for no apparent reason, accelerating down Pleasant Street as if drag-racing an invisible opponent. His minivan had surprisingly good pickup; the speedometer shot up to fifty in what felt like a couple of seconds. Todd was both startled and relieved when he jammed on the brakes at the intersection with South

Street, belatedly obeying a red light. Both men lurched forward and back along with the van.

"So now I'm fucked," Larry said. "It's gonna be lawyers, and custody rights, and child support. Then she's gonna marry someone else, and some stranger's gonna raise my kids. That's what happens to assholes like me."

"Maybe you can still work it out. Get counseling or something."

"We been down that road. There's nothing left to talk about."

The light turned green. Larry was driving slowly again, as if unfamiliar with the area. Todd felt tired and a little buzzed; he searched his cloudy mind for conversational gambits unrelated to the game or his friend's domestic troubles. What he really wanted was to talk about Sarah, and the beautiful strangeness of their affair, the way it seemed to fit so perfectly with the contours of his life—*the morning and night belong to my family, the afternoon belongs to her*— but something told him that Larry wasn't the right audience for his confession. Then something else popped into his mind, something he'd been meaning to mention anyway.

"You hear about the pervert? He went swimming at the Town Pool."

"What?" Larry whipped his head in Todd's direction, turning his attention completely away from the road. "Who told you that?"

"I saw him myself. During the heat wave."

"The Town Pool? That place is crawling with kids. Sometimes my boys go there."

"It was just that one time. I don't think he came back."

Larry just kept shaking his head and muttering to himself, as if something were very, very wrong. Even before he stepped on the gas and spun the wheel hard to the left, pulling a cop show U-turn in front of the Pet Palace, Todd had already come to the conclusion that he would have been better off keeping his big mouth shut.

———

Lately, Kathy had found herself thinking a lot about a particular incident in her past, the moment when she had the first vague inkling that her future and Todd's might somehow intersect. It happened during the spring semester of their junior year in college, in a class called Sociology of the American Family.

It wasn't like they were total strangers. They'd attended the same small school for two and a half years at that point, and shared a handful of mutual acquaintances. They bumped into each other every so often on the compact, bucolic campus, and exchanged the obligatory smiles and slightly labored small talk of people who lived in the same world but had made a tacit decision not to become friends.

At least Kathy had made that decision, very early in their freshman year. She'd been hearing about this gorgeous football player ever since her first night in the dorm, when she and her three roommates stayed up late, comparing notes about the people they'd met. When Todd's name came up, it inspired a chorus of ecstatic recognition.

"Oh my God, did you *see* him?"

"He is sooo hot."

"Doesn't he look like that J. Crew model?" the friendly one named Amy asked, glancing at Kathy for support. "The blond guy?"

Kathy shrugged, unable to offer an opinion. She was the only member of the group who hadn't caught a glimpse of the magnificent, apparently ubiquitous Todd. Amy's eyes narrowed thoughtfully.

"You know what?" she told Kathy. "You should go out with him. You're like the two best-looking people in the whole class. You'd be, like, the perfect couple. Wouldn't they?"

The other roommates agreed, and Todd was immediately designated Kathy's boyfriend-in-absentia. *I saw your boyfriend today*, one of them would invariably say. *Your boyfriend's in my bio lab.*

But all it took was a single conversation at a party a few weeks later to convince Kathy that her "boyfriend" would never be her boyfriend. He was handsome, all right, but he seemed less like a person than a type, the epitome of the dashing scholar/athlete, a category whose charms Kathy felt like she'd exhausted in high school. She hadn't come to college to waste her time with another guy like *that*, the square-jawed captain of the team, the boy most likely to succeed.

No, Kathy was through with jocks, weary of the preening and self-congratulation, the minutely detailed recaps of yesterday's game. She was on the lookout for scruffier, less conventional lovers, artists and intellectuals, unshaven guys in thrift-store paisley shirts who could help her to transform herself into the serious person she meant to become, someone her airheaded high school pals wouldn't even recognize.

By the end of her sophomore year, she'd worked her way through a blues guitarist, an abstract expressionist painter, a pothead photographer, and an anthropology major who'd hitchhiked his way across Australia. Each of them was exciting for a while, but once the novelty wore off, she had to admit that the bohemians had just as little interest in actually getting to know her as the football players did. They didn't want to spend hours discussing the finer points of art history or aboriginal culture; they just wanted to get her stoned and take her clothes off.

Then, in the beginning of junior year, she met Jason, a short, curly-haired guy whose parents were both history professors at a state college in Wisconsin. He was a fiery, unrepentant Marxist, one of the few on campus, with a passion for social justice and a seemingly inexhaustible appetite for conversation. All through the fall, he and Kathy stayed up late into the night, drinking black coffee and talking about politics. They disagreed about almost everything—Jason believed that the East Germans were justified in building the Berlin Wall, for example, and that a dictatorship of the proletariat couldn't, by definition, be considered a repressive form of government—but that wasn't the point. He was the first smart guy she'd ever been with who treated her as an intellectual equal, who listened to her opinions and tried to respond to them with reasoned arguments of his own. He didn't act like these discussions were mere foreplay, a preliminary to the main event. For Jason, the talking *was* the main event. He never flirted, never tried to kiss her, and ignored her increasingly unsubtle hints that he no longer needed to be so respectful of her physical boundaries.

Needless to say, she fell madly in love with him. Once a source of pleasure and excitement, their chaste, endlessly unspooling conversations about Maoism and the Sandinista Revolution became a form of erotic torment. Finally, Kathy couldn't take it anymore. She got him drunk on vodka one Friday night and took him to bed. The sex was everything she'd hoped for—intense and tender at the same time, full of sustained eye contact and whispered commentary, a physical and emotional dialogue. When it was over, she poked him in the chest and demanded to know what in the world had taken him so long. Jason looked away, scowling with embarrassment.

"I don't know," he muttered. "It's stupid."

"What? You can tell me."

He forced himself to meet her eyes.

"You're too tall," he said.

She laughed out loud. *Was that all?*

"Jay," she said, "I'm like three inches taller than you."

"Closer to four."

"Whatever. It doesn't matter to me."

Kathy waited for him to echo her sentiment, but he couldn't bring himself to do it.

"Say what you want," he said. "It just doesn't look right when the girl is taller."

"Look right to who?"

"To people. Everybody."

"My God," she said. "You're a revolutionary socialist. You hand out copies of *The Daily Worker*. Since when do you care what people think?"

"It just bothers me, Kathy. People are gonna laugh. And they won't be laughing at you."

"Let them," Kathy whispered, leaning forward and kissing him. "Let the idiots laugh."

They tried to make a go of it, but they didn't last a month. Jason wouldn't take her on dates, wouldn't be caught dead holding hands with her in public or stepping onto a dance floor. Instead of arguing about dialectical materialism, they ended up wasting their time fighting about whether she was trying to "undermine" him by wearing a pair of cowboy boots to Sunday brunch. He finally dumped her on her first day back from Christmas vacation, apologizing profusely as he did so.

"I'm an idiot," he said. "I'm probably gonna regret this for the rest of my life."

"Then don't do it," she said, her eyes welling with hot, humiliating tears. "I'll throw out the boots. I won't ask you to dance anymore."

"I'm sorry," he said. "It's just not gonna work."

She was still smarting from the break-up two months later, on that afternoon in sociology when her life veered suddenly in a whole different direction. The professor, a bearish ex-radical with an immense potbelly and a salt-and-pepper-beard, was pacing back and forth in front of the blackboard, on which he'd scribbled the enigmatic phrase, "Gender Expectations/Conflict. Insoluble Problem?"

"At this particular point in time," he said, "I think it's fair to say that we are experiencing an era of definitional instability. The whole concept of a quote unquote just and equitable marriage is pretty much up for grabs. Your generation has no choice but to reinvent the wheel and discover workable new ways for men and women to live together in a long-term domestic relationship."

To illustrate his point, he took an impromptu poll of the students, asking how many of them expected to marry and have children. About half the class raised their hands. The professor waited patiently, an amused look on his face. After a brief hesitation, Kathy joined the second wave of future procreators.

"About three-quarters of you. That sounds about right."

Next the professor asked how many women in the room expected to pursue a full-time career during their childbearing years. About half of the prospective mothers raised their hands, Kathy among them.

"Okay, then," continued the professor. "That's a pretty substantial number of women who expect to follow a traditionally male career path. I ask this next question simply out of curiosity. How many of you men would be willing to stay home and raise the kids while your wives go off to work? Change the diapers, take care of the cooking and the laundry?"

The guys glanced around—many of them were football players, a tribute to the professor's well-deserved reputation for generous grading and a shockingly light reading load—trading *Yeah, right* smirks, leading the women to shake their heads and roll their eyes in mock exasperation.

"Any takers?" the professor asked.

By that point, though, the whole class was already in the process of turning to face Todd, who was sitting in the back row, between two other football players, all three of them dwarfing their little wooden chair-desks. Unlike his teammates, however, Todd's hand was raised high over his head, his long arm stretching toward the ceiling.

Kathy thought at first that he must be joking, pulling a little prank for the amusement of his buddies. Her indifference to Todd had remained constant over the past couple of years, as he fulfilled his early promise to the letter, developing into an old-fashioned B.M.O.C., the object of much swooning speculation and feverish pursuit from the sorority girls and sports groupies who made up the least imaginative sector of the undergraduate female population.

Oh, grow up, would you? she thought.

As if responding to this request, Todd looked right at her and smiled. Not the smug, mocking smile she expected, but something sweeter and more complicated, as if he were apologizing for not being the person she thought he was, for failing to embody her low expectations.

I'm not kidding, his face replied.

Memory has a way of distorting the past, of making certain events seem larger and more significant in retrospect than they ever could have been at the time they occurred. This was certainly the case with the silent communion that passed between Todd and Kathy in sociology class on that dreary March afternoon. The whole episode couldn't have lasted more than a couple of seconds, during which Kathy was aware of nothing more than a pleasant sense of possibility, the beginning of an unexpected flirtation. Ten years later, however, as she lay in bed beside her sleeping son, it seemed to her that everything that had happened afterward—the whole course of their lives—had been contained in that single charged moment,

Todd's hand in the air, his eyes on Kathy, almost as if he were volunteering to be her husband.

"There he is, ladies," the professor had announced, in a tone of mild but genuine surprise. "There's the man you're looking for."

———

The old woman answered the door after the third ring. She didn't seem unduly surprised to find two men—one of them with a bruised and puffy eye, the other with a bag of ice pressed against his cheek—standing on her front stoop at two-thirty in the morning.

"What now?" she demanded. Her gaze was sharp and alert; she must not have been sleeping.

"Good evening, Mrs. McGorvey." Larry sounded like a polite drunk, the kind of guy who wasn't fooling anyone but himself. "We were wondering if Ronnie was home."

"You leave him alone," the woman snapped.

"We just want a moment of his time." Larry smiled, as if to underscore the modesty of this request. "Just a little chat."

Mrs. McGorvey turned to Todd as if he were the one who had spoken. He shrugged, but what he really wanted to do was apologize—for bothering her so late, for the eggs, the posters, the burning bag of shit. The poor woman just looked so sad and ravaged standing there in the doorway, breathing raggedly through her nose, all the indignities of her advancing age nakedly on display—the hamhock arms, the thinning, badly colored hair, the Ace bandages wrapped around her swollen ankles. If she had dentures, they were floating in a glass somewhere. With a certain amount of amazement, it occurred to him that she probably wasn't much older than his stepmother, who played tennis three times a week and kept standing appointments with a masseuse, an acupuncturist, and a personal trainer. Helena's dental work alone could have put a couple of kids through college.

"This is my house." The old woman spoke firmly, her head held high. "I paid the mortgage, and I say who is and isn't welcome."

Larry cupped his hands around his mouth. His voice sounded playful and commanding at the same time.

"Yoo hoo, Ronnie! Get your sick, perverted ass down here!"

Mrs. McGorvey tried to slam the door in his face, but Larry caught it with his foot and kicked it open even wider. A musty odor of hard-boiled eggs and stale ashtrays—the warm, rancid breath of the house—came surging out, mingling unpleasantly with the leafy coolness of the summer night.

"I'm calling the police," she said.

Larry laughed. "I hear they're well disposed to child molesters." All the air went out of the old woman.

"Ronnie didn't hurt anyone. Why can't you just leave him in peace?"

"Ronnie didn't leave that Girl Scout in peace. Do you think he deserves any more consideration than he gave her? And what about little Holly?"

Before Mrs. McGorvey could reply, Ronnie himself appeared in the hallway behind her, blinking and bewildered, wearing a short-sleeved pajama top over blue work pants. He looked like a loser in the sickly yellow light, a middle-aged dork with a hopeless combover and a slouching, cringing demeanor, as if he expected to be beaten at any moment. It was hard for Todd to connect him with the otherworldly creature he'd seen at the pool, the masked and flippered invader who'd struck fear into the hearts of grown-ups and children alike.

"It's okay, Ma." He came forward, gently insinuating himself between his mother and the visitors. "Can I help you gentlemen?"

"Hey," said Larry. "Aren't you gonna show me your dick?"

Ronnie appeared to give the matter some serious thought before shaking his head.

"I'm sorry." Larry affected a puzzled expression. "It's just that I was told that you like to show your dick to people who ring the doorbell."

Todd looked down in embarrassment and found himself staring at the old woman's boat sneakers, one of which had a jagged hole cut into the canvas, apparently to relieve the pressure on her big toe.

"Maybe I'm too old," Larry speculated. "Maybe you only show it to little kids. Is that how it goes?"

Todd tried to fight off a rising wave of sympathy for McGorvey by picturing his crime, but his imagination faltered. Did he answer the door with his pants already down? Or did he talk to the Girl Scout a little while, place an order for Thin Mints, and then spring his little surprise on her? Did he say anything? Did he try to touch her? The fear and horror on the little girl's face, that was easier to imagine. Little Holly—Todd didn't even want to think about that.

"You listen to me, you piece of shit." Larry grabbed Ronnie by his ears and yanked his face forward until it was within an inch of his own. "You stay the fuck away from the Town Pool, you hear me? Or I will personally fix it so that you no longer have a dick to show anyone, is that clear?"

Todd laid a gentle hand on Larry's arm.

"Come on, Larry. Let's go home. I think he gets the point."

"I fucking hope so." Larry made a hawking sound deep in his throat, and spit in Ronnie's face before shoving him backwards into his mother. "You got the point, scuzzball?"

Ronnie nodded. His face was blank, as if none of this bothered him in the least. From the way he acted, you wouldn't have known that another man's saliva was sliding down the bridge of his nose.

"Okay, then." Larry took a deep breath and tipped an imaginary hat at the old woman, who was holding one hand over her sunken mouth and making a strenuous effort not to cry. "You have a nice night, Mrs. McGorvey."

BOOK GROUP

SARAH AND JEAN WERE THE FIRST GUESTS TO ARRIVE AT THE JULY meeting of the Bellington Ladies' Belletristic Society. The gathering was being held in a townhouse on Waterlily Terrace, a small development of six attached units sharing a grassy yard and a fenced-in swimming pool. The complex felt far more pleasant and secluded than Sarah could have imagined from its location, just off a busy street leading into Bellington's downtown business area.

Their host, Bridget, was a bright-eyed, squat-bodied woman in an African-print mumu; her haircut looked like it had been administered by a blind barber working with toy scissors. She hugged Jean, then moved on to Sarah without missing a beat, closing her eyes and purring with pleasure as she gathered the younger woman into the lumpy cushions of her body.

"So good to *see* you," she murmured, as if Sarah were a long-lost member of her family. "We're looking forward to your insights."

She led them into her living room, an airy, art-filled space lit solely by the evening sun, which filtered in through floor-to-ceiling glass doors opening onto a tiny patio. Kitchen chairs supplemented the regular furniture, creating an intimate circle around a coffee table brimming with wine, cheese, fruit, and crackers.

"So how are you liking the new place?" asked Jean.

"I love it," said Bridget, who was having some trouble opening a bottle of white wine. "It already feels like home."

"Did you just move in?" Sarah asked. "It doesn't feel like it."

"February." Bridget grimaced as she extracted a crumbling cork from the neck of the bottle. "My husband passed away last fall."

"I'm sorry."

Bridget gave a philosophical shrug. "It was such a relief to escape from that stuffy old house." She filled three glasses with chardonnay and handed two of them to her guests. "I could hardly breathe in there."

Trying to ignore the flecks of cork floating in her glass, Sarah sipped her wine and thought of her own mother, still living in the musty old house on Westerly Street, the last holdout on the block. She didn't know any of her neighbors anymore, and spent entire days locked up like a fugitive from justice, the windows shut, the shades pulled down. She talked about soap opera characters as if they were real people, and wondered why her plants kept dying.

"Maybe I'll move here," said Jean. "If something happens to Tim, I mean."

"We're all widows on Waterlily Terrace." Bridget smiled, as if this were somehow a comical idea. "Four of us were schoolteachers, Ellen was a social worker, and Doris was a housewife. She has a degree from Smith, though."

"Do you get along?" asked Sarah.

"Most of the time. There's been some tension this summer about the pool. There's a heater, but I don't like to use it. The cold water is so much more invigorating."

"Especially when you're skinny-dipping," Jean added knowingly.

Bridget laughed. "I don't even wear a bathing cap. I'm such an outlaw."

Jean looked around, surveying the cozy interior of the townhouse with a wistful expression.

"Must be nice, not having to clean up after anyone."

"And eating whatever you want." Bridget smeared a generous quantity of goat cheese on a Swedish cracker that looked like a rectangle of stiffened burlap. "My late husband, Art, God rest his soul, thought it was his mission in life to keep me thin." Bridget looked down, contemplating her plumpness with affection. "Does this look like a body that was meant to be thin?"

Jean dipped a carrot spear in a bowl of hummus. There was a barely perceptible edge in her voice.

"So how was Provence?"

Bridget flashed Jean a quick look of sympathy.

"Heavenly. I didn't want to come back. In my heart of hearts, I believe I'm actually a French peasant."

"She went with Regina and Alice," Jean explained to Sarah. "You'll meet them later on."

"We're going back next year," Bridget told Jean. "This time you'll have to come."

Jean turned to Sarah. "Tim wouldn't let me go. He said it was too expensive."

"Life's too short," Bridget huffed. "What's the old fart saving his money for? A silk-lined coffin?"

"The super-premium cable package." Jean didn't sound like she was joking. "He's going to die right there on that recliner, switching back and forth between that A&E biography of Churchill and an infomercial for a stain remover."

"Art was big on exercise shows." Bridget smiled sadly. "Not that he ever exercised."

"I've never lived alone," said Jean. "Not even for a day."

"It can get lonely," Bridget allowed, though it sounded to Sarah like she was just trying to cheer Jean up. "But that's the nice thing about a place like this. There are always people around if you want some company. Doris and I are taking a ceramics class. You should join us."

"Maybe I will," said Jean.

Bridget shifted her attention to Sarah.

"Jean says you have a Ph.D. We're honored that you decided to join us."

"I don't actually have a doctorate," Sarah explained, sorry to disappoint her. "I did all the coursework, but I never wrote my thesis."

Bridget shrugged this off as a mere technicality.

"I'm so curious," she said. "Did you like the novel?"

"It's complicated," Sarah began. "I had such a strong reaction that it doesn't seem right to just say I liked it or I didn't like it, you know what I mean? It just goes way beyond that."

Bridget seemed pleased by this response. She reached across the table and squeezed Sarah's hand.

"I think we're going to get along just fine," she said.

The doorbell rang. Bridget set down her glass and extracted herself with some difficulty from the deep indentation she'd made in the couch.

"Drink some more wine," she said, caressing Sarah's shoulder on the way to the door. "We find the conversation's livelier that way."

Jean flashed Sarah an I-told-you-so look as she refilled their glasses.

"See?" she said. "Aren't you glad I dragged you here?"

For weeks now, on their nightly walks, Jean had been bugging Sarah about *Madame Bovary*. Had she obtained a copy of the Steegmuller translation? Had she started reading it yet? Had she given any thought to the five discussion questions each "little sister" had been asked to contribute to the meeting?

Until a couple of days ago, the answer to all these questions had been a resounding no. Because she felt like she was being rail-roaded—to the best of her knowledge, she had never actually agreed to be Jean's "little sister"—Sarah had avoided the novel for as long as possible, in the hope that an unexpected circumstance would arise and free her from the obligation: Maybe Richard would get sent on a last-minute business trip, or Lucy would catch a cold; maybe she herself would go blind or get run over by a bus.

It wasn't just the book group she dreaded; it was the book itself. She had read *Madame Bovary* in college, for a seminar called Sexism in Literature, which cataloged the multifarious strategies male writers had used throughout the ages to oppress and marginalize their female characters. Emma Bovary was Exhibit A—right up there with Ophe-lia and Isabelle Archer—a dreamy, passive, narcissistic figure en-thralled by paralyzing bourgeois notions of "love" and "happiness," utterly and indiscriminately dependent upon men to rescue her from the emptiness of her useless life. To make matters worse, she turned her back on the empowering consolations of sisterhood: She had no female friends, mistreated her servant girl and wet nurse, and ne-glected her poor little daughter.

Even if Sarah had been inclined to revisit this depressing ma-terial, it wouldn't have been easy. Despite its racy subject matter, *Madame Bovary* was densely written and slowly paced; like any nineteenth-century novel, it placed serious demands upon the reader's time and concentration. Ever since she'd begun her affair with Todd, Sarah had developed some sort of adult-onset attention deficit disorder. She'd pick up the newspaper and get maybe two paragraphs into an article before finding herself completely at sea, the words on the page dissolving into a fantasy of travel, just herself and Todd, no children, complete freedom—two lovers laughing on a crowded bus in India, sipping champagne in a first-class train compartment in Europe, barreling down the interstate in a red convertible, singing along with the radio. She'd turn back to the paper and reread the same two paragraphs, only to be waylaid by a daydream of grocery shopping, cruising down the aisles of Bread & Circus with Todd at her side, filling a cart with organic produce, fresh pasta, free-range chicken, sinful desserts, Australian wine. She'd force her attention back on the paper with a feeling of growing annoyance—what did she care about a shark attack in Florida, rolling blackouts in California, George W. Bush's love affair with his Texas ranch? All she wanted to think about was hiding in the balcony of an old-fashioned movie palace, Todd's hand inching up her thigh as the calvary charged across a Western landscape. Finally, she just tossed aside the paper and turned on the TV, which seemed so much more accommodating of her fantasy life, and not nearly so judgmental.

Knowing that she was no match for Flaubert, she'd resigned herself to winging it at the meeting, skimming the novel for an hour or two, scrawling down a handful of boilerplate questions, keeping her mouth shut during group discussion. But then something happened on Saturday morning that put her in a serious funk. In an effort to distract herself, she picked up *Madame Bovary* and discovered an entirely different novel from the one that existed in her memory.

"What does your wife look like?"

Todd seemed surprised by the question, at least partly because he was licking Sarah's navel when she asked it.

"My wife?"

"The woman living in your house?" Sarah said, attempting to make a joke out of a subject that had become a source of obsessive speculation on her part. "The one you sleep with every night?"

"What does she look like?" Todd repeated skeptically.

"I'm just curious, that's all."

After several evasive maneuvers, Todd attempted to describe Kathy as if she were a criminal suspect—five-nine, straight brown hair, brown eyes, no visible scars or tattoos—but Sarah remained unsatisfied.

"Is she pretty?"

He gave the matter some serious consideration, as if it were open to debate. Sarah found this encouraging.

"I guess so," he said. "Objectively speaking."

"Is she a knockout?"

"We're married. I don't think about her like that."

"What about other guys? If they saw her walking down the street, would they think she was hot?"

"Depends on the guy, I guess."

"Do you have a picture?"

In a transparent attempt to distract her, Todd kissed her from the base of her throat down to her sternum. With a gentle tug on her bikini top, he freed her left breast, flicking his tongue playfully at her nipple, waking it from its afternoon slumber.

"Come on," she persisted. "You must have one in your wallet."

"Jesus." Todd looked up in bewilderment. "Why is this so important to you?"

Sarah felt a warm flush of shame surging into her face. She knew it was a bad sign, this jealousy she was feeling toward a woman she'd never met, who'd never done anything to hurt her.

"I don't know," she confessed, wondering if she was about to burst into tears. "I wish it wasn't."

Todd pressed a finger to his lip, shushing her as if she were a small child. Looking straight into her eyes, he slipped his other hand inside the waistband of her bikini bottom and reached between her thighs, cupping her gently from below, exerting a slight upward pressure. It always came as a shock when he touched her down there, the pleasure of it so much more intense than she'd anticipated. She opened her legs to give him room.

"She's a knockout," he confessed, slipping one finger inside of her, then another, making her gasp out loud. "But beauty's overrated."

At the time, Sarah barely registered the comment, giving herself up to the strong sensations flooding her body. Later that night, though, it came back to her: *Beauty's overrated.* He'd meant it to be comforting, but at three in the morning it had precisely the opposite effect. He had a beautiful wife, *a knockout*, and she was sleeping beside him right now, their legs intertwined beneath the covers. And where was Sarah? Wide-awake in the dark, listening to the wheezy, tedious breathing of the man she no longer considered her husband. *Beauty's overrated.* Only someone who took his own beauty for granted could have been able to say something so outrageously stupid with a straight face.

Richard liked to sleep in on the weekends; he was still in bed when Sarah left the house on Saturday morning, leaving Lucy in front of the TV with a big bowl of dry Cheerios for company and instructions to wake Daddy if she needed anything.

"Mommy has to run some errands," she said.

Her first stop was Starbucks, a journey back in time she preferred to avoid whenever possible. For years after she stopped working there, just a glimpse of that tasteful beige-and-maroon interior— the bags of featured coffee, the shelves full of upscale accessories, the customers lined up like addicts at a yuppie methadone clinic—could throw off her whole day, stirring up a sediment of bad memories that otherwise lay dormant in her mental attic, covered by several protective layers of dust. (She used to feel the same way about her old high school, devising all sorts of elaborate detours to keep from having to lay eyes on it.) But she'd slept badly and was suffering from a low-level headache that only a serious dose of caffeine could cure.

"Vente house," she said to the girl at the register, a punky earth mother with a jet-black pageboy and a tongue stud.

"Vente house," the girl repeated a moment later, sliding the gigantic paper cup across the counter.

"Don't worry." Sarah smiled in rueful solidarity. "You won't work here forever."

"It's not that bad," the girl said, eyeing Sarah with suspicion, as if she were some sort of troublemaker.

Todd's address, Sarah had learned from the phone book, was 24 Angelina Way. She found the place without much difficulty and parked across the street in front of Number 19, in what felt to her like an unobtrusive patch of shade beneath a maple tree. Sipping her coffee and listening to NPR's *Weekend Edition*, she settled back in her seat and stared at the house where her boyfriend lived.

It was nothing special, what would have been an average-sized colonial if it hadn't been divided into two mirror-image condos, powder blue with pale yellow trim. Instead of a lawn there was a large driveway sloping down to a two-car basement garage. On either side of the driveway, cement walks led to the respective entrances, identical except for the fact that one said 24 and the other 26. The higher number also sported a decorative straw hat on the door.

Sarah shouldn't have been surprised to find Todd living in a duplex with a beat-up Toyota on his side of the driveway—she knew that his wife supported the family with some kind of low-paying work as a documentary filmmaker for public TV—but the house just didn't fit into her idea of his stature in the grand scheme of things. He carried himself like a natural aristocrat, a person for whom nice things came as easily as good looks. In some fundamental way, it didn't make sense that someone as unremarkable as she was should be living in a bigger house and a better neighborhood than Todd.

It wasn't an awful house, not by a long stretch. It had skylights and scalloped woodwork over the front doors and windows, the sort of small touches that marked it as a "quality home," modest though it was. Maybe it felt right for them to be living there at that particular point in their lives. Maybe it was even romantic in a way, to be a young family together, sharing burdens, moving up in the world. Years from now, Todd and Kathy would be able to drive Aaron down Angelina Way and say, *There's the old condo, can you believe we ever lived like that?* Sarah had skipped that particular phase of life, moving straight from a shared apartment with annoying roommates into a mini-Victorian full of furniture from Pottery Barn, and she couldn't help resenting Kathy for the fact that she got to suffer with Todd through their lean years, creating a history they could look back on with pride and maybe even a touch of nostalgia.

Unless he leaves her, she thought, her chest swelling with a strange feeling of lightness, as if hope were helium. *Unless he leaves her to be with me.*

It wasn't the first time she let herself consider this scenario, of course, but it was the first time she'd let herself believe it was a real possibility. *He could divorce Kathy. He could marry me. I could divorce Richard. Todd could marry me.* She kept extending the sequence, playing out the permutations, imagining the logistics involved to the best of her ability—the lawyers, the custody battles, the financial arrangements, the emotional trauma—until Todd startled her by stepping out the front door, hugging a picnic cooler to his chest, his brow furrowed with worry. *He can divorce her.* He carried the plastic box down the steps and placed it in the trunk of the Toyota. *I can divorce him.* It took all of the self-restraint she possessed to stay inside the car, to keep herself from running over to him and shouting out the wonderful news.

We can divorce them and marry each other!

He made three trips in all—beach umbrella, toy pail and shovel, two canvas totes, a football—and had just shut the trunk when Aaron emerged from the front door, looking serious and oddly unfamiliar without his jester's cap, and joined his father by the car. Kathy stepped out into the sunlight a moment later. She was barefoot, wearing tight blue jean shorts, a black bikini top, and Italian movie star sunglasses, looking taller, thinner, and more glamorous than Sarah had let herself imagine in her worst self-loathing insomniac nightmare. She was one of *those* girls, the ones from high school who made you stick your finger down your throat after lunch, the ones who made you look in the mirror and cry.

Kathy stood on the porch for a long time, giving Sarah a fair chance to contemplate her folly. She interlaced her fingers overhead and tilted her lithe torso from side to side. Then she spread her arms wide and yawned, the way people do when they're sleepy but happy, and ready to embrace the day.

"Okay, boys," she called out. "Let's get moving."

Sarah felt herself deflating, a Thanksgiving Day float pierced by an arrow. *Oh God.* Her dream of happiness suddenly seemed cruel, a joke she'd played on herself. *He'll never leave her.* She barely managed to hold herself together until Todd and his family had backed out of the driveway and headed off down the street. *Not for me.* She covered her mouth politely with one hand, as if she were coughing instead of sobbing. *Not for anybody like me.*

Long after she'd stopped crying, Sarah sat in the parked car on Angelina Way, wondering how she was going to get through the next two days. Weekends were brutal under the best of circumstances, forty-eight-hour prison stretches separating one happy blur of weekdays from the next. But this one was going to be unbearable, now that she'd be able to torment herself with the thought of Todd spending every second of it in the company of his gorgeous wife—at the beach no less—while she was stuck at home with the panty sniffer.

Richard was sitting on the front lawn with Lucy when she pulled into the driveway, and just the sight of him filled her with disgust—his pleated shorts and Italian sandals, the polo shirt with the collar turned up as if it were 1988 on Nantucket, his little potbelly. They were having a tea party around a red-and-white-checkered tablecloth, along with one of those hideous American Girl dolls and a stuffed frog named Melvin (both the doll and the miniature ceramic tea set were gifts from Richard's mother, a woman who still believed that "dainty" and "ladylike" were the conditions to which all little girls should aspire). He looked up from the game as she approached, a demitasse of nothing raised halfway between a saucer and his mouth, his pinky sticking out with a primness that didn't seem satirical.

"Where were you?" he asked, his face artfully blank, no hint of accusation in his voice. Ever since the incident in his office, he'd been a lot less imperious around the house, a little more considerate of his wife and child.

"I had some things to do."

"You could have left a note. I didn't know if you were coming back in fifteen minutes or two hours."

You're lucky I'm back at all, she thought. She looked from Richard to Lucy, smiling as if touched by the sight of them.

"Well, I'm glad to see the two of you having so much fun. I think you needed a little father-daughter bonding time."

He nodded, as if to concede her the round.

"It's been wonderful," he said. "But I was hoping you could take over in a few minutes. I have some work to do for that Chinese restaurant. The presentation's next week."

"Could you do it later?" she said. "I need a little time to myself."

"Sarah." She could hear the irritation creeping into his voice. "This is a big account."

"Spend the day with your daughter," she snapped. "It won't kill you."

"I don't think this is fair," he spluttered. He seemed genuinely baffled, as if Sarah had no business in life beyond taking care of Lucy and making things convenient for him. "Is there something particular you need to do?"

She only had to hesitate a second or two.

"I joined a book group," she told him. "We're reading Flaubert."

———

Based on the name alone, Sarah had developed a completely erroneous impression of the Ladies' Belletristic Society. She'd expected it to be stuffy and pretentious, fatally suburban, a garden club nightmare of watercress sandwiches and polite snobbery, well-preserved matrons in golf visors and pearls who used the word *darling* as an adjective.

Instead, the atmosphere inside Bridget's condo was warm and welcoming, full of laughter and intellectual curiosity. Over here an informed conversation about the films of Mike Leigh. Over there an impassioned discussion of third-world debt relief. Despite the age of the members—the "ladies" were in their sixties and seventies—Sarah sensed a collective vibrancy in the air that seemed vaguely reminiscent of something she couldn't quite put her finger on.

As the only little sister present—everyone kept assuring her that another was on the way—Sarah found herself in great demand. Jean ushered her around the room like a visiting celebrity, introducing her to each new arrival: Regina, a tall bony woman with a hearing aid and an owlish smile; Alice, whose iron gray hair only emphasized the uncanny youthfulness of her face; and now Josephine, plump and frumpy, with a tight helmet of curly hair and mismatched orthopedic splints on her forearms.

"Oh no," said Jean. "Don't tell me you got carpal tunnel."

"Repetitive stress," Josephine replied with a sigh. "Too much typing."

"She's writing a novel," Jean explained to Sarah. "She always said she would."

Josephine gave a rueful nod. "Only forty years behind schedule."

"This is Sarah, my neighbor," said Jean. "She's a literary critic."

"In my dreams," said Sarah. "In real life I'm the mother of a three-year-old girl."

"An *adorable* three-year-old girl," added Jean.

Josephine stared at Sarah for a long moment. There was something probing in her gaze, but tender too, as if she were attempting to move beyond conversation into some more intimate realm.

"She won't be three forever, honey. When she goes to school, you can get back to your work."

"My work," said Sarah. The words felt good in her mouth. She just wished she knew what they referred to.

"Don't be like me." Josephine reached for Sarah's hand and gave a feeble, but still somehow encouraging squeeze. "Don't let your whole life go by."

Before Sarah could reply Josephine was besieged by concerned friends peppering her with questions and medical advice. Regina recommended acupuncture. Alice said she should try dictating her novel into a tape recorder. Bridget said she hoped Josephine's grip was strong enough to support a wineglass. Jean said she knew lots of people with similar injuries who had complete recoveries, no disability whatsoever.

"You just have to be patient," she said.

And all at once, it came to Sarah: It was like being back at the Women's Center. For the first time since she graduated from college, she'd managed to find her way into a community of smart, independent, supportive women who enjoyed each other's company and didn't need to compete with one another or define themselves in relation to the men in their lives. It was precisely what she'd been missing, the oasis she'd been unable to find in graduate school, at work, or even at the playground. She'd searched for it for so long that she'd even come to suspect that it hadn't actually existed in the first place, at least not the way she remembered it, that it was more a product of her romantic undergraduate imagination than anything real in the world. But it had been real. It felt like *this*, and it was a huge relief to be back inside the circle again.

The feeling didn't last long. The doorbell rang, and Bridget escorted two more women into the room, both of them in expensive floral dresses. The older one had a pretty, but somewhat leathery face and the toned legs of a tennis player.

"See," said Bridget, presenting the younger woman to Sarah with an air of triumph. "I told you you'd have a comrade."

Sarah tried to look pleased, but her face wouldn't cooperate. She just hoped her smile wasn't as stiff and phony as the one plastered on her comrade's face.

"Nice to see you again," said Sarah.

"What a surprise," said Mary Ann. "We miss you at the playground."

The two little sisters eyed each other warily across the coffee table. Sarah still hadn't recovered from the shock of Mary Ann's arrival and how completely it had spoiled what had been shaping up as a very nice evening. This couldn't be the Women's Center, not with *her* here. She felt like she'd been given a beautiful birthday present, only to have it ripped away a moment later and handed to someone else. Her only consolation was the look of raw discomfort on Mary Ann's face. She must have realized that she'd strayed onto alien turf, that for once she was the one who was outnumbered.

"Which one of you would like to start?" asked Bridget.

"She's the bookworm," said Mary Ann. "Let her go first."

"No, you go ahead," said Sarah. "I can wait."

Mary Ann took the measure of her audience before speaking. The ladies of the Belletristic Society were smiling at her like kindergarten teachers overseeing the year's first installment of show-and-tell, fully prepared to be fascinated by a broken clam shell or a worn shoelace.

"Did anybody like this book?" Mary Ann screwed her face up into the look of offended disapproval Sarah knew so well. "Because I really just hated it."

She hesitated, waiting for someone to take the baton and run with it, but the ladies seemed startled by this unexpected salvo of negativity. They didn't look upset, exactly, but their smiles were in retreat.

"I mean, isn't it kind of depressing?" Mary Ann continued, her voice growing in confidence, as if she were sitting at the picnic table on the playground, lecturing Cheryl and Theresa. "She cheats on her husband with two different guys, wastes all his money, then kills herself with rat poison. Do I really need to read this?"

This question was met with an uncomfortable silence. It was Laurel, Mary Ann's sponsor, who finally ventured a response.

"There's a lot of good descriptive writing," she said hopefully.

The ladies nodded in vigorous agreement.

"It's supposed to be depressing," Josephine pointed out. "It's a tragedy. Emma's undone by a tragic flaw."

"What's her flaw?" Bridget inquired.

"Blindness," Josephine replied. "She can't see that the men are just using her."

"She just wants a little romance in her life," Jean ventured. "You can't really blame her for that."

"It's about women's choices," Regina added. "Back then, a woman didn't have a lot of choices. You could be a nun or you could be a wife. That's all there was."

"Or a prostitute," added Bridget.

"She had a choice not to cheat on her husband," said Mary Ann, staring rudely at Sarah.

"Mary Ann's got a point," admitted Laurel.

"Usually it's the man who cheats," said Alice. "I found it refreshing to read about a woman reclaiming her sexuality."

"Reclaiming her sexuality?" Mary Ann repeated with disdain. "Is that a nice way of saying she's a slut?"

"Madame Bovary is not a slut," said Regina. "She's one of the great characters in Western literature."

"Hello?" said Mary Ann. "She's sneaking off to the city every week to screw her husband's friend."

"I found some of the sex stuff a little cryptic." Josephine paged through her paperback. "Like here on page 216. 'Rodolphe discovered that the affair offered still further possibilities of sensual gratification. He abandoned every last shred of restraint and consideration. He made her into something compliant, something corrupt.' "

"See?" said Mary Ann. "She's a slut."

"Does anybody know what that means?" Josephine asked. "Do you think he's tying her up or something like that?"

Alice leaned forward and mouthed the words, "Anal sex."

Josephine looked horrified.

"Really?" she asked, glancing around the room in embarrassment. "Did everyone get that but me?"

"Why don't we hold off on that for the moment," suggested Bridget. "Let's see what our other little sister has to say."

Back when she was teaching, the prospect of public speaking had filled Sarah with dread. She always felt like she was faking it, unsuccessfully impersonating an authority figure. But tonight, for some reason, she felt calm and well prepared, an adult among her peers. Maybe she'd grown up in the past five or six years without realizing it. Or maybe she was just happier now than she'd been back then. She looked at Mary Ann with what she hoped was a kind of empathy.

"I think I understand your feelings about this book. I used to feel the same way myself." She shifted her gaze around the circle, making eye contact with each of the older women. It was okay being the center of attention; it was even kind of fun. "When I read this book back in college, Madame Bovary just seemed like a fool. She marries the wrong man, makes one stupid mistake after another, and pretty much gets what she deserves. But when I read it this time, I just fell in love with her."

Mary Ann scoffed, but the ladies seemed intrigued. Jean smiled proudly, as if to remind everyone who was responsible for Sarah's presence at the meeting.

"My professors would kill me," she continued, "but I'm tempted to go as far as to say that, in her own strange way, Emma Bovary is a feminist."

"Really?" Bridget sounded skeptical, but open to persuasion.

"She's trapped. She can either accept a life of misery or struggle against it. She chooses to struggle."

"Some struggle," said Mary Ann. "Jump in bed with every guy who says hello."

"She fails in the end," Sarah conceded. "But there's something beautiful and heroic in her rebellion."

"How convenient," observed Mary Ann. "So now cheating on your husband makes you a feminist."

"It's not the cheating. It's the hunger for an alternative. The refusal to accept unhappiness."

"I guess I just didn't understand the book," Mary Ann said, adopting a tone of mock humility. "I just thought she just looked so pathetic, degrading herself for nothing. I mean, did she really think a man like that was going to run away with her?"

Sarah couldn't help smiling. Just yesterday, for the first time, she and Todd had discussed the possibility of divorcing their respective spouses. Sarah had floated the subject cautiously, after he'd told her about his miserable Saturday at the beach, how he and Kathy had argued the whole time, how fragile and unhappy their marriage had become. *She's losing patience with me,* he confessed. *I'm going to leave Richard,* she replied. And then they had made love tenderly, almost fearfully, as if trying to absorb the meaning of what they'd just told each other.

"Madame Bovary's problem wasn't that she committed adultery," Sarah declared, in a voice full of calm certainty. "It was that she committed adultery with losers. She never found a partner worthy of her heroic passion."

Mary Ann shook her head sadly, as if she pitied Sarah, but the other ladies were beaming, nodding in fervent agreement with this unexpected and thought-provoking assessment of the novel. Sarah sipped her wine, basking in the glow of their approval. *Maybe I should go back to graduate school,* she thought. Josephine raised her hand.

"Could we get back to the sex now?" she asked.

DREAM DATE

RONNIE WAS BEING A LOT MORE COOPERATIVE THAN MAY EXpected. He was ready at six-thirty, shaved and showered, looking quite presentable in the beige Dockers and jungle-print polo shirt she and Bertha had picked out for him at Marshall's. His hair was combed, and his shoes were polished. If not for his eyeglasses, which were thick and ugly and sat crookedly on his nose—May had been bugging him for years to get contacts—he would have seemed completely normal.

"You look handsome," she told him. "She won't be disappointed."

"Wait'll she hears about my criminal record," said Ronnie, mimicking May's bubbly tone. "That'll really seal the deal."

"I don't think you need to get into that just yet. Why don't you stick to the small talk?"

"Right. I can tell her why I don't have a job and why my face is plastered all over town."

"Just keep it light, honey. Chat about the weather, the foods you like to eat, your favorite TV shows. If you hit it off and start going steady, then maybe you can get into . . . you know, the other stuff."

"I'll do my best." Ronnie clapped his hands and rubbed them together like he was eager to get down to business. "I'll work the old McGorvey charm on her. It hasn't let me down yet."

May let that one pass. She couldn't blame him for being nervous; she was nervous herself. As far as she knew, this was the first time Ronnie had ever gone on an actual date. It reminded her of the excitement that used to brighten up the house back when Carol started having boyfriends, the burst of activity when one of them came over for dinner, the heart-in-your-mouth feeling of prom night, when your little girl suddenly transformed herself into a princess. Ronnie had never had any of that. He was always hiding in his room with the door locked, doing God-knew-what.

"She's late," he said, squinting at the digital clock on the VCR. "Maybe she chickened out."

"Be patient," May told him. "She probably just hit some traffic."

Ronnie's personal ad had worked like a charm, drawing twenty-seven responses the first week alone. Bertha tried to take credit for the success, insisting that her addition of the word *handsome* had made all the difference, but May knew better. Ronnie had read the letters out loud, and almost all of them referred directly to the line, *I'm not perfect and don't expect you to be, either.* There must have been a lot of men out there demanding perfection, judging from the relief the women felt at the absence of this requirement.

I'm overweight, the very first letter began, *but I have a lot of love to give. I do hope you'll give me a chance.* One correspondent spoke of her double mastectomy scars; another detailed her long struggle with unwanted facial hair. *I tried electrolysis, but it hurt like anything!*

I am currently making an effort to accept myself for who I am, and your ad made me think you might treat me with the compassion and respect I deserve.

"Jesus Christ." Ronnie tore the letter into shreds with the thoroughness that characterized all his actions. "Just what I need. A date with the bearded lady."

Jenny had SEVERE acne. Patricia's cellulite was so bad she'd rather die than wear a bathing suit. Diana was suffering from female pattern baldness. Chronic foot pain made it hard for Angela to get around. Sharon had headaches that felt like dull spikes being pounded into her skull. The world was riddled with imperfections.

"It's a freak show," Ronnie muttered. "They should all run away and join the circus."

May hated when he talked like that. She wanted to believe that her son was good at heart, that his own suffering had at least made him sympathetic to the suffering of others. But there was a coldness in him that scared her sometimes. One woman had included a photo of herself taken at an amusement park. She was standing beneath a Ferris wheel, holding a cloud of cotton candy on a paper cone. She would have been pretty enough, May thought, if not for the buckteeth. Ronnie held up the picture and burned the woman's face away with the tip of his cigarette.

"There," he said. "A little cosmetic surgery."

In short order, he had whittled the stack of letters down to three finalists: Arlene, a divorcee with three kids, two of whom had life-threatening allergies to peanut products; Gina, "a teenager in her late thirties" with "a passion for miniature golf"; and Sheila, who had been "out of circulation for too long," and was making "a sincere effort to come out of my shell and reconnect with other people."

Arlene was his first choice, but May talked him out of it. Life was complicated enough without having to deal with someone else's kids. So he'd written to Gina and Sheila, identifying himself only as "R.J.," and inviting them to give him a call, if they didn't mind the fact that he didn't have a car. Only Sheila took him up on the offer. She hadn't included a photo with the letter, and hadn't provided much in the way of physical description (*Slender SWF, 29*), so there was an added layer of suspense when the doorbell finally rang.

"She better not be a dog," Ronnie said, stubbing his cigarette into the ashtray and rising without haste from the couch. "I'm not gonna be seen in public with some dog."

"Ma," said Ronnie, "this is Sheila."

May was pleasantly surprised. The girl was no beauty, but she was attractive enough, a slightly mousy brunette of medium height wearing a sleeveless pink dress. She wasn't heavy, exactly, just a little wide in the hips and thick in the ankles, but May didn't hold that against her. She was "slender" the same way that Ronnie was "handsome." But they made a nice-looking couple.

"Pleased to meet you," said May.

"Hello," said Sheila.

All it took was that one word for May to realize that something wasn't quite right with her. Part of it was her voice, flat and dreamy, as if she were talking to herself, and part of it was her eyes, which were staring vacantly, but insistently, at the wall above May's head. Also the way she hugged her purse so tightly to her stomach with both hands, as if she were walking through a bad neighborhood late at night.

"Are you cold?" asked May.

"Why?" said Sheila. "Are you?"

"No," said May. "I thought maybe you were."

"It's the middle of summer." Sheila laughed nervously, her eyes darting around the room. "Why would I be cold?"

The poor girl's terrified, May thought. *Maybe she recognizes him from the poster.* But when he sat down on the couch, she sat down right next to him, as if they were old friends.

"Can I get you something?" May asked. "A wine cooler, maybe?"

"Just water," said Sheila. "This medication I'm taking gives me the dry mouth. I can hear the spit crackle when I talk."

Ronnie winced, making a face of exaggerated disgust. May gave him a sharp look.

Sheila smiled sweetly. "When I wake up in the morning, I feel like I've eaten a jar of paste."

"I'll get you a nice tall glass of ice water," said May.

She took her time in the kitchen, giving them a few minutes to get acquainted, but she didn't hear any voices. When she returned to the living room they were both staring straight ahead, like strangers waiting for a bus.

This is a date, May wanted to tell them. *You're supposed to talk to each other.*

She handed one glass to Sheila, the other to Ronnie. Sheila drained hers in a single thirsty gulp.

"How was traffic, dear?" May inquired. She glanced pointedly at Ronnie, as if to say, *See? It's really not that hard.*

Sheila seemed perplexed. "Excuse me?"

"The traffic? On your way over here."

"Oh." She nodded, but her expression remained vague. "I didn't really notice."

Ronnie twirled his index finger by his ear, indicating that Sheila was a little batty. He seemed pleased by the idea.

He knew, May thought suddenly. *He must have known it from her letter.* Ronnie had a radar for that sort of thing. A feeling of unease spread through May's body.

"Come on." Ronnie patted Sheila on the knee. "Let's get this show on the road."

May followed them to the front door. She pinched Ronnie's arm.

"You be nice to her," she whispered.

Ronnie crossed his arms on his chest and drew back as if she'd offended him.

"When am I not nice?" he asked her.

————

Sheila didn't see it coming.

As far as she could tell, the date had been a dud, and the ride home was worse. R.J. hadn't said a word the whole time, just sat brooding in the passenger seat, encased in a bubble of his weird nervous energy, plucking repeatedly at the dark hair on his wrist. But then, when they were only a couple of blocks from his house, he spoke up suddenly, his voice clipped and urgent, striking an unexpected note of command.

"Take the next left."

She obeyed without thinking, pulling into a small parking lot built alongside what appeared to be an elementary school, judging from the playground lit up by the beam of her headlights. It had those bucket swings, the ones that kept the little kids from falling out. The slides were made of molded plastic in bright, primary colors, and the ground around the structure was covered by some kind of spongy rubber material. It was a far cry from the playgrounds of her own childhood, rusty monkey bars embedded in cracked asphalt, metal slides baking in the sun, sharp edges and exposed screws.

"Everybody's so careful now," she said.

R.J. stared at her like she was kind of alien life-form. She wondered if her words weren't coming out right, if they were slurred or mechanical-sounding, or maybe she was talking too fast or something.

"Cut the headlights," he told her.

At one time in her life Sheila had been a good conversationalist. She'd had friends. She remembered sitting with them in the high school cafeteria, laughing about silly things. She and her college roommates used to stay up till all hours, trading secrets, giggling about sex, trying to figure out the meaning of life.

But not anymore. The damn medication had fogged her brain, made it seem like everything was happening twenty feet away, on the other side of a gauze curtain. If she stopped taking it, though, everything was too close, way too bright, pressing in on her until she forgot how to breathe. That was how she'd ended up in the hospital again this past fall. She just wished there was some middle ground, something that didn't muffle everything and make her feel like English had become a foreign language.

She and R.J. had spent the first half of dinner floundering around, trying to make conversation. But what was there to talk about? Neither one of them had a job. He wasn't interested in sports or music, and showed no interest in travel.

"I'm broke," he said. "Where am I gonna go?"

The sad part was, she kind of liked him. He wasn't like the other guys she'd met through the personals, big forty-year-old babies.

Joel, who asked her to squeeze his bicep and then seemed hurt when she wasn't as impressed as he thought she should be. Gary, who went on and on about the boat he would have built if he'd had access to an unlimited amount of money. And that awful one with the beard, who kept calling her for weeks after their date, trying to convince her to upgrade her cell phone, apparently unaware of the fact that she didn't have one.

"I'm offering five hundred anytime minutes a month. Can your current plan compete?"

R.J. didn't have much to say, but at least he seemed smart, like there was something going on beneath the surface. He watched her with those shrewd eyes—the glasses made them seem too big, too observant—smiling in a way that seemed encouraging, but then suddenly did not. He laughed a lot, too, usually when she wasn't trying to be funny. There were moments when she could have sworn he was emitting radio signals from the center of his forehead, beaming them right across the table.

We have a connection, she thought.

But when the food arrived, he lost interest, stopped even trying to talk to her. She kept waiting for him to look up from his gigantic bloody steak, to say *something*, if only to acknowledge the fact that she was still sitting right in front of him.

Of course she'd panicked and started blathering about her illness, the way she always did, just to fill the silence. *That* she could talk about for hours. She told him about her first so-called breakdown, the one that came out of nowhere during her senior year in college. One day she's normal, a sociology major on the dean's list, and the next she's standing naked on the quad, trying to set a pile of her clothes on fire.

"They were itchy," she explained. "I thought they were full of bugs."

That got his attention. Chewing slowly, he pondered her with the neutral expression of a psychiatrist.

"Maybe you just wanted to get naked," he suggested. "Maybe the breakdown was just an excuse."

"I wanted to kill the bugs," she insisted. "I didn't even realize I was naked until the police came and made an issue of it."

R.J. flagged down the waiter and ordered dessert, apple pie and ice cream, which he shoveled into his mouth while she continued the saga of her hospitalization and treatment, the five years of relative lucidity followed by a second so-called breakdown, which was actually a very positive experience. She was about to tell him why—it was something she enjoyed talking about—when he looked up and yawned right in her face, not even bothering to cover his mouth. Then, when the check arrived, he said he'd forgotten his wallet.

"Wouldn't you know it?" he chuckled.

She didn't mind paying. It was her father's money anyway. A thank-you would have been nice, though, a simple word of gratitude. But R.J. just acted like it was his due, the least he deserved for sitting through dinner with a crazy woman.

But maybe she'd misread his signals, she thought, as they sat quietly in the car, staring at the shadowy playground. Maybe he liked her. Maybe he was as shy and awkward as she was, and simply didn't know how to behave around women. He didn't seem like a guy who'd had a lot of girlfriends.

She smiled, to let him know that it would be all right to kiss her or just hold her hand. It wasn't that she wanted to kiss *R.J.*, exactly. She just wanted to kiss *someone*, to remember what it felt like, to know that she'd taken one more step in the direction of a normal life.

R.J. smiled back. She must have been a little more encouraging than she'd meant to be, because instead of kissing her, he started undoing his belt, and then his zipper.

"I want to show you something," he said.

"I'm sorry," she said. "You must have misunderstood."

"Don't be scared," he told her. "It's not gonna bite."

If R.J. had been a little more interested back at the restaurant, Sheila would have told him about the vision that had triggered her second so-called breakdown, the most beautiful and important thing that had ever happened to her.

She was driving on the highway during the evening rush hour, coming home from a temp job, a mind-numbing eight-hour shift of data processing for a payroll company. It had rained all day, but now it was clearing, a strong breeze erasing the bad weather from the sky so quickly that it looked like time-lapse photography.

The sun was sinking, ducking in and out of the scudding silver-gray clouds. At one point, she happened to be looking straight at it as it emerged from hiding, inexplicably transformed into something glorious. A moment before it had been a pale yellow orb, but now it was an enormous red fireball, its rays separating into four rosy beams, one of which—the second from the left—was directed right at Sheila's windshield. The touch of that crimson sunlight through the glass, the sudden reassuring warmth, landed on her skin like a blessing.

She knew it was a bad idea to look directly at the sun, but she couldn't avert her gaze. A face had emerged from the clouds, and it was trying to speak to her. She rolled down her window to hear the words, but it was no use; the road noise was just too loud.

She slammed on her brakes, right there in the center lane, setting off a chain reaction of violent swerves, squealing tires, and furious horn-blowing, capped off by the sound of one crash, then another, behind her and off to the right. She gave the collision no more than a passing glance—a three-car pileup, nothing too serious—as she climbed onto the warm hood of her car and from there onto the roof, so she could get a better look at the face in the clouds.

It was a boy, seven or eight years old. Brown hair. Freckles and a cowlick. An innocent but mischievous expression. A face she'd seen before, or imagined she had.

"Hello!" she called. "I can see you!"

"I can see you, too," he replied.

By then he wasn't just a face anymore, but an entire body, his blue jeans and black-and-orange-striped shirt standing out vividly against the flat gray background. And suddenly it was obvious: He was her child, the one she'd aborted during sophomore year. But he was more than just her unborn son.

"You're God, aren't you?"

"I am," he told her. "And you're my special mommy."

"Will you forgive me?" she asked.

"You're already forgiven."

She felt so much better knowing that, relieved of the burden she'd been lugging around for so long, the terrible guilt of not having given him a chance. But he was God, so of course he was okay.

"I'd like to know you better," she told him.

"You will," he promised her.

She sat with her hands resting in her lap, and comforted herself with the thought of God's sweet face while R.J. finished his ugly business in the passenger seat. At least he wasn't touching her. He wasn't even looking at her, just staring straight ahead at the playground as he yanked on himself, once in a while muttering something disgusting in a threatening voice.

"You bitch . . . you whore . . . little crybaby . . . piece of shit . . ."

After a while the words dissolved into whimpers and R.J. exploded with an angry bark of relief, lurching forward as if he'd been shot, bracing himself with his free hand against the glove compartment. He rested his head on the dashboard, breathing in hiccupy spasms that sounded like sobs. After a while he straightened up, wiping his dirty hand on her seat. He studied Sheila with cold eyes as he zipped up and fixed his belt.

"You're not gonna tell on me, are you?" His voice was soft and taunting, but worried nonetheless.

Sheila shook her head. He pressed his index finger against the base of her chin, forcing her head back until she was staring up at the padded ceiling of the car.

"I hope not," he whispered. "Because I don't like tattletales."

He removed the pressure. She lowered her head cautiously and looked at him. He put his hands over his face like a child playing peekaboo and started moaning into his palms, making a sound she interpreted as a kind of apology.

"Let's get you home," she told him.

PART THREE

LOVEBIRDS

TRUANTS

THE BAR EXAM WAS A TWO-DAY MARATHON, AS MUCH A TEST OF physical endurance as legal knowledge. Day One was the MBE, two hundred nitpicking, densely worded multiple choice questions, a mental root canal that made the SAT seem like a routine cleaning by comparison. Once they had you thoroughly battered and demoralized, they made you trudge back on Day Two for the essay section, which for Todd, at least, was even worse: an eight-hour confrontation with the blankness of his own mind, the white noise of his inability to think made even louder by the furious scratching of his fellow test-takers' pens and pencils. It was as if he'd never gone to law school at all, as if he were living through an endless, real-time version of the nightmare in which you find yourself naked in an unfamiliar classroom, taking a final in Swahili or electrical engineering, some subject about which you know exactly nothing, except that you'd enrolled and somehow not managed to attend any classes.

"Eat your breakfast," Kathy told him on the morning of Day One. "You don't want to fade in the home stretch."

Todd took an obedient bite of toast. Despite her frequently—and, at times, angrily—expressed worries about his preparation and motivation in recent weeks, Kathy had slipped back into the role of supportive spouse as the actual exam date approached. She smiled at him as though he were a child returning to school after a brief illness.

"I have a good feeling," she said. "They say the third time's a charm."

They also say, "Three strikes and you're out," Todd thought, but he didn't say it out loud. There was no reason to make this any worse than it already was.

"I'm going to buy a bottle of champagne," she continued. "We'll put it in the fridge and open it as soon as you get the good news."

As far as Todd was concerned, there was only one upside to this whole ordeal: The results of the bar exam wouldn't be announced for several months, so Kathy wouldn't know until late November or early December that he'd failed for a third time. Maybe by then it wouldn't matter so much.

"Don't get your hopes up," he warned her. "We've been down this road before."

"This time it'll be different," she said. "I'm sure of it."

She sustained this stubbornly optimistic mood all through breakfast and the short drive to the commuter rail station, and Todd did his best to play along. It was a relief to kiss her and Aaron goodbye and step out of the car, a relief to finally stop pretending. He stood in the parking lot, briefcase in hand, waving as they drove away.

A flight of metal stairs led up to the platform, but Todd remained below, pacing in front of the pay phone, forcing himself not to keep checking his watch every fifteen seconds. Sarah pulled up at 7:45 on the dot, just as the train rumbled into the station, its horn blaring a wake-up call to a herd of lethargic commuters. He climbed into the Volvo and kissed her hello.

"Right on time," he said.

She studied him for a moment, trying to detect a trace of ambivalence beneath his cheerful demeanor.

"You sure about this?" she asked.

Instead of answering, he flipped open his briefcase, spinning it a quarter turn on his lap to reveal the contents: a bathing suit, a container of heavy-duty sunscreen, and a bottle of chilled white wine, still sweaty from the refrigerator.

"Quite the Boy Scout," she told him.

It was a gorgeous summer morning, hot but not yet muggy, with a gentle intermittent breeze stirring the air, the kind of weather that made you wish you had a sunroof or convertible. They lit out for the North Shore, moving freely against rush-hour traffic, the radio turned way up to compete with the rush of wind and road noise through the open windows. Sarah reached across the gearshift console and squeezed Todd's hand. She looked prettier than he'd ever seen her, her eyes bright with adventure, stray ringlets and unruly corkscrews of hair blowing across her face.

"I never did this in high school," she confessed. "Not even when I was a senior."

"I'm corrupting you."

She laughed. "Better late than never."

The idea had come to them just two days ago, and had blossomed into a plan with only the slightest coaxing. Todd had been agonizing about the test to the point where he'd become tedious even to himself. He knew he was going to fail, so why go through the motions? Why waste two whole days of his life on a hopeless and unpleasant quest? Why not spend them on the beach? Why not spend them on the beach with Sarah?

From there it was only a short journey to here. Kathy was taking both days off to watch Aaron, so Todd was clear on that front. And wasn't Jean always volunteering to baby-sit Lucy? All Sarah had to do was concoct a little story about an old friend from college, an unexpected layover in Providence, a welcome chance to catch up.

"How was Lucy?" he asked. "She cry or anything?"

"Are you kidding? She just about shoved me out the door. How was it at your place?"

"The usual," he said. "Everybody happy but me."

They were on the beach by nine, their blanket spread on the cool sand, anchored at the corners by Todd's shoes and briefcase, and a small cooler Sarah had filled with fruit and sandwiches and a six-pack of bottled water. Todd lay back, cradling his head in his hands, and smiled up at the perfect morning sky. Whatever guilt he was feeling was muffled by an immense feeling of relief: The sun was shining, the surf crashing, the gulls banking and crying out over-head, and he wasn't sitting in the sickly light of a cavernous con-ference center surrounded by five hundred other would-be lawyers, sharing a table with some Ivy League whiz kid who was going to ace the test on his first try and be ruling the world by the time he was thirty.

"Can you believe it?" Sarah's hand moved lightly over his thigh. "It's our first real date. Without the kids, I mean."

Todd raised himself on his elbows and looked around. It was still early, the beach mostly empty. The only other people out were solitary joggers and dogwalkers and a few families with small chil-dren.

"Think we should've brought 'em?"

She leaned forward like a penitent, her face momentarily eclipsing the sun, and kissed him on the shoulder.

"Not today. Today's just for us."

They rode the waves, then walked the length of the shore holding hands, stopping to examine the occasional shell or stone, marveling at the speckled beauty of a crab claw, shaking their heads at the sight of a washed-up tampon applicator tangled in seaweed, a pair of safety goggles with a broken strap. A tanned retiree jogged past, his potbelly wobbling over a pair of inadvisably skimpy Speedo trunks.

"Richard took me to a nude beach once," she said. "Back when we were dating."

"Around here?"

"In New Jersey. At one of the state parks. He found it in a guidebook."

Todd wasn't surprised. Sarah had recently told him about her husband's sexual proclivities—the panties, the way he'd try to pressure her into attending a "swingers' party" back when she was still breast-feeding.

"Did you take off your clothes?"

"Just my top."

"Very European of you."

She smiled. "I like to think so."

"What about Richard? Did he go for the full-body tan?"

"Are you kidding? He was naked in the car on the drive down. Just a towel draped over his lap. Got some pretty funny looks from the toll collectors."

They fell silent for a moment, smiling their greetings to a frustrated father about their own age, a big sunburned guy who'd been trying for a least a half hour to get an unwieldy box kite airborne, while his beautiful twin daughters—they were five, maybe six—looked on with expressions of withering contempt. He'd just finished a thirty-yard sprint, trying to create an updraft, the kite dragging along behind him, plowing the sand.

"No breeze," he panted defensively, as if he suspected the strangers of laughing at him. "Yesterday it worked fine."

Todd and Sarah made sympathetic faces and continued down the beach.

"So tell me," he said. "Did it turn you on?"

"The nude beach?" Perhaps unconsciously, she reached down and pinched the sweet roll of fat perched above the waistband of her bikini bottoms. "God, no. You want to feel young and thin and attractive, go spend a day with some nudists."

After lunch they checked into the Sea Breeze, a justly inexpensive motel tucked between a propane supply store and a seafood shack on a soulless commercial strip half a mile west of the beach. It was the real deal, an old-fashioned, independently owned and operated fleabag, fully equipped with moldy wall-to-wall carpeting, a hideous synthetic bedspread that felt oily to the touch, and an unambiguously phallic painting of a lighthouse hung over the bed as if for inspiration. They toasted each other with Todd's wine, poured into plastic cups liberated from sanitary plastic wrappers, and made love without showering, their bodies sticky and gritty with the obligatory day-at-the-beach coating of sand and salt and sunscreen residue.

"We're like two pieces of Shake 'n Bake chicken," he told her.

Todd was pleased by the metaphor, but Sarah shook her head, as if he'd said something offensive.

"No jokes," she said. She was lying on her side, her legs scissored across the highly flammable sheets. "Not today. I want to concentrate."

"On what?"

"On you. I want to feel you inside me."

She closed her eyes, her face tightening into a grimace that suggested effort more than pleasure. All morning long he'd been fantasizing about being alone with her in a private place, no kids to worry about waking, a chance to finally cut loose. He imagined her shouting his name with the breathy gusto of a porn queen, startling the clerks at the propane outlet, making the waitresses blush at Ricky's Chowda Pot. But instead she seemed oddly subdued, even quieter than usual. When he moved into her, she released a soft sigh. His retreats elicited an even softer whimper.

"Are you okay?" he asked.

She nodded, harder than necessary, as if she'd lost the power of speech and needed to be extra emphatic.

"I want to help you," she said.

"How?"

"You're sad." She torqued her neck to look him in the eyes, daring him to disagree. "I want to make you happy."

"You do." He gave her more accessible breast a friendly squeeze. "This is about as happy as I get."

"She puts too much pressure on you. I wouldn't do that."

"It's not her fault."

"Give me a chance," she pleaded. "I know I'm not as pretty as she is."

"You're beautiful."

"Liar."

"You have a hot ass."

She smiled naughtily, bucking her hips to meet his thrust.

"You think so?"

"Oh, God. I'm gonna come."

"I want to feel it."

A wave of energy surged up from his toes.

"Now," she commanded.

His body lurched, arching at the waist. A big shudder buckled his arms, followed by a smaller one. She gave a yelp, as if she'd been scalded. For an immeasurable amount of time, he was nothing but suspense and release, clenching and unclenching, until one last fluttery spasm turned his arms to jelly, and he collapsed on top of her, crushing her beneath his bulk. She gave a throaty chuckle and wriggled herself free.

Todd woke with a start, head foggy, body infused with dread. For a moment or two, nothing made sense—the dingy room, the labored wheeze of the air conditioner, the stark afternoon light pouring in around the edges of the curtains, the unfamiliar dead weight of the arm across his chest.

"Whuh?" Sarah's face was bleary, vaguely alarmed. "Something wrong?"

Todd's eyes shot to the digital clock/radio on the bedside table. It was only two-fifteen. They still had plenty of time. He let his head drop back onto the pillow.

"Just a bad dream."

"What about?"

"I don't know. It's already gone."

All that remained was an image of a conveyor belt, an endless procession of identical yellow flashlights, but how could that account for the odd thumping in his chest, the panicky shortness of his breath?

"Was it about the test?" she wondered. "Maybe you're feeling bad about that."

He wished she would shut up about the goddam test. Of course he felt bad about it. He had paid four hundred dollars just to sign up, four hundred dollars that were gone forever, and had wasted countless spring and summer evenings pretending to study for it. He had convinced his hardworking, ever-hopeful wife that he was making a good faith effort to pass it at this very moment, when, in reality, he was in bed with a woman he'd just fucked in a cheap motel, speculating about a dream.

"It wasn't the test," he explained. "I think I was supposed to be doing some kind of quality control, but I didn't know how to tell the good flashlights from the bad ones."

She sat up and nodded, as if this made perfect sense. She looked sweet, he thought, totally absorbed in the conversation, unconscious of her own nakedness. Her nipples were hard from the AC, just begging to be sucked. Without trying, he pictured her on the nude beach in New Jersey, unwilling to remove her shorts, her husband-to-be browbeating her for being a prude.

"What happened?" she said. "Did you ever even *want* to be a lawyer?"

"It was kind of an accident," he admitted. "This guy in my frat, Paul Berry—he was the one who wanted to be a lawyer. He had this idea that it was an exciting, glamorous career, like on *LA Law*. He registered to take the LSAT, but he didn't want to do it alone. We got drunk on tequila one night, and he convinced me to sign up, too, just to keep him company. We went to Stanley Kaplan, studied together for a few weeks, and sat next to each other at the test. When the results came back, it turned out I did way better than him. With the scores I got, it was stupid *not* to go to law school."

"Not if you didn't want to be a lawyer."

"I didn't know what I wanted. I put it off for a couple of years after college, worked a couple of different jobs, nothing too interesting, then finally put in the applications."

"Law school must have been pretty tough."

"It was okay. Just school, you know? You do the homework, you take the test."

"So what went wrong with the bar exam?"

"I don't know."

"You could always take it again in the winter," she told him. "I could help you study. I could grade your practice tests, and you could explain the answers to me. Sometimes it helps to talk things through."

He was touched by the offer, impractical as it was, but he knew he was finished with the bar exam. He was never going to be a lawyer. He'd told Sarah he didn't know what had gone wrong, but that wasn't precisely true. He knew, he'd just never been able to put it into words. Something had happened to him over the past couple of years, something to do with being home with Aaron, sinking into the rhythm of a kid's day. The little tasks, the small pleasures. The repetition that goes beyond boredom and becomes a kind of peace. You do it long enough, and the adult world starts to drift away. You can't catch up with it, not even if you try.

"Mind if I suck your breast?" he asked.

In every way Todd could think of, the day had been a success, one of those rare occasions when your elaborate plan comes off without a hitch. He'd avoided the drudgery and humiliation of the bar exam and replaced it with a relaxing morning at the beach and an afternoon of uninhibited grown-up sex, a new milestone in his relationship with Sarah.

And yet the ride home was a somber journey, as if something had gone badly awry. But what? As far as Todd could determine, the only shadow on the whole experience had been cast by his cryptic half-remembered dream about the flashlights. Rather than offering some specific commentary about his romantic and professional dilemmas, the dream seemed to issue a more general—and somehow more disturbing—warning about the unpredictability of life, the impossibility of knowing or controlling your own feelings. You go to sleep happy, you wake up sad. You have no idea why, and there's nothing you can do about it.

Unlike Kathy, who no longer took much of an interest in the nuances of Todd's emotions, Sarah seemed all too keenly aware of the shift in his mood. As she had in the morning, she reached across the console and took his hand; but this time the gesture felt more supportive than conspiratorial, as if he were a patient in a hospital, someone in need of cheering up.

"Remember that guy you were talking about? Your best friend from college?"

"Paul Berry."

"Are you still friends?"

"We kind of drifted apart senior year. I started seeing Kathy, and the two of them didn't really get along."

"Did he ever become a lawyer?"

"Didn't have the grades. He got into real estate in Westchester County just in time for the boom. Last I heard, he was driving a BMW and dating a TV reporter."

Sarah checked her mirrors and changed lanes. She struck Todd as a trustworthy driver, neither too cautious nor too emotional. Ka-

thy drove slowly, almost like an elderly person, but her whole personality changed the moment she felt that another driver was trying
to take advantage of her, cutting her off at a tollbooth, or deliberately not allowing her to merge. In a split second, she transformed
herself into a tailgating, bird-flipping demon, fully capable of pulling
up beside the offender and loudly berating him or her through an
open window, despite Todd's frequent reminders that people had
gotten themselves and their families killed for less.

"You don't talk much about your friends," Sarah observed.

"I don't have many. There were a couple of guys from law
school I was friendly with, but they've scattered. We exchange e-
mails every once in a while, but that's it. I think they're embarrassed
for me. They're all working now, making real money, and I'm—"

"What about around here? Is there anyone you hang out with?"

"Just the cops on my football team. Most of the people I've met
the past couple of years are women. I can't just call them up and
say, 'Hey, let's grab a beer.' "

She nodded and fell silent. A couple of times she opened her
mouth, as if to ask a question, then stopped herself. Todd wasn't
surprised. He'd never had a girlfriend who knew how to be quiet in
the car, especially if he seemed distracted or upset, or just not in
the mood for conversation. It was some kind of female compulsion,
this need to fill the air with talk, as if words could somehow paper
over his feelings of sadness or discontent.

"It's okay," he said. "If you want to ask me something, go ahead
and ask it."

"I was just wondering about your frat."

"What about it?"

"I don't know. I never went out with a frat guy before. When
I was in college, I thought they were all a bunch of sexist assholes
and brainless party boys."

"We probably were," he said with a laugh. "I know Kathy thought so."

"Did you like it?"

"Sophomore year I loved it. Junior year I put up with it. By the time I was a senior I was pretty much sick of the whole thing."

"Was it like people think? Wild parties, date rapes, all that stuff? There was a frat at my school that got suspended after some townie high school girl drank herself into a coma at one of their parties. The Women's Center used to hold these annual protests on fraternity row."

"We weren't like that," he explained. "We were known around campus as the boring frat. A lot of our guys were science majors."

"That's so typical," she said. "I had this whole stereotype of you as this arrogant frat boy with a hundred different girlfriends. I think it even kind of turned me on. Sleeping with the enemy or something."

"There was this one weird thing that happened," Todd said, after a moment's hesitation. "Spring of junior year, this girl from the University of Connecticut came to one of our parties. Her friends left, but she stayed late, after everyone else had gone home. Pretty girl, a little bit chubby. Drunk as anything."

"Oh God," said Sarah. "I don't know if I wanna hear this."

"All right," he said. "Forget it."

She shot him a look.

"Come on, Todd. You can't stop now."

"I don't want to upset you."

"I'm a big girl. It's not gonna *upset* me."

"I mean, you can imagine what happened. At a certain point in the festivities, she just sort of volunteered to give everyone a blowjob. The whole frat."

"She *volunteered*?"

"I swear, the whole thing was her idea."

"Right."

"I was there," he said. "You weren't."

"She was drunk."

"Everyone was drunk."

"So what happened?"

"Nothing. We talked her out of it. We told her it wasn't a good idea."

"Really?"

He gave her a look. *Yeah, right.*

"So did you—?"

"I didn't want to. But she made me feel guilty, like I was insulting her if I didn't."

"I can't believe you're telling me this."

"That's not even the weird part."

"What could be weirder than that?"

"She stayed the whole weekend."

"Oh, God."

"No, it wasn't like that. She ended up sleeping in this one guy's room, Bobby Gerard. Really nice guy. Total nerd. Never had a girlfriend before in his life."

"And?"

"They're married now. Three kids."

"Come on."

"I went to their wedding. So did a lot of our frat brothers."

"Guys who were there that night?"

"Yup."

"What was that like?"

"Like the whole thing never happened. Nobody joked about it or even referred to it indirectly. When people asked the bride and groom where they met, they just said, 'At a frat party,' as if it were the most normal thing in the world."

"That's creepy."

"It was actually a nice wedding," he said.

Kathy was in a talkative mood at the dinner table. She and Aaron had had a wonderful day. They had followed the usual routine, visiting a playground in the morning, swimming at the Town Pool in the afternoon. After that they'd come home and worked on the math cards.

"He's getting really good," she said. "He can put the numbers in the proper order all the way from one to twenty."

"Really?"

"Almost." She lowered her voice. "He had a little trouble with fourteen. But otherwise he did great."

"Wow," said Todd. "We've got a prodigy on our hands."

"Very funny."

"I'm serious," he said. "I couldn't do that until I was sophomore in high school."

It took him several hours to understand his mistake. He and Kathy were lying in bed. She'd put Aaron to sleep in his own room, for once, apparently not so worried about keeping him close by after spending the whole day in his company. She was wearing excellent underwear, skimpy pink panties with a matching tank top, cut to show a lot of midriff. She read Stephen Ambrose for about five minutes, then clapped the book shut as if she had better things to do.

"I'm really encouraged," she said.

"About what?"

She laughed, as if he were teasing her.

"The test, dummy. You seemed so relaxed at the train station. The last two times you were a complete wreck when you came home. You wouldn't talk to me, wouldn't play with Aaron. Tonight you're like a different person."

"I guess I'm getting used to it."

To his surprise, her hand went straight to his cock.

"It's been a long time," she said, rubbing him through his boxers. "I know I've been a little uptight lately."

"That's okay," he told her. "We've been under a lot of stress."

She kissed him and he kissed her back. He felt himself stirring beneath her touch, but with a telltale soreness that reminded him that he'd already had sex twice that afternoon. He might be able to get hard again—it was already happening—but he wasn't going to be able to come, at least not in a timely fashion. He reached for her wrist.

"You know what?" he said. "We better not."

She released a groan.

"Why not?"

"I still gotta get through tomorrow. Better conserve my energy."

"Maybe you're right," she said. "Can I get a rain check?"

"Absolutely."

The following afternoon he made sure to look grim and exhausted when she pulled into the station. It wasn't that hard. Day Two of the bar exam had been long, muggy, and aimless. Sarah had stayed home with Lucy—there was no way to arrange another day of babysitting on such short notice—so Todd was on his own, wandering around Boston like a tourist. He killed the morning on Newbury Street and the Common, then sat through a matinee in an empty theater after lunch. After that, he read a couple of magazines in a Starbucks before trudging back to North Station.

Kathy tried to hide her disappointment when he climbed into the car. She was subdued at dinner, watchful. When she asked him how the test went, he answered with a single word: "Terrible."

In bed that night, she didn't try to redeem her rain check. Instead she read for about an hour before putting down her book. She turned off her lamp, and rolled onto her side, facing away from him. After a long interlude of silence she flipped onto her back.

"Todd?"

"Hmm?"

"Tell me about Sarah."

CHURCH ON SUNDAY

AS A SEVERELY LAPSED CATHOLIC, LARRY MOON DIDN'T ENJOY waking up on Sunday morning, putting on nice clothes, and heading across town for eight-thirty mass at St. Rita's. He much preferred the leisurely donuts-and-newspaper routine he'd inherited from his late father, a low-stress ritual that, oddly enough, seemed perfectly in keeping with the biblical injunction to make the Lord's Day a day of rest. But his lawyer said go, so he went.

He'd met with Walt Rudman of Rudman & Bosch shortly after receiving written notification from his wife's attorney that she was filing for divorce. A plump, silver-haired guy who actually wore striped suspenders, Rudman seemed less like a lawyer than an actor playing one on TV. He listened to Larry's account of his marital woes with the sympathetic expression of an old friend.

"I don't care about the money," Larry told him. "I just don't want to get cut off from my kids."

"Do you have any reason to believe that your wife may try to limit your contact?"

"I've got a bad temper," Larry admitted. "Sometimes I say things I should probably keep to myself."

"To the children?"

"To their mother."

"In their presence?"

Larry gave a contrite nod.

"Does this happen frequently?"

"Just a few times."

"And you've been married how long?"

"Eight years. She gets on my nerves sometimes." Larry sighed, trying to be fair. "Sometimes I get on hers, too."

"It happens," said Rudman. "Even in happy marriages."

"I've got some anger management issues," Larry admitted. "I'm fully aware of that."

Rudman tapped his pink cheeks like he was applying aftershave.

"I hate to have to ask this, Mr. Moon, but it's relevant to the situation. Have you ever been physically violent with your wife or children?"

"Absolutely not," said Larry. "Never."

"I'm relieved to hear it." Rudman allowed himself a cautious smile. "So basically your wife's main concern is with your occasional verbal indiscretions?"

"To be honest, that's probably just the straw that broke the camel's back."

Larry filled Rudman in on the major tension in his marriage: The fact that he, a physically healthy thirty-three-year-old male, was retired, and collecting a disability pension from the police department. It drove Joan crazy, he explained. She thought he was stagnating, sinking into a swamp of laziness and self-pity. She wanted him to get a job, reengage with the world, get out of the house a little.

"Can you meet her halfway on this?" Rudman inquired. "It wouldn't hurt to make a good faith effort to look for work in the next couple of weeks. Even a part-time position would be helpful. Candidly, a man your age, unemployed, the judge may not look favorably on that."

"I'm not unemployed," Larry pointed out. "I'm retired."

"What about school?" said Rudman. "Maybe you can take some classes, learn a new skill."

"I'd rather spend the time keeping an eye on my kids. You heard about Ronnie McGorvey, right?"

"I'm not familiar with the name."

"The child molester."

Rudman grimaced in recognition.

"I saw something in the paper. Or maybe on a telephone pole."

"Scumbag's right in our neighborhood," said Larry. "That's priority number one: keeping my kids safe from this pervert."

"That's completely understandable. I'd be nervous, too." Rudman checked his watch. "Any other issues I should know about?"

"She wants me to go to church," said Larry. "She thinks I should set a better example for the kids."

"This is important to her?"

"Very," said Larry. "She's a big-time Catholic."

"Why don't you do it? At least for the next couple of months, until we work out the custodial arrangements."

"But I'm an atheist," Larry objected.

Rudman considered him from across the desk. Despite his pudgy, jovial face, he had a way of turning his eyes into steely slits that must have been quite effective with the jury.

"Do yourself a favor, Mr. Moon," he advised. "Drop that word from your vocabulary for a little while. And go to church on Sunday."

On the night they met, a little more than ten years earlier, neither Larry nor his soon-to-be-ex-wife would have won any prizes for being an especially observant Catholic. Had they hewn more closely to the precepts of the Church in which they'd been raised, Joanie probably wouldn't have been competing in the Thursday Night Miss Nipples Contest at Kahlua's, and Larry—along with his fellow bouncer, a huge taciturn guy known only as "Duke"— probably wouldn't have been dousing the four finalists with buckets of extremely cold water. (Joanie received the somewhat disappointing honor of second runner-up, but that was only, as Larry explained to her after closing time over multiple shots of tequila, because he was just the water tosser and not one of the judges, who, in his humble opinion, needed to get their frigging eyes checked.)

And yet, despite their enthusiastic embrace of contraception and premarital sex (that very night!)—not to mention their theoretical willingness to terminate an unwanted pregnancy should such an unfortunate situation arise—both Larry and Joanie considered themselves to be good Catholics in some rock-bottom, immutable way that had less to do with religious practice than cultural identity. They were Catholics like they were Americans—it was their birthright, a form of citizenship that their parents had passed on to them and that they would pass on to their children, regardless of whether they toed the Vatican line on morally fraught issues like abortion and wet T-shirt contests.

Unlike Joanie, Larry had actually gone to Catholic school, attending the now-defunct St. Anthony's through eighth grade—they still allowed the ancient, crazy nuns to teach in those days; it was a miracle he and his classmates could even read—and serving a brief stint as an altar boy, usually assisting Father MacManus, a young, virile priest who enjoyed a sweaty game of pickup basketball and eventually ran off with Dave Michalek's hot mom, a deeply pious, ripely sexual woman who parted her lips and presented her tongue for communion in such excruciatingly slow motion that it always gave Larry a boner beneath his cassock (it apparently had the same effect on Father Mac, though the two of them never discussed the subject over Danishes and OJ after mass). After scandalizing the entire parish, the athletic ex-priest and the erstwhile Mrs. Michalek moved a few towns away, where they opened a video store called Mr. Movie, which did a great business until Blockbuster arrived and sent them into bankruptcy within a matter of months.

Although they'd started out in more or less the same place with regard to their Catholicism, Larry and Joanie had drifted far apart over the past decade. He could pinpoint the exact moment the theological rift had opened up between them. It was a Saturday morning early in their marriage, when they'd already been trying for well over a year to make a baby. On that particular morning, Joanie's period was almost a week late, and both of them believed they'd finally been blessed by conception. They made love with unusual tenderness, in honor of the vast mystery of life, only to find blood on the sheets and themselves when they were finished. Joanie went to the bathroom to clean up; Larry could hear her sobbing behind the closed door. When she emerged, however—now wearing an old pair of flowered panties over a maxipad—her tears were dry.

"I'm sorry," he said, stroking her hair when she lay back down beside him. "I thought we were home free."

She rolled onto her side and stared at her husband with a brave expression.

"I've been thinking," she said. "Maybe God doesn't want us to have children."

Her remark stung Larry like a slap.

"What the hell does God care? All over the world, millions of people are having children. What's He got against us?"

"I'm not sure," she admitted. "We can't always know what He wants. We just have to accept it."

"Maybe we should go to that fertility clinic John and Karen recommended. It could just be a mechanical problem, a blockage or whatever. Something they could fix with surgery."

"Or it could be God's will."

"Listen," he said. "Not everything is God's will. If your VCR doesn't work, it's not because God doesn't want you to watch a movie."

"Don't make fun of me, Larry."

"I'm just saying, if your VCR's broken, you don't take it to a priest. You take it to the VCR guy."

"We're living creatures," she pointed out. "We're not VCRs."

"Our bodies are machines," he said. "Sometimes they just need to be tweaked a little."

Joanie went to confession that afternoon, her first one in years, and to mass on Sunday. But on Monday she called the fertility clinic and made an appointment for a preliminary workup.

To their relief—though also to Larry's lasting dismay—the problem was easily diagnosed: His sperm count was so low that conception was deemed "highly unlikely" through normal sexual intercourse. The doctor recommended in vitro fertilization, and Joanie didn't object, despite the fact that a test-tube pregnancy was a highly dubious expression of "God's will."

"I wish I'd known this years ago," he said as they left the clinic. "Woulda saved me a fortune in condoms."

Joanie got pregnant on their first try, but miscarried early in the second trimester, a painful and horrible experience that she bore with a stoicism Larry found both admirable and a little worrisome.

"I'm leaving it in God's hands," she said. "It's not something I can control."

With some financial help from her parents, they tried a second round, and this one resulted in a successful, if difficult, pregnancy. Joanie was confined to bed rest for the last eight weeks of her term, a seemingly endless period of time she endured by saying the rosary and reading the Bible, as well as watching lots of TV (she had a weakness for the Home Shopping Network and reruns of *Taxi*). When the twins were born, her first words were addressed not to the doctor or the nurses who'd delivered the babies, or to the father of her children who'd held her hand and cheered her on through an eleven-hour labor, but to the Man Upstairs.

"Thank you, Jesus!" she'd gasped, as the two tiny infants were placed upon her breast. She sounded ecstatic, like a gospel singer from Alabama. "Thank you, Lord!"

Even at that sublime moment, Larry could barely hide his irritation. *What happened?* he wanted to ask her. *Did God change His mind? Did He suddenly decide it was okay for us to have children?*

At the same time, his heart was so full of joy—the boys were healthy and beautiful, and he was going to teach them how to play football and baseball, and take them camping—that Larry almost wished that he shared his wife's faith. He would have been more than happy to turn his gaze toward heaven and give thanks and praise to the all-knowing, all-powerful, sternly loving God of his childhood, if only he could have done so with a straight face.

———

He figured Joanie's religious fervor would subside once she'd gotten her babies, but it only intensified. She turned into a fanatically regular churchgoer, and started badgering him to attend mass with her and take communion, partly for his own good, and partly because she wanted to present a united front to the twins. Figuring that an hour of hypocrisy a week was a small price to pay for domestic harmony, Larry went along with the program for about a year, until the fall of 1998, when his life got turned upside down and shaken hard.

In the winter of that year, his father was diagnosed with lung cancer. The cancer spread quickly, but killed him slowly—he died a miserable death, spared no pain and no humiliation, a hell-on-earth ending fit for a Hitler or a Jeffrey Dahmer, not for a good-humored guy who'd worked his ass off in his father-in-law's auto parts store for thirty-seven years and got to enjoy maybe three months of retirement before the doctor read him his death sentence. Then, barely a month after they laid his father in the ground, Larry found himself standing in the food court of the Bellington Commons Mall, breathing hard and looking down at the gun-wielding criminal he'd just shot through the neck in a moment of adrenaline-filled terror, trying to absorb the fact that the "criminal" was a sweet-looking kid, and the gun in his hand a cheap toy, so fake-looking it was almost like some kind of cosmic joke.

The twin tragedies that blasted through his life in such quick succession—in his memory it was like they'd happened on the same day, like he'd gone straight from the cemetery to the mall—only confirmed the dark suspicions he'd been harboring for a long time: i.e., that the world was a cruel and senseless place where horrific things happened to good and bad people alike with no regard whatsoever for their goodness or badness. They just *happened*. And if some kind of God was in control of it all in the service of some inscrutable divine purpose, as Joanie liked to insist, then God was an asshole or at best an incompetent, and in either case was of absolutely no use to Larry Moon or any other human being who simply wanted to live a decent life and protect his or her loved ones from misery, injury, or death.

"Are you kidding me?" Joanie asked him, when he tried to explain this to her. "You think God is an *asshole?*"

"Pretty much."

"I got news for you," she told him. "He probably doesn't think too highly of Larry Moon, either."

"As far as I'm concerned, God can burn in hell," Larry said. "Soon as He's finished kissing my ass."

"I swear," she told him. "If I ever hear you talking like that in front of the boys—"

"What? What're you gonna do?"

She started to say something, then stopped. Larry walked away feeling like he'd won the argument. But later, when he felt like being honest with himself, he understood that from that moment on, things were never the same between them again.

———

With an adorably guilty expression on her tomboy face, Sandra Bullock removed a chocolate-covered donut from the bodice of her evening gown and surrendered it to what's-his-name, the British actor, who was not a very convincing homosexual. May chuckled, casting a hopeful sidelong glance at Ronnie.

"That was cute," she observed.

Ronnie turned slowly, appraising her with that lofty look of his, like he was some kind of Harvard professor instead of an out-of-work custodian with a criminal record.

"It doesn't make sense," he told her.

"She's hungry," May explained. "She's trying to sneak some goodies behind his back."

"I understand that, Ma. But it's the middle of the night."

"So?"

"Why's there a tray of donuts sitting out in the middle of the night?"

"It's a beauty pageant. They leave the food for the girls."

"The girls are supposed to be asleep."

"Someone must have put it there and forgot all about it."

"What planet do you live on? Nobody *forgets* a tray of donuts."

"Don't be such a pill."

"What do you want from me? It's a stupid movie."

A familiar feeling of failure, the sludge of deflated hope, spread through May's body like an illness. All she'd wanted was a pleasant Saturday evening at home, a movie and a bowl of microwave popcorn to take her son's mind off his troubles. Because something was eating at him, making him more depressed and discouraged every day.

When he first came home, Ronnie had at least made an effort to look for work, to imagine a future for himself, to address his mother in a pleasant tone of voice every once in a while. But ever since that blind date a couple of weeks ago, the optimism had leaked out of him. He had given up. He wasn't even pretending to read the Help Wanteds, and flatly refused to contact any more of the women who'd responded to his personal ad. All he did was mope around the house and complain that nothing was on TV. Tonight he seemed particularly agitated. He kept jiggling his leg and rocking his upper body back and forth, sighing like he was stuck in traffic and late for an important meeting.

"I can't believe it," he grumbled. "A whole store full of movies, and this is the crap we end up with."

Sandra Bullock was talking to the handsome guy, telling him she was going to quit the beauty pageant. You could see how much the handsome guy liked her, even if he did bite into a candy bar right when you thought he was going to kiss her.

"She looks pretty in that dress," said May. "She seemed so drab at the beginning, but now you can see how attractive she is."

"She's the ugly duckling," said Ronnie. "A retard could have written this movie."

"Well, *I* like it."

She'd chosen *Miss Congeniality* because it seemed like nice, light entertainment, nothing too serious or depressing, without the sex and bad language you found in so many of the movies these days. She and Bertha had rented it a couple of months ago and laughed themselves silly. *Maybe that was it*, May realized. Maybe she shouldn't have mentioned Bertha's name. Anything that came with her seal of approval was immediately poisoned for Ronnie. He'd make himself hate it out of spite.

"This part's funny," May said, as the talent competition began. "You're gonna love this."

Sandra Bullock was dressed in some kind of crazy getup, pigtails and a ruffled dress. She made music by rubbing her fingertip on the rims of partially filled water glasses, and it actually sounded pretty good. The crowd loved her. But then some creepy guy in a cowboy hat started moving toward the stage. When his coat fluttered open, you could see that he was carrying a gun.

"I hope he shoots her," Ronnie muttered. "Put us all out of our misery."

"If you don't like it, go read a book or something. And stop fidgeting already. You're driving me crazy with that leg."

Ronnie made an effort to sit still, but she could see that he was jumping out of his skin. He was like a restless teenager, one eye on the door, body in constant motion. May didn't like it; he'd been antsy just like this the morning he exposed himself to that poor little Girl Scout.

"I don't know what it is," he said. "I can't read anymore. It's like I forgot how to concentrate or something."

She gave him a taste of his own medicine, turning back to the movie. The British guy was tucking falsies into Sandra Bullock's bathing suit, jamming his hand right down her top. Ronnie laughed, but there was something in the laugh that bothered her, that reminded her of things she didn't like to think about.

"I wish you'd been nicer to that girl," May said. "The one you took out to dinner."

"Would you forget about her? I told you, she wasn't my type."

"I know all about your type," said May.

"You don't understand, Ma. She's a wacko."

May bit her tongue. Ronnie didn't know it, but she had called Sheila a few days after the blind date. She hadn't wanted to pry, but she was curious, and Ronnie refused to tell her anything, not even what they'd eaten for dinner. The girl hadn't been too clear on the details—Ronnie was right on that count; she *was* a bit loopy—but it was clear to May that her son had not conducted himself like a gentleman.

"You need to give people the benefit of the doubt," she said. "It's not like there's some perfect woman out there, just waiting for your call."

"You know what we need?" Ronnie said suddenly. "A computer."

"What would we do with a computer?"

Ronnie gave the matter some consideration.

"E-mail," he said.

"Who are you gonna e-mail?" May wondered.

"Not just that." Ronnie counted on his fingers. "You can pay your bills on-line, play games, make plane reservations, all kinds of stuff. Everybody has one."

"They're too expensive."

"If I learned to use a computer," Ronnie told her, "I'd have a much better chance of finding a job. You see it in all the ads. If you're not computer literate in this day and age, you're operating at a severe disadvantage. We could probably get something used for about five hundred dollars."

May got scared. She knew how Ronnie's mind worked. When he started talking like this, so smooth and reasonable, producing clever arguments like they'd just popped into his head, he was probably up to no good.

"I know what you want a computer for," she said. "You think I don't read the papers?"

"What?" Ronnie played Mr. Innocent, one of his favorite roles. "I have no idea what you're talking about."

"You want to look at those pictures."

"What pictures?"

May didn't answer. She had found some of Ronnie's pictures a few years ago, after he'd gone to jail. He had a whole library of them packed inside an old suitcase in his closet. She'd burned them in the bathtub, crying the whole time, admitting to herself for the first time that her son really was sick, that he might actually be some kind of monster.

"I don't want to look at pictures, Ma. I swear to God. I'm done with all that."

Ronnie was such a good actor, May almost let herself believe he was telling the truth. But she knew him too well.

"You stay away from computers," she told him sternly. "And I'll tell you what else, I want you to come to church with me tomorrow morning."

"No way," Ronnie said. "I'm not going to church."

"Come," May told him. "You need something positive in your life."

"That's why I want a computer."

"Would you stop it with the computer?"

"I'm gonna get one sooner or later," Ronnie told her. "Whether you like it or not."

"What's that supposed to mean?"

"I hate to say this, Ma, but you're not gonna be around forever to say no."

"That's right," she told him. "I might be gone sooner than you think."

Something cracked inside May when she said that. Because it was true: Something *was* wrong with her. The headaches that the aspirin couldn't fix. The dizzy spells when she stood up. Twice in the past week she'd woken up on her bedroom floor, without a clue as to how she'd gotten there.

"What are you gonna do when I'm gone?" she demanded in a quivering voice. "Who's gonna take care of you?"

Ronnie slid closer on the couch. He put his hand on her shoulder and gave a little squeeze, the first time he'd touched her in weeks. Tears spilled out of her eyes as if she were a big wet sponge.

"What's the matter, Ma?"

"I don't feel good, Ronnie."

"Why don't you go to the doctor?"

"What are they gonna do? I'm old. Maybe it's my time."

May placed her hand on her son's cheek. She could see how scared he was.

"Come to church tomorrow. Say a prayer for your old sick mother."

"All right," he said. "But I don't think God's gonna pay too much attention."

"He listens to everyone," she insisted. "We're all His children. Every last one of us."

Ronnie squeezed her shoulder again.

"You'll be okay, Ma. I know it."

May sniffled and gave him a smile.

"Watch the movie," she said. "This is the best part."

————

The only thing Larry really liked about going to church was how confused and upset Joanie got when she saw him there. He caught it in her expression the very first Sunday, when he'd gone up to take communion—he'd skipped confession, but as an atheist he felt free to ignore the finer points of Catholic doctrine—and passed her pew on the way back to his own. The boys' faces lit up with joy at the sight of him; they tugged on their mother's arm, whispering and pointing in his direction, forcing her to abandon her strategy of staring straight ahead and pretending not to notice him. She glanced at him in feigned surprise, squeezing out a tight little smile that wasn't quite enough to cancel out the suspicion and hostility in her eyes.

She was a little more composed by the time he "bumped into" her after mass, an encounter he pretty much assured by stationing himself on the sidewalk that led from the main exit to the parking lot. He had to wait there for nearly fifteen minutes while she mingled with friends and acquaintances in front of the church, eventually becoming entangled in what seemed like a much-too-chummy conversation with the Nigerian priest, a skinny, bug-eyed guy with a snooty accent and an unpronounceable name, Nagoobi or Ganoobi, something like that. Larry had figured him for gay—it was the accent, plus something swish and theatrical in his gestures—but he revised that opinion in light of the close attention Father Ubangi was paying to Joanie, who, as usual, had dressed for church as if Dirty Dancing were the Eighth Sacrament—short skirt, sheer black hose, tottery high heels, and a tight red top that made it quite clear why she had once been a plausible contender for the title of "Miss Nipples." She and Larry had clashed over her Sunday wardrobe in the past; the unfortunate "fucking whore" comment that had led to their separation was inspired by a cleavage-baring dress she'd worn to mass during the July heat wave. Her excuse was always the same: As a nurse, she spent most of her time trapped inside an ugly uniform; didn't she deserve to look nice one day a week?

Father Banoogi certainly seemed to think so. He kept touching her arm and nodding with such an emphatic downward motion that you would have thought it was her tits talking to him instead of her mouth. Then they started laughing about something, their mirth so prolonged and exaggerated Larry could hear it clearly from thirty yards away. He couldn't help getting irritated. What could be so goddam funny at nine-thirty on a Sunday morning? Weren't there millions of kids starving in Africa? He was all set to walk over there and break up the little lovefest when they did it themselves. Joanie and Father Nooganbi hugged on the sidewalk with such uncalled-for intensity that Larry flashed on the scandal from his own distant past.

Jesus Christ, he thought, *she's the next Mrs. Michalek. In a day or two, they'll be opening a video store.*

This whole time the twins had been standing obediently at their mother's side, somber little angels in short-sleeved white shirts and clip-on ties, but as soon as the priest turned his back they started shoving each other and airing some sort of grievance that Joanie refused to acknowledge. With her usual unflappable efficiency, she took each of the boys by a hand and tugged them along with her as she started down the path that led smack into Larry.

The boys whooped when they saw him, breaking free of their mother and charging into his arms. Only a day had gone by since he'd seen them—Joanie was letting him take the kids on Saturday—but Larry still felt starved for their company, the mere sight of them. It had been like this ever since they'd started preschool last September, and he'd been forced to muddle through the empty weekdays without their raucous company. He gathered them up, one twin under each arm, and calmly walked toward Joanie. It felt good, the whole family together on a sunny morning in a wholesome environment. If it hadn't been for the worshiping God part, he would have happily attended church on a regular basis.

"Well, well," said Joanie. "If it isn't the prodigal son."

Larry presented his cheek for a hello kiss, but she just brushed right past him and continued toward the parking lot, forcing him to pivot and hurry after her, which wasn't that easy, given that she was a fast walker, even in high heels, and he was weighed down by an unbalanced seventy-pound load of squirming twin boys. By the time he caught up, she had already popped the automatic locks on her Camry.

"Aren't people supposed to be happy to see the prodigal son?" he asked, loosening his arms so his sons could escape.

Joanie opened the back door.

"Inside, guys."

The boys clambered in, but not before Gregory asked if Daddy was joining them for lunch. Larry shrugged hopefully.

"Not today," said Joanie.

She shut the door on the twins' disappointed groans, shaking her head in mock admiration.

"Not bad," she told him. "Communion and everything."

"You look great," he told her. "Why don't we go out for a drink some night, talk things over?"

Her mouth hardened. "Don't do this to me, Larry."

"I miss you. Is that a crime?"

The thing about Joanie was that she could be tough, but not for very long. All of a sudden, she looked like she wanted to cry.

"You should have treated me better when you had the chance."

"I'm trying, baby. Can't you see that?"

"I see it, Lar. It's just too little, too late, that's all."

She circled around to the driver's side, putting the bulk of the car between them, as if she feared for her safety.

"I bet that priest's kicking himself," Larry said.

Joanie opened her door, but didn't get in. She sighed, to let him know she was losing interest.

"Why's that?"

"I saw the way he was looking at you." Larry grinned, daring her to deny it. "That vow of celibacy must be a real bitch."

This was only Larry's third week at St. Rita's, but already he felt like a regular. Slipping into what was rapidly becoming his usual spot—right side, fourth row from the back, seat closest to the aisle—he nodded a friendly good morning to the neighbors. The whole gang was there: the sloppy guy with the problem dandruff and the barbershop quartet baritone, the nervous middle-aged lady who wore an asthma inhaler on a chain around her neck, the straight-backed senior citizen with the military brush cut who, if the past two weeks were any guide, would weep quietly throughout the entire mass, pausing only to blow another majestic honk into his dirty handkerchief.

He'd chosen this particular spot less out of solidarity with the misfits and loners who favored the back of the church—not that he was ashamed to count himself among them—than for the clear angle it afforded on Joanie and the boys, who made it a habit to sit on the left side of the aisle, about a dozen rows from the front, in the section of the church favored by families with young children. He liked the feeling of power it gave him, being able to see without being seen, knowing that she probably wanted to turn around and get a fix on where he was sitting but that her pride and stubborness wouldn't allow it. Luckily, the boys had no such scruples. One or the other of them would check on Larry every few minutes, flashing him a shy smile or a quick wave that he'd acknowledge with an equally discreet thumbs-up of his own.

The processional began, and Larry rose along with the rest of the audience. He was pleasantly surprised to see that Joanie was wearing pants, the tight black ones with no pockets to spoil the rear view, and her miracle underwear that functioned exactly as promised on the package, making "unsightly panty lines vanish!" (If he hadn't known better, he would have thought she'd dispensed with the underwear altogether.) In any case, her ass was on full display in all its ample glory, and he'd have lots of opportunity in the next forty-five minutes to give it his rapt and reverent attention. This was probably not the kind of Sunday worship the Pope would have approved of, but Larry had a feeling His Holiness was not an Ass Man.

Larry's enthusiasm for his wife's tits had waned a little over the years—pregnancy and breast-feeding had changed them, both physically and conceptually—but his admiration for her ass had remained constant, even as the inevitable middle-aged spread had begun to set in. As Joanie would have been the first to admit, her ass had expanded, but it had done so in a nice, welcoming way, becoming ever rounder and softer without losing its essential shapeliness. And for all that she fretted about it, she never tried to hide her ass the way lots of women her age did. Her pants were tight, her skirts short, her shorts even shorter. Even at church, she was happy to give the world an eyeful. And don't think the world—or at least Larry Moon—wasn't grateful.

In a funny way—a sadly ironic way, really—Larry wanted her more now that they were separated than he had during the last two years of their marriage. Ever since he'd fired the shots that had killed poor Antoine Harris, he'd lost his taste for sex, among other pleasures. Joanie was always the one trying to initiate things, and Larry had been frequently unable to perform. It got to the point where she started bugging him about going on Viagra, which, in retrospect, was probably a good idea but seemed like an insult at the time. After a while he started resenting her sexuality, and even feeling a little threatened by it, which is probably why he freaked out so much when she dressed like a slut. At the same time, though, he'd taken a certain amount of pride in having such an overtly sexy wife, knowing that he'd once been man enough to win her, even if he didn't quite know what to do about her anymore.

Now that she had left him, though, and he could no longer take her body for granted—he didn't see her getting dressed in the morning, or peeling off her rumpled uniform at night—he found himself hungering for her again, in the same simple way he'd hungered for her back when he was a bouncer at Kahlua's, or a bridegroom in a tuxedo, or a rookie cop on lunch break, with his gun belt around his ankles. Viagra would not be necessary, he was pretty damn sure of that. But it was all moot, because she was slipping away from him, and there was nothing he could do but watch her from a distance and wish things were otherwise.

Thus preoccupied, he didn't notice when Ronald James McGorvey and his mother entered the holy sanctuary. They arrived late, maybe ten minutes after mass had begun, and must have walked right past him.

Why they didn't just take a seat in the rear was a mystery he wondered about later. If they'd just slipped quietly into the back row, maybe nothing would have happened. But instead they marched straight down the center aisle, where everyone could see them, and squeezed into a pew a couple of rows behind the one where Joanie and the twins were kneeling.

Larry registered the disturbance they created without understanding its cause. It started as a kind of collective whisper that increased in volume until it all but drowned out Father Mugabe—Larry had finally figured out his last name—who actually pressed a finger to his lips and shushed the congregation, as if they were a bunch of unruly schoolchildren. But the hubbub only intensified, the angry buzz of voices accompanied by an abrupt surge of movement, whole families fleeing their pews as if someone had released a stink bomb, indignantly clogging the center aisle.

"What happened?" Larry asked his neighbor.

"Dunno," said the sloppy guy. Dandruff frosted the shoulders of his navy suit like a light snowfall. "Heart attack, maybe."

The weepy senior citizen turned around.

"Someone probably threw up," he speculated with a sniffle. "Saturday night at the gin mill."

Larry leaned into the aisle to get a better view. The displaced worshipers were migrating across the aisle, their counterparts on the right side skooching over to make room. This process had left an odd hole on the left side of the church, three rows more or less vacant now, except for an old woman and a bald guy who was partially obstructing his view of Joanie.

"Nobody threw up," said the lady with the inhaler. "It's that disgusting man from Blueberry Court. He's probably playing with himself."

As if to assist in confirming this ID, McGorvey turned like a perp taking his mug shot, displaying his profile for Larry's benefit. He was wearing a hideous suit, a beige polyester monstrosity with big lapels and the kind of stitching you usually saw on blue jeans. As McGorvey pivoted back to the front of the church—Father Mugabe was continuing the mass as though nothing had happened— Larry's son Phillip turned around and waved, revealing his beautiful, innocent face to the pervert.

Instead of flashing his customary thumbs-up, Larry gestured angrily for the boy to turn around. Phil seemed confused at first, then a little hurt, but he did what his father wanted. He whispered something to Gregory, who appealed to Larry with a quizzical expression on his broad, flat face. Barely four years old, and he already seemed so much less vulnerable than his brother, so much better able to take care of himself. Larry shook his head, waving both arms as if signaling to an airplane.

"Something wrong?" asked the sloppy guy.

"My kids are up there. Just two feet away from that shitbag."

"Excuse me?" said the asthmatic woman. "Did you just say what I thought you did?"

"Sorry," said Larry.

What he couldn't understand was why Joanie hadn't moved with the others. Why stay behind, letting a convicted sex offender feast his eyes on your children—*my children!* Larry thought—so he could think about them later when he went home and jerked off to some hideous fantasy. It was like she was doing it to spite him, to remind him of the fact that she'd never approved of what she called his "obsession" with Ronnie McGorvey.

"You've got to let go of it," she'd told him. "It's not healthy."

"I'm just trying to protect our kids."

"Are you sure? Because it seems like this is more about you than it is about them."

"What's that supposed to mean?"

"I don't know, Lar. Maybe if you had a little less time on your hands—"

"Maybe I should do a little more yard work," he proposed. "That way our lawn would look really nice while our kids are being raped and murdered."

"Forget it," she told him. "Forget I even mentioned it."

He managed to keep his cool all the way into the homily, telling himself that he wasn't going to make a scene, not in church, not in front of his kids. But then the priest started talking about Jesus, how He loved absolutely everyone, even the lowest of the low, the lepers and prostitutes and convicted criminals, the reviled and despised, the forsaken and friendless. The way Father Mugabe talked, you would have thought Ronnie McGorvey was a character from the Bible, a pal of Barabbas and a neighbor of Mary Magdalene.

What about Holly Colapinto? he wanted to shout. *Jesus sure had a funny way of showing His love for her.*

He tried to distract himself by examining the stained-glass windows, but his eyes strayed to one of the stations of the cross, Jesus bent double under the weight of His terrible burden, being jeered by the soldiers. *That's the problem with these people*, he thought. *They worship suffering. They want the worst to happen.*

"So please ask yourself," Father Mugabe intoned. "Am I truly loving my neighbor as myself? Is my heart open to the grace of God, or is it sealed shut by the glue of anger, the nails of vengeance?"

Larry stood up to leave, he couldn't bear another word of it. But just as he was rising from his seat and stepping into the aisle, Phillip turned again, smiling so sweetly that Larry couldn't help but mirror the expression, which would have been perfectly fine except that Ronnie McGorvey turned at the exact same moment, so that Larry found himself smiling, with a heart full of love, right into the face of the child killer. As if to mock him, the child killer smiled back.

Don't you dare, Larry thought. Instead of heading for the vestibule he found himself moving forward, toward the altar, toward his family, toward the grinning pervert.

"Don't you dare fucking smile at me!"

Larry hadn't wanted it to come to this. He'd asked McGorvey to leave in a polite voice, but the son-of-a-bitch refused. Then the old lady started in, telling Larry he should be ashamed of himself, disrupting mass like this, violating a holy sacrament. And then Joanie joined the chorus, pleading with him to stop, to not do anything stupid in front of the boys. *As if I'm the problem*, Larry thought bitterly. He'd taken hold of McGorvey's arm, but the pervert had resisted, squirming out of his grasp and diving to the floor. Now he was cowering at his mother's feet, his arms wrapped tightly around the kneeler.

"Stand up like a man," Larry told him. "Don't make me come and get you."

"Just leave him alone," said the old lady. "He never did anything to you."

"Really," said Joanie. "This is not the time or the place."

Larry had no choice but to squeeze into the pew and grab hold of Ronnie's legs, down by the ankles. He squatted and pulled, but McGorvey's grip was tenacious.

"Please," the old woman squealed. "Please don't hurt him!"

"Ushers!" the priest was shouting. "Remove this man."

Larry wasn't sure which man they were talking about. He pulled even harder.

"Lawrence Moon," Joanie said, employing that overly rational tone favored by people talking to lunatics or very small children. "You need to stop this right now."

Larry glanced up at his wife.

"Not now, Joanie." He gave another pull, and felt the pervert's grip start to loosen. "I've almost got him."

"Oh my God!" the old woman screamed, an edge of hysteria entering her voice. "You can't do that!"

Larry shifted his attention back to the business at hand, suddenly understanding what had gotten the mother so worked up. It wasn't Ronnie's fingers that had given way, it was his pants. They were sliding down right in front of his eyes, revealing the hairy crack of the pervert's ass, the blasphemous pallor of his butt cheeks. Larry twisted his neck hard, averting his gaze from the grisly spectacle.

"Oh, Jesus," he groaned, loosening his grip so abruptly that he almost lost his balance.

Ronnie scrambled awkwardly to his feet, yanking up his pants, his face flushed with embarrassment. He looked at Larry as if he was about to cry.

"You're the pervert!" he shouted. "You trying to rape me or something?"

"Shut your goddam mouth," said Larry.

He glanced sheepishly at Joanie, who was staring at him in stern

254 | TOM PERROTTA

disapproval, hugging the boys close to her body. She'd actually placed her hands over their eyes, as if shielding them from some unspeakable horror.

"I'm sorry," he explained. "I wasn't trying to pull his pants down."

Larry felt a hand on his shoulder. It was one of the ushers, an old man with a frightened expression.

"Please," he said. "Please just leave."

"We'll both go," Larry said.

He grabbed Ronnie by the ear and yanked him out of the pew, surprised by his sudden lack of resistance. Twisting the cartilage between his thumb and forefinger—just like the nuns used to do—and moving at a brisk pace, he led the cringing pervert down the aisle like a misbehaving child, past the startled but not disapproving faces of the parishioners. As he approached the vestibule, he saw his own neighbors—the sloppy guy, the asthmatic woman, the sad old fellow—nodding with quiet satisfaction as he ejected the evil man from the Lord's House.

"Some Christian," Ronnie muttered, contorting his head in what looked like a painful way to make this observation.

"That's where you fucked up," Larry told him as he kicked open the exit door. "I'm no more of a Christian than you are."

The sunlight seemed harsh and baleful after the dimness inside, and Larry was suddenly at a loss. You couldn't just drag someone out of church by their ear and then simply release them as if nothing had happened. You needed to *do* something—or at least say something—that would bring a sense of closure to the situation, do some kind of justice to the drama you'd just enacted. But his mind was blank. He stood paralyzed at the top of the stairs, squinting into the merciless glare.

"You wanna let go of my ear?" Ronnie inquired.

"Not yet," Larry said.

They stood like that for another moment or two, Larry distracted, McGorvey bent double, bearing his pain and humiliation without complaint. Even his patience was annoying. For lack of anything better to do, Larry twisted the ear a little harder, amazed by the flexibility of human cartilage. Ronnie gave a soft whimper, his knees buckling.

"That's for little Holly," Larry told him.

This is the moment I've been waiting for, he thought. McGorvey finally in his power, just the two of them, man-to-man. He had a lot to say to him, stuff he'd been saving up for months. But for some reason, all he could think about was his father's funeral.

The sun had been blinding that morning, just like it was now. Larry remembered how lost he'd felt, stepping into the cruel brightness after the funeral mass, seeing the hearse at the curb, the driver in his dark suit standing so casually by the open back door. The desolation of that moment had imprinted itself on his skin and gotten absorbed into his blood. It was permanent now, as much a part of him as his hair or his teeth.

"I'll let you look at my ass again," Ronnie offered.

Larry didn't remember pushing him, just a flash of anger and the blur of Ronnie tumbling down, the sad *whump* when he hit the sidewalk. And the awful way he lay there, face to the concrete, not moving, the arms and legs at all those weird angles.

Larry barely had a moment to absorb the shock of what he'd done—*OhmyGod, not again*—when he was distracted by a surge of activity at his back, the church doors flying open, the people spilling out, the oppressive sensation of being surrounded by an angry mob, an accusatory chorus of gasps and exclamations, Father Mugabe grabbing him angrily by the shoulder and demanding to know what he'd done.

"I didn't mean to hurt him," Larry said, and the words sounded lame even to himself, worse than dishonest. He'd said the exact same thing in the mall, staring down at the awestruck face of Antoine Harris.

When he finally worked up the courage to turn back around, he saw, to his amazement and immense relief, that Ronnie was not dead, or even very badly hurt. He was sitting on the sidewalk with his legs splayed out, his right arm dangling limply from its shoulder, falling across his chest as if he were reaching for a sword. He grabbed the injured arm by the elbow and raised it slightly, the palm upraised, as if making some sort of offering to the spectators. He appeared to be in terrible pain, but not so terrible that he couldn't muster a smile.

"I am gonna sue your ass so bad," he told Larry. "When you get outta jail, you can come visit me in my mansion."

REASONS IT MIGHT BE TRUE

KATHY'S FIRST REACTION WAS RELIEF. FOR OVER A WEEK, SHE'D been obsessing over this mysterious Sarah, mother of Lucy, and the possibility that Todd was having an affair with her. But the moment her imaginary rival limped into the house with her daughter clamped to one leg and her much older husband at her side, Kathy's fears seemed misplaced and exaggerated, the product of an overheated imagination. Despite the many warning signs—there were six, to be exact; she'd listed them yesterday during a lull at the VA Hospital— it was hard to believe that Todd could be cheating on her with such a plain and frazzled-looking woman. It just wasn't like him. His entire romantic history—she'd made it her business to know this— had consisted of one stunningly pretty girl after another after another (herself included, she wasn't ashamed to admit it), and she was convinced that old habits like that died hard.

"Welcome," she said, her voice animated by a sudden infusion of friendliness. "It's so nice to finally meet you."

Sarah trudged forward with awkward tenacity, dragging her human ball and chain. Her hair was frizzy from the humidity, and her lipstick was the wrong shade of red, clashing both with her skin tone and her shirt, as though she were a teenager who still hadn't quite mastered the grown-up art of color coordination. Kathy almost felt sorry for her, she had so completely failed to live up to the paranoid image she had concocted of the Other Woman, the Stay-at-Home Mom/Sex Goddess at the Town Pool.

"This is for you," Sarah said, holding out a bottle of chilled white wine.

"Thanks." Kathy glanced at the label, an Australian chardonnay, more expensive than what she and Todd were used to drinking. "That's sweet of you."

The husband thrust out his hand and introduced himself as Richard Pierce. He was a skinny, potbellied man with close-cropped gray hair and a neatly trimmed salt-and-pepper beard, wearing pleated navy shorts, a pink Ralph Lauren oxford with the sleeves rolled up, and Topsiders with no socks. Kathy didn't approve of any of these choices in isolation, but taken together they gave him a confident, surprisingly distinguished air.

"Nice place," he remarked, with obvious insincerity.

"We just rent," Kathy explained. "We'd love to buy something, but we're not quite ready yet."

"It's a tough market," Richard observed. "Even the little starter homes are way overpriced."

"Tell me about it. It's hard to keep up with our monthly expenses, let alone save for a down payment."

She glanced away from Richard just in time to see Lucy peeking out from behind Sarah's right leg, a delicate elfin thing with rosy cheeks and silky blond hair, so different from her dark, curly-haired mother, who, despite her small size, gave off a strong impression of squat peasant solidity. Being the willowy child of plump parents,

Kathy was familiar with the fluky nature of genetic transmission, and knew better than to comment on the apparent lack of resemblance. She got down on one knee to address Lucy on her own level.

"And who is this pretty girl?"

In lieu of responding, Lucy pressed her face into the back of her mother's thighs.

"She's a little shy," Sarah explained.

"Well, I know someone who's very excited about your visit."

Kathy beckoned to Aaron, who was watching from the hallway, his face a horror movie mask of dread and despair.

"Come on, honey. Come say hello."

He held up both hands and shook his head no, as if Lucy were a goon who'd come to collect a large sum of money he was in no position to repay.

"Aaron, you've been waiting for this all day."

Richard knelt down and placed his hand on Lucy's shoulder. In this position, his face was only a few inches from Kathy's, and she saw that he'd grown his beard to artfully compensate for a weak chin.

"Is that your little boyfriend?" he asked, directing a sly wink at Kathy.

Kathy forced herself to smile, even as she hurried to stand up. She didn't like being winked at, especially by older, bearded men. It was a constant thing at the VA Hospital, an epidemic of not-so-subtle innuendo. She got it from everyone—these battered, geriatric vets, toothless and shell-shocked, their limbs missing or palsied, some drooling and incontinent, all of them winking at her like sleazy British game show hosts. And now this guy, right in her own house.

"Not *boyfriend*," Lucy said with bitter vehemence, as if she'd been accused of a crime she hadn't committed.

Kathy smiled at Sarah.

"They just nap together," she quipped. "It's not like it means anything."

Sarah smiled back, but only a little, and only after an uncomfortable hesitation. It was odd, Kathy thought. She didn't look like a prude.

"Todd's getting some beer," she reported. "He should be back any minute."

Kathy had never been one of those women with a thing for older men. She'd always been a little grossed out when one of her girlfriends confessed to a crush on a gray-haired professor, or an affair with a "senior colleague." It seemed perverse to her, depriving yourself of the best years of your lover's life, fast-forwarding to the inevitable period of decay and decline, the saggy pecs and expanding waistline, the cholesterol and blood pressure medicines, the godawful snoring they all did, the ear wax and nose hair, the need to be compassionate and understanding if the plumbing didn't work the way it used to.

The thing that really gave her the willies, though, was the idea of the guy having a massive heart attack in the middle of sex, Nelson Rockefeller-style, dying while he was still inside you. Everybody thought about it from the man's perspective, like it was some kind of triumphant exit (*What a way to go,* they'd sigh. *At least he died happy*). Did anybody consider the poor woman? Could there be anything more horrible? It would probably take a few minutes for you to even realize what had happened—you might just think he'd had an especially intense orgasm or something—and the whole time you'd be lying there, hugging an old man's corpse, talking dirty into its waxy ear. Just the thought of it was enough to make you start sleeping with teenagers again.

"Forget the old geezers," she'd said, after her friend Anna had described a fantasy in which her sixty-eight-year-old father-in-law seduced her at the family vacation house. "Stick with the young studs."

"But he's so vital for his age," Anna replied. "And he's done so much with his life. You really feel like he appreciates things. Good food, good books, a vigorous morning walk. I'm sure he'd be like that with a younger woman. Polite and appreciative, and maybe even passionate, but in a dignified way."

Oddly enough, Kathy found herself flashing back to this conversation while listening to Richard talk about his experiences as a restaurant consultant. Despite his yucky clothes and weak chin and annoying tendency to wink, there was a kind of expansive ease about him, a wealth of experience and opinions that reminded her of something else Anna had said about her father-in-law.

"He's a man of the world in the old-fashioned sense. Guys our age don't have the same sort of gravitas."

Todd didn't, that was for sure. He was a thirty-one-year-old man who'd accomplished nothing with his life except to father a child and avoid paying work for longer than she'd imagined possible. It wasn't so much that Richard had achieved anything particularly significant, or even that he'd reached some especially impressive level of financial success, it was simply that he had some experiences to share, some stories to tell about his interactions with the world. All Todd could do was sit there and ask the occasional question.

"Are these guys Chinese?"

"Of course not," said Richard. "That's the beauty of it. They're a bunch of fat cats from Tennessee. But they think they can create a chain of Chinese restaurants authentic enough to fool the average American boob. After all, people just like them have already gotten rich doing the same thing with Mexican and Italian food. Why not Chinese, right?"

"It just doesn't seem right," Todd reflected. "Chinese people should run Chinese restaurants."

"That's why they want to call it Charlie Chopsticks. They figure they can have a cartoon logo of this bucktoothed Chinaman, maybe even use him as a spokesman in commercials, and that would some-how convince the dining public that Chinese people are actually involved in running the restaurant. I keep telling them that it's a racist image that's going to cause them no end of trouble, but they just don't get it. They say, what's racist about buckteeth? And Char-lie, what's the problem with that? It's just a name, it has nothing to do with Vietnam. I say, what if a bunch of northerners started a chain of Southern restaurants called Redneck Roy's House of Grits? How would you feel about that? And they all nod their heads like, Hey, great idea! Let's do that next year!"

"Have you suggested alternatives?" Kathy asked.

"That's my job. I've given them at least a hundred. My favorite is Chow Down Here. It kinda sounds Chinese while actually com-municating in idiomatic English. To me, it's a home run, but the clients hate it."

"I liked Chairman Mouth," said Sarah. "That was clever."

Richard shook his head sadly.

"You can imagine how that went over. No one's going to get it, they said, and anyway, we're not naming our restaurants after a communist dictator. So I said, you want something American, how about Wok 'n Roll?"

Todd laughed. "You could do Rock Around the Wok, or Wok Around the Clock. Or Wok Star."

"Wok Steady," added Richard. "Wok On By. I have two solid pages of wok puns."

Sarah smiled fondly at her husband. "You've been wokkin' overtime."

It was such a lame joke, Kathy couldn't help laughing. She sipped the excellent wine her guests had brought and thought about how long it had been since they'd spent an evening like this, meeting new people, enjoying some interesting adult conversation while the kids played quietly at their feet. It wasn't what she'd expected—it was, in fact, quite the opposite of what she'd expected—but she was more than happy to admit that she'd been wrong, that she'd gotten herself all worked up over nothing.

The only thing that still bothered her was this: If Sarah was what Todd said she was—i.e., a casual acquaintance, the mother of one of Aaron's playmates, a parent he occasionally bumped into at the pool; in short, no one she needed to worry about—then why all the secrecy? Why the denial? (Those were the first two entries on her six-item list, entitled *Reasons It Might Be True*.) Why had she had to hear about Sarah from her three-year-old son, instead of her husband? And why, when she first mentioned Sarah's name, had Todd pretended not to know who she was talking about?

"Sarah?" he said. "I don't know any Sarah."

"Sarah from the pool? She has a little girl named Lucy?"

They were lying in bed in the dark, so she couldn't see his face. But there was a hesitation before he answered, a slight pause that smacked of calculation.

"Oh, Lucy's mom. That's right. I forgot her name was Sarah."

"Aaron says he plays with her every day."

"Not every day."

"He says he takes naps at her house."

"One time," said Todd. "We got caught in a rainstorm. The kids fell asleep in the stroller."

"He made it sound like an everyday thing."

"That's an exaggeration. Maybe two or three times, but not every day."

Now it was Kathy's turn to pause.

"So what do you and this Sarah do while the kids are napping?"

"What do you think we do? We hang out. We talk."

"Is that all?"

"Jesus, Kathy. If you're accusing me of something, just come out and say so."

"I'm not accusing you of anything. I'm just trying to figure out why you never told me."

"It didn't seem like earth-shattering news. Am I not allowed to make friends with the other parents?"

"You go to her house, Todd."

"Just a couple of times. Mostly we just see each other at the pool."

"What kind of bathing suit does she wear?"

"I don't know."

"You haven't noticed? Because in my experience men are pretty much aware of what a woman's wearing at the pool."

"I'll take notes tomorrow and bring you back a full report."

"Is she pretty?"

"Not really," said Todd, with surprising quickness. "Not like you."

"Right."

"Come to the pool tomorrow. See for yourself."

"I can't just come to the pool tomorrow, Todd. I have a job, remember? I'm the only person in this family who has one."

"You think it's not work, caring full-time for a little kid? You should try it sometime."

I'd like to, she wanted to tell him. *I'm happy to switch places whenever you say the word.* But she didn't want to change the subject to the bar exam, and their less-than-perfect domestic arrangements. She just wanted to know what the hell was going on between him and Sarah while she was stuck inside the hospital all day, interviewing broken old men about Midway and Guadalcanal.

"I've got an idea," she said. "Why don't we invite Sarah and her husband over for dinner next week?"

"I don't think so," Todd mumbled.

"Why not? Doesn't she have a husband?"

"She has one. I just don't think he's the nicest guy in the world."

"Oh, so she complains to you about her marriage, does she?"

"Not exactly. I'm just reading between the lines."

Kathy's stomach hurt, and she wasn't breathing right. She hadn't felt this sort of sexual panic since high school, when she found out that Mark Rovane had cheated on with her with slutty Ashley Peterson a week before the junior prom, making out with her at a crowded party while Kathy was home with the flu. She should have told him to fuck off, but she was weak, and didn't want to miss the prom. So she went with Mark and hated herself the whole time. When she got home that night, she made a vow never to be put in that position again.

"Invite them to dinner, Todd. I'd like to get to know my son's friends. And my husband's, too."

Todd dragged his feet for a couple of days.

"I'll do it," Kathy said. "Just tell me her last name so I can look it up in the phone book."

"I don't know her last name."

"All right," she said. "I'll take tomorrow afternoon off. I'll meet you at the pool."

"Calm down," he said. "I'll take care of it. Now would you just chill out already?"

The kids ate first—hot dogs and Tater Tots and baby carrots—then migrated into the living room to watch *Thomas and the Magic Railroad*, a movie Kathy found disturbing on any number of levels. It was a cinematic catastrophe, shifting clumsily between the inane antics of the talking trains and a bewildering psychodrama starring Peter Fonda, of all people. As a filmmaker, Kathy felt insulted and even polluted by the sheer awfulness of the storytelling; as a parent, she was mystified that her normally rambunctious three-year-old could tolerate, let alone enjoy, its art house pacing and dark Freudian overtones. But Aaron would have watched it every day if she let him, and Lucy seemed willing to trust his recommendation.

In the past couple of years, as if in apology for his failure to pass the bar exam, Todd had become a surprisingly talented cook. Tonight he'd grilled salmon, and it was done to perfection, a vivid tic-tac-toe board of grill marks seared into the flesh of each moist, flaky fillet. He beamed as the compliments poured in.

"This is delicious," said Sarah.

"You could start a restaurant," said Richard. "House of Todd."

"Your wine is terrific," Todd replied.

"Speaking of wine . . ." Richard raised his glass. "Here's to the chef, and to his lovely wife. *Salud.*"

There was a slightly awkward pause after the toast, a moment of collective floundering they masked with tentative, encouraging smiles. Kathy was about to fill the space by asking Richard if it might be possible for her to film some of his meetings with the

Charlie Chopsticks executives. For too long, she'd put off planning a new project, on the assumption that Todd would pass the bar and find a good job, freeing her to take a break for a couple of years, spend a little more time with Aaron, maybe have another baby. But recently she'd come to accept the possibility that it might not happen, and it had occurred to her that it might be fun to do some kind of comic documentary, something lighthearted but socially engaged, a little hipper and edgier than her current project. The creation of a nationwide chain of Chinese restaurants by a bunch of clueless white guys seemed like just the sort of vehicle she was looking for, a way to shine an amusing light on what was actually a troubling phenomenon: the voracious march of American business, its insatiable need to devour everything in its path—other people's history, their cuisine, their ethnic identities and cultural traditions—and then spit it back out as bland commodities for sale to middle America. But she needed to be diplomatic, to figure out a way not to tip her satirical hand, and while she was pondering her strategy, Richard shifted the conversation in an entirely different direction.

"Lots of sturm and drang in our quiet little town, eh?"

Nobody had to ask what he was referring to. In the past couple of days, the papers and TV news had been full of Larry Moon and Ronald James McGorvey, the sensational tabloid drama of the pervert expelled from church by "the killer cop," the assault and battery charge filed against a man some people considered a hero and others a dangerous vigilante.

"It's crazy," said Sarah. "He's lucky he didn't kill the guy."

"And in church of all places," agreed Kathy. "I'm not religious myself, but I was like, is nothing sacred?"

"What I want to know," said Richard, "is what a creep like that was even doing in church."

"Which creep?" asked Sarah.

"Larry's not a creep," said Todd. "McGorvey was sitting near his family. Larry didn't like the way he was looking at his kids."

"Todd's biased," Kathy explained. "He's friends with the cop. They're both on that Committee of Concerned Parents. That's why he's defending him."

"Well, who am I supposed to defend?" Todd wondered. "The poor little child molester?"

"Nonviolent protest is one thing," said Kathy. "Throwing a man down a flight of stairs is something else."

Sarah was staring at Todd in apparent perplexity.

"I didn't know you were on that committee."

Todd shrugged. "I kinda got sucked into it. I play on Larry's football team, and he asked me to distribute some flyers."

"He's on your team?" Sarah said. "You never told me that."

Kathy heard something jarring and oddly familiar in Sarah's tone, almost as if she were a wife who resented being kept in the dark about her husband's activities. It was a tone Kathy herself had been striking a lot in the past week, and it was odd to hear it coming out of another woman's mouth.

"I just wanted to play football," said Todd, a bit defensively. "There turned out to be a little more baggage than I bargained for."

"What kind of football do you play?" asked Richard.

"Tackle," Kathy interjected. "Without pads. He comes home looking like he was in a bar fight with Mike Tyson. It's very responsible behavior for a grown man."

"It's not that bad." Todd sounded proud of himself. "Just a few bumps and bruises."

Richard plucked a piece of bread from the basket in the middle of the table.

"What's he like? Your friend the cop."

"Decent guy, I guess. Bit of a hothead."

"As a general rule," Richard said, buttering his bread as though it were an especially delicate operation, "I don't condone throwing people down the stairs, but in this particular case I can't say I feel too bad about it. Especially if this S.O.B. gets the message and finds somewhere else to live."

"Where's he gonna go?" Sarah asked. "The same exact thing will happen in the next place."

"Fine with me," declared Richard. "Just as long as it's not in my backyard. If that makes me a selfish yuppie, so be it."

"Mr. Liberal." Sarah's voice was laced with disgust. "I thought you, of all people, would be a little more tolerant."

"I am tolerant," Richard replied. "I just happen to draw the line at child molesters."

Sarah seemed more upset than the conversation merited.

"But everything else is okay, right?"

"Pretty much." Richard spoke with an air of icy calm that Kathy found unpleasant. "If consenting adults are involved, I say go for it."

Todd was studying Richard with almost as much intensity as Sarah was, and Kathy couldn't help feeling like she was missing something important. She spoke more to dispel her own discomfort than anything else.

"You know what's weird? I've never even seen this McGorvey guy."

"We did," said Sarah.

"No, we didn't," said Richard.

"Not you," said Sarah. "Me and Todd. That day at the pool, remember?"

Todd looked momentarily stumped.

"Oh yeah. I forgot about that."

"He went swimming with flippers and a mask," Sarah continued. "Everybody got out of the water. It was the middle of a heat wave, and he had that whole gigantic pool to himself. But then the cops came and kicked him out." She looked at Kathy. "He wasn't scary or anything. He was just this pathetic loser, you know?"

Richard shook his head. "Those are the ones you have to worry about."

Kathy turned to Todd. Her voice came out sharper than she'd meant it to.

"You never told me about that."

"Sure I did."

"You did not."

Todd shrugged. "I thought I did."

"I took Lucy swimming last year," said Richard, "and a kid threw up in the water. That cleared the pool pretty quick, too."

Sexual tension is an elusive thing, but Kathy thought she had a pretty good radar for it. All through dinner she'd been watching Sarah and Todd and not picking up on any suspicious behavior—no furtive eye contact or flirty repartee, no nervous laughter, nothing. But suddenly—it happened the moment Sarah said "we" in reference to herself and Todd as though it were the most natural thing in the world—it was like someone had turned a knob a hair to the right, and the radio station clicked in, so loud and clear it almost knocked her over.

Wham.

Once she became aware of the connection between them, it seemed impossible that she'd missed it before. Todd and Sarah didn't even need to *look* at each other. There was just this thick fog surrounding them, engulfing the table, the mini-climate generated by two people sharing a powerful physical and emotional bond, a force field that turned everyone else into outsiders—mere footnotes—even their lawful spouses. Kathy felt embarrassed by the realization, as if she were seeing a stranger naked, and for a couple of seconds she couldn't think of anywhere to look except straight down at her plate.

"I really respect that you're a filmmaker," Sarah was saying. "I'd give anything to be able to do something creative like that."

Kathy forced herself to look up, and when she did, Sarah seemed to have been transformed into an entirely different woman. Not beautiful, but powerful nonetheless. Maybe it was the wine she'd drunk, or the pressure of the situation—she'd been dealing with it all night, of course, while Kathy had just tuned in—but whatever the cause, her face was full of color, a feverish flush of excitement. Her eyes were glittering with what Kathy couldn't help but recognize as sexual triumph, a kind of animal pleasure. So what if she envied Kathy's career? There was only one contest between them, and Sarah had won by a mile. The most galling part of it, Kathy thought, was that her mother had been right all along.

"It's really not that creative," she replied. "It's more like an oral history."

"Still," Sarah insisted. "You're making something, contributing to the culture. What am I doing with my life?"

"You're raising a child," said Richard. "There's nothing more important than that."

On a hunch, Kathy dropped her fork and quickly ducked under the table to pick it up. She thought she would catch Todd and Sarah playing footsie, but she was mistaken. All she found down there was a forest of bare motionless legs—Todd's muscular and downy, Richard's scrawny and covered with coarse hair, Sarah's bare and tanned. She had okay legs, nothing special. Nice calves, knobby ankles, boring Birkenstocks. The only surprising thing was the polish on her toenails—somehow Kathy hadn't noticed it before—a hideous metallic blue, the kind of color a trashy twelve-year-old would have loved, nothing you'd ever expect to find on the feet of a grown woman, the mother of a young child. You would have to be crazy to wear nail polish like that, or so deeply in love that you were beyond caring.

"Kathy?" Todd's voice seemed far away, like he was talking through a cement wall. "Are you okay?"

It was getting embarrassing, she understood that. She had been hiding under the table for too long, way longer than it should have taken to simply retrieve a fork. But she didn't really want to get up just yet, to sit in her chair and carry on a civil conversation with the woman who'd stolen her husband.

She would do it, though, she knew she would. She wasn't going to make a scene, not in front of guests, not with two three-year-olds in the next room. She was going to have to get off the floor and somehow make it through dinner with her dignity intact. No tears, no accusations. She'd do it if it killed her.

"I'm fine," she said, still on her hands and knees, still staring dumbstruck at the other woman's toes. "Just give me a second."

BULLHORN

AFTER THREATENING ALL DAY TO GO TO THE FOOTBALL GAME, Todd's mother-in-law decided against it at the last minute.

"You sure?" he asked, trying to keep the pleasure out of his voice. "You're welcome to come."

"I'd like to," Marjorie lied, "but I'm a little tired. You and Aaron sure kept me hopping this afternoon."

"Looks like you're on your own," said Kathy, who was sitting beside her mother on the couch. The two women looked nothing alike—Marjorie was short and thickly built, with permed gray hair and little octagonal eyeglasses—but both were staring at him with the same unfriendly expression, like he was a grounded teenager unworthy of the trust they were placing in him.

"Suit yourself," Todd muttered. "It's your choice."

What a fool he'd been. Todd had convinced himself that the dinner party had gone okay, that he and Sarah had managed to put Kathy's suspicions to rest, at least temporarily. She certainly hadn't accused him of anything, or behaved in a way that made him think she'd noticed anything untoward. All she'd said before going to bed that night was that she'd enjoyed meeting Sarah and Richard, and thought that Lucy was a sweet little girl.

Two days later, however, her mother had showed up with three suitcases for a "surprise visit" of ominously indeterminate length, and from that moment on, Todd's activities and whereabouts couldn't have been more closely monitored if he'd been a psycho making death threats against the president. Marjorie accompanied him and Aaron everywhere—the playground, the library, the supermarket, the Town Pool, the movie theater. If Todd wanted to go for a walk after dinner, Marjorie invariably could use a little air herself. He was surprised she didn't squeeze into the bathroom with him, making small talk while he sat on the toilet, offering to scrub his back in the shower. When he managed to escape for a run in the evening, he kept expecting her to pull up beside him in a slow-moving vehicle, checking a stopwatch and shouting encouragement through the open window.

Aside from the occasional lovesick e-mail he managed to fire off while Marjorie wasn't looking, Todd hadn't had any substantial contact with Sarah for five days. He was beginning to consider desperate measures—sneaking out in the middle of the night, tossing pebbles at her bedroom window. Anything, just to be able to steal a couple of minutes alone with her, a handful of kisses. He'd gone so far as to think about applying for some kind of mindless job at Home Depot, so he could arrange to meet her during his lunch hour.

The worst of it was the pool, seeing her in their usual spot, in her little red bikini—the briefest glimpse of her shocked him like a defibrillator—and not being able to spread his towel next to hers or rub sunscreen on her back, not being able to do anything but trade lingering doleful glances from afar, conducting a short wordless conversation that always ended up with Todd offering a helpless little shrug in response to her unspoken question: *When can I see you?*

"Besides," Marjorie said, patting Kathy affectionately on the leg, "I need to spend a little time with my daughter. I've hardly said two words to her since I got here."

Todd bent over to tie his sneaker, wondering if he could slip upstairs and call Sarah from his cell phone. Maybe she could leave the house on a supermarket run or something, spend a couple of minutes with him before the game. Even that would be better than nothing. But before he could figure out the logistics, a horn sounded in the street outside.

"That's my ride." Todd leapt up and headed for the door, hoping to complete his exit before Marjorie changed her mind.

"What time will you be home?" Kathy asked.

"Hard to say. One or two, something like that."

"Be careful," Marjorie warned him, smiling like it was all in good fun. "And stay out of trouble."

You might have thought that having a felony assault charge and a potentially ruinous civil lawsuit hanging over your head would spoil your appetite for a football game, but Larry was fired up for the Guardians' season finale against the Controllers. Todd sensed it the moment he stepped into the minivan. The guy was high on adrenaline, itchy for combat. Instead of saying hello, he punched Todd in the sternum.

"You ready?" he demanded. There was a harsh, nonrhetorical intensity to the question. "You better fuckin' be ready."

"I'm ready." Todd held his gaze, but spoke in a quieter, more probing voice. "How about you? How you holding up?"

If Larry understood this as a reference to his legal problems, or the relentless media scrutiny he'd endured as a result of his arrest, he wasn't letting on.

"I'll tell you something," he said, his expression relaxing a little as they pulled away from the curb. "I've always liked being the underdog. I like stepping onto the field knowing that the other guy thinks I'm going to roll over and play dead, especially if the other guy's an arrogant, overconfident asshole. I like seeing the look on his face the first time I knock him on his ass, and he realizes he's in for a street fight."

It was an understatement to say that the Guardians were underdogs. At 0–5, they were the basement dwellers of the Midnight Touch Football League, a low-scoring, error-prone gang of amateurs who always managed to find a new way of snatching defeat from the jaws of victory, at least on those rare occasions when victory was even a vague possibility. The week before, they'd been whupped by the lowly Technicians, a team that hadn't won a game in three seasons, by a score of 20–0. The Controllers, on the other hand, were 4–1, with an explosive big-play offense that regularly racked up forty and fifty points a game. In all likelihood, they were already looking past the Guardians to next week's championship showdown with their archrivals, the Auditors.

"These guys are good athletes," Larry conceded, "but they're a bunch of crybabies. You clean their clocks a few times, they just wanna pick up their ballie and go home."

"Be nice to pull off an upset," said Todd, gazing sadly down Sarah's street as they drove past, wondering what she was up to, if she missed him as badly as he missed her.

"We gotta shut down their running game early. That's the key. Their passing game's more erratic than it looks on paper."

It seemed surreal that Larry was so focused on football at such a turbulent moment in his life. Todd's own situation wasn't half as dire, and he'd barely given the game a passing thought all week.

"How's your lawyer?" he asked. "Are you satisfied with your representation?"

"He's no Johnnie Cochran," said Larry. "But I'm no O.J. Simpson, either."

"Must be a pretty scary time for you."

"Scary?" Larry turned to Todd in what appeared to be genuine surprise. "You think there's a jury in the world that's going to convict me of assaulting Ronnie McGorvey? No wonder you failed the bar exam. They'll probably give me a medal."

Larry circulated among the Guardians during pregame warmups, accosting and cajoling them as they did their jumping jacks and hurdler's stretches. He was head cheerleader one minute, Vince Lombardi the next.

"We're tougher than they are!" he proclaimed, batting Tony Correnti vigorously on both sides of his head, as if he were wearing a helmet. "Am I right? I said, AM I RIGHT?"

"Fuckin' A," Correnti replied, hauling off and smacking Larry right back. "They're a bunch of shithead stockbrokers."

Grinning, Larry moved on to his next victim, hammering DeWayne on his unpadded shoulders with both fists, as if trying to pound him into the ground.

"Who we gonna beat?" he demanded.

"Controllers!" DeWayne bellowed.

Pete Olaffson was next in line. As if performing a dance they knew by heart, Larry and Pete locked hands and slammed their bodies together, three times on the right, three times on the left.

"Who's a winner?"

"I'm a winner!"

"Go Guardians!"

"Go Guardians!"

"Kick some ass!"

"Kick some ass!"

Larry swaggered over to Todd with a bravado that would have been comical if not for the look of stone-cold conviction on his face.

"Who's scoring the first touchdown?" he yelled, pummeling Todd's stomach as if working on a speedbag.

"I am!" Todd sang out obediently, tightening his abs to deflect the blows.

"I got second!" cried DeWayne.

"I'll take number three," volunteered Bart Williams.

It felt like a joke at first, a parody of the high school coaches they all remembered with varying degrees of fondness and resentment, but after a while—the evolution was so gradual as to be almost imperceptible—it turned serious. Todd had seen this phenomenon in every sport he'd ever played, ever since he was old enough for Little League. The mood of a team was a delicate, volatile thing—it only took one person to change the whole chemistry.

Larry's feverish optimism spread among his teammates like a virus. By the time they lined up for the opening kickoff, the Guardians—Todd included—had worked themselves into a frenzy of barely suppressed excitement. As if he'd drunk some sort of magic potion, Bart Williams, an indifferent placekicker, charged forward and connected with a monster boot. The football rose high above the lights and into the night sky, soaring over the heads of the dumbstruck return men, and bouncing out of the end zone for a touchback.

If the Auditors were the thugs of the Midnight Touch Football League, the Controllers were the pretty boys, spandex-clad twenty-somethings from the financial industries who arrived at the field in a caravan of BMWs, Lexuses, and Cadillac SUVs, bringing along a platoon of hot women who apparently didn't mind staying up late to cheer the boys on, a sure sign they were girlfriends instead of wives.

There was a cockiness about them as they broke the huddle and lined up for first down, a palpable air of command. The quarterback—he was lanky and sandy-haired, with chiseled features and a deep beach-house tan—gazed across the line of scrimmage with the unquestioned self-assurance of a guy who'd been pulling down six figures since the day he graduated from B-school, a hotshot with a Palm Pilot, a German luxury car, and another fat bonus right around the corner.

That could have been me, Todd thought, shifting uneasily from foot to foot in the secondary. He made this observation without shame or regret, accepting the truth of it with an almost perverse sense of pride. He felt okay about where he was, over on this side of the line with Larry and DeWayne, men who eked out forty or fifty grand a year and struggled to scrape together the down payment on a two-bedroom cape that needed work, men for whom a new car was a twice-a-decade extravagance.

On the first play from scrimmage, the Controllers ran straight up the middle. From his godlike perspective at free safety, Todd watched a hole open in the Guardians' front line, a momentary gap between Olaffson and Correnti just big enough for the Controllers' halfback—a wiry speedster who supposedly competed in Iron Man triathalons in the off-season—to shoot through. Reading the play perfectly from middle linebacker, Larry rushed forward on a collision course with the ballcarrier. Somehow, though, the collision never occurred. Dancing a quick little stutter step that left his would-be tackler with two handfuls of air and a faceful of artificial turf, the Iron Man slipped into the open field, loping straight toward Todd, the defender of last resort.

He was one of those shifty runners, a virtuoso of jukes and misdirection, eyes going one way, shoulders another, legs somewhere else, but Todd knew enough to stay put and focus on the hips, (*Gentlemen,* Coach Breeden used to say, in one of his rare aphorisms that had worn well over the years, *the hips don't lie. Not in the boudoir and not on the field of play.*) Realizing he wasn't going to elude his man with fancy footwork, the halfback tried to do it honestly, veering toward the sideline with a sudden and disheartening burst of speed. He almost turned the corner, but Todd just managed to trip him up from behind with a desperate, diving tackle that almost certainly saved a touchdown.

The girlfriends on the Controller bench rose as one, whooping it up like cheerleaders as the Iron Man bounced to his feet, brushing nonexistent dirt off his hairless, freakishly muscled legs with his gloved hands.

"Way to go, Zack!"

"Controllers rule!"

"Go team!"

Todd picked himself up a little more gingerly, trying to ignore the burning sensation in his right knee, which he'd skinned on the unforgiving carpet. The Iron Man pulled out his mouthpiece and grinned.

"Dude," he said, bestowing a comradely pat on Todd's shoulder, "I'm gonna keep you busy."

Jogging back to the huddle, Todd couldn't help noticing the wilted expressions on the faces of his teammates, the sense of impending doom that had replaced their irrational exuberance of a moment ago. All it had taken was one bad play to wake them from their collective dream, to remind them that they were a bunch of losers due for an ass-whipping. But Todd wasn't in the mood to fold just yet.

"Come on!" he said, clapping his hands sharply. "Buckle down! Let's play some D!"

"That was my bad," Larry said, picking up the thread. "It won't happen again."

"Damn straight," said DeWayne. "Next time you *hit* that sucker."

"Let's tighten the fuck up!" Correnti growled.

Like the cocky bastards that they were, the Controllers repeated the exact same play on the next snap, and it unfolded in the exact same way, except that this time Larry didn't fall for the stutter step. He plugged the hole like Dick Butkus in some grainy highlight film from 1971, slamming into the halfback with a chest-to-chest tackle so bone-crunchingly ferocious that Todd felt a shudder of sympathy pass through his own body from ten yards away. The Iron Man took his time getting up, and when he did he had the look on his face that Larry had described in the van: the woozy, unhappy expression of a guy who suddenly realizes that his cakewalk has just turned into a street fight.

To Todd's amazement—not to mention the amazement of the Controllers and their girlfriends—it turned out to be a game, a low-scoring, evenly matched slugfest that stayed interesting right to the end. The Controllers scored first, after recovering a Bart Williams fumble deep in Guardians' territory near the end of the second quarter. The Guardians evened things up early in the second half, moving methodically down the field on an eighty-yard touchdown drive. Late in the fourth quarter, the Controllers kicked a short field goal, leaving them with a precarious 10–7 lead as the Guardians took possession of the ball for what was probably their last offensive series of the game.

On a rational level, the Guardians were the team who should have been worried. They were losing; time was running out. But as Todd stepped up to the line on first down, he understood, along with everyone else on the field, that it was their opponents who were running scared. With a little under two minutes to go, the Controllers looked battered and demoralized. The Iron Man's right eye was swollen shut; the quarterback sported a fat lip that made it increasingly difficult for him to call signals. The wide receiver—an Asian guy with a buzz cut and blazing speed—had his jersey ripped open halfway down to his waist, as if he'd inexplicably failed to complete his transformation into the Incredible Hulk. All through the second half, the whiz kids had been carping at one another, taking their frustration out on themselves instead of on the Guardians. Even more telling, their foxy cheering section had fallen into a stunned and gloomy silence.

The Guardians, on the other hand, had jelled as a unit for the first time all year, coming together in a spirit of teamwork and mutual admiration. They'd played over their heads the entire game, shutting down the league's most fearsome offense and moving the ball up and down the field with surprising authority, despite their frustrating inability to put more than seven points on the scoreboard. Everyone had contributed—DeWayne had caught six passes from Todd, including one for a touchdown; Olaffson and Correnti had had five sacks between them; Bart had saved a touchdown with a spectacular interception—but Larry had outdone them all. He was all over the field, making plays he had absolutely no right to make, batting down passes, anticipating reverses, one time even catching the Iron Man from behind on a crucial third down sweep. If the game ended with the Guardians still down by three, they'd go to a bar afterward and celebrate a job well-done, while the victorious Controllers would drink in gloomy silence, knowing they'd taken a thrashing from a team they were supposed to dominate.

With nothing to lose, the Guardians went for broke on first down. Todd faked a handoff to Bart and lofted a bomb down the left sideline, overthrowing a wide-open DeWayne by a heartbreaking couple of inches. On second down, he completed a quick slant pass for a pickup of five. The Controllers blitzed on third down, forcing him to throw the ball away to avoid a sack.

So this was it, their last chance—fourth and five on their own thirty-five, fiftysomething seconds to go. Todd called for a flood pass, all three of his eligible receivers breaking toward the right sideline, each about five yards deeper than the other. He took the snap and bootlegged right, looking first for Richie Murphy, his short man. Covered. Ditto on Bart, the middle receiver. He cocked the ball, ready to throw to DeWayne, his last and best chance, only to watch him slip and fall as he made his cut.

At almost the same moment, Todd heard footsteps from his left, the unmistakable thunder of a rampaging defensive lineman. He held his ground a little longer, standing up straight and gazing doggedly downfield, letting his assailant zero in on his upper body. It was the oldest trick in the book. He ducked at the last possible second, crouching as low as he could go, and the Controllers' 250-pound defensive tackle flew right over him, landing with an elephant-sized thud near the sideline.

Now it was anarchy, an official broken play. Todd looped back to his left to avoid the rest of the pass rush, hoping to scramble long enough for his receivers to reverse course and get themselves open. But what he saw as he drifted back toward midfield forced him to rethink his plan on the fly. There was so much green in front of him that it felt like a dream, yards and yards of open field, way more than he needed for a first down. He tucked the ball and ran.

He was ten yards downfield before anyone even seemed to understand what he was up to. Fifteen yards, twenty, twenty-five, the field pitching toward him and away from him with each pounding stride. He heard a dull drumbeat off to the right, the staccato of hot pursuit.

Don't look, he told himself, *just keep going. One leg in front of the other. Big steps. Eat the yardage.*

Someone was breathing down his neck by the time he crossed the Controllers' thirty yard line, a development that didn't surprise him—there were at least two of them he knew he wouldn't be able to outrun. What did surprise him, as he gave in and glanced over his shoulder, was the sight of DeWayne pulling up beside him to run interference, his stumpy arms and legs pumping at a cartoonish frequency, his breath coming in big raggedy gulps. A little bit farther away, but gaining with every step, were the two Controllers he'd expected, the Iron Man and the Asian guy, each of them moving with long, graceful strides and expressions of fierce determination.

He had just crossed the twenty when DeWayne turned suddenly and took out the Asian guy with a textbook open-field block, a tumbling blur in the corner of Todd's eye. Now it was a footrace, Todd and the Iron Man, a race he knew he'd lose. Calculating the angles as he ran, he came to the conclusion that he'd be pushed out of bounds around the ten yard line, an outcome that seemed as unacceptable as it was inevitable.

Unless.

Crossing the fifteen, Todd slammed on the brakes, somehow managing to slow down so drastically and unexpectedly that the Iron Man simply went zooming past him with a desolate cry of protest, stumbling out of bounds and pitching face first onto the synthetic lawn, leaving Todd with a clear path to the end zone.

He spun on his heels and jogged backward across the goal line, the ball raised triumphantly overhead, a gesture that looked arrogant when the pros did it on TV but felt right just then, allowing him to watch his teammates as they came charging joyfully down the field to join him. Todd spiked the ball and waited for them, his arms stretched wide, his chest heaving as if he were trying to suck the whole night into his lungs. All he wished was that Sarah had been there to see it, to know him as he'd known himself streaking down the wide-open field, not as some jock hero scoring the winning touchdown, but as a grown man experiencing an improbable moment of grace.

And then he saw her.

He wasn't sure what made him glance up just then at what he thought were the empty bleachers—a reflex of habit or hope, some kind of magnetic charge she was emitting—but there she was, a wish made flesh, sitting by herself in the top row, in the shadow of the announcer's booth. She was waving to him, her face shining like a beacon, her mouth forming words he found he could understand quite clearly, as if there were no distance between them at all, words he would have said right back to her if he hadn't been buried just then beneath a stampede of ecstatic teammates, a swarming pile of jubilation.

———

"What the hell happened to Todd?" Correnti wondered. "I wanted to buy him a drink."

Larry shrugged. "He said he was coming."

"Guess he got a better offer," said Richie Murphy.

"Shit." Bart Williams shook his head in wistful reflection. "Was that a beautiful run or what? Sixty-five yards on a broken fourth-down pass play. They should put it on ESPN."

"He couldn't have done it without the little man's help," Olaffson pointed out, polishing DeWayne's already gleaming scalp with a paper napkin. "You see him take that sucker out? Pow! He hit the ground like a tumbleweed."

"Ol' Todd was truckin'," laughed DeWayne. "That white boy was running for his life."

"I don't care what anybody says," declared Bart. "I don't begrudge him a thing. Guy deserves to get laid after a touchdown like that."

Correnti raised his beer bottle.

"Here's to the Toddster. Even if he did ditch us for a little late-night pussy."

Larry joined the toast, but his heart wasn't in it. He didn't think it was right, Todd skipping out on their only victory celebration of the year, especially since he was the man responsible. The whole thing felt half-baked without him, a party with no guest of honor.

"You sure that wasn't his wife?" asked Olaffson, his brow furrowed with concern. Pete was a born-again who refused to watch R-rated movies, abstained from alcohol, and never forgave Clinton for that blowjob.

"I got news for you," said Correnti. "You wanna grab your wife's ass, you don't need to do it at midnight on a football field."

Larry was no prude like Olaffson, but even he was shocked by the brazenness of his friend's behavior. He'd lost track of Todd in the immediate aftermath of the game, distracted as he was by the highly gratifying spectacle of the Controllers slouching off the field, heads bowed in shame, their sexy girlfriends comforting them with maternal pats on the back. It wasn't until the Guardians began drifting toward the parking lot that he realized he'd misplaced his passenger.

"Anyone seen Todd?" he asked.

DeWayne pointed downfield, toward a couple of shadowy figures in the end zone, a man and a woman making out like teenagers beneath the goalposts. Even from that distance, Larry realized right away that the woman wasn't Todd's wife. He'd met Kathy in the supermarket about a year ago, and though he'd be the first to admit she was a total babe, he'd also found her to be disturbingly tall— i.e., taller than he was. The woman in the end zone had to stand on her tiptoes and crane her neck just to be able to kiss Todd on the mouth.

Larry gave them a few minutes to finish their business, but they showed no sign of winding down, let alone wrapping it up. Not seeing any choice in the matter—he'd be damned if he was going to stand there all night, watching Todd fondle a short woman's ass— he strolled back onto the field and made his way over to the lovebirds. He stopped near the ten yard line, at what struck him as a reasonably discreet distance, and cleared his throat as loudly as he could.

"What?" Todd sounded pissed, as if Larry had barged into his bedroom. "Whaddaya want?"

"The guys are going to Casey's. You comin'?"

"Oh, Christ." Todd's sigh was audible twenty yards away. "I'm gonna be a little while. Why don't you go ahead. I'll catch up later."

"You're gonna come, right? We need to celebrate."

"Yeah, yeah, I'll be right there. Just give me fifteen, twenty minutes." He hesitated, and it was possible the woman had whispered something. "Half hour tops."

"You promise?"

"Jesus, Larry. I just told you."

"I don't mean to bother you," Larry said. "It's just—I'm head-ing over to Blueberry Court later on. I was hoping you could ride shotgun."

"What about the other guys? Why don't you ask one of them?"

"They're cops. They can't get involved with this kinda shit."

Todd let go of the woman and took a few steps in Larry's direction.

"Do yourself a favor, Larry. Just stay away from there. You're gonna get yourself arrested again."

Larry stared at the woman for a second or two, trying to place her. He was pretty sure he recognized her from somewhere, that messy hair and cranky expression. *She should be with someone like me*, he thought, *not someone like him.*

"I don't care," he said. "Let them arrest me. They wanna lock me up for protecting my kids, then bring it on. Make me a fuckin' martyr."

Long after the rest of the Guardians had gone home, Larry sat like a jilted lover on the hood of his minivan in the almost empty park-ing lot of Casey's Bar and Grille, knowing that Todd had blown him off but waiting for him anyway.

It wasn't like he needed help. On a purely operational level, Larry had no doubt that he was better off working solo. All Todd ever did was hide in the car and try to talk him out of whatever it was that needed to be done. *It's late, Larry, you can't ring the doorbell now. You're not really gonna set that bag of shit on fire, are you, Larry? Come on, Lar, give the old lady a break. She's not a criminal.* But maybe that was what Larry needed—a reality check, a voice of rea-son whispering in his ear, keeping him from doing something that he'd end up regretting. If Todd had been with him at St. Rita's, maybe he wouldn't have lost his temper; maybe he wouldn't be in the shitload of trouble he was in right now.

On the other hand, stupid as that had been, Larry didn't exactly regret hurting Ronnie. He wasn't going to spill any tears over a pervert's broken arm—even if it was a nasty compound fracture— and the majority of his fellow citizens seemed to feel the same way. Most of them were more upset with the D.A. for pressing charges against a Concerned Parent than they were about the fact that a convicted child molester had suffered a few bumps and bruises during an involuntary trip down the stairs. For every letter to the editor criticizing Larry's "rash and violent behavior," and demanding to know who had elected him "judge, jury, and executioner," there were two more defending him for his "completely justified reaction," and a third going so far as to call him a hero.

After living through an ice age of private hell and public disgrace, Larry had, in the past week and a half, begun to notice a distinct thaw in the air. Women waved to him when he walked down the street; men went out of the way to shake his hand. He felt like he was entering a new phase of his life, shedding the image of Larry Moon, the trigger-happy, possibly racist cop, and trading it in for something a whole lot better: Larry Moon, the avenging father, defender of the innocent, the guy who'd enacted the whole town's secret fantasy.

"Don't give up," his neighbors told him. "Keep on fighting."

That was exactly what Larry intended to do; he just couldn't help wishing Todd was there to do it with him. It must have been a holdover from his cop days, the feeling of security he got from having a partner, the knowledge that someone he trusted was watching his back. Tonight, though, he wasn't going to have that luxury.

———

"WAKE UP!"

Just for a moment—that strange way station between dreaming and not—May McGorvey thought she heard the Voice of God calling to her from the sky, finally coming to take her home.

"WAKE UP!!" the Voice repeated.

"Okay." May sat up in bed, her heart pounding rapidly, but not with fear. "I'm awake."

"OPEN YOUR EYES!" The Voice was harsher than she'd expected. "GET YOUR GODDAM HEADS OUT OF THE SAND!"

My heads? thought May. *My goddam heads?*

She stood up too quickly and had to sit back down until the dizziness passed. By the time she made it to the window, she understood quite clearly that she was not listening to the Voice of God.

"DON'T YOU PEOPLE LOVE YOUR CHILDREN? DON'T YOU WANT TO PROTECT THEM FROM EVIL? THEN WHY AREN'T YOU OUT HERE DOING SOMETHING ABOUT IT?"

May pulled up the shade. That awful man was standing in front of her house, spreading his poison through some kind of loudspeaker.

"BLUEBERRY COURT, THERE'S A PERVERT IN YOUR MIDST!"

He had no right. No right to strut across the lawn—*my lawn,* May thought bitterly—trampling the grass and saying those horrible things, not after what he'd done at church.

"YOUR CHILDREN ARE NOT SAFE!"

May hadn't been feeling well for a long time—her legs were weak, something was wrong with her breathing—and the demands on her energy had increased to the breaking point now that Ronnie had his arm in a cast. He couldn't tie his shoes, or button his shirt, or cut his meat. It was like he was a child again, needing her for everything. She was tired, more tired than she'd ever been in her life.

"A MURDERER LIVES IN THIS HOUSE! DON'T YOU PEOPLE CARE?"

You bastard, she thought. *I see what you're up to.*

A wave of righteous anger spread through May's body like a wonder drug. Her legs were steady as she moved through the upstairs hall, her breathing deep and regular. She felt like her old self as she scurried down the stairs and pulled open the front door.

———

"You dirty son of a bitch! Get off my lawn!"

The old lady was in some kind of frenzy, hobbling toward him in bare feet and a short nightie, her enormous bosom jiggling in a way that made Larry embarrassed for both of them.

"Who the hell do you think you are?" she demanded. "Mr. High-and-Mighty."

Larry ignored her.

"NO PERVERTS AT THE PLAYGROUND! NO PERVERTS AT THE PLAYGROUND!"

"You think you're God?" the old lady shouted, her toothless face contorted into a fright mask of rage and loathing. "You're not God. Far from it!"

"I KNOW I'M NOT GOD," Larry replied, inadvertently addressing her through the bullhorn. "I NEVER SAID I WAS."

The old lady cracked a nasty smile. Her voice was soft and hateful.

"You're the murderer. You killed that boy at the mall."

Larry lowered the bullhorn.

"I didn't murder anyone," he said, making a real effort to control his temper. "Now why don't you go back inside and put some clothes on?"

To his amazement, the old bitch made a lunge for the bullhorn, grabbing hold of the flared end and trying to rip it out of his hands. Luckily, his grip on the handle was secure.

"You shot him through the neck," she said, spreading her feet and giving another tug. "I read it in the paper."

Larry tugged back, but she was stronger than she looked, or maybe just angrier.

"That was a mistake," he said. "It wasn't murder."

He dug his heels into the grass and tried again. By this point they were locked in a full-scale tug-of-war, crouching low and revolving in a slow circle on the lawn, yanking on the bullhorn with all their strength. Larry felt the old woman's grip slip a little at almost the same moment he heard the voice.

"You need to go home, Mister."

He glanced over his shoulder and saw two men standing by the curb—a big guy in lightweight pajamas, and a little guy in suit pants and a T-shirt. It was the big guy who had spoken.

"The police are coming," the little guy added.

The big guy glared at Larry.

"You're scaring my kids," he said. "I wish you'd cut it out."

"Your kids need to be frightened," Larry grunted, tightening his grip on the handle. "They live across the street from a child molester."

He heard a siren in the distance as he gathered his strength for one last monster tug. Before he could wrench it free, though, the old lady suddenly let go, sending Larry stumbling backwards onto his ass, the bullhorn cradled to his chest.

When he got back to his feet, he saw the two men crouching on the grass, looking down at the old lady and shaking their heads. She was flat on her back, like a boxer who'd taken a knockout punch.

"Now look what you did," the little guy said, as Larry approached.

A cold shiver of fear ran through him as he looked down at Mrs. McGorvey. She was alive, at least, her limbs twitching, an awful gurgling noise coming from somewhere deep in her throat. Her eyes were wide-open, staring straight into Larry's. Her lips were moving, too, but there weren't any words coming out, just a few foamy bubbles of spit.

"Oh Jesus," Larry said. "This is all I need."

————

They were lying on their backs at the fifty yard line, gazing up at the sky as if an answer to their unspoken question might appear there at any moment, yellow letters blazing against the black dome of infinity. Todd fumbled for Sarah's hand, feeling her sweaty fingers intertwine with his own.

"I don't want to go home," he said. "I want to stay right here forever."

She didn't answer; it wasn't necessary. They'd said everything that needed to be said in the first five minutes. For the last two hours they'd just been repeating themselves.

"Thank God you came," he continued.

She rolled onto her side to look at him. Her eyes were wet and puffy, her voice husky with emotion.

"I was going out of my mind."

"Me too." He lifted his head and shoulders off the ground and planted a soft kiss on her kiss-swollen lips. "When I looked up and saw you—"

He stopped. There was no use trying to put it into words, the perfection of that moment, the way she seemed to have been conjured by his touchdown, as if she were the physical incarnation of his happiness. He gave a heavy sigh, letting his head sink back down to the artificial turf.

"I can't do this anymore," he said. "I can't go another week without kissing you."

A subtle change came over Sarah's expression as she gazed down at him, and Todd felt his mind grow suddenly alert, as if a cool breeze had blown all the confusion away. It was as if the whole summer—his whole life—had been imperceptibly narrowing down to this very moment, the slight widening of her eyes, the little catch in his breath, the sudden realization that they'd crossed a line so big and bright it was hard to believe he hadn't seen it coming.

PART FOUR

MEET ME AT THE PLAYGROUND

SWING ME

THE PLAN WAS LOVELY IN ITS SIMPLICITY. AFTER WRITING NOTES to explain their sudden absences and concealing them in places where they were certain to be found, Sarah and Todd would slip out of their respective houses, rendezvous at the Rayburn School playground, and head north for a few days at the seashore, giving all the interested parties some time to absorb the shock of their departure and begin the difficult process of orienting themselves to a new alignment of the domestic planets.

For the fleeing lovers, of course, this adjustment period would also be a honeymoon—premature by one standard, overdue by another—a celebration of the miracle of their finding one another, a hard-earned opportunity to savor the fruits of their daring. For three whole days, at the very least, they'd have nothing to do but eat, sleep, and make love whenever they wanted to, free from the banal responsibilities of child care, the ceaseless petty time pressures of family life. The sweetness of the prospect was almost too much for Sarah to contemplate.

Todd had originally proposed Monday as the date for their getaway, but it wasn't doable. Richard was returning that night from a weekend business trip to California, and wouldn't be home until close to midnight under the best of circumstances. After that, though, the coast was clear: He would begin a two-week vacation upon his return, leaving him free to watch Lucy for as long as Sarah needed him to. So they pushed the plan back to Tuesday, despite their eagerness to get the messy part over with as quickly as possible.

Sarah endured an excruciating weekend alone with Lucy, her mind a million miles away from her daughter's annoying questions (*What you favorite color? Why they call it raisin?*) and highly specific requests (*Hang me upside downy. Now drop me on the couch*). But there was never any way she could see of deflecting the questions or ignoring the requests, so she said, *Blue*, and *I don't know, that's just what they call it*, and carried Lucy into the living room by her ankles and dropped her on the couch, and then did the same thing five more times without a break, all the while thinking, *In two days I'll be in a motel room near the beach with the man I love. In two days I'll be a different person. In two days I'll finally be happy.*

It was unbearable to be so close to something so momentous and have nothing to do but wait, and no one to talk to about it. She was besieged by worries—*he's going to change his mind, he'll never be able to leave her*—and in desperate need of reassurance, but Todd had made her promise not to call or e-mail him if she could possibly avoid it, as he had reason to believe that his communications were being monitored (it didn't help that he shared a cell phone and an e-mail account with his wife). She had no contact with him until Monday afternoon, when they made cautious eye contact at the Town Pool, separated by a distance of about fifty feet. His mother-in-law was sitting right next to him, but she was momentarily distracted by a problem with one of her sandals.

We still on? she asked with a hopeful grimace.

You bet, he replied, the vehemence of his nod undercut by the slightly fearful grin that accompanied it. But why shouldn't he be scared? She was scared, too. It was okay, though. Just a glimpse of him steadied her nerves, made her feel like she wasn't about to explode into a million tiny pieces after all. For the first time in days, she remembered how to breathe.

I love you, she mouthed, but he must have misread her lips. His face contorted into an uncomprehending slack-jawed squint, like he was a kid who didn't yet realize he needed glasses to see the blackboard.

Oh, forget it, she mouthed. *I'll see you tomorrow.*

————

Richard had come to San Diego not for business as he'd told Sarah, but for Beachfest 2001, the summer meeting of the Slutty Kay Fan Club. It had not been an easy decision to make. He'd resisted the temptation for weeks, just as he'd done with the panties, telling himself that it was out of the question, not even worth thinking about: Grown men didn't belong to fan clubs, and even if they did, they didn't lie to their wives and plunk down a couple of grand to attend a meeting on the other side of the country. And what if his plane went down on the way? Would people read about his idiotic mission on the obituary page? *Richard Pierce, 47, died last week when his plane crashed in the Nevada desert. Pierce, a successful branding consultant for Namecheck, Inc., was on his way to a gathering of the Slutty Kay Fan Club, a web-based group of perverts that he had recently joined. He leaves behind a wife and a three-year-old daughter, as well as two grown daughters from a previous marriage.*

But it was no use trying to scare himself straight. As the big weekend approached it became painfully clear to him that nothing was going to deter him from making the pilgrimage—not the dishonesty, not the expense, not even the possibility of shameful public exposure. Partly it was jealousy that motivated him: He couldn't stand the thought of other men—braver, less self-deluding men—cavorting with Kay while he sat home, stewing in the juices of his own cowardice masquerading as virtue. But there was something else, too: the desperate hope that doing something so extreme might somehow cure him. Maybe the way out of his obsession with Slutty Kay was through it. Maybe some contact with the flesh-and-blood person would release him from his bondage to the virtual woman.

It was worth a try. Partying on a beach in California with his fellow weirdos couldn't be any more embarrassing than sneaking into the bathroom at work five times a day to sniff a pair of panties whose odor had grown so faint that he was no longer even sure if he was smelling anything at all beyond the fumes of his own sick imagination.

An oddly familiar-looking man—he was white-haired, with a big belly and a ruddy, incongruously youthful face—was waiting among the chauffeurs at the airport, holding up a sign on which the word *Beachfest!* had been scrawled in a notably shaky hand. When Richard did a double take, the guy stepped forward.

"Here for S.K.?" he asked in a soft, conspiratorial voice.

Richard cast a quick glance at the air travelers and professional drivers milling around him. No one seemed particularly interested in his business. He nodded discreetly. The red-faced man stuck out a meaty, slightly humid hand.

"Walter Young. I'm president of the fan club."

"Richard Pierce. Jeez, it was nice of you to come all the way out here."

"It's not that far," Walter said, balling up the sign and jamming it in his pants pocket. "Besides, I know what it's like to show up in a strange city at night, no one to meet you. I spent a lot of years on the road, trade shows, sales conferences, client meetings, all that shit. I'm retired now, thank God. I go where I want, when I want."

"Good for you," said Richard. "I've still got a few years on the chain gang."

"Counting the days, huh?"

"You know it."

On the way to the baggage claim, Walter persuaded Richard to cancel his rent-a-car. He explained that the club had arranged for a van to shuttle everyone from the hotel to the beach and back.

"Saves a lot of trouble," Walter said, wrenching the suitcase out of Richard's hand as soon as he hefted it up off the conveyor belt.

"Don't be silly," said Richard. "You don't need to carry my bag."

"It's not a problem," said Walter, yanking up the pull-handle and dragging the bag along as he headed for the exit doors. "I'm sure you're tired from your trip."

"Thanks," said Richard, hurrying to keep up.

"Yeah, like I said, we started doing the van last year. Carla got tired of all the headaches. People getting lost, showing up late in a pissy mood. Who needs it, right? Plus, this way you can have a few beers and not have to worry about the drive home, you know?"

Richard was happy to hear it. He had long ago reached the age where having to make his own way around an unfamiliar city had lost all its charm and had become a genuine source of anxiety.

"This is great," he said, following his guide out into the balmy night. "You guys thought of everything."

"That's Carla for you. She insists on doing things first-class. That's just the kind of lady she is."

"I'm a little behind the curve. Who's Carla?"

Walter glanced at him for a second, apparently to see if he was kidding.

"Kay," he explained. "In person she's Carla. Slutty Kay's more like a stage name or something. You know, just for the web site."

Walter clicked the remote and the trunk of his white Chrysler Concorde popped open.

"That's weird," said Richard. "She doesn't really seem like a Carla."

Walter heaved the suitcase into the trunk.

"That's what her mama named her."

"I don't know. It just doesn't seem right to me."

"You'll get used to it."

The hotel was only a fifteen-minute drive from the airport, and Walter talked the whole way about recent club events, many of which Richard knew about from photos archived on sluttykay.com. They were just pulling into the parking lot of the Holiday Inn when he suddenly realized why his companion looked so familiar. In one of the "Hot Tub Encounter" photos that Richard knew so well, Walter was sitting naked on the edge of the tub with a beer in one hand and his other hand resting on the shoulder of a naked old guy with leathery skin and a sad little tuft of white hair on his chest. The two of them were leaning close together, engaged in a lively conversation, apparently oblivious to the fact that Kay was having sex with a bald man just a couple of feet away.

"You want to get a drink or something?" Walter asked as he pulled up in front of the office. "After you check in, I mean."

"I don't think so," said Richard, "I'm kinda beat. Still on East Coast time."

Walter nodded. "Yeah, that jet lag's a bitch. Just be in the lobby tomorrow, eleven o'clock sharp. You snooze, you lose."

"I'll be there," Richard promised, holding up his right hand. "Scout's honor."

Walter returned the salute.

"Scout's honor," he laughed. "I like that."

———

Carol told him he needed to get to the hospital *right away*.

"Call a cab," she said. "And tell them it's an emergency."

Ronnie hung up the phone, gripping the edge of the counter for support while he waited for the strength to return to his legs. This was it. He could sense it in his sister's voice, in the very fact that she'd lowered herself to speak to him personally, which she had not done for years. For the past week, even with their mother in critical condition, Carol had somehow managed to arrange it that they were never at her bedside at the same time. If she needed to communicate with him, she used Bertha as an intermediary, adding insult to injury.

He looked around the kitchen in a fog of dread and disbelief, his mother's unmistakable presence radiating from the avocado tea-kettle and toaster; the peeling wallpaper with illustrations of various herbs and spices, their names written helpfully below; the brown medicine containers lined up like good little soldiers on the windowsill, the prescription labels all facing out. It didn't seem possible that she wouldn't be coming home. Just the thought of it made him feel dizzy and imperiled, as if he were standing on a high balcony with no railing, looking straight down at an empty parking lot.

"Please," he said, turning his gaze to the ceiling, in the direction of a God he considered his mother a fool for believing in. "Don't you fucking let her die."

————

The cab driver was a senior citizen who had something wrong with his nose, these multiple lumpy growths sprouting out of it, like a flesh-colored cauliflower had taken root in the middle of his face. Ronnie felt for the guy. It couldn't have been easy going through your golden years like *that*.

"Where to?" he grunted.

"Presbyterian Hospital. My mother's in the ICU." The driver didn't respond, didn't say *Too bad*, or *I'm sorry*, or any of the crap people usually spouted when you told them something like this, but Ronnie kept talking anyway. "She had a stroke last week. Bad one. We don't know if she's gonna make it."

He directed these remarks not so much to the driver himself as to his hack license, which was affixed by rubber bands to the flipped-down sun visor on the passenger side. WENDELL DEGRAW, it said, next to an ID photo showing the poor guy's face in a highly un-flattering profile that looked like it could have been ripped out of a medical textbook.

Wendell himself was listening to talk radio, a familiar voice that Ronnie couldn't quite identify, one of those professional know-it-alls with a smart-ass comeback for everything. Ronnie used to listen to a lot of that stuff before he went to prison, used to fantasize about going to broadcasting school, getting a radio show of his own. *Smart Talk with Ron McGorvey*. Two hours a day to speak his mind and humiliate the uninformed idiots who called in, barely able to form a grammatical sentence. *Pardon my asking, Frank, but do you have shit for brains or what?*

"They had to put her on a ventilator," he continued. "She can't talk or anything. Just lies there all day, staring up at the ceiling."

Fuckface Wendell turned up the radio, as if purposely trying to drown out Ronnie's voice. The talk-show guy was ranting about Gary Condit, how if he had a shred of decency he'd resign from Congress and tell everybody what he'd done with his girlfriend. Ronnie spoke up even louder.

"She's a good woman. Raised two kids all by herself, not a mean bone in her body. You couldn't find a nicer lady."

The bastard didn't even grunt. He cranked down his window, hawked up a loogie from deep in his throat, and spat it onto the pavement.

Nice, Wendell. Real classy.

"What about you?" Ronnie inquired, while they waited at an endless red light. "Your mother still alive?"

Wendell whirled around in the driver's seat. Full on, he looked even more hideous than he did in profile.

"You think I don't know who you are?" he demanded. "You're lucky I don't toss you out on your ass."

"Sorry," Ronnie muttered. "I was just making conversation. You don't have to be so goddam sensitive."

Wendell turned off the radio, and they rode in silence the rest of the way to the hospital. When they pulled up in front of the main entrance, Ronnie gave the guy a twenty for a fourteen-dollar fare.

"Keep the change," he said. "Buy yourself a new nose, okay?"

————

Sarah should have known there would be a hitch. There was always a hitch. As soon as kids were involved, the simplest plan had a way of turning complicated on you. She hadn't been home from the pool for fifteen minutes when she got the call from Richard. He made small talk about the California weather for a minute or two before abruptly shifting gears.

"So listen," he said. "I don't think I'm coming home."

"Why? Is your flight delayed?"

"It's not about the flight. It's about us."

He said he was going to spend the rest of his vacation in San Diego, give some thought to moving there permanently. He'd been thinking about making a change for a long time now, and had always wanted to give a California a shot.

"We never should have gotten married." His voice was sad when he said this, and the sadness made her remember how much she'd liked him before everything turned awful. "You know that as well as I do."

"Oh, shit," she said suddenly. "Damn it."

"Are you upset? I thought you'd be relieved."

She was; she was more than relieved. On any other day she would have broken out the champagne and tap-danced on the kitchen table. But right then, all she could think about was her honeymoon on the beach, how the whole plan depended on his being home to take care of Lucy.

"I'm fine," she said. "The timing's just a little inconvenient."

"There's never a good time for something like this. But we've both been miserable for too long."

"What am I supposed to do with Lucy?" she asked, thinking out loud.

"Please," he told her. "Don't worry about that. I'm going to take good care of her. Of both of you. You can keep the car and the house. All I want is a fresh start."

"Okay," she said. "Fine. Whatever. We don't need to hash this out over the phone. I guess I'll have to hire a lawyer or something."

"Absolutely. Sure. That would be the smartest thing." He hesitated. "Sarah?"

"Yeah?"

"I came out here to meet a woman. Someone I've been in touch with on the Internet. I just wanted you to know."

She took a moment to absorb this information, wondering if she'd feel even the smallest flicker of jealousy or betrayal. But there was nothing. Nothing at all.

"Okay," she said finally.

"Okay?" He seemed almost hurt. "Is that all you can say?"

Jesus, she thought. *What does he want from me?* Was she supposed to tell him the truth, that she felt sorry for the woman, who wouldn't find out until it was too late that Richard was not as nice a guy as he seemed? And besides, who could tell with these things? Maybe a new woman would turn Richard into a new man.

"You do what you have to do," she said.

Lucy entered the kitchen, still in her damp bathing suit, the toy stethoscope hanging around her neck, her hair sun-bleached and matted. She was watching her mother with ominous intensity, as if she'd been listening to the conversation on another line.

"Daddy?" she inquired.

Sarah nodded. "Your daughter's here," she informed Richard. "You want to say hi?"

"Not right now," he said. "I gotta run. Just tell her I love her, okay? I'll be home in a couple of weeks, and we can break the news to her then. You know, do it as a family."

"Sure," she murmured, her head buzzing with a swarm of conflicting emotions. Something wonderful had happened at the worst possible time. Everything was all messed up, but she was free. Richard was leaving. She could keep the house. "That's a good idea. We'll do it as a family."

"Do what?" Lucy asked, after Sarah clicked off the phone. "What we do?"

"Nothing," said Sarah, averting her gaze from her daughter's watchful face. "Nothing you need to worry about, sweetheart."

————

Richard hadn't expected her to take the news so calmly. He had no doubt that they'd reach an accommodation over time, but he'd braced himself for a lot more anger and recrimination in the short run, the kind of abuse that comes with the territory when you take a hike on your wife and kid. At least that was how it worked with his first marriage; Peggy had made him suffer for years before she found it in her heart to forgive him. But Sarah belonged to a different generation. Women her age were more independent, less freaked-out by the idea of divorce or single parenthood. She'd reacted so agreeably, in fact, that he was almost sorry that he'd offered her the house and car without running it by his lawyer. He'd just blurted it out, no strategic thinking whatsoever, the kind of impulsive, self-defeating behavior he never would have permitted himself in a business situation.

Oh well, he thought, *no sense getting all stressed out about it*. He closed his cell phone and took a moment to savor the mellow touch of the Southern California sunshine on his skin, so much less antagonistic than the midday glare back home. It was a cliché, but it struck him with the force of transcendent truth: *Things are easier out here.* His lungs expanded as he drew in a deep breath of eucalyptus-tinged air. An exhilarating sense of lightness spread through his body, as if he'd just stepped out of a lead-lined suit.

Maybe this is what life feels like for happy people, he thought, *the obstacles falling down in front of you before you even get close enough to give them a push.*

————

It was weird, but Ronnie actually liked going to the hospital. People were friendly there. They smiled at him in the elevators and corridors, and treated him as if he had as much right to be there as they did, an attitude he didn't often encounter in public places.

He understood that they weren't smiling because of the warm feelings they harbored in their hearts for Ronald James McGorvey, Registered Sex Offender. They were smiling because his right arm was encased in a fiberglass cast, suspended in a cloth sling. That was all they saw when they looked at him—a man with a broken bone, a medical problem that was obvious and eminently fixable. He wasn't one of those mystery patients who looked fine on the outside but must have had some terrible disease gnawing at their innards. In the hospital, those were the scary ones, the ones who made you wonder what kind of time bomb was ticking away in your own apparently healthy body. Ronnie was dreading the day when the cast came off his arm, when he'd no longer have that one small claim on people's sympathy. He was thinking about doing a little research, finding out if he couldn't get some sort of fake cast he could wear to the supermarket or public library, maybe even a waterproof one for the Town Pool. If not, maybe he could just get that asshole to throw him down the steps again.

He walked more and more slowly as he approached the ICU, as if his legs were filling gradually with cement. The waiting room seemed quieter than usual; the extended Puerto Rican family who'd been camping out around the TV for the past week had disappeared. They'd been taking turns visiting this comatose guy in his midtwenties—supposedly he'd fallen off a scaffold at a construction site—standing around his bed in pairs and weeping so melodramatically Ronnie couldn't help shooting them dirty looks when they started to get on his nerves. He sat down in an armchair and watched a couple of minutes of CNN, wondering if the Puerto Ricans had relocated their moaning and hair-tearing to a private room or a funeral home, then got up and announced himself over the intercom. One of the nurses told him to come in.

You'd think a moment like that would be unbearable, but it wasn't as hard as he expected. You just do that thing, that thing where you kind of shut off your mind for a little while. You see what's in front of you—your sister and her husband, the priest in black, the doctor in his white coat, Bertha, the nice Jamaican nurse, every last one of them ringing your dead mother's bed, shaking their heads in unison, as if you've asked a question, when really you're just standing there taking it all in with a blank expression, not feeling a thing.

————

Richard had to fight off a persistent sense of unreality as he and Carla made small talk while looking over their menus. It hardly seemed possible that this was actually happening, that he was having lunch with the woman who had presided over his fantasy life for more than a year, a woman whose thong he'd been carrying around in his briefcase for most of the summer. And yet here she was, sitting right across from him, cursing softly to herself as she tried to wipe a salsa stain off her silk blouse with a damp napkin.

"I'm such a slob," she said. "I should wear one of those yellow rain slickers when I eat in public."

"I'm the same way," said Richard. "I find these spots on my ties sometimes, I don't have a goddam clue how they got there."

She gave up and tossed the napkin on the table.

"My dry cleaner's gonna yell at me. He's this old Chinese guy, always giving me a hard time when I bring him something with a stain on it. *Why you do that? You not careful! Why you so messy?* He's worse than my mother."

Richard felt a foolish smile spreading across his face.

"What?" she said, a bit defensively. "I got something in my teeth?"

He shook his head. "I can't tell you how weird this is for me. Like I'm out with the queen of England."

"I've seen pictures of the queen. I'm not sure if I should take that as a compliment."

"You're a lot prettier," he assured her.

"I know, I know," she said, as if she'd had this conversation a hundred times, "but she gives better head."

Richard let out a guffaw that drew the attention of his fellow diners.

"You're too much," he told her.

Carla shrugged, her open hands held at shoulder level as if to say, *I can't help myself*. But then her face turned serious, as if she'd suddenly remembered why they were here.

"So you have a business proposition for me?"

"I wouldn't call it a proposition at this point," he said. "I just want to brainstorm a little. About the mail-order panties."

"Oh, wait," she said. "Hold that thought. Before I forget."

Carla lifted a bulky tote bag onto the table, dirty white canvas with a blue PBS logo on the side. The sight of it surprised him.

"You give money to public television?"

She shook her head, an expression of distaste flickering across her face.

"It's a freebie. My ex-husband used to work at the station. I must have a dozen of these things."

"Your first husband?"

"My only."

"But the web site says you're married."

"It's easier that way. Keeps some of the weirdos away." Carla smiled sadly. "Dave tried to be supportive when I started the business, but it got to him after a while. He didn't want to share me."

Richard nodded thoughtfully.

"You'd have to be a pretty evolved human being," he said.

Carla seemed pleased by this insight. She withdrew a pale yellow folder from her bag and passed it across the table.

"This is for you. A little memento."

The folder was made of stiff, high-quality paper. On the front cover, a decent amateur calligrapher had printed the words, *Beachfest 2001: "Thanks" for the Memories.* Richard opened it to find a five-by-seven print of the team picture taken on Saturday afternoon, along with the inscription, *To Richard, One of my* biggest *fans. With love and kisses, Carla (aka., "Slutty Kay").*

In the picture, everyone was naked, but Richard thought that was a bit misleading. For most of the day, the Beachfest was just innocent fun, no more scandalous than your average company picnic. Carla and her seven fans wore bathing suits and T-shirts as they whiled away the afternoon drinking beer, playing beach volleyball, tossing a Frisbee, and even engaging in a hilarious round of three-legged races. Richard took some time to get acquainted with his colleagues, most of whom he recognized from photos on the web site. Aside from himself, the only newbie was Claude, a French-

Canadian schoolteacher with a thick accent and a scar from open-heart surgery running down the center of his chest.

"They're a nice bunch of guys," Richard commented.

"I know," said Carla. "I feel really lucky to know them."

The other part of the festivities didn't begin until much later in the day, after Walter fired up the grill for the evening barbecue. Carla went for a quick dip in the ocean—they were on a beautiful crescent of beach, a secluded cove north of La Jolla that Richard wouldn't have been able to find on his own in a million years—and when she came back to shore she unsnapped her bikini top without fanfare and tossed it to Marcus, the twenty-eight-year-old software designer who was the youngest member of her entourage. As if that were the agreed-upon signal, the men of the Fan Club began pulling their shirts over their heads and stepping out of their swim trunks. Richard didn't hesitate to join them. This was why he had come, after all. To be a part of this community, a tiny vanguard who had moved beyond shame and hypocrisy, at least for one day of the year.

For a long time after the clothes came off, nothing else happened. Walter kept watching the grill; Richard kept tossing the Frisbee in a triangular formation with Claude and Roberto, the only black man among them (he was a retired army master sergeant); and Marcus continued debating theology with Fred, a middle-aged Lutheran minister whose wife believed he was on some sort of spiritual retreat.

"And I am!" Fred had insisted, when reporting this fact to Richard. "Just not according to my wife's cramped definition of the phrase."

At some point, though, the Frisbee floated over Richard's head, and when he turned to chase it he saw Carla kneeling by the grill, her head bobbing back and forth against Walter's crotch. As if he'd been taken by surprise, Walter was still clutching the spatula, pressing the flat part of it against the top of Carla's shoulder. Marcus was squatting nearby, recording the action with his high-resolution digital camera, the many impressive features of which he had explained to Richard in great detail earlier in the afternoon, almost like he was making a sales pitch.

"Don't let the burgers burn!" shouted Earl—he was the old guy, a retired trucker from Nebraska—inspiring widespread laughter from the onlookers.

When Carla was finished with Walter, she took care of Claude, Earl, and Fred in short order. And then it was Richard's turn. It felt like a dream as she knelt before him, the Pacific glinting a majestic purple and gold in front of him, the tantalizing smell of grilled meat mixing with the salty ocean air. It was almost as if he'd stepped inside his computer, into one of those images that had burned themselves into his brain, making him permanently unfit for normal life.

"Thank you," he whispered, after she had planted a friendly kiss on his knee.

"No," she said, looking up with the sweet, earnest expression he had memorized a long time ago. "Thank *you*."

After they'd eaten, everyone lined up for the picture Richard was looking at now. Seven men in a row, of varying heights, weights, body types, ages, and skin colors, each of them grinning at the camera as if competing to see who could look the happiest. Claude, Marcus, Walter, Roberto, Richard, Earl, and Fred. In front of them, Carla on one knee, her arms spread wide, as if she were trying to embrace the world.

"Wow," said Richard. "That was a great day."

"It sure was," said Carla. "Now tell me about the panties."

Bertha's jaw kept flapping all the way home from the hospital, telling Ronnie not to feel bad, that his mother had gone to a better place, that she no longer had to suffer the aches and pains of lonely old age in a town where everybody hated her.

"Nobody *hated her*," he said, breaking his vow to just sit quietly the whole way home, not to utter a single word to the toxic old bitch. It was bad enough that he had to breathe the same air as her, that his own sister wouldn't even offer him a ride home in her minivan *on the day their mother died*, like he was going to foul the seats just by touching his ass to them, like he'd leave an invisible slime of sex offender germs on the surfaces her kids had to touch on the way to school every day. *Well, fuck her.* One day she'd wake up and her precious fucking Mercury Villager would just be a smoking hulk in her driveway.

Oh, gee, Sis, sorry to hear it. Too bad you weren't sleeping in it.

The thing that really pissed him off was that she hadn't even hugged him good-bye. She thought about it for a second, he saw it, saw her move toward him and then suddenly draw back, as if realizing what she'd been about to do. She patted him on the shoulder instead, patted him the way you'd pat an ugly dog, standing as far away as you could, looking away so you wouldn't have to smell its rotten breath.

"She was an old woman," Bertha said, shooting him an accusatory sidelong glance. "She had no business fighting off intruders in the middle of the night. No business at all."

"I have a broken arm," Ronnie reminded her, shifting on the seat to show her his cast. "There was nothing I could do."

Bertha shook her head, and Ronnie couldn't help marveling at how pickled she looked, even after a day spent in the hospital. You could almost see the fumes rising off her skin, like she was a sponge soaked in cheap wine.

"She seemed so strong this morning." Bertha dabbed a Kleenex at her eyes. "She was awake and alert, her vital signs were good. And then God called her."

Ronnie shut his eyes and pretended his ears were clogged with melted wax. He reminded himself that he'd never have to spend another minute with Bertha in his life, never have to arrange his schedule around her daily visits.

Everything would turn out okay, he was pretty sure of it. His mother had set things up so that he could remain in the house for as long as he wanted. If he and Carol decided to sell it someday, they would split the proceeds, just like they would split the money in her bank account and the CDs and the annuities. The way he figured it, he'd have at least a year before he needed to worry about money, even if he went ahead and splurged on a new computer like he planned. A guy in prison had told him about some web sites he was interested in checking out.

"They're from Amsterdam," he'd said. "Those fucking Dutch people are *sick*, man."

It was amazing to think about, a computer of his own and no one to bother him. He could just surf the web all day, look at whatever he wanted.

The cab pulled up in front of his house. He reached for his wallet, but Bertha told him his money was no good, not today.

"I'll get it," she said. "I promised your mother I'd keep an eye on you."

Yeah, right, Ronnie thought, *you and the Gallo Brothers.*

"Oh wait," she said. "I almost forgot."

Bertha reached into her purse and handed him a folded sheet of paper that had been ripped from a spiral notebook.

"Your mother wrote it this morning. She wanted me to give it to you."

"What do you mean, she wrote it?"

"She wrote it," Bertha insisted. "I held the pen between her fingers and the nurse held the clipboard. But she did all the letters. She fell asleep right afterward. And then she had the hemorrhage."

Ronnie stuck the paper into his shirt pocket and slipped out of the cab, glad not to have to look at Bertha's nasty face for a second longer.

"See you at the wake," she called out, as the cab pulled away from the curb.

Inside the house, Ronnie unfolded the note. The letters were big and sloppy but he could tell the handwriting from a single glance. His eyes filled with tears as he read the brief message, a mother's final plea to her wayward son.

Please, she begged him. *Please be a good boy.*

———

As much as she hated to admit it, Mary Ann was rattled. Isabelle had gone to sleep according to plan, under the covers by seven, asleep by quarter after, but Troy had rebelled, pitching a kicking and screaming fit on the living room floor, the likes of which she'd never seen before.

"I'm not tired!" he shrieked. "Get that through your stupid head!"

She decided to ignore the insult for the moment.

"I don't care if you're tired or not. When it's our bedtime, we go to bed."

"Why?" he demanded. There was a wild look in his eyes, an expression Mary Ann might have called terror if it hadn't sounded so ridiculous. "Why do I have to go to bed *if I'm not tired?*"

"Because I say so," Mary Ann replied calmly. "And your father does, too."

She cast a pointed glance at Lewis, who was sitting on the couch reading *National Geographic,* an activity she would have approved of under less pressing circumstances (she'd gotten him the subscription for Christmas, but he usually just let the magazines gather dust on the coffee table). He looked up with a carefully neutral expression, as if to say, *You're on your own, honey.* He had never been as supportive about enforcing bedtimes as she would have liked.

Troy seemed emboldened by his father's failure to intervene.

"None of the other kids go to bed at seven," he declared, spreading his arms wide in a plaintive demand for an explanation.

"And you know what?" Mary Ann shot back. "None of the other kids are going to get accepted into Harvard, either. But you are. And do you know why? Because we do things differently around here, understand?"

She grabbed him roughly by the arm and marched him upstairs to his room, watching from the doorway as he crawled beneath the covers, muttering softly into his pillow. Mary Ann turned off the light.

"Good night, honey."

Instead of answering, he rolled onto his side, face turned to the wall. She moved closer to the bed.

"Troy Jonathan, I just spoke to you."

After a tense moment of defiance, he flopped onto his back.

"Mommy? Will you read me a story?"

"No," she said. "I most definitely will not. Mommies don't like it when little boys call them stupid."

———

Sarah unwrapped a Hershey bar and handed it to Lucy, whose eyelids were beginning to droop. The little girl accepted the treat without a word of comment, despite the fact that her mother normally enforced a strict no-chocolate-after-dinner policy. She took a tiny bite and chewed with unusual deliberation, keeping her vacant gaze glued to the TV screen like a pothead contemplating a lava lamp. Sarah couldn't tell if she was mesmerized by the movie—Dick Van Dyke was leading his fellow chimney sweeps in their big broomstick number—or simply too tired to turn her head.

"Mommy's going upstairs for a couple of minutes," she said. "Whatever you do, don't fall asleep. You keep those little eyes open, okay?"

"Okay, Mommy."

Sarah got dressed with what she considered to be admirable efficiency given the circumstances, trying on only three outfits before settling on the stretchy black skirt and cropped white T-shirt (which she'd pretty much known she was going to wear all along). She brushed her teeth, put on a little makeup, and was back downstairs by eight-forty-five.

But she was too late. Lucy was conked out on the couch, the barely nibbled Hershey bar clutched to her chest like a stuffed animal, the chocolate already beginning to ooze between her fingers. She made sweet little puffing noises as she slept, as if she were reading a book consisting only of the letter "P."

This was not good.

Sarah had gone to great lengths to avoid just this scenario, doing everything she could think of short of force-feeding her daughter a double espresso to keep her awake past the nine o'clock deadline, but it was all for naught. Lucy's sleep schedule had gone haywire ever since she'd stopped napping with Aaron.

Sarah turned off the TV and considered her options. She could call Jean, ask her to come over and keep an eye on Lucy while she ran a quick errand, but the last thing she wanted was to bring Todd into the house on tonight of all nights and have to introduce him to her chatty next-door neighbor. It was theoretically possible to have him wait in the backyard or something, but Sarah knew Jean well enough to know that the payment she'd extract for a half hour of last-minute baby-sitting was an hour-long conversation about her husband's shortcomings, how crabby and forgetful he'd become, and how difficult it was to buy him clothes now that he'd put on so much weight. It was trying enough to suffer through these monologues on a normal night; to know that every tiresome word out of Jean's mouth was another second without Todd would be nothing short of torture.

Of course, none of this would have mattered if she'd been able to contact him and notify him of the change in their plans. It hardly seemed possible at this point in human history that you could try all day and not find a way to reach a person living less than a mile away to pass along the simplest bit of information—*come to my house, not the playground*—but that was precisely the position in which Sarah found herself.

He hadn't come to the pool that afternoon, which eliminated the possibility of direct communication—a stolen conversation, a passed note, or, at the very least, the transmission of some sort of warning signal. Sarah called his house five times during the day from different pay phones—his home system was equipped with caller ID, supposedly to flush out solicitors—but each time the mother-in-law picked up, her voice growing harsher and more suspicious with each subsequent episode.

"Who's there? Stop calling here. Leave us alone."

Sarah considered breaking the cyber component of her promise as well, but that seemed even more dangerous. An e-mail in the wrong hands could have ruined everything. She believed she'd exercised heroic restraint in not exposing them to that risk, but it left her without any alternative beyond parking in front of Todd's house and hoping to catch him if he left the house without his bodyguard. Unfortunately, it was an oppressively hot day, and all the shady spots were taken. Lucy's complaints put an end to the stakeout after a mere twenty minutes.

For a fleeting second, Sarah thought about letting her daughter sleep. She wouldn't need much more than fifteen or twenty minutes, would she? All she had to do was rush over to the playground, collect Todd, explain the circumstances, and bring him back here for the night (it wasn't a seaside motel, but she was pretty sure he'd understand). Chances were, Lucy would sleep straight through till morning, and never even know her mother had been gone.

It was a tempting solution, but Sarah knew better. Every so often—a little more often than you'd expect—you'd hear these stories about tragic fires, very young children playing with matches, left alone in an apartment without adult supervision (the baby-sitter out looking for crack or whatever), or toddlers wandering across busy intersections with no shoes on their feet, their mothers subsequently arrested for neglect or endangerment (always the mothers, of course, hardly ever the fathers). And aside from these melodramatic risks, Sarah simply couldn't stand the thought of Lucy waking up and spending even a couple of minutes trying to figure out where her mother had gone, why she'd been left all alone in an empty house.

Waking her up wasn't such a great alternative, either. The last thing Sarah wanted on the way to what was supposed to have been the most romantic assignation of her life was a cranky and confused three-year-old whining in the backseat. Her only hope was to some-how transport Lucy out to the car, drive to the playground, pick up Todd, and carry her back inside without waking her. She was a deep sleeper; it could be done.

Sarah thought of everything. She opened the house and car doors beforehand, and removed a small plastic dog from the car seat. After prying the chocolate bar from Lucy's grip and wiping her fingers clean with a wet paper towel, she slipped both hands under her daughter's warm and compliant body and lifted her off the couch. Lucy stirred in her arms, uttering a drowsy syllable or two of protest, but she didn't wake. Sarah carried her out the front door, pulling it shut behind her, and tiptoed down the stairs and across the lawn to the Volvo. As carefully as if she were transporting a ticking time bomb, she tilted her daughter's body to avoid the door-frame and lowered her into her seat, pressing her head gently back-ward while she lowered the safety restraint and clicked the buckle into the slot. Lucy kicked her legs a couple of times, as if trying to free herself from tangled blankets, then let her head loll heavily to the right. Sarah released a deep sigh of relief and satisfaction.

Yes.

Everything would be all right now, she just knew it. She would get to the playground on time—well, maybe a couple of minutes late—and Todd would be waiting. They'd come home, put Lucy to bed, and go right to bed themselves, celebrating the beginning of a whole new phase in their lives. She couldn't help it, she touched herself between her legs as she drove, just letting her hand rest there lightly, nothing too distracting.

"Hey," came a tiny, unhappy voice from the backseat. "Where my chocket?"

With a groan of disbelief, Sarah checked the rearview mirror.

Lucy's eyes were wide-open, as if it were the middle of the day, as if sleep were the furthest thing from her mind.

"It's home," Sarah said. "You can eat the rest of it tomorrow."

"I want it now!"

"I don't have it," Sarah explained.

Lucy squeezed out an angry face for the mirror. Sarah braced herself for the inevitable tantrum, but somehow it passed. The little scowl softened; it looked more curious than angry.

"Where we going?" Lucy asked.

"To the playground," Sarah told her. "But not to play."

———

After all those years of being watched, first by the prison guards, and then by your mother, you would have thought it would be nice to be alone for once, nobody looking over your shoulder, making sure you were keeping out of trouble, but it was actually kind of weird and even a little scary. All these thoughts racing around your head, these impulses you no longer had to control.

It wasn't that Ronnie didn't *want* to be a good boy; he would have liked nothing better than to make his mother proud, to live a normal healthy life, be a solid citizen with a car, a good job, and a loving family. He could coach Little League, take his players out for ice cream after the games . . .

Yeah, like that was gonna happen.

He just wished he had the computer already. Then maybe he could look at a few pictures, keep himself occupied that way, maybe figure out how to navigate through those chat rooms you heard so much about. But right now he was in limbo. He tried to stick to the usual routine, dinner at six, the news, *Wheel of Fortune*, but it wasn't the same without his mother sitting next to him on the couch, muttering about Dan Rather's jowls or Vanna's crazy getups, studying the puzzles like they would reveal the mystery of life rather than a stupid proverb or the name of a celebrity no one had thought about for decades.

"Abe Vigoda!" she'd shout in triumph. "The heart is a lonely hunter!"

It was the phone he kept staring at, as if it held some sort of magnetic attraction. He wished there was somebody he could call, a friend or a relative, somebody who'd want to hear his sad news, somebody he could invite over for a cup of coffee, a little company. But there was only one number in his head, a number he hadn't used in years.

Don't do it, he told himself, but his finger was already pressing the buttons. *Don't be stupid.*

It rang three times, his heart going absolutely bonkers in his chest, the way it always did.

"Hello?" He could tell right away it was the mother, Diane Colapinto. He remembered seeing her on TV after the girl had disappeared, those black rings of grief encircling her dark eyes. "Hello?"

She sounded good, actually—cheerful, almost, like she'd given up crying over spilled milk and had finally gotten on with her life. He could hear laughter in the background, and realized that Holly's two younger siblings weren't so young anymore. The sister would be eleven, the brother ten, older than Holly was the day she got into his car.

"Hello?" Diane said again, this time more tentatively. "Who's calling?"

It would have been easy to do it, to whisper what he used to whisper after sneaking out to a pay phone in the middle of the night, when he'd startle her out of a deep sleep, enjoying the confusion of terror and hope in her voice. *I know where she is,* he'd taunt. *But I'm never going to tell you.*

Not tonight, though. Out of respect for his own dead mother, if for nothing else.

"Sorry," he said. "Wrong number."

He hung up, feeling sweaty and light-headed. There was one more person he could call, come to think of it. He had the number in his wallet, scribbled on a sticky note. She wasn't home, though— probably out on another blind date, boring some guy silly. All he got was her spacy voice on the answering machine. *This is Sheila, please leave me a message.* Ronnie waited for the beep, which took way longer than it should have.

"You are one loony bitch," he told her. "Why don't you put *that* in your personal ad?"

After that he was at a loss. It wasn't even nine o'clock, and he didn't have a fucking clue what to do with himself. He couldn't just sit around the house all night, making prank phone calls, could he? It would have been easier if he was a drinker. Then he could at least go out and get plastered, then come staggering home to sleep it off. If that had been his problem, everything would have been so goddam simple.

"Hey, Ma," he said, as if she were standing right there beside him, "I think I'm gonna go out for a while."

————

Lewis didn't even look up when she returned to the living room, taking a seat on the other end of the couch and picking up the copy of *Family Circle* that had just arrived in the mail.

"What are you reading about?" she asked after a moment or two, unable to tolerate the silence.

"Las Vegas."

"In *National Geographic?*"

"It's a history of the city. How it's evolved since the fifties."

"That's not right," she said. "You'd think *National Geographic* would have better things to report on. The rain forest or something."

"It's actually very interesting."

At eight-thirty, she put down her magazine and told him she was going upstairs to get ready. He grunted, still absorbed in his article.

She took a long bubble bath, closing her eyes and breathing deeply, trying to clear the clutter from her mind and will herself into a sexy mood. She'd recently come across an article (*Five Zesty Ways to Spice Up Your Marriage!*) that recommended fantasizing about partners other than your husband, and decided to give it a whirl. Bruce Willis didn't work, for some reason, and neither did Brad Pitt, but that was probably because he was in dire need of a haircut and a shave, and, quite possibly, a hot shower. But then, out of nowhere, she found herself thinking about Tony Soprano, a man she found completely repulsive, with his big hairy belly and gutter mouth, the way he bent that girl over a table with his pants around his ankles, a cigar clenched between his teeth as he pounded away.

Disgusting.

She yanked the drain plug, forcing the image out of her mind, wishing Lewis had never convinced her to get HBO. After she brushed her teeth and dabbed some perfume on her neck, she slipped into a pink satin slip with a lacy bodice, ran a brush through her hair, and stepped into the bedroom, pausing to let herself be admired.

Her husband should have been sitting on the bed in his glasses and boxer shorts, nodding in fervent approval, but he wasn't there. A queasy, almost desolate feeling came over her as she contemplated the undisturbed bed, the clock on the end table reading 9:02. She headed straight downstairs to see what was keeping him.

"Honey?" she said. "Aren't you forgetting something?"

"You know what?" he said. "Why don't we give it a rest?"

"But it's Tuesday. It's our date night."

He stared at her for what felt like a long time. There was the oddest look on his face, like he pitied her for something.

"I really don't feel like it."

Mary Ann gulped. It took an enormous effort to remain composed, to keep the tremor out of her voice.

"You don't love me anymore."

Lewis didn't answer right away. He seemed to be giving her statement some serious consideration, as if he hadn't thought about it in a while.

"Our son is four years old," he said. "You have to stop talking to him about Harvard."

———

Hands clammy and heart pounding, Sarah pulled into the Rayburn School parking lot at seven minutes after nine, not nearly as late as she'd feared. She kept her headlights on, their dusty beams shining on the deserted playground—the seesaw and slide, the play structure with its swaying bridge and festive little gazebo, the fateful swing set—waiting in an ecstasy of suspense for Todd to step out of the shadows, the sight of him always so startling to her after even the briefest of separations, the way he had of seeming so matter-of-factly present and so utterly fantastical at the same time.

At eleven after nine she shut off her headlights. *It's all right,* she told herself, *he's only ten minutes late.* She had to make a conscious effort to ignore the flutter of panic in her belly, the little voice reminding her that he'd never been late before. It was something they'd joked about at the Town Pool, the invariable pattern of their relationship—the boys always early, the girls always late.

But maybe it was a good thing, this little break in protocol. This way Todd would owe her an apology, and he'd be that much less likely to hold it against her that they weren't going to the beach after all, that they'd be stuck in her house with Lucy, still trapped within the suffocating borders of Bellington and parenthood.

"What we doing?" Lucy inquired.

"Waiting for Todd," she replied. "He should be here any minute. He's going to sleep over at our house tonight."

Lucy didn't seem unduly troubled by this answer. Sarah had never really been able to figure out just how much she understood—even in her limited three-year-old capacity—about her relationship with Todd. All through the summer, she had just accepted whatever happened as if it were well within the natural order of things. When they were hanging out with Todd and Aaron every day, that was fine with her. When they stopped, she asked about it once, and seemed to find her mother's explanation—*Aaron's grandma wants them all to herself*—completely satisfactory. Sarah couldn't help hoping that Lucy would show the same flexibility toward the much larger changes that were about to shake up her life, but she couldn't quite suppress the suspicion that she was being a bit too passive as a parent, not doing enough to prepare her daughter for the immediate future.

"Honey," she said. "Do you like Aaron?"

"Sometimes."

"He's a nice boy, isn't he? You play so well together."

"He likes cars," Lucy said, a trace of contempt in her voice.

"Would you like him to be your brother?"

Lucy giggled nervously. She seemed to think Sarah was playing some sort of game with her.

"Him not my brother."

"He might be." Sarah turned in her seat and looked her daughter straight in the eyes, hoping by this to make her understand that they were having a very serious discussion. "Someday. Not your real brother, but your stepbrother. That means we would all live together in the same house, at least some of the time."

"I don't like that." Lucy sounded angry.

"Sure you will. It'll just take a little time to get used to it."

Lucy shook her head in ferocious denial.

"Not get used to it."

Sarah decided not to push it. You just had to take these things one step at a time. Given enough time and love, kids would adapt to anything. And Sarah couldn't help thinking that, however Lucy felt about it right now, she'd be better off in the long run with Todd as the father figure in her life than she would be with Richard.

"Mommy?" Lucy asked a couple of moments later. Her voice was soft and tentative, as if she'd been thinking things over.

"Yes, honey?"

"Can you swing me?"

"Sure," Sarah said, before she'd even realized what she was agreeing to. "But just for a little while, okay?"

————

Todd had left his house at nine o'clock sharp, but he got sidetracked at the library. The skateboarders were out, and he stopped for a minute to see how they were doing. To his surprise, they greeted him like an old friend as he assumed his once-familiar post by the mailbox.

"Dude," this gruff-voiced kid called out. "Where the fuck you been?"

"We missed you," another one added, somehow managing to sound sarcastic and sincere at the same time. "We thought you didn't love us anymore."

"Yeah," said G., the skinny leader of the pack. "Thought maybe we were boring you."

"Not at all," he explained, oddly flattered by the attention. "I've just been going through some weird shit."

He hadn't watched them for weeks, not since before the bar exam, and was amazed at how much they'd improved in the interim, as if they'd all gone to skateboard camp or something. Kids who'd looked like beginners in June were whipping around like experts. The ones who were good then had blossomed into virtuosos, though G. remained in a league of his own.

As always, there was something hypnotic about the spectacle of the boys on their boards, the steady flow of riders gliding past him, each following the one before in almost metronomic regularity, the insistent hum of wheels on pavement. They were improvising these overlapping figures in the street, six of them weaving in and out of each other's paths, crouching and standing like human pistons, shifting directions on a dime with these abrupt pivots and trick spins, performing nimble, almost monkeylike, maneuvers with their feet, flipping their boards into the air, then landing gracefully on top when they reconnected with the ground.

He knew Sarah was waiting, but he couldn't quite bring himself to leave. Every time he did a gut check, it always felt like he needed another minute or two to clear his head, to gather up his courage for the big and terrible step they had agreed to take together.

He'd meant it on Thursday when he told her that they should run away together, meant it like he'd never meant anything in his life. In that sublime moment, the two of them lying on their backs on the fifty yard line, gazing up at the star-studded emptiness of space, the words had emerged from his mouth with a conviction that startled both of them. He remembered the thrill that had passed from his fingers into hers, then back again, an electrical current filling him with the conviction that a life with Sarah—a life rearranged and made whole—was not only possible but absolutely necessary.

Four days had passed since then, four strange and painful days during which this conviction had been tested in a hundred different ways. It started first thing on Friday, when Kathy shook him awake at eight o'clock in the morning and told him that they were going away for the weekend, just the two of them, to the same inn in the Berkshires where they'd spent their honeymoon.

"I'm taking the day off," she said, running her hand over his forehead as if checking for a temperature. "We need a little time alone."

He could have said no, of course, could have told her right then that he'd made other plans for his life, but he was still in too much of a daze to put up a struggle.

"Yeah, sure," he said, raising himself up on his elbows and blinking away the harsh morning light. "Whatever."

"Don't get so excited," she told him. "It's not good for your heart."

By the time they left, shortly after noon, he had decided that maybe the little trip wasn't such a bad idea. One way or another, he was going to have to get through the next few days, and at least this way he'd be able to spend a couple of them without his mother-in-law breathing down his neck. Not to mention the fact that he was finding it extremely difficult that morning to look Aaron in the eye. It was almost a relief to leave him standing on the porch in his bathing suit and jester's cap, waving good-bye along with his grand-mother.

"What a cutie," Kathy said, looking wistfully over her shoulder as they pulled away. "I kinda wish he was coming with us."

They had been driving for about an hour in companionable silence—they'd always traveled well together, just as long as Kathy wasn't driving—when she suddenly reached forward and turned down the stereo. He could feel her eyes on him, the tension gathering.

"Just tell me one thing," she said. "Do you love her?"

"I don't know. That's what I'm trying to figure out."

She laughed, sounding a little more amused than he might have expected.

"Let me know when you decide, okay?"

"It's not funny," he muttered.

"Oh, that's right. I almost forgot."

They hiked and swam after checking in, then ate a sunset dinner on a terrace overlooking the lake. It was all so pleasant—so much like their idea of a good day—that Todd had to keep reminding himself that he was leaving her, that their marriage was over. He only drank one glass of wine at dinner and refused a bite of her chocolate mousse cake, as if he no longer had a right to it. Before bed, she asked him if he'd like her to try on some new lingerie she'd bought for the occasion, but he said no, he'd prefer it if she didn't.

"Are you sure? It seems like a waste to drive all the way out here and not even make love."

"I'm kinda tired," he explained.

"Fine," she said, pretending not to care. "Suit yourself."

He caved on Saturday morning, when she woke him with a long sloppy kiss and guided his hand between her legs. Before he even had a chance to remember why it wasn't such a good idea, he was hard, and she was straddling his prone body, smiling down at him with an expression that mingled triumph and apology.

"This isn't so bad, is it?" she whispered.

"It's okay," he conceded.

Actually, it was way better than okay, a greatest hits medley of their entire relationship, Kathy reprising every mind-blowing bedroom move she'd ever performed for him, vividly illustrating the cornucopia of pleasures he was on the verge of giving up. It was an amazing performance, marred only by the slightest trace of smugness on her face, a cool erotic confidence that he couldn't help resenting on behalf of Sarah, whose undeniable enthusiasm for sex was often accompanied by a strange, almost adolescent clumsiness, as if she were acting on the basis of vague schoolyard rumors and half-remembered passages from dirty books, rather than years of hard-won adult experience.

A heavy silence descended upon the room when they were finished, Todd staring up at the ceiling with a profound sense of melancholy, trying to process the realization that this was it for them, that he and Kathy would probably never make love again. As if reading his mind, she rolled over and punched him in the arm as hard as she could.

"You shithead," she said.

"What?" he replied, trying to look casual as he massaged his tricep.

"You think I don't want a summer boyfriend? You think I don't want to spend my days at the pool, holding hands with some cute guy I just met yesterday? How come you get to do that, but I have to spend my time in a smelly VA Hospital, listening to old men explain how they lost their legs?"

"I thought you liked your job."

"It doesn't matter if I like it or not, does it? I'm gonna have to do it regardless, unless somebody else in this family has a better idea."

Todd had nothing to say in response. He didn't have a better idea. All he had was a debt to Kathy he'd never be able to repay. Especially now, when he was on the verge of declaring bankruptcy.

"She's not a summer girlfriend," he muttered, more to himself than to his wife.

Kathy laughed, as if she were enjoying this in spite of herself.

"And let me tell you something else," she said. "Summer's just about over, in case you hadn't noticed."

———

There was a sour taste in Larry's mouth as he walked up to the front door of 44 Blueberry Court. The thought of what he was about to do sickened him. If he could have done otherwise and still figured out a way to live with himself, he would have been a very happy man.

But there was no choice for him. He had lived through something like this once before with the Antoine Harris shooting, and he had learned his lesson. Hard as it was for even his close friends to believe, Larry never really regretted pulling the trigger in the food court that awful afternoon. He had made a tragic mistake, of course, but he would go to his grave knowing it had been an honest one. In his own mind, he'd seen a man with a gun, not a kid with a toy, and he'd reacted accordingly, the way any cop would. No matter how many times he'd turned it over in his thoughts, he could never see his way out of firing that fatal shot, not unless he'd been an entirely different person.

But he could have apologized. He could have ignored his lawyer's advice and presented himself to the family, told Rolonda Harris how heartsick and sorry he was for her unimaginable loss and for his own part in causing it. Maybe she wouldn't have believed him. Maybe she would have slammed the door shut, or called him an evil racist, or even spat in his face, but so what? At least he would have tried, and trying would have been better than keeping silent, acting like the boy's death meant nothing to him, like all he cared about was saving his own skin.

Still, apologizing to Rolonda Harris was one thing, and apologizing to Ronnie McGorvey another. Rolonda was an innocent woman whose worst nightmare had come true. Ronnie was Ronnie, a repulsive human being who dragged his mother into a mess she had nothing to do with. If it hadn't been for him, Larry would have had no reason to be standing on the poor woman's front lawn, shouting into a bullhorn at two in the morning.

You killed your mother, Larry could have argued. *You did it, not me.*

But he wasn't going to go there, wasn't going to let himself sink into that futile swamp of blame-shifting and self-justification. Ronnie would have to live with his own conscience, if he even had one, and Larry would have to do what he could to accept responsibility for his own undeniable role in May McGorvey's death.

He rang the bell, steeling himself for the moment when Ronnie appeared in front of him. He wasn't going to shake hands or make small talk. All he was going to do was look the pervert in the eyes and say, *I'm sorry for your loss.* Just that, not another word. And then he was going to turn around and drive home.

He rang a second time, but still no one answered, even though all the downstairs lights were on. If this had been any other house, any other errand, he would have given up right then. But it had cost him too much to get this far; he couldn't bear the thought of having to do it all again tomorrow. He tried the knob, pushed the door open just enough to stick his head inside.

"Ronnie? It's Larry Moon. I'm not here to hurt you."

Maybe he was sleeping. Larry remembered how bone-tired he'd felt after his own father's death. He'd collapsed right after the funeral, slept for almost twenty hours.

"Yo, Ronnie?"

He stepped cautiously into the hallway and peeked into the living room. The TV was going, the sound turned way down. Someone had left a dirty plate on the coffee table, a half-eaten chicken leg and some peas.

"Ronnie?" he called again, this time from the base of the stairs.

He thought about checking the second-floor bedrooms, but decided against it. A bad feeling had suddenly come over him, the kind of feeling a cop learns to ignore at his own risk. If there was something ugly to find in this house, Larry didn't want to be the one to find it.

He circled through the kitchen on his way out. It was cleaner than he'd expected, a lot like his own mother's before she'd gotten it renovated. An old gas stove, pictures of the grandkids on the fridge. Everything in order except for an open liter bottle of 7-Up on the table, alongside an ashtray full of cigarettes that had been smoked down to the filter.

And a note under the ashtray, a creased and crumpled piece of paper with frayed edges on one side. Two different people had written on it, almost like they were having a conversation. The first message was a plea, written in faint blue ink by someone with a shaky hand.

Please please be a good boy.

The response was in black, in jagged block letters that could have been scrawled by a child.

I'M SORRY, MOMMY, I DON'T THINK I CAN.

————

Sarah pushed Lucy on the annoyingly creaky swing, forcing herself not to check her watch again. She already knew it was close to nine-thirty, how close she didn't want to know.

Please, she thought, glancing over her shoulder to see if he might be approaching from the athletic field instead of the parking area. *Would you just get here already?*

It had been a romantic flourish, this plan to meet at the play-ground, to revisit the scene of their first kiss, that impulsive trans-gression that had changed everything for both of them. Right now, though, the playground felt anything but romantic. Never having been here at night, Sarah hadn't realized how creepy and isolated it would be, backed up against the school building and overhung by shade trees, separated from nearby streets by a parking lot on one side and a vast grassy field on the other. It wasn't pitch-black out—there were a couple of floodlights shining on the parking lot—but the weak grayish glow barely made it to the swing set.

"I sleepy," Lucy murmured. "We go home?"

"In a minute," said Sarah. "As soon as Todd gets here."

He's coming, she insisted to herself. *He just got held up.* Maybe Kathy had to work late. Maybe she and her mother went out shop-ping or something.

Or maybe Todd had just chickened out.

She knew he was worried about money, about the financial re-sponsibilities he assumed would fall on his shoulders if he and Sarah decided to make a go of it. If he had been here, though, she would have told him not to worry. She had come up with the perfect solution to their problem.

"I'm going to be a lawyer," she told her daughter. "What do you think of that?"

Lucy didn't answer, but Sarah kept talking anyway.

"I could go to law school. I used to think it would be too boring and too hard for me, but now I don't feel that way anymore. All you really need is an organized mind, and I think I have an organized mind, don't you, sweetie?"

The decision had crept up on her over the weekend, while she was sitting in bed, plowing through *A Civil Action*. She'd been reading a lot of books about the law and legal education over the past couple of weeks—*One L, The Paper Chase, The Brethren*—thinking they might help her muster some good arguments to convince Todd to take the bar exam one last time, to not let his education go to waste, the way she'd done with her master's in English. And then it suddenly occurred to her: *Why not me? Why can't I be the lawyer in the family?* Todd could stay home, ferry the kids back and forth to school and music lessons and soccer practice, take care of the cooking and the housework if that was what he preferred. *I'll get a job with a small public interest firm, do environmental or sexual harassment law, take on the big corporations on behalf of the little people.* She cultivated an appealing vision of herself standing in front of the jury box in a tailored blue suit, all those heads nodding as she made her elegant closing argument, asking her fellow citizens not to let big money trample on simple fairness, on America's noble promise of justice for all.

"I don't see why the man always has to be the breadwinner," she continued. "That's not the only way to do it. That's not—Oh, thank God."

Her pleasure at the sound of his footsteps was so strong that it took her a second or two to process the surprising fact that he wasn't approaching from either the parking lot or the grassy field, which were the two obvious ways to access the playground from the street. Instead, the footsteps were coming from her right, almost as if he'd been hiding in the bushes by the school.

"What are you——?" she began, turning just in time to see a man step into the light between the seesaw and the twisty slide, a man with a cast on one arm and a far too familiar face. For an odd moment, she felt no fear at all, only the most profound, crushing disappointment of her life.

"Wait a minute," she said, as if he were trying to pull a fast one on her. "You're not Todd."

————

The boys were catching air, zooming down the handicap ramp and launching off a small wooden platform at the edge of the street. The best ones, like G. and the gruff-voiced kid, actually managed to spin around in the air and still stick the landing. Their less skillful comrades usually got separated from their boards soon after liftoff; only the lucky ones landed on their feet. Because they were so young, though, even the unfortunates who did swan dives and belly flops bounced right up from the pavement, laughing like it was all in the service of an excellent time.

A slow surge of panic crept from Todd's feet up through his chest and shoulders. He understood quite clearly that time was running out; Sarah wouldn't wait forever. And yet he couldn't bring himself to move. It was the same inexplicable paralysis that used to root him to this very spot on nights when he was supposed to have been studying for the bar.

The past two days with Aaron had been way harder than his weekend away with Kathy. They'd stuck to their well-oiled routine on Monday—playground, lunch, pool, supermarket, Train Wreck—dogged as usual by Marjorie and Big Bear. The whole time, Todd was tormented by an urgent need to explain himself, to pull Aaron aside and give him some advance notice of the tidal wave that was about to crash into his life, but he didn't know how to do it without placing the entire plan in jeopardy—vague hints and obscure warnings just weren't going to cut it with a three-year-old. So instead of putting it into words, Todd found himself hugging and kissing his son all day long, behavior Aaron tolerated from his mother, but apparently found worrisome, and even a bit unseemly, coming from his father.

"Da-ad!" he'd say, fending off the embrace with a stiff-arm that would serve him well in Pop Warner in a few years. "Why you do that?"

On Tuesday Todd tried a different approach, taking Aaron and Marjorie on an impromptu trip to an amusement park just over the New Hampshire border. He bought Aaron a bracelet good for a day's worth of unlimited rides and let him call the shots. If he wanted to ride the Chinese Dragon kiddie coaster six times straight, Todd had no objection, nor to the cotton candy, SnoCone, and corn dog Aaron downed in quick succession, while his grandmother looked on, silently scandalized.

"This is your day," Todd kept telling him. "You're the boss."

Right before they left, Todd and Aaron took a spin on the Ferris wheel. After a couple of continuous revolutions, they suddenly found themselves stopped at the top, swaying gently over the treetops in their green metal cage, looking down on the festive chaos below. Todd turned toward his son, gazing into his lovely, trusting eyes.

"Aaron? Whatever happens, I just want you to know one thing."

"Something happen?" Aaron asked suspiciously.

"No, nothing happened. I'm only speaking hypothetically."

Aaron frowned; Todd couldn't help laughing.

"Forget it," he said. "I'm not even going to try to explain that. I just want you to know, no matter what happens, that I love you very much and wouldn't do anything to hurt you. Do you understand that? And if anything does happen, it's not your fault, okay? You didn't do anything wrong. Not a single thing."

Aaron thought this over for a while as the operator released the brake and the wheel lurched forward and down.

"You mad at me?" he asked.

"No," said Todd. "Not at all."

"I thought you were mad."

Todd reached for his son's hand. Aaron let him take it.

"I'm not mad. I just love you so much."

"Okay." Aaron nodded thoughtfully, as if to say, *Fair enough.*

They held hands the rest of the ride, neither one looking at the other or saying a word. Even then, though, Todd's resolve hadn't weakened. He sang along with Raffi the whole way back to Bellington, never doubting for a second that he would be leaving with Sarah later that night, heading for the seashore and a new version of his life.

After putting Aaron down for his nap, Todd locked himself in his bedroom and wrote a long letter to Kathy, explaining what he was about to do and why he was doing it. The letter ended with a long postscript to Aaron that he asked Kathy to please read aloud to him in the morning. He sealed the note in an envelope, folded it, and slipped it into his back pocket.

A little before nine that night, Todd went upstairs and sat on

Aaron's bed for a few minutes, watching him sleep, trying to convince himself of what a luxury it would be to wake up tomorrow morning in a motel room far from here, no responsibilities, no fights about breakfast or getting dressed or turning off the TV, but he couldn't quite pull it off. He *liked* dressing Aaron, as much as he complained about the relentless dailiness of it, and the extreme challenge posed by the socks. It was sad to think of him being dressed in the morning by someone else, especially in a house full of gloom and confusion.

Still, he pressed forward. He rose from Aaron's bed with a weary sigh and ducked into his own room to hide the letter on Kathy's pillow, a place where she'd be certain to find it, but not until after he and Sarah had ample time to make their getaway. He peeled back the bedspread just far enough to expose the pillow, and then froze.

That was when his courage faltered. Not completely, but just enough that the letter was still tucked into his back pocket when he bent down to pick up the errant skateboard that had banged into the curb by his feet, dislodging him from his reverie. It must have belonged to the kid who was sitting in the middle of the street, laughing and whimpering as he rubbed his knee.

"You okay?" Todd asked, walking toward him.

The kid nodded and stood up, but he shook his head when Todd tried to return the skateboard.

"Keep it," he said. "I think I'm done for tonight."

"Keep it?" said Todd. "What do you mean?"

"Take a run," the kid told him. "It's pretty fucking cool."

"Yeah," the gruff-voiced kid called out from the opposite curb, as his comrades nodded and muttered their agreement. "Give it a shot, dude."

"You guys are crazy," Todd said, trying to sound amused rather than intrigued. "I don't know how to ride a skateboard."

"Sure you do," said G. "You been watching us all summer."

————

Mary Ann stood beneath the streetlight at the edge of the soccer field, her hand shaking as she tried to light the cigarette. It was the first one she'd smoked since she was fourteen, the summer when she and two of her fellow counselors-in-training at Camp Mesquantum used to sneak down to the lake after lights-out, trading puffs on a single Marlboro and concocting clever plans for seducing older boys. It should have been a pleasant memory, but it wasn't; Mary Ann hadn't liked the other girls very much and was terrified of getting caught breaking two camp rules at the same time. Not to mention that she had absolutely no interest in seducing anyone at that point in her life, especially an older boy.

The cigarette wasn't hers. It came from a pack of Camel Lights that had accidentally spilled out of Theresa's purse at the playground a couple of weeks ago, when she was looking for a Band-Aid. Mary Ann had snatched it up from the picnic table before any of the kids had a chance to notice.

"I thought you quit," she said, surprised by the anger in her voice.

"I've been backsliding," Theresa admitted.

"I'm keeping them," Mary Ann had told her. "For your own good."

Ignoring Theresa's feeble protests, she dropped the cigarettes into her own purse. And there they'd sat since the beginning of August, as if waiting for this very moment, when sneaking one would suddenly seem like an inspired idea, the perfect accessory for her mood of reckless desperation. Luckily, she'd confiscated a lighter, too, a yellow Bic some irresponsible parent had left lying on the edge of the sandbox.

It took her three tries just to get the thing lit. The first puff seared her lungs, triggering an extended coughing fit that brought tears to her eyes. Reminding herself not to inhale, she set off across the soccer field in the direction of the playground.

It was more force of habit than conscious intention that had led her to the Rayburn School after she'd barged out of the house, telling Lewis she needed a little fresh air. But it was the right place, she realized right away, a secluded spot where she could sit for a while without worrying about anyone she knew seeing her with a cigarette in her hand. She just needed a little time to think things over, to absorb the significance of what had just happened and what it might mean for her future.

Her marriage was floundering—there was no use denying it—but the truth was, it hadn't been that great to begin with. She had never loved her husband, not even on the day when he raised her veil and kissed her in front of two hundred applauding people. She had married him in a fit of impatience that bordered on panic, after being dumped by the man she considered her soul mate. Sure, her career had been going well—she had just been named VP of Employee Relations—but what good was that? She vowed not to let herself get stranded, not to turn into one of those pathetic middle-aged spinsters she sometimes talked to at work, the ones who were always going on in these weirdly insistent voices about how much they loved their cats.

Lewis was a decent man, quiet and solid, a certified financial planner. Even when they met, when he was still in his early thirties, she'd wished that he had a little more hair and a flatter stomach, but what was the alternative? *The last train's leaving*, she told herself. *Better get on board.*

She'd been reasonably satisfied with the trade-offs in her life until this past spring, when the Prom King started showing up at the playground. He reminded her so much of her beloved ex-boyfriend, Brian, the only man she'd ever loved—same height, same broad shoulders, same easy smile. Brian, the man she'd lived with for two years and fully expected to marry, and who'd left her, he said, because she didn't know how to have any fun. *Show me*, she'd begged him, *I want to know*, but he said it was impossible, you either knew how to have fun or you didn't.

Every day she sat at the picnic table with her friends and watched that ridiculously handsome man playing with that beautiful child in his jester's cap, and it was like they were taunting her with an image of what might have been, the life that had been snatched away from her and replaced by something decidedly inferior. And then for that awful Sarah—Sarah, of all people—to become his girlfriend, it was just a little too much. She couldn't help but take it out on Lewis. Poor schlubby Lewis. The good provider. Mr. 401(K). Talk about a person who didn't know how to have any fun. It got to the point where she could barely look at him, let alone touch him. They wouldn't have made love at all if it hadn't been for the custom of the unbreakable Tuesday night date. And now he'd gone and broken it. *Him*, she thought bitterly. *Him rejecting me*. It was almost funny.

There are times when you know you're awake, but can't shake the feeling that you must be dreaming, because the world is suddenly showing you something that makes no sense whatsoever. That was how Mary Ann felt as she approached the playground, angrily puffing on Theresa's cigarette and reflecting on her hopeless marriage. There was something peculiar happening by the swing set—it was hard to make out at first, but growing clearer with each step— something so disgusting and inexplicable it could only have emerged from her feverish and vengeful brain, rather than any possible version of objective reality.

————

This was *so* not the man Sarah wanted to be embracing right now. She tried to disengage, but he held on tightly with his one good arm, his ungainly body heaving against hers in great hiccupy sobs. It smelled like he hadn't showered in a couple of days.

"Take it easy," she whispered, turning her head to avoid contact with his wiry hair, her heart still pumping like crazy. "It's gonna be okay."

"No," he replied, snorting and sniffling the way Lucy did when she was trying to regain control of herself after a tantrum. "It's not . . . gonna . . . be . . . okay."

He dropped his head onto her shoulder, his mouth alarmingly close to her breast. Patting him awkwardly on the shoulder blade, she tried to block out the unpleasant sensation of warm moisture seeping through the fabric of her shirt.

She took a couple of deep breaths, trying to calm down a little. Distasteful as it was to be hugging a hygienically challenged child molester, it was way better than the other possibilities that had flashed through her mind when he'd materialized so swiftly and unexpectedly out of the darkness. She'd been momentarily paralyzed by the sight of him—more out of bewilderment than fear, she thought—but then her maternal instincts had kicked in. Rushing around to the front of the swing, she grabbed her daughter under the arms and tried to yank her out of the rubber seat, but Lucy had fallen asleep, and her dangling foot got caught in the opening. Sarah was frantically trying to extract it when she felt an oddly gentle hand on her shoulder.

"Please," Ronald James McGorvey had said, in this tremulous, almost beseeching voice that made no sense to her, as if she were the one calling the shots. "Don't run away from me."

She let go of Lucy and turned slowly, preparing herself to scream like she'd never screamed before, only to discover that her assailant was in a pitiful state. He was rocking back and forth on his heels with a dazed expression on his face, broken arm pressed across his chest like he was about to recite the pledge of allegiance.

"Do you need help?" she asked him.

"I just wanna talk to someone," he said, his bottom lip quivering.

"Okay," she said. "I'm listening."

"I lost my mother!" he wailed, stepping forward and throwing his arm around her neck. "Just this afternoon!"

She tried a second time to step away from him, but he had a handful of her shirt and wasn't letting go. Her whole shoulder felt wet, almost like he was drooling on her.

"It's hard," she said, squinting in the direction of the empty parking lot, her impatience with Todd suddenly metastasizing into anger. "It's really hard."

McGorvey lifted his head to look at her, his eyes swollen with grief behind his thick glasses. She had to make a conscious effort not to avert her gaze.

"I didn't even say good-bye." His voice was calmer now, only cracking on the last word. "She was dead when I got there."

"It's okay," Sarah said, glancing over her shoulder to check on

Lucy. She was still sleeping in the motionless swing, thank God, oblivious to the world. "I'm sure she knew how you felt about her."

"I don't know what I'm gonna do," he said. "I just don't know."

Sarah didn't answer, distracted by the sight of a silver minivan pulling into the parking lot, its headlights sweeping across the playground. At almost the same moment, she heard a siren in the distance and footsteps approaching from the soccer field. She turned quickly, hope surging through her body with such force that it almost knocked her down. But instead of Todd it was Mary Ann who emerged from the darkness. She stopped at the edge of the playground, where the wood chips met the grass, and stood there for a moment with a lit cigarette in her hand and the strangest look on her face.

"Sarah?" She sounded more puzzled than angry. "Why are you doing that?"

Before she could reply, McGorvey stepped out of her arms and turned toward the parking lot. A man—he was too stocky to be Todd—was running toward them at a furious clip, like he had an important message to deliver.

"Oh great," said McGorvey. "Now he's gonna break my other arm."

———

Just for a second, Todd thought he must be at a football game. He was lying on his back on the hard ground, and DeWayne was staring down at him with a concerned expression.

"Todd?" he said. "Can you hear me?"

It couldn't have been a football game, though. DeWayne was wearing his police uniform, hat and all, and some kids were standing a bit behind him, wearing unbuckled helmets.

Oh shit, he thought. *The skateboard.*

He tried to sit up, but DeWayne restrained him, pressing gently on his shoulder.

"Don't move. The ambulance is on its way."

"It's okay. I'm fine."

"You sure? Can you move your fingers and toes?"

Todd tested his digits.

"Everything's okay," he said. "Everything except my head."

DeWayne shook his head. "Least it's nothing important."

It was a little more difficult than Todd expected to shift into a sitting position. When the dizzy spell passed, he reached up to rub his sore jaw, and was startled to find blood on his hand.

"Jesus," he said. "What happened to me?"

"You had an intimate encounter with the street," DeWayne informed him. "These kids say you've been out cold for the past five minutes."

"You caught some monster air," G. chimed in, with real admiration in his voice.

"Dude, you were fucking awesome," echoed the gruff-voiced kid. "Like that ski jumper on TV."

DeWayne shooed the kids away, telling them to give the man some breathing room, or better yet, get on home to their parents.

"No more skateboarding tonight," he said. "Why don't you clear out of here."

The kids grumbled a little, but began to disperse, leaving Todd and DeWayne alone in the street. It was coming back to him now, the amazing sensation of rolling down the wheelchair ramp, gathering speed, his feet rooted to the board, as if this were the way he'd been meant to travel through the world. The launch platform wasn't much higher than a curb, but it was steeply pitched, and he must have hit it with more momentum than he'd realized. Even through the thrumming pain in his head, he held on to a vivid memory of finding himself suddenly aloft, his arms spread wide, his body suspended above the street. And then pitching sideways, rolling over until he was staring straight up at the sky, floating on a cushion of air. The only thing he didn't remember was hitting the ground.

"How you feeling?" DeWayne asked.

"Okay," said Todd. "A little woozy."

Fingering a tender bump on his skull, he flashed on Sarah, wondering if she'd left the playground. He hated to think of her still standing there in the dark, wondering what the hell had happened to him.

"They're probably gonna take you to the hospital. Don't like to take no chances with head injuries."

Todd nodded. It was painful to admit it, but the main thing he felt right now was an overwhelming sense of relief to be here in the street with DeWayne, instead of in the car with Sarah, rushing down the highway into the next big mistake of his adult life. Sure, he felt guilty for disappointing her, for making her wait around for nothing, for promising something he couldn't deliver. But what he suddenly understood—it seemed so obvious now, as if the truth had been jarred loose when his body hit the pavement—was that he'd never actually wanted to start a *new* life with her in the first place. What he loved most about Sarah was how beautifully she fit into his old one, distracting him from his imperfect marriage and the tedious obligations of child care, supercharging the dull summer days with a sweet illicit thrill. Outside of that context, he couldn't imagine them ever being as happy with each other as they'd been this summer.

"Hey, DeWayne," he said. "You think I'd make a good cop?"

DeWayne studied him for a moment, apparently trying to decide if it was a serious question.

"Yeah, sure," he said, raising his voice to compete with the bloopy siren of the approaching ambulance. "You could patrol the town on your skateboard."

———————

Sarah felt like a fool. When she saw Larry Moon sprinting toward the playground, she'd let herself believe that Todd had sent him, that he was coming to deliver a message to *her*. But he went straight for McGorvey, grabbing him roughly by the collar.

"You sonofabitch!" he said, his voice trembling with rage. "Didn't I tell you to stay away from playgrounds? Didn't I?"

McGorvey nodded politely, as if responding to a civil question. "I'm sorry," he said.

The apology just seemed to make Moon angrier.

"Sorry?" He cuffed McGorvey hard on the side of his head. "You're a sorry piece of shit is what you are."

McGorvey just continued nodding, as if he were in complete agreement with this assessment of his character. Moon raised his hand again, but Sarah stepped in front of him before he could strike another blow.

"Would you just leave him alone?" she said. "He wasn't hurting anybody."

Mary Ann chose that moment to step beneath the crossbar of the swing set and join the group. She smiled cheerfully, taking an awkward puff on her cigarette and blowing out a mouthful of smoke right away, as if she hadn't yet mastered the art of inhaling.

"They were sharing a tender moment," she explained to Moon. "Until we so rudely interrupted."

You bitch from hell, Sarah thought.

"His mother just died, okay? He's upset."

As if to confirm this report, McGorvey sniffled and rubbed a hand across a cheek.

"Oh, you're upset, are you?" Moon taunted McGorvey. "Well, now you know how they felt. Except a million times worse."

"How who felt?" said Mary Ann.

"The parents of that little girl. The one he killed. I bet they were pretty upset."

McGorvey hung his head. Sarah wanted to tell Moon to stop hounding the man, to just leave him in peace for one single day, but McGorvey spoke up before she had a chance.

"I didn't want to hurt her," he muttered, still staring at the ground. "She made me."

"What?" Moon cupped a hand around his ear as if he wasn't sure he'd heard right. "What did you just say?"

McGorvey looked up. He held his good arm out like an actor, the way he had at the Town Pool on the day of the electrical storm.

"I didn't want to," he repeated in a wounded tone. "She said she was gonna tell on me."

"She was gonna tell on you?" Moon repeated incredulously. "You killed a little girl because she was gonna *tell on you?*"

McGorvey lowered his arm. A strange whimper escaped from his throat. He shifted his gaze from Moon to Mary Ann to Sarah, as if searching for a more sympathetic listener.

"I didn't want to get in trouble." McGorvey's voice trailed off as he said this, as if he suddenly realized how ridiculous it sounded.

"Did you hear that?" Moon asked Sarah and Mary Ann in an excited voice. "Did you hear what he just said? You two are witnesses."

"I heard it," said Mary Ann.

Sarah nodded. She wasn't sure a hearsay confession would hold up in court, but she didn't say so. She just watched silently as Moon clapped McGorvey on the back, almost like he was offering his congratulations.

"Oh-ho, man. You are so fucked."

McGorvey shook his head.

"Doesn't matter," he said. "I'm fucked any way you look at it."

A stunned silence descended upon the playground, a hush so sudden and profound that Sarah was momentarily startled by the sound of her own breathing. She stared at McGorvey with an open-mouthed expression of bewilderment that would have seemed unthinkably rude under any other circumstances, trying to comprehend the fact that this harmless-looking man—this man she'd just *hugged*—was a murderer.

Of a child.

More out of embarrassment than anything else, Sarah turned away from him to check on her daughter, who was still dozing peacefully in the swing, her head slumped to one side, her lips parted as if she were about to speak.

Poor girl, Sarah thought, reaching out to brush a strand of hair away from Lucy's clammy cheek. *I'm all you have.*

She knew she'd been a bad mother, that she'd signed on for a job that demanded more of her than she knew how to give. If she'd been alone, she might have gotten down on her knees to beg her daughter's forgiveness.

I'll do better, she promised the sleeping child. *I have to.*

Sarah smelled chocolate on Lucy's breath as she leaned forward to plant a soft kiss on the tip of her cute little nose. A vision came to her as her lips touched Lucy's skin, a sudden vivid awareness of the life they'd lead together from here on out, the hothouse intimacy of a single mother and her only child, the two of them sharing everything, breathing the same air, inflicting their moods on each other, best friends and bitter rivals, competing for attention, relying on each other for companionship and emotional support, forming the intense, convoluted, and probably unhealthy bond that for better and worse would become the center of both of their identities, fodder for years of therapy, if they could ever figure out a way to pay for it. It wasn't going to be an easy future, Sarah understood that, but it felt *real* to her—so palpable and close at hand, so in keeping with what she knew of her own life—that it almost seemed inevitable, the place they'd been heading all along. It was enough to make her wonder how she'd ever managed to believe in the alternate version, the one where the Prom King came and made everything better.

She smoothed Lucy's hair again, then turned back around, rejoining the circle of adults, none of whom had spoken for some time. What was there to say, really, after someone had confessed to a murder? Another endless minute ticked by before McGorvey finally addressed Mary Ann.

"Mind if I bum a cigarette?"

With a certain reluctance, Mary Ann reached into her purse and withdrew a pack of Camel Lights.

"Since when do you smoke?" Sarah asked her.

"I don't," said Mary Ann, taking another amateurish drag. "This is just a one-time thing."

"Got an extra?" Sarah asked.

Mary Ann extended the pack first to her, and then, out of politeness, to Moon. He waved her off, but then suddenly reconsidered.

"Ah, what the hell," he said.

The four of them stood in a circle on the playground, smoking and exchanging furtive glances. Every couple of puffs, Sarah reached back and gave Lucy's swing a gentle push.

"Hey, Ronnie," Moon said, after a long interval of silence.

"Yeah?"

"I'm sorry for your loss." He sounded sincere. "I wish it hadn't happened like that."

"Thank you," said McGorvey. "She was a good woman. Took good care of me."

Mary Ann dropped her cigarette on the ground and stepped on it with unnecessary vigor. McGorvey turned to Sarah.

"Can I ask you something?" he said. "I mean, I wouldn't want you to take this wrong, but it's not such a great idea to be out here with your kid after dark."

"Yeah," said Moon. "I was kinda wondering about that myself."

"You want to know what I'm doing here?" Sarah said, as if she hadn't understood the question.

Moon and McGorvey nodded, while Mary Ann looked on with an oddly sympathetic expression. Sarah started to speak, but instead of words, only a small, embarrassed giggle escaped from her mouth. How could she explain? She was here because she'd kissed a man in this very spot, and tasted happiness for the first time in her adult life. She was here because he said he'd run away with her, and she believed him—believed, for a few brief, intensely sweet moments, that she was something special, one of the lucky ones, a character in a love story with a happy ending.

Tom Perrotta is the author of several works of fiction, including *Joe College* and *Election,* which was made into the acclaimed 1999 movie starring Reese Witherspoon and Matthew Broderick. He lives with his wife and two children in Belmont, Massachusetts.

AUTHOR PHOTO CREDIT: DEBI MILLIGAN

READING GROUP GUIDE

1. Is *Little Children* an appropriate or deceptive title for this novel? Can you think of the different ways the phrase is employed within the book? To which characters does it best apply? In the end, is the title simply descriptive, or does it work on multiple levels?

2. Which characters do you sympathize with most in the novel, and why? Which characters are the least sympathetic? Do your sympathies shift over the course of the novel?

3. What does Todd want from Sarah? What does Sarah want from Todd? Are they in love, or simply using each other to escape from bad marriages and/or unhappy lives?

4. What do you make of the portrayal of Ronnie McGorvey? Is he a uniquely evil character in the novel? Or is he more similar to some of the other characters than they'd like to admit? Is he treated fairly by the people in the town?

5. How are children portrayed in this novel? What do you make of such details as Aaron's jester's hat, Big Bear, and the games Train Wreck and Car Doctor? Do Todd and Sarah have different attitudes toward their children, and toward themselves as parents?

6. When Sarah and Mary Ann argue about *Madame Bovary* at the book group, what are they really arguing about? Which one makes the most convincing argument about Emma Bovary, and by extension, about the characters in *Little Children*?

7. A critic has suggested that "all the noncriminal [characters] in this story are better off in the end than they were at the start." Is this true? Can you think of any exceptions?

8. Critics have differed a great deal in characterizing the tone of the novel. One called it a "gentle satire," while another claimed that "Perrotta has moved into the suburbs with a wrecking ball." Which critic do you agree with? How do you account for this discrepancy in these descriptions?

For more reading group suggestions visit
www.ReadingGroupGold.com

St. Martin's Griffin